Born in Malta and christened in the upturned bell of a ship, Jon Courtenay Grimwood grew up in Britain, the Far East and Scandinavia. He currently works as a freelance journalist and lives in Winchester. He writes for a number of newspapers and magazines, including the *Guardian* and *SFX*.

Visit the website
http://www.j-cg.co.uk

Other books by Jon Courtenay Grimwood

neoAddix

Lucifer's Dragon

reMix

redRobe

Pashazade
The First Arabesk

Felaheen
The Third Arabesk

Effendi

The Second Arabesk

Jon Courtenay Grimwood

POCKET
BOOKS

LONDON · SYDNEY · NEW YORK · TOKYO · SINGAPORE · TORONTO

First published in Great Britain by Earthlight, 2002
This edition first published by Pocket Books, 2003
An imprint of Simon & Schuster UK Ltd
A Viacom Company

1 3 5 7 9 10 8 6 4 2

Simon & Schuster UK Ltd
Africa House
64–78 Kingsway
London WC2B 6AH

www.simonsays.co.uk

Simon & Schuster Australia
Sydney

A CIP catalogue record for this book is available from the
British Library

ISBN 0-671-77369-0

Typeset by Palimpsest Book Production Limited,
Polmont, Stirlingshire
Printed and bound in Great Britain by
Cox & Wyman Ltd, Reading, Berkshire

For EMC G
from Singapore to England, via Afghanistan
(a hard act to follow)

I saw three faces on one head. One was an angry red, another between pale and yellow, the last like those who live where the Nile rises . . .

Dante *Inferno* Canto XXXIV

Prologue

27th October

'Of course,' said Ashraf Bey. 'We could just kill the defendant and be done with it . . .' He let his suggestion hang in the cold air. And when no one replied, Raf shrugged. 'Okay,' he said. 'Maybe not.'

It was getting late and autumn rain fell steadily on the darkened streets outside, while inside, sat around their table, Raf's visitors continued to chase the same argument in tight circles. A Grand Jury was in session. If three judges plus a senior detective in a damp, third-storey office could be called anything so imposing, which seemed doubtful.

'An accident,' suggested Raf. 'The steps in this precinct are notoriously slippery. Or perhaps suicide . . . Shoe laces, an unfortunately overlooked belt . . . ? One of my people would have to be reprimanded obviously.'

Raf looked from Graf Ernst von B, the German boy, to a sour-faced politician from New Jersey who insisted everyone call her Senator Liz, neither of whom met his eye. There was also an elderly French oil magnate, but he sat so quietly Raf mostly forgot he was there. Which was probably the man's intention.

'Alternatively,' said Raf, 'I could have him taken out to the courtyard and shot. Or, if you like, we could lose the body altogether and just pretend he never existed. One of the old Greek cisterns should take care of that.'

They didn't like this idea either; but then the young detective with the Armani wrap-rounds and drop-pearl earring hadn't expected them to . . . He was acting as *magister* to their judges. And no one as yet, least of all him, seemed very sure what that actually entailed.

'*Justice*,' Senator Liz said loudly, '*must be seen to be done.*' Her voice remained as irritating as when the session began several hours earlier.

'Lord Hewart,' Raf pulled the quote from memory. 'One of the worst judges in history. And even he never suggested putting a North African trial on American television.'

'That's not . . .' Ernst von B's protest died as Raf flipped up a hand.

'Let's hear what St Cloud thinks,' he said and turned to the Frenchman. 'Do *you* think justice needs to be televised?'

'Me?' Astolphe de St Cloud slid a cigar case from his inside pocket. And though the iridescence of its lizard skin was beautiful, even by the light of a single hurricane lamp, what they all noticed was the enamel clasp: an eagle spreading its wings, while jagged thunderbolts fell from between the bird's sharp claws.

As if anyone there needed reminding that St Cloud would have been Prince Imperial, if only his father had bothered to marry his mother.

'It depends,' said St Cloud, 'on what Your Excellency means by *justice* . . .' Shuffling a handful of prints, he stopped at one which showed a young girl with most of her stomach missing. 'If we decide the evidence is convincing enough, then obviously the prisoner must stand trial. Like Senator Liz, my only reservation is that, perhaps, El Iskandryia is not quite . . .'

Raf caught the wry amusement in the Marquis' voice and glanced round the room, trying to see it through the eyes of a man whose own business empire was run from a Moorish palace overlooking Tunisia's Cap Bon; and who now found himself in a third-floor office, without electricity, on the corner of Boulevard Champollion and Rue Riyad Pasha, in a tatty four-square government block built around a huge courtyard in best Nationalist Revival style.

At street level the exterior walls to Iskandryia's Police HQ were faced with cheap sheets of reconstituted marble, while glass hid the exterior of the two floors above. Black glass obviously. The architect had been on loan from Moscow.

It showed.

As for the level of comfort on offer . . . A fire burned in a bucket in the centre of the floor, filled with logs from a dying carob. Apparently, the tree had been not quite alive and not yet dead for as long as even Raf's oldest detectives could remember.

Two men from uniform had hacked it off just above the roots, using fire-axes. Now chunks of its carcass spat and spluttered as thin flames danced across the top of their makeshift brazier.

Directly above the brazier, suspended from the centre of the ceiling like an inverted red mushroom, hung a state-of-the-art smoke detector. Like almost everything else in Iskandryia since the EMP bomb, it no longer worked.

And behind Raf's head, a window unit that once adjusted electronically to lighting conditions had been rendered smoke friendly, also with a fire-axe. Through its shattered centre came flecks of rain and a salt wind that blew in from the Eastern Harbour.

'Justice,' said Raf, 'is whatever we decide . . .' His voice lost the irony, became serious. 'And since the killing occurred within the jurisdiction of the Khedive, I demand that the trial take place in El Iskandryia.'

Senator Liz shook her head. 'Absurd,' she said. 'We have to change the location. You cannot expect us to work in these conditions . . .'

'I don't remember anyone asking you to work on this at all.' Wrap-round dark glasses stared at the woman. The other two he'd chosen. The Senator was different, she'd practically demanded to sit on the Grand Jury.

Actually, there was no practically about it.

On her breath Raf could smell gin, while a non-too-subtle miasma of sweat rose from her compact body. If von Bismarck and St Cloud could manage to bathe in rain water, then so could the American.

'Your Excellency,' said Ernst von B. 'Senator Liz has a point. It will not be easy . . .' The young German spoke slowly, in schoolboy Arabic, supposedly out of respect for Ashraf Bey's position as *magister*, though Raf suspected his real reason was to annoy the American, who spoke no languages other than her own.

'Nothing is ever easy. But the decision is made.' Raf stood up from his chair. And it was his chair because they were in his office. His was the name engraved on an absurdly-long brass plate on the door. *His Excellency Pashazade Ashraf Bey, Colonel Ashraf al-Mansur, Chief of Detectives*.

He'd told his assistant a plastic nameplate was fine but that wasn't how things were done in El Iskandryia. The long plaque had turned up the day after Raf took the job, and once a week, on Thursdays, a Cypriot woman from maintenance came up from the ground floor to polish the sign.

'Excellency?'

Raf turned to find St Cloud stood next to him, leaning on a cane with a silver top.

'You *were* joking about those steps, the accidents . . . I have your word this trial will actually take place?'

The blond detective nodded. 'You do.'

The trial would happen and it would happen soon. In all probability the defendant, one Hamzah Effendi, would be convicted. Raf just wished Hamzah wasn't father to the girl he should have married.

Chapter One

18th October

Nine days before the Grand Jury met in an upstairs office at Champollion Precinct, Ashraf Bey sat through a warm Iskandryian evening, bombed out of his skull, at a pavement table outside Le Trianon, drinking cappuccino and listening to DJ Avatar wreck havoc on the words of a Greek philosopher.

The afternoon call to prayer had finished echoing from the mosque on Boulevard Sa'ad Zaghloul and the bells from l'Eglise Copte had yet to begin. If it hadn't been for a sense of dread hanging over El Iskandryia, this could have been a Monday in October like any other.

Horse-drawn calèches, their brasses shined and wheel bosses polished, rumbled up the Corniche, from the fat sea wall known as the Silsileh all the way north to Fort Qaitbey, where the ancient Pharos lighthouse once stood.

And at both ends of the sweeping Corniche, at Silsileh in the shadow of Iskandryia's famous library, and at Fort Qaitbey, groups of tourists watched as fishermen set hooks or mended and untangled nets, waiting for the evening tide.

It was a tourist who'd taken the taxi that stopped outside Le Trianon, with its window down and sound-system up too loud, giving Raf the chance to hear the city's favourite DJ one more time.

'And remember. . .' Avatar's voice was street raw. 'Rust never sleeps. Coming at you from the wrong side of those tracks, this for the Daddy, the Don . . .'

Most of Raf's officers thought DJ Avatar came up with *SpitNoWhere* on his own; if they thought at all, which Raf considered unlikely. So they happily stamped the corridors at

Police HQ, humming along, not knowing that the unchopped original went, 'In a rich man's house, there's nowhere to spit but his face.'

Raf hadn't known that, at least not until recently, but the fox in his head did. And while the fox couldn't say why, the General's *aide de camp* had just delivered to Raf an engraving of hell, inscribed with the words, *'At its centre hell is not hot.'* It had at least been able to identify the picture as late Victorian, unquestionably by Gustave Doré . . .

'. . . *ou know,*' said the fox, before all this happened. '. . . *ese things, they occur.*'

The fox had a grin like the Cheshire Cat, except that no cat ever owned so many teeth or carried its tail wrapped up round its shoulders like a stole. Come to that, few cats took afternoon tea at Le Trianon.

These things could have been Raf becoming Chief of Detectives by default, or his recent refusal to marry the daughter of a billionaire.

'Why?' Raf asked. '*Why* do they occur?'

But the fox didn't answer.

Sighing, Raf took a gulp of cold cappuccino to wash away the taste of cheap speed and fixed his gaze on the pedestrians who streamed past his café table, separated from the terrace where he sat by a silk rope and the assiduous attention of two bodyguards.

The only pedestrians to meet Raf's stare were those, mainly tourists, who didn't realize who he was. They just saw a blond young man in dark glasses, wearing an oddly old-fashioned suit, the kind with a high collar.

'Come on,' said Raf, searching inside his head. 'You can tell me.'

He ignored his two guards, who looked at each other and then hurriedly looked away. Raf didn't doubt that they could see tears trickling from under his glasses, but he didn't much care either.

The fox was saying goodbye.

The beast had been dying for years. Its abilities limited by memory conflicts, failed backup and the fact that, these days, the animal could only feed on neon light.

Once Tiri had been state of the art. Feeding on daylight, infrared and ultraviolet, or so it told Raf. White light, black light – back then anything went. The fox sharpened Raf's reflexes, steadied his nerves and gave him good advice. It was what Raf had instead of parents . . .

A small ceramic box set into his skull behind one ear which kept him sane, sort of, and gave him a definable centre. And once, when Raf was very young and in another country, it had helped him walk out across a steel beam through flames and crumbling walls.

Only life wasn't simple; because the fox, of course, refused to admit that it existed. The fox's view was that Raf had a number of unresolved issues.

'Your Excellency . . . ?'

Someone hovered at his shoulder.

'Go', said Raf and the waiter went, grateful to have been waved away.

Raf went back to watching the tourists who fed off from Place Sa'ad Zaghloul, and headed south down Rue Missala, searching for bars and theatres or just in a hurry to get back to their hotels.

After a hundred and eleven days in the city, Raf could now identify tourist groups as clearly as if they wore labels: waddling Austrians, dark-haired French men, the odd bunch of shore-leave Soviets in mufti and, rarer still, an occasional pink-skinned English woman with silk scarf and sensible shoes. But mostly Iskandryia got nice couples, as befitted a famously romantic city.

The fuck-me singles, with their piercings, tattoos and trailer chic, came out only after dark, and then only in closely-defined areas. Places like PeshVille, where Scandinavian kids hosed lines of coke off toilet rims, while girls shuffled in darkened corners on the unzipped laps of boys too blasted to know they weren't safely hiding out in student halls back home.

But that wasn't really Iskandryia, just how it went, with

the limo-delivered international DJs as interchangeable as the clientele. It could have been Curitiba or Berlin, Punta del Este or Kota Baru. And anyway those clubs weren't Raf's business. The tourist police dealt with that stuff.

'*You in there?*'

Raf counted off the seconds, listening carefully for an echo inside his head. One winter night, when he was maybe ten and feeling sorry for himself, something that happened less often than Raf remembered, he'd asked the fox if he (Raf that was) had a soul . . . And the fox had gone all silent.

That was the weekend Raf refused to go to chapel. For five weeks he'd been made to run round a field in the sleet at the back of his school, while the others sang hymns in the dry. And the fox's only comment, months later, had been to point out that he should have waited until summer to lose his faith.

Maybe it was one of his schools that first put the fox in his head. Or perhaps it was his mother. Alternatively, just maybe the fox was right and it didn't exist, maybe it had never existed outside of Raf's imagination.

Raf sighed. 'Do I get an answer?' he demanded. 'Or do I sit talking to myself like an idiot?'

'*Your Excellency?*' It was the maître d' this time. Raf tried to wave away the thin man but the maître d' stayed rooted to the spot, urgency winning out over embarrassment. 'The General is on the line from New York . . .' In his hand the man held an old-fashioned telephone. 'He says it's very urgent.'

Raf shook his head and almost laughed as shock flooded the maître d's face. No one refused to talk to General Saeed Koenig Pasha, not even His Excellency Ashraf Bey.

'What do I tell him?' The maître d' begged frantically.

Raf thought about how to answer for so long that the thin man holding the telephone actually began to squirm with agitation.

'I know,' said Raf finally, 'tell him my fox is dying.'

Chapter Two

19th October

An early tram rattled up Rue Moharrem Bey towards Misr Station, jinked around the silent taxi rank at Place Gumhuriya and continued west along Boulevard Sherif, passing the open front door of the al-Mansur Madersa.

On the madersa's second floor, in a small room in the haremlek, a nine-year-old girl, nicknamed Hani, slept badly while a Catholic cook watched over her. The cook spoke just enough Arabic for her closest friend to be the skeletal Sudanese porter who sat, cross legged, on worn stone steps at the front of the house talking slowly into an ancient cell phone.

'Yes Hamzah Effendi,' he said, watching the almost empty tram go by. 'I know where His Excellency is. He's still at Le Trianon.' Khartoum listened again. 'Wrestling with evil djinn,' he answered and broke the connection.

Two of the tram's fares were tourists late home to bed, the other three Iskandryian, headed to work. A short-order cook, a chambermaid, a stall holder from a minor souk. Travel was cheap in the city. For most of those who worked in the service industries it needed to be.

At some hours of the day gulls could be heard everywhere across the city, but this early in the morning they circled tightly over the Shambles, rabid for any entrails that might be tossed from gutting table to harbour.

(Years before, when the women with their razor-edged filleting knives had been children, or maybe it was when their mothers had been children, the Khedive had declared it illegal to discard the guts and tailings of each night's catch. Every scrap not sold had to be ploughed into the barren edges of the delta to improve the soil. Then came the first flu epidemic and with too few *felaheen* to gather in crops that lay spoiling in the existing fields, increased maize yields ceased to matter. So now the entrails went back into the water.)

And when the gulls finally dispersed and first light finished staining the horizon, the sun rose out beyond Glymonopolo Bay and another Tuesday morning began.

Shutters were opened, doors unlocked. In red-brick tenements everywhere, middle-aged women looked at pot-bellied men and remembered dark-eyed boys, marriage vows and lost virginity. Men mourned the slim-hipped girls they'd married and, catching sight of themselves in the mirror, wondered how they'd never noticed they'd become someone else.

And on the edge of Glymonopolo Bay, in a stuccoed villa as arrogant as any conquistador's palace, a barrel-chested industrialist turned off his phone, sighed heavily and picked up a revolver.

Again.

In front of Hamzah Effendi was a naked angel. Wings spread wide and breasts full, like those of a distantly remembered mother. Except that the angel was pale and fair-haired and elegant, things untrue of anyone in his family.

She hovered within a page torn from a book, written in a language he couldn't read and inscribed on the back, '*Only here will you find peace*' and '*Apollyon*'. General Koenig Pasha had penned these in his immaculate copperplate just below a half-title which read '*Divina Commedia di Dante Alighieri: Paradiso*.'

With the engraving came a gun. They were the governor's answer to Hamzah's desperate plea for help.

Shooting himself would ruin his looks, Hamzah knew that. Regretted it. A long succession of twenty-something mistresses had assured him that he had the dark eyes of a hunter, the mouth of a poet and the profile of an emperor: the founder of a dynasty, not one of those weaklings that came later, slope-chinned and nervous, the kind who got strangled with a golden rope as they slept.

Hamzah's chin jutted so proudly that the eye almost slid past his heavy jowls and neck. His face had a flabbiness now that business partners seldom recalled when they thought back to meeting him; somehow imperfections got forgotten, leaving only a memory of his strength.

A gulp from his crystal tumbler later, Hamzah put down the gun.

Again.

'*Coward.*'

Alcohol tells the truth. '*I didn't mean it,*' that's the lie. People do mean it, every time. Hamzah did, even if the person at which he swore was himself. Of course, he'd have preferred to bawl out Ashraf al-Mansur but the recently appointed Chief of Detectives wasn't taking calls.

Downing another gulp of neat Laphroaig, Hamzah topped up his glass and carefully hid the bottle in the bottom drawer of a burr-walnut desk. Alcohol was illegal in Iskandryia, except for tourists and in certain bars attached to the bigger international hotels, or unless one had written permission from the General. It was a prohibition of which Hamzah heartily approved since one small sliver of his diverse interests involved supplying illegal alcohol to illegal clubs, many of which he owned anyway.

There were no early memories for him of a high-breasted, thin-hipped girl. Any more than his wife had memories of a smouldering-eyed boy who turned her body to fire. Their marriage was arranged and the only thing odd about it was that, in theory at least, Hamzah did the arranging. Rahina's useless father had owed him a debt and she was part payment.

Hamzah would have preferred the money.

He wondered, but only briefly, how well his wife would cope as a widow. Maybe her life would be improved? Money would be no problem and Villa Hamzah had never been Rahina's first choice as a home, so his guess was that she'd leave the city entirely. Either to live on a country estate in the delta or else move to Tunis or Algiers, where his disgrace might not follow her.

Hamzah ran through the check list in his mind.

Will, signed and witnessed.

Accounts, doctored obviously; the real ones were bleached to NSA standards, overwritten and then bleached again.

Deeds to the villa.

Share certificates . . . Those were mostly for Hamzah Enterprises, the Midas Refinery, Quitrimala Industries and the offshore and Sudanese oil fields. The French and the Germans had recently offered to buy him out, but any deal could be done with his executor.

Bank accounts, both known and previously hidden.

Suicide note. Words weren't what he was good at, so he'd quoted from a poem he'd once learnt, long ago beside a river when he was a boy. *'I loved you so I wrote my will across the sky in stars . . .'* He'd probably got half of the words wrong, but they'd expect that.

Everything was in place for what came next. Shares in Hamzah Enterprises would dip on the Bourse but bounce back. Oil prices were rocketing and the Midas Refinery would continue turning crude to cash, whoever owned it. Only in the illegal clubs, brothels and dance halls would there be a fight for succession, and that would have happened someday, whatever . . .

The revolver he held stank of oil, which was his own fault. Every gap in the previous week he'd spent cleaning and recleaning the .38, until the rifling shone metal-bright and the cylinder spun as cleanly as if the weapon was new rather than a hundred and twenty years old.

Now was the point for him to suck silence from its muzzle. Only he couldn't.

He'd been maybe ten years old when he acquired his first gun. *Felaheen* back then didn't know their age. Often they didn't know their families either. Some nights he'd wished he was one of them. But later he found excuses for the beatings as he tried to imagine what life must have been like for his uncle in Abu Simbel at the height of the little war, to be penniless, illiterate, with a dead wife, dead sister and a small nephew.

No, Hamzah shook his head slightly – children, responsibility, the past – those were places he wouldn't revisit. Because then he'd start thinking about . . .

Bite on darkness.

The revolver's handle looked odd, held upside down like that, with three of his fingers wrapped round its ivory stock and one curled tight across the trigger. All but one of the chambers were empty, because he'd only need the single bullet, the one waiting for the fall of the hammer.

Watch the knuckles whiten.

Every step of his life had been leading to this point. From a shack on the Nile's bank to a study panelled in pale English oak in a vast stone villa, on the edge of Glymonopolo Bay. Symmetry was what his daughter Zara would have called it. Perhaps a paradigm. She was fond of big words and bad politics.

From nothing back to nothing.

Only he couldn't do it, for reasons as ugly as the reason he had to do it in the first place. All that was left for him was to accept what came.

Hamzah yanked the taste from his mouth, spun his study chair in a half circle and blasted the head off a taut-hipped marble girl with the blank eyes of a victim and the tight buttocks of a Renaissance catamite.

Flying splinters from her crystalline hairdo ricocheted off bomb-proof glass in the far window and splintered English oak panelling. Alarms exploded and before the marble dust had even begun to clear Hamzah could hear running footsteps in the corridor outside.

Alex would be upset. His wife would be furious. And her French chef would be quietly disapproving. The only one Hamzah cared about was Alex. Good bodyguards were hard to find in North Africa and he was going to need one.

'Boss.' The big Russian skidded to a halt, automatic already drawn and laser sight lit. A red dot danced across the walls, coming to rest when Hamzah's bodyguard realized the wrecked study was empty.

'Nothing to kill,' said Hamzah. 'Unless you want to slot

her?' He jerked his heavy chin towards the damaged dryad and blinked as Alex blasted off first one arm, then another. Finishing with two rapid shots that took the statue off at her knees.

'Okay?'

'Yeah,' Hamzah coughed. 'Pretty good.'

The statue was a fake, a Victorian copy of a Renaissance original, provenanced from the Russell-Coates museum in Bournemouth, which apparently was a spa somewhere in England. Hamzah had loathed the carving on sight, only buying it when he realized how much it would upset his wife. She thought all statues were an abomination in the eyes of God, never mind naked ones, and still hadn't forgiven her husband for having his portrait painted.

'You bored, Boss?' The ex-Soviet *Spetsnaz* had taken in the empty glass on the table. 'You want maybe we should have some fun . . . Check out one of your clubs?'

'What clubs?' The small woman in the doorway glared at Hamzah's ruined statue and then at Hamzah. 'You told me you'd got rid of the clubs.'

Madame Rahina wore her wealth in gold bangles up both arms and in large sapphire earrings that made up in sheer worth for what they lacked in elegance. And even over the acrid dust, her cologne was heavy and obvious.

All her irritation was focused on her husband. Somewhere down life's journey from local schoolmaster's daughter to wife of a major industrialist she'd learned the essential Iskandryian art of walking into even the most crowded room and seeing only people who mattered.

Five years on, she was still smarting from the only time she'd been invited to one of the General's soirées and Koenig Pasha had chosen not to see her.

'Well?' demanded Madame Rahina. 'Did you sell the clubs or not?'

Hamzah nodded. Yeah, he'd sold them all right. To himself in another guise and then leased them straight back.

'Yes, of course I did.' Well, the *himself* in this case was actually a DJ called Avatar. Partly his choice of the boy was sentiment, and Hamzah knew he was sentimental (he'd yet to meet a gangster who wasn't), but mostly it was plain common sense. He'd needed to reward Avatar for an essential service the kid had performed three months earlier, one summer night near the beginning of July. When the shit was still waiting for someone to switch on the fan . . .

Chapter Three

7th July

At the eastern end of the city's sweeping Corniche, where the expensive palladian villas built from imported limestone boasted gardens that reached down to the sea, a girl swam under a warm dome of summer stars.

She was naked and out of her head on redRiff. Which was better than a few years back when her crutch of choice had been amphetamine sulphate, the pharmaceutically-pure kind dished out by the sort of diet clinic that double checked your credit rating and forgot to measure your weight.

The blond man leaving the grandest of those villas had yet to notice her because he had other things on his mind, like being wanted for murder. But he would.

Inside the villa that Ashraf al-Mansur had just left, a boy flicked silver dreadlocks out of eyes that were angry and forgot about the flick-knife he'd been using to clean his nails.

Avatar had stolen that habit from an old film, but Hamzah already knew this. Recognizing his own faults in somebody younger either made for Hamzah losing his temper or keeping it. He was working hard to keep his.

'Zara's out there. You got that?'

Hamzah Effendi nodded.

'And you know she's, like . . .'

Hamzah said nothing but, yes, he knew. She was naked. They were discussing Hamzah's only daughter, the one who was meant to be upstairs in bed, asleep. The girl who'd recently been dumped-on, very publicly, by the very man Hamzah had just sent down to the beach.

'Well . . . whatever.' It was Avatar's turn to shrug. Things

he thought would worry the old man sometimes didn't . . .
And things Av considered nothing often did. So the boy trod
carefully, but tried hard not to reveal the fact.

'You heard what Ashraf Bey said?' said Hamzah, his voice
hoarse with good cigars and better whisky.

Yeah, Avatar had.

'You believe him?'

The boy shrugged. How did he know who looked like a
killer and who didn't . . . ? The bey was some blond-haired
princeling, half Berber and half something *nasrani*; all silk
suits and Armani shades. That put him way outside Avatar's
frame of reference. Until Hamzah's daughter, defaulting to her
'Comrade Zara' mode, had tracked Av down and dragged him
off the street, he'd thought sleeping in his own bit of doorway
was posh.

'Me,' said Avatar, 'I believe nobody.'

Hamzah smiled.

Avatar had entered via a window, seconds after Raf exited
through the French doors, headed without knowing it towards
the rocks where Zara swam, phosphorescence smoothing across
her adolescent body like slipstream.

'Kamil . . .'

'DJ Avatar, Av, Avatar, 2Cool Kid,' the boy corrected his
father without even thinking about it. The options tossed out
machine-gun fast. He didn't answer to Kamil, any more than
he used the door at Villa Hamzah. This last was his present to
the man sat on the other side of the desk.

Four years back – after Avatar had kicked her – Madame
Rahina, the woman who very definitely wasn't his mother,
had made her husband promise never to let Avatar through
the door of Villa Hamzah again.

So Hamzah hadn't.

'Av . . .' Hamzah Effendi paused and picked a cigar. Remembering just in time to use a tiny gold guillotine to circumcise its
end. A life's worth of biting off the end and spitting was a habit
he found hard to break. Hamzah wanted to explain to Avatar
exactly why he'd sent the bey out of that door, down to where

his daughter swam naked: but he couldn't put *'needs must'* into words. At least not words he found acceptable. So instead, the big man took another pull on a Partegas and thought about his lawyer waiting nervously in the hallway.

He could wait. Whatever it was Avatar had come to say wouldn't take long.

'You need money?'

Avatar grinned. Of course he needed dosh. Didn't everyone? Apart from the industrialist sat in front of him. All the same, that wasn't why Avatar was there.

'Some journalist's been asking about you . . .'

'A *nasrani*?' It had to be. Hamzah already kept most of the local press in his pocket, and the few who were not lapping up his hospitality missed out, not from any misplaced moral backbone but because he already had them by the balls.

'English. Well, probably. You know . . .'

Hamzah knew. It was unfashionable to say so, but telling one from another was difficult until *nasranis* started flashing round their passports or local currency.

'So let me guess,' the big man smiled and let cigar smoke trickle towards the ceiling; though the smile didn't reach his eyes and a breeze through the open window dissipated the smoke before it reached the height of a picture rail.

'Organized crime the Ottoman way?'

Avatar shook his head.

'Well it can't be the refinery, because then they'd just go through my press office . . .' His refinery was situated to the west of Isk, at the point where slums met desert. In an industry working hard to improve its image, Midas Oil was an entire lap ahead. Bursaries, research grants, third-world scholarships, a whole marine-biology, anti-pollution programme at Rutgers.

Accidents got apologized for the moment they happened, critics were greeted with open arms, research papers were put to peer review and then released, copyright free, straight onto the web. It was a long-term game and, as Hamzah had hoped, it was driving even the softest ecological pressure groups insane.

'What then?'

'Your childhood . . .'

To the man's credit, Hamzah did little more than blink.

'Think you can deal with this?' Hamzah asked Avatar.

'Sure,' said Avatar. 'You want him killed?'

Hamzah raised his eyebrows, amusement driving out the last echoes of anger.

'No,' he said with a smile. 'I don't want him killed. Whatever you've heard, whatever the police whisper, that's not how I do things.'

Avatar looked for a brief second like he wanted to disagree. Then he shrugged. 'It's your party,' he said. And left without glancing back, exiting through a window larger than the front door of most of the places in which he'd lived.

Chapter Four

Sudan

'Safety off,' said the gun.

Stood beside Sergeant Ka, Zac said nothing. He'd spoken little enough when he was alive and now he was dead he talked even less . . .

Ka thought that strange, because Zac's sister Ruth had also said little from the time she'd been captured to the moment she died. But now she talked so much that Ka couldn't concentrate on watching the growling trucks that rolled across the scrub towards him.

'Distance?'

'Half a klick and closing . . .'

Status and range. That was all the plastic H&K/cw could manage. It was an incredibly stupid weapon and the boy with the bone cross, feather amulet and boots several sizes too big didn't know why the manufacturer had bothered.

There was meant to be some way to turn off the voice but to do that you needed to be able to read. So instead Ka had ripped the tail from his shirt and tied it to the stock, right over the little plastic grille behind which the speaker hid.

Before Ka began this mission, Colonel Abad had ordered him to be sure to check his weapons each morning. Then, when that was done, to inspect the weapons of the rest of his troop. Only there was no rest any longer. At least, Ka didn't think so.

He was it.

So Ka inspected his own weapons, trying to remember what he was meant to be looking for . . . Dirt, maybe, and rust. Except rust wasn't a problem because it hadn't rained in a year in this part of wherever he was, somewhere between Bahr

el-Azrek and the Atbarah. At least, that's where he thought
he was.

Untying the lanyard that fastened a revolver around his neck,
Ka checked it. It was as clean as any weapon could be in a
country where most of the earth had turned to red dust and
half of that had been stripped away from the rock beneath.
The revolver was his favourite. He'd have liked it even more
if any of the bullets he carried in his truck had been the right
calibre.

H&K21e clean and freshly oiled. Tripod fixed and belt ready.
H&K/cw . . . spotless. His knife wasn't clean but that was
because Ezekiel's blood had ruined the leather of its handle.
Everyone had warned Ezekiel not to pick up bomblets, but the
boy was six and the cluster bombs came in red, green and
yellow.

Ezekiel had always loved bright colours.

Their most junior soldier had been left under a blanket of
stones where he died, on the side of a hill just below the
cracked eggshell memorial to where a functioning mosque
once stood. Ka had refused to kill the boy until the others
stopped talking to him, because he was a sergeant and that
was his job. In the end, Ka had given in, gone back to where
he'd rested Ezekiel in the shade of a broken wall and found the
small boy already dead.

But he buried the blade deep and carried it back to camp to
show them the deed was done. Things had been different after
that. They all wanted to be with Ka but he no longer wanted
to be with them.

Now he was alone, with his back to the empty village. Well,
it was two villages really. One built from grey brick which
looked heavy but turned out to be solid froth, like ossified
spit. That version had been constructed ten years before by the
government and destroyed by them as well, a few years later.

The older village was behind the new one, jammed into a
space between the start of a hill and a scar of rock. But most of
its mud-walled huts had fallen in, from age this time. According
to the Colonel, there was no water for miles, what with the wadis

drying up and the nearest bore-hole being both barren and filled with corpses from an earlier battle.

Ka lifted his H&K/cw and snapped free the lower clip. It was loaded with 5.56mm, each kinetic round dipped in holy water and polished with snake skin. His old AK-49 had been altogether better, less flashy. But an older boy had wanted Ka's AK-49 and given him the plastic gun in return. The boy was dead now. Ka didn't feel too bad about it.

Chapter Five

7th July

'You need to be here . . .'

Avatar's call came through as Hamzah was getting ready for bed. His wife was upstairs sleeping, and his daughter . . . Wherever Zara had gone after her swim, she'd taken her little F-type Jaguar and left a wet towel on the hall floor by way of goodbye.

'Where's here?'

'Sarahz . . . Corner of Place Gumhuriya.'

Hamzah knew exactly where the club was. There might be a dozen bars and restaurants he owned without knowing exactly where they were, but Sarahz had been one of his early acquisitions, maybe the first. It got hard to remember.

'I'm about to turn in.'

'Not now, you're not . . . Believe me, I've got something you'll want to see.'

Avatar put down the club's payphone and went back to his decks. Building on a breakbeat *sambassimba* anthem that cut the heavy overdub/techno fusion that was ol'sko drum'n'bass with lighter Sao Paolo rhythms, weirdshit polka, vicious Fender licks and syncopated snare.

SpecialBeatService, the near original PatifePorto mix.

He was working a late Wednesday crowd, upstairs at Sarahz. Mostly poor little rich boys from St Mark's plus a handful of over-dressed, hard-eyed kazuals from Moharrem Bey. The girls were tourists, mostly. A smattering of au pairs, exchange students, teenagers glad to get away from their distant families.

Avatar got the gig on merit. The manager didn't know his new DJ was the bastard of Hamzah Effendi. Until ten minutes ago,

Amici hadn't known that his club was owned by Quitrimala Enterprises – and he was still getting over that shock.

Hamzah sighed and pushed himself up off his *bateau lit*. The mahogany bed had been imported eighty years earlier from Marseilles, found the previous year in a souk in El Gomruk and repaired for Hamzah by a sullen carpenter from Mali who spat, chain-smoked and forgot to wash but had the hands of an angel and the eye of an Italian polymath.

Hamzah forgave the carpenter his bad habits because he actually made things by hand, instead of using machines. Madame Rahina hated the *bateau lit* but that was fine. As Hamzah frequently pointed out, nothing required her to sleep in it.

Habit had made such things easy for them; and Hamzah's practice of working late justified his need for a bed in the room off his study.

Within the standards set by culture and religion, he was a good husband and he tried to be a good father. He'd never once raised his hand to his daughter and had only occasionally slapped his wife, and that not recently.

It would never occur to him to hit his mistress, but then Olga used to assassinate Americans for a living, in the days before she came to work as his PA. Olga was *Organizatsiaya* and also a Soviet spy, but she knew that Hamzah knew, and they both understood that Commissar Zukov at the Soviet Consulate now required little more than a daily report on Hamzah's movements.

Tomorrow she'd report that, after a good breakfast, he voluntarily presented himself at Champollion Precinct, the Police HQ in Rue Riyad Pasha, to be questioned about the murder of Lady Nafisa, aunt of Ashraf Bey. She'd mention that he'd taken his lawyer and been released without charge . . . Because Hamzah would be released, that was why he kept tame lawyers.

Quite apart from the fact that, for once, he was totally innocent.

Hamzah hit a button beside his bed and waited.

'Boss?'

'I'm going out.'

'Very good. I'll get the car.'

It was obvious which vehicle Alex would select. Hamzah's Rolls-Royce Silver Ghost. Like Olga, Alex was Soviet and so, bizarrely, was the Rolls. At least its modifications were . . .

'If you're ready, Boss.' The big man slammed shut the rear door and Hamzah felt, rather than heard, the solidness of bomb-proof steel and a thud as heavy locks slid into place. The car was originally built for Lenin, one of six that the revolutionary leader ordered from London when the fledgling Menshevik Alliance was at its lowest ebb.

With Cossacks advancing from the Crimea and Siberia already lost to Admiral Kolchak, Vladimir Illych had ordered his secretary's secretary to write to Charles Rolls ordering six models of his latest car, the cars to be paid for in advance, in gold. Three weeks later, the British PM reluctantly agreed to the dismemberment of the old Tsarist empire . . . Prussia, France and America followed.

Hamzah had purchased the vehicle at Commissar Zukov's suggestion, during one of the CCCP's habitual bouts of bankruptcy. And had spent the first six months having various illegal listening devices taken out. Alex had come with the vehicle.

'We got trouble, Boss?'

Good question. And if he did have trouble, was it the kind that mattered? Hamzah hired people to keep trouble at arm's length but Avatar wasn't one of them. The boy was grief of a different kind.

'Let's find out,' said Hamzah and leant back against black leather, remembering the boy's mother, a dark-skinned slip of a girl who spoke three languages and didn't know her own age. Hamzah did, knew it to the very month, but never admitted it, except occasionally to himself.

Rammed was how tourists described Sarahz. Rammed to the rafters, to the gills, rammed tight. The same thing happened every Wednesday, the El Anfushi clubs closed up and hardcore clubbers headed south looking for the real thing. Sarahz gave it to them. Detroit techno, down & dirty Chicago house, breakbeat . . . even trance, so epiphanic it came with a built-in halo. Chemical sainthood.

And DJ Avatar bestowed the radiance, from battered Matsui decks that had been rebuilt so many times that the only original component left was a cheap plastic logo glue-gunned to the front. Av learnt fast. His first real sound system comprised a triple deck, reconditioned 303 and original theramin. The lot got ripped off his second week playing clubs, at some cellar behind Maritime Station.

Now he had a deck that looked shit and sounded like it was wired direct to God. And when he wasn't riding his Wild Star, Avatar drove an old VW camper with one side caved in from front arch to rear fender. Prayer beads hung from the front mirror and the back window was stickered with quotations from the Holy Qur'an. No one looked twice. Certainly no one looked and thought, 'Ah, there goes enough rare vinyl to open a shop.'

Which was the point, obviously.

Sarahz had an all-night licence. The result of astute blackmail, a little bribery and the impossibly convenient fact that it was directly opposite Misr Station, with a huge taxi rank to one side and Place Gumhuriya to the front. Since the nearest apartment block was a hundred metres away and inhabited by people who really didn't matter, there were no complaints. At least none that made it onto the record books.

'D'bozzizzere . . .'

Which Avatar quickly translated as, 'The Boss is here . . .'

Nodding, Avatar killed the lights in his booth and slid a disc into one slot and a slab of samples into another and put the deck on auto. He didn't figure on being gone longer than it took to build up and break down and, to be honest, most of the floor were so caned it was doubtful they'd even notice.

'Out of here,' he told his throat mike and heard an acknowledgement through his earbead. If whatever looked like taking longer than it should, Smugs would work the crowd. Smugs was a house regular, ten years older than Avatar, with half the following. Av tolerated the other guy's lack of skill and in return Smugs didn't object to Avatar claiming the decks when fancy took him.

'On the roof,' said the manager as Av unlocked the booth's rear wall and stepped into a darkened corridor. All shaved skull, pearl-stud and shiny black suit, Carlo Amici stood back politely and Avatar sighed. This afternoon the man had regarded Av as a lower form of life, some kid who got overpaid for pushing buttons and spouting crap. Now, suddenly, he'd discovered that Av had a direct line to Hamzah.

There went another good gig.

'I'll find my own way up,' said Avatar, heading for a steel door.

'You could use the lift . . .'

'No, this is quicker.' Cooler too, more in keeping, though Avatar didn't mention that.

The fire escape brought Avatar out on a flat roof that overlooked a darkened square. Over on the far corner of the roof, a small man was lashed to a radio aerial. The aerial was illegal but, equally obviously, no goons from RadioAuthority came by with angle grinders and chopped $15,000 of pirate transmitter into metal spaghetti as happened in other clubs. Next to the naked journalist stood Hamzah Effendi, elegant in Homburg and camel-hair coat.

'Old man.' Avatar stepped out of the darkness.

Hamzah smiled and held out a hand. The big man's grip was firm but controlled. What he offered was a greeting, not a test of strength.

Avatar was being publicly acknowledged in front of Alex, Carlo Amici and a couple of the doormen. Without wanting to be ungrateful, he did wonder why . . .

'Okay,' said Hamzah, 'I'm here. Who's this . . . ?'

'Remember the shitweasel I was talking about . . .' The boy nodded towards the naked man. 'His name's Mike Estelle. He came in earlier, still asking questions. So I figured it might be a good idea if you two actually met. You know, socially . . .'

'You did this to him?'

'Did what?' Avatar looked at the quivering Englishman who was lashed to the mast by his testicles. There wasn't a bruise on the man. And the only blood came from where the little shit had chewed out the inside of his own mouth.

'I barely touched him . . .'

Hamzah smiled. 'You,' he said to the man. 'Here I am. You want to tell me what this is about?'

A sniffling silence was Hamzah's only answer. Sniffling silence and frightened eyes that stared back, wide and defenceless. Well, Hamzah had news for the Englishman. Defencelessness didn't impress him and it certainly didn't punch any buttons.

'No questions?' Hamzah sighed. 'Your choice . . . Throw him off the roof,' Hamzah ordered in English, turning away.

The rising thud of acid house from the floor below mixed neatly with Mike Estelle's rising scream. And apart from Alex, only Avatar saw the tiny, sideways chop of Hamzah's hand which negated the order.

'You hear me?' Hamzah demanded crossly. 'Do it now.'

'Sure, Boss. Sorry, Boss.' Alex produced an evil-looking pair of pliers from his pocket. 'Let me just snip this wire.'

Between them, Avatar and Alex freed the struggling journalist and dragged him to the edge of the roof. The fall was barely twenty feet but the ground below was concrete.

'He should be dressed,' Avatar said suddenly. 'Less suspicious.'

'No,' said Alex, voice casual. 'Foreign tourist gets blasted, weirds out and jumps from club roof. Check out the local newsfeed. Happens all the time . . .'

'Yeah, really,' he added, seeing Avatar's doubtful look. 'Besides, no problem, the Boss will tell the police what to decide . . .' Alex began running the sobbing man backward and forwards, like an athlete limbering up for some Olympic event. 'Okay,' he said to Avatar. 'You ready?'

That was when the *nasrani* shat himself.

Hamzah sighed. 'Okay,' he said heavily. 'Let's try it a different way.' He took a fresh Partegas from his pocket and paused as both doormen bounced forward with lighters. Waving them away, Hamzah bit off one end and spat it over the edge. Only then did he nod to the one nearest.

'Last chance,' Hamzah told the journalist. 'My name is Hamzah Effendi. I own the company that owns this club. I also own an oil field, the Midas processing plant and a shipping line. All this you can get from any trade directory . . . So tell me, who sent you and what do they really want to know?'

Chapter Six

Sudan

Sergeant Ka turned towards the truth and raised a fist above his head in formal salute:

> *I will ascend to heaven*
> *I will raise my throne above the stars*
> *I will sit on the mount of assembly . . .*

Before the silver talisman he wore around his neck became an amulet, it was briefly a bride piece in a dusty city with empty streets and a broken-down bazaar. South of the city lived the Dinka, cattle people, who once roamed the cracked earth between here and the upland forest, where fever trees glow and scrub lies lifeless, until rains come and the underbrush explodes.

Originally, the talisman was recognizable as a Maria Theresa dollar, but the touch of a thousand hands had worn it flat. The coin, however, was never Austrian. It was minted in Stambul, a hundred years after the empress died, at a time when silver dollars were a common currency in the Sahara, Arabia and the Sudan.

Having been taken south as payment for slaves, the coin become a bride price before coming north again, around the neck of a child who stabbed the grandson of the Dinka who originally received it in marriage.

She used a blade because that day's bullet ration was gone . . . Later, she swapped the talisman for a bone crucifix taken from a nun; but that was months later, long after the little war started in Abu Simbel. Mostly Ka avoided thinking about the little war and how he became a soldier.

And sometimes he forgot.

Before Ka was a soldier, he was a camel boy which was an easy job and one he liked. Foreigners came by gleaming barge to the great temple and he and boys like him led them by camel up the thorny slope from the river's edge to the foot of the cliffs, where great carvings had stood undisturbed for well over three thousand years.

Back then, Ka wore tattered shorts and no top or shoes, because that way the tips were better. Once he'd worn a Pepsi tee-shirt and a pair of Nikes that a pink-skinned girl had left behind and hardly any of the foreigners chose him. They rode with the bare-footed boys.

He'd have learnt his lesson from this, even without the beating he got from his uncle. Next day, Ka went back to no shirt or shoes. He also began to listen to the guides when they were too busy to notice.

Soon he knew all the best stories about the great king and his wife. He could explain why the four big statues all wore the double crown of Upper and Lower Egypt, while inside the cliffs, in the darkness of the inner chamber, the king wore only the white crown of Upper Egypt or the red crown of Lower Egypt, depending on whether he was in the northern or southern part of the temple.

And he learnt what interested the foreigners, those people who wasted water as if it was endless. Who washed under flowing showers, shat in unused water and giggled as they tipped full bottles over their heads and let clean water drain away into the dust.

He told them of kings marrying their daughters, brothers sleeping with sisters, mothers with sons. It kept the magic sacred, kept the river flowing and renewed the dark silt that lined the banks and fed the kingdom, but he didn't explain that. The reasons were never as important to the nasrani as the actions themselves.

When Ka told of battles where the king's army collected

testicles to help his scribes count the number of captured, the men would look sick and the bare-headed women either quizzical or appalled. And Ka would smile and look happy when they tipped him, pretending to be surprised. As if he'd spend his whole morning telling them tales just because he loved foreigners.

No one loved the foreigners, not really. Except, maybe, the government because they brought in francs, marks and American dollars. The poor, the felaheen would rather the foreigners didn't wander unasked into mosques, still wearing their shoes, that they didn't choke the desert roads with coaches that threw dust into the faces of those walking and, most of all, that they didn't need endless hotels along the river, because now the areas richest in silt were closed to those who used to sharecrop them and landlords got their money from the tourists instead.

In one month, at the start of the little war, the army beat to death forty-eight people because they came from a distant village where the headman's son had gunned down five foreign tourists. Forty-eight for five. That was the exchange rate.

The son, Samir, whose name meant one whose conversation in the evening is lively, but who was never heard to say more than two words together, lived away from his father's village in a brick house on a rocky islet somewhere unimportant between Aswan and Wadi el-Sebua. He was a strange man, educated first at a local school and then at el-Azhar College in Al Qahirah. He left el-Azhar to work for the Société de Géographie d'Egypte, only to leave that in turn a few months later.

After his reappearance near the village, Samir adopted a family of ungainly chicken-sized birds. There was nothing very special about the birds other than the fact that they lived in a reed bed and were entirely purple, except for their stilt-like legs, which were pink. They weren't even rare.

Before he died under torture, Samir was questioned by a major from the Al Qahirah military police. The local police were happy to do the job themselves but had been ordered to *leave the job to an expert. One reason, some suggested, for their lack of action after the dead Samir's cousins ambushed the major's car, shot dead his eighteen-year-old driver and cut off the major's hands, then beat him to death.*

By then, the disc of Samir's questioning was on its way to regional HQ at Aswan for transcription and analysis. It made no sense at all.

Splashing water, that came first. The clank of something, probably an empty bucket hitting a concrete floor. A slap. Another slap.

'I'm asking you again. When did you join the Sword of God?'

'Never. I'm not a member.'

'Then why kill foreign tourists?'

The sound of a ragged sigh. Part pain, part exasperation.

'They shot the gallinule . . .'

'The tourists?'

'No, the contractors. They cut down the acacia, grubbed up the tamarisk and shot my . . .'

A thud, leather on flesh.

'NO, WAIT.' The voice is foreign, the accent atrocious. Whoever is wielding the whip, they do what they're told. Silence follows.

'You want me to believe you shot five tourists because contractors killed a few wading birds?'

'The river doesn't need another hotel and it doesn't need more tourists. Besides the birds were there first.'

'So you are Sword of God.'

'No, I'm an ornithologist . . .'

That was the start of the little war, which lasted a month. The big war came afterwards and went on for much longer, but Sergeant Ka never quite worked out who the government were fighting. No one important, obviously. And most of the fighting wasn't in Egypt anyway, it was in Sudan.

The little war, which was what his uncle called it, didn't seem so little once the tourists stopped coming to Abu Simbel and the soldiers arrived. Inside of forty-eight hours the whole of Ka's village had been rounded up and marched into the desert. Only a handful of adults survived the first week's march. Most died of heat or succumbed to the cold at night. Very few made it into the second week to reach the holding pen at El Khaschab.

Ka's uncle was one of those. With his wife, parents and own son already dead in another place, the man no longer believed in God, only this lack of belief was so shocking that all Ka's uncle registered was an emptiness as his midday prayers escaped between parched lips and ascended to a silent heaven.

Above him the same cruel sun that turned half-fertile earth to dust and killed the crops in the year Ka was born blistered his skin. A swarm of freshly-hatched flies draped his shoulders like a heavy mantle but he hardly noticed them. Just as he failed to notice the watching boy or the white-plumed vultures that hopped and shuffled through the dirt, a hand's breath away.

They are excluded by a single question. Should he shoot himself or should he shoot his nephew, since, with only one bullet remaining, it was impossible to do both . . .

Chapter Seven

1st August

Zara got arrested for indecency on the 28th July. The first Hamzah knew of it was a day later, from a local paper. Front page, single column.

Rebel Daughter Restrained.

Since Hamzah relied on bribes, blackmail and his fearsome reputation to ensure such things never happened, never mind got reported, he was obviously furious: particularly since the shot used in *Iskandryia Today* showed his daughter crop-haired and naked under a tight coat.

It would be fair to say that he was also troubled. The police were paid handsomely to leave anything that might connect to Zara or her friends well alone.

So far as Hamzah was concerned, *leaving alone* meant not arresting his daughter at some illegal/political dance club. And if the Club de Hashishan really was hers, and the police were probably right about that, then that was even more reason for letting things be.

Unfortunately, the offending picture of Zara turned up again, slightly larger in *Iskandryia on Sunday*. This was the paper which his daughter had just tossed in the bin, before stamping out of his marble and red sandstone office . . .

'Well,' said Olga Kaminsky, 'you deserved that.' She smiled as she removed Zara's cup from Hamzah's desk and wiped up icing sugar with one easy sweep of a linen napkin.

Stating the obvious to Hamzah was living dangerously but he paid her to tell him the truth and so Olga did. Besides, the man looked too shocked to fire her. Which happened about once a month, only for him to say nothing when she turned up the following day, as if the argument had never taken place.

Another PA might have convinced herself that this was because he prized her opinion, that the unusual leeway Hamzah gave her had nothing to do with those half-dozen occasions each year when they slept together, but Olga lied neither to Hamzah nor herself. All the same, she knew their relationship wasn't based on anything as simple as sex.

It was her lack of avarice that had captured Hamzah's imagination. Other mistresses had taken the diamond chains, the Cartier watches, the inevitable mink. Olga took nothing but her salary and returned every gift, opened but unused. She wanted nothing from him but his company and, occasionally, his presence in her bed. And it was *her* bed, a single one with metal frame, because she'd refused his offer of a flat as well.

'Olga, where did I go wrong?' Hamzah's grin was rueful but admiring. There couldn't be another daughter in Iskandryia who'd stamp unannounced into her father's HQ, spin on the spot and slip off her jacket to show her naked back, lash marks and all, when asked why she refused to come home.

But then, daughter and mother had never been close. And it hadn't helped that Rahina's only advice to Zara before her abortive engagement to Ashraf Bey was, 'Never undress in front of your husband.'

If Hamzah could have stopped the whippings, he would have done so years back; but mothers dealt with daughters and fathers with sons. And his boast that he'd never lifted his hand to Zara lost out to the fact he'd never actually raised his voice to protect her either. Tradition strangled him, Hamzah knew that. Under the silk shirt and Gucci suit he was still a *felaheen* at heart.

Zara, however, was not a *felaheen* daughter. Proper schools, two years in New York and a career at the Bibliotheka Iskandryia had seen to that. She was brave, beautiful and smitten with Ashraf Bey, although Hamzah was prepared to bet almost anything she hadn't let Raf know that.

He understood what drove his daughter. What was even

weirder, he actually admired her while knowing full well it was meant to be the other way round.

'Olga, I've got a problem . . .'

Her laugh was instinctive. 'You've got lots of—' Then she stopped. 'You mean you've got a problem I don't know about?' Olga paused in the doorway, then quietly came back to where Hamzah sat. She didn't perch on the edge of his desk or casually grab a chair and straddle it. She waited for Hamzah to nod towards a leather sofa. And when she sat it was elegantly, with her stockinged legs crossed at the ankle.

Hamzah wondered what Olga saw when she looked at him. A filthy capitalist? A self-deluded gangster? A parvenu so desperate for baubles he bought his own title? Or a father unable to safeguard a daughter who refused all protection?

'Okay,' said Olga briskly. 'Problems I do know about . . . Your daughter's been busted by the *morales* for running an illegal club. She's in love with some spoilt little princeling who doesn't know his arse from his elbow. There are rumours of a strike at the refinery. And, despite a full and frank talk, someone's still asking around about your childhood, according to Kamil . . .'

'Avatar,' Hamzah corrected, without even thinking about it. 'He calls himself DJ Avatar.'

'Whatever. He could still become a problem . . .'

'No,' said Hamzah. 'Ashraf Bey's a problem. Avatar just wishes he was.'

'You believe the bey's for real?'

'I know he is,' Hamzah said heavily. 'And he's a trained killer, government issue . . . A bit damaged round the edges but still under guarantee.' The big man laughed. 'Well, that was how he described himself.'

'And you actually *wanted* this man to marry your daughter?'

'*I want*,' Hamzah corrected her. 'More than want, *I need* this man to marry Zara.'

'I see,' said Olga. 'Can I ask why?'

Hamzah shook his head. There were, in his experience, immutable laws about how fathers felt regarding the suitors who sent flowers and elegant cards to their daughters. The first feeling of hatred gave way to one of regret. Third, and finally, came loss as the daughter became a woman. So was it written.

Laws, equally immutable, governed the behaviour, if not the actual feelings, of those courted. Whoever came calling, daughters pretended to despise them. Presents were returned unopened, letters sent back unread. Mashrabiya shutters were slammed tight against each and every serenade. No touch was sought or permitted.

Yet Hamzah knew beyond doubt that his own daughter had spent a night with this man. And while he should have been furious, he was merely worried and oddly sad. It was hard to know if his tenderness for Zara and her willingness to turn to him was a sign of success or proof of failure.

And beyond these things he barely ever thought about, like his own feelings, was a real threat to his wealth, his happiness and to his own and Zara's life. Because when Iskandryian newsfeeds began running stories they shouldn't and the police stopped contacting him at the first sign of trouble then the threat was real.

Someone somewhere reckoned they could change the balance of power.

'Look,' said Hamzah, relenting slightly. 'At its most basic, I need Ashraf to marry Zara to give her protection . . . Protection I may not be able to provide for much longer. And if she doesn't marry the bey, I have to find someone else. The big problem is that I may not have time.'

Behind her heavy spectacles, Olga's blue eyes were large. She understood exactly what he was saying. If Hamzah could no longer protect his daughter then he couldn't protect her either. If he couldn't protect her, then what hope had he of protecting the refinery, Hamzah Enterprises or any other of the myriad shells within shells that made up the story which justified the last thirty years of his life . . .

'Have you upset the General?'

'No.' Hamzah shook his head. He and Koenig Pasha had a

better understanding than most people realized. All the General required of Hamzah was that he recognize who was in charge of El Iskandryia, which wasn't the young Khedive and wasn't him. In return, the General kept Interpol at bay, played Washington's investigators off against those from Moscow, and shamelessly ignored or flattered Paris.

'Tell me,' said Hamzah, 'Is there such a thing as a normal childhood?'

'No,' Olga replied, without having to think about the question.

'Then, even allowing for the fact no one has a normal childhood,' said Hamzah, 'mine was different.'

Standing up from his desk, he walked to a window, leant out and watched a sweeper in the playground of St Mark's College. The fact that Hamzah's marble and red sandstone office was built next door to the college was not an accident.

He'd worked the kitchens at St Mark's, long ago, when he first arrived in the city. The name *Hamzah* came from a faded board listing every pupil killed in the war of 1914–15. The *Quitrimala* that became his surname was borrowed from the gilded spine of a book in the library.

He wasn't meant to leave the kitchens but no one saw a young boy in a jellaba with a split broom in one hand and a dustpan in the other. To the pupils and masters of St Mark's, Hamzah was so invisible that he might as well have been made from glass.

No one would ever look through Zara.

'Follow her,' Hamzah demanded.

'Me?' Olga sounded surprised.

The thick-set man briefly considered that option. There were advantages but the disadvantages were greater. 'No,' he said, 'get someone from security. Have them report back every five minutes.'

At noon Hamzah received a report that Zara had been admitted to the General's house and had seen not the General but the young Khedive himself. Two hours later she was shopping for children's clothes accompanied by a small girl, described as anxious and scrawny. The child had just demanded a haircut, one enough like Zara's own for them to be taken for sisters.

At six, both Zara and Raf's niece Hani were being driven aimlessly back and forward along the Corniche in a calèche, one of those open-top, horse-drawn carriages loved by tourists. Shortly after that, they disappeared through the door of a warehouse at the back of an old market near Rue Tatwig.

A quick and dirty skim through the land-registry revealed that it was owned by a holding company. An even dirtier skim anchored the ownership to Madame Sosostris, a known agent of the *Thiergarten*, Berlin's infamous intelligence service. An organization with whom Koenig Pasha was believed to have close, if occasionally-fractious, links.

But it was only when Zara was joined by Lady Jalila, wife of the Chief of Police, aunt to Hani and cousin to a woman Ashraf Bey was rumoured to have murdered, that Hamzah began to get really worried.

Chapter Eight

Sudan

'Don't be ridiculous.'

'I'm not.'

'Yes, you are . . .'

It was Zac who came up with the idea of turning off the river, a few days after antiquated F-111s bombed Masouf Hospital with his brother inside.

Ka had found a small radio and a pair of spectacles. The radio was one of those old, wind-up things made of blue plastic. Like the spectacles, its case was cracked, and the dial didn't work too well, but it still got Radio Freedom, which was the government, and Radio Liberty, which wasn't . . .

An old woman was talking about war. She sounded cross and upset. Close to tears. She didn't think the hospital had been an arms depot at all, she thought it was a hospital.

Did she have any proof she was right?

Did anyone have any proof that she wasn't?

How long did Madame Ambassador think the war would go on? The woman asking all the questions was younger, her voice brittle.

'As long as there's water to be fought over,' replied the old woman tiredly. 'As long as . . .'

'. . . the Nile flows,' Zac repeated, for about the fifth time. 'That's what she said.'

'Rivers aren't taps,' said Sarah, flicking long black braids out of her eyes. Being reasonably open to new ideas, Sarah wasn't contemptuous like Saul, just doubtful. She looked across their small camp fire to where the sergeant sat, and casually asked Ka what they were all wondering . . .

'What do you think?'

It was Ka's job to know.

'Well,' Ka poked at the embers with a stick, sending sparks flicking skywards. 'Rivers get bigger, right Saul?' That was what he remembered being told.

Saul shrugged. He was older than Ka and bigger, only not as clever. And Saul wasn't his real name any more than Sarah was Sarah or Bec was actually Rebecca. But they'd fought with Ras Michael and those were their given names. The shoulder patches might have changed after they swapped sides at Aswan, yet the biblicals had stuck. Mostly because they'd been with Ras Michael for so long their original names were lost.

'Gets bigger? Says who?' Bec's voice sounded aggressive but then it always sounded aggressive. Hers was still a real question.

'I do,' said Ka, more confidently. 'Rivers start as streams and then get bigger on the way down the mountain. So they must begin small.'

'What mountain?' Zac asked.

'There's always a mountain,' said Ka said. 'Or a hill. So if we find the start we can block it . . .'

'And just how do we do that?' Bec demanded.

It was Zachary who answered. 'With ash,' he said, then blushed. 'You build the dam with stones, put twigs behind it and then throw ash in the water. That blocks the small holes.'

'Okay,' Saul said heavily. 'Suppose we decide to turn off the Nile . . .' His tone made it obvious how stupid he found that suggestion. 'How do you suggest we get to where it starts?'

'Follow it,' said Sarah, as if that was blindingly obvious.

'Rivers wiggle,' Zac protested.

Sarah looked at Zac, trying not be cross with the small boy. 'Then we'll just have to follow the wiggles, won't we?'

'Not necessarily,' said Ka, then stopped. Only he'd said too much already. And Sarah was looking at him, openly interested.

Reaching into his shirt pocket, Ka pulled out the dark glasses.

They were warm beneath his fingers. From the moment he'd found them, day or night, whatever the temperature in the desert they were always slightly warm. As if their temperature was controlled by a tiny spider's web of gold threads that ran beneath the surface of the frame.

'Wow,' said Saul. 'He's got shades.'

Ka kept his temper.

'Where am I?'

'What . . . ?'

Flipping up one hand, Ka cut dead Sarah's question. He could still see the others but now the fire had become a white blaze. A split second later, the flames fell into focus and it was the others who backed into shadow. And then in front of Ka's eyes, the picture changed. Maybe it altered inside his head or maybe the new picture happened on the lenses. It was hard to tell.

All Ka knew was that suddenly he looked down at himself. A boy with too-big boots, sat at a crude fire beside a girl in a vest and combats. Opposite sat another heavier girl, a small boy hugging a gun, and a large boy who was clearly the eldest but whose poorly-mended arm put him at an obvious disadvantage.

Around them were dotted other fires, other groups. Ka was slightly shocked at just how many fires there were. Further away began real tents, where the real soldiers slept, their camp fires fuelled by gas, not scrub or camel dung. Beyond this, a slope began and at the bottom was a wide river. And though the water level was low, fat hippopotami still hung heavy near the muddy banks, ignoring the jackals that slunk out of the darkness to drink.

Black birds with white crowns roosted in the ruin of an old tomb, its broken walls split apart so long ago that it looked like a natural formation, an outcrop of crumbling mud brick.

Lions were meant to sneak down from the highlands, ridden by white-whiskered monkeys who spoke a real language and lived high on a cliff face, secure from humans. Ka could see neither of these.

Though he could see movement, away to his right, human movement where dry wadis fed from mountains that ran the distant coast like a spine. Beyond this, a thin strip of towns and small cities separated the spine from more water than Ka could imagine.

RED SEA.

The letters lit across his vision, but he didn't need to read them because the name was spoken softly into his ears. Which was as well because Ka hadn't been taught reading, though he could remember anything if he knew it was important. And sometimes he remembered things anyway, just in case they turned out to be useful later.

So he knew, without being told, that the white markings on the bonnets of the 4x4s racing down the dried oueds towards their camp belonged to the government.

They left their fire banked up and burning brightly. Their rucksacks made a huddle under Saul's old blanket. At ground level it looked like they were still there and sleeping.

Ka led them through the early morning, heading west. Pickets were stationed at regular spots around the camp, but those on guard duty sat talking or smoking kif, which they hid in their hands so that ends stayed hidden from the grown ups. Who, if they were wise, stayed away. Two nights back a ten-year-old picket had fragged a one bar, ostensibly for refusing to give the password. Word was, she'd tried to confiscate his cache.

'This way.' Ka slid down a gravel bank to where silver water spread away into forever. Reality was less far than it looked, but far enough. Now was where he learnt if he actually had control over the group or not.

'We have to cross the river,' said Ka, his voice calm. As if asking them to brave the water was a perfectly reasonable request. For a second, he wondered whether to mention the armed trucks racing across the desert on the other side of the camp, each one filled with a dozen heavily-armed soldiers.

Saul might want to stay to fight and Ka could live with that. It mattered very little to him what Saul did, or where. But

Sarah might stay too, and that mattered much more. Bec, as ever, would do what was the least effort.

'What about crocodiles?' Zac asked.

'There aren't any,' Ka said firmly.

'How do you know?'

'I just do.'

Obviously enough he was lying, because he could see at least three. Log-like flickers of warmth that grew brighter the harder he looked. Crocodilus niloticus, according to the glasses, five hundred paces away. With luck, the reptiles would remain asleep. Without luck . . . Well, that applied to everything.

'Come on,' insisted Ka. 'Move it. And hold your weapon over your head so water doesn't go down the barrel.'

'I can't move it,' said Saul quietly. Sounding, for once, less than certain.

'Why not?

'Because I can't swim.'

'Oh . . .' Ka hadn't thought of that. 'Anybody else?'

'I probably can,' Zac said brightly. He paused, suddenly aware that Ka, Sarah and Bec were staring at him. 'I mean I've never tried but . . .'

Bec sucked at her teeth, crossly.

'Sarah?'

She was the only one Ka was really bothered about.

'Of course I can swim. My father was a fisherman.'

'So?' His father had kept camels and Ka hated the animals and they hated him. He never rode when there was an option to walk.

'So I can swim,' said Sarah. 'Okay?'

'Well, I can't.' Saul's voice was getting angry.

The picture shifted and tightened, an overlay of wavy lines hanging ghost-breath in front of Ka's eyes. Some spoke of height, being set tight to the edges of scars and cliffs. Others mapped the river. It took Ka a while to realize that these indicated depth, but that was because his attention was on something else.

Sarah volunteered to get the boat.

'Turn your backs,' she demanded, waiting until they had. Beneath her vest and combats she wore nothing except a ragged thong cut high at the hip. A Norwegian nurse had given the thong away, along with the rest of her spare clothes the day before returning to a family farm outside Namsos. The new owner died of a gut shot. Sarah had swapped the thong for a half packet of Cleopatra and an amulet from the person who owned it after that.

'Be back soon . . .'

Ka heard the slight splash, as they all did: but he was the only one able to watch as Sarah struck out across the dark expanse of water, head bobbing and legs kicking to the side. Except it wasn't her head he watched but her back and buttocks, flesh thinned by hunger and endless marches that trailed the Ragged Army up and down the river.

Fifteen minutes later, Sarah was on her way back, puffing slightly but happy. Although what the others saw was a boat that glided towards them as if by magic.

'Turn round,' she demanded, scrambling up the bank and into her dusty clothes, ignoring the water that ran down her legs and between her small breasts.

'What's with you?' Saul demanded.

Ka jumped.

'You're standing weird . . .'

'I was listening,' Ka said hastily and regretted it the moment Saul asked him the obvious question.

'To trucks,' said Ka.

Which got their attention. Zac went fly catcher, mouth hanging open, Bec looked round and even Sarah shot him a sideways glance as she squeezed water from heavy black braids. That was when Ka remembered he wasn't going to mention the government.

'Blue hats?' Saul's voice was raw.

'No idea,' said Ka, although he had. There were blue hats, militia and regular government troops. Plus two open trucks full of nasrani wearing black uniforms and swirling face paint. 'But I don't plan to hang round to find out.'

'You just going to run away then?

Ka stepped back. 'Which is more important?' he asked Saul. 'Staying here or going to turn off the Nile?'

'We can do that later,' Saul protested.

'What if we're dead?' Ka said. 'Who'll go then?'

The deck of the tiny felucca had been bleached white from a lifetime's sun, the sky sail was rotten and the sycamore sides were warped. Cracks above the water-line had been ignored but any gaps below were stuffed with rope and crudely gummed over, both inside and out, with dollops of bitumen.

'It looks great,' Ka told Sarah.

Together they launched her boat and then stood back, up to their hips in the wide river as Zac pulled himself up over the side. Bec followed, hooking her dress above wide hips to keep it out of the water. Ka guessed she knew she wasn't wearing any pants.

Chapter Nine

7th October

The earlier collective gasps of a city in orgasm were silent, although the crunch of exploding fireworks still tripped car sirens, providing a counterpoint to the dogs which found themselves tethered for the evening.

October 7th was *Ashura*, tenth day of Muhram and the date of El Iskandryia's biggest firework display. A night when rockets rose so often from parties along the Corniche that they ceased to attract the eye; and only the grandest waterfalls of silver sparks raised even slight interest. At midnight, having fasted for two days the city turned its attention to feasting.

Cafés spilled out onto pavements, restaurants were overbooked months in advance and only money or influence could get you a late table.

Heading west on Boul Isk, a dining car swayed over rails beaten silver with use and water slopped from a carafe. In a kitchen so small that the evening's menu was limited to only five dishes, a sous chef dropped his steamer of asparagus . . .

But all of that was only background. Maxim's was still the only place to dine at the end of *Ashura*. A single restaurant car with, bizarrely enough, its own liquor licence; crowded out with people who mattered. Which, in Zara bint-Hamzah's considered opinion, meant monied *and* stuck up, as opposed to her dad, who was just obscenely rich.

As of this morning, Zara's hair was blue, almost purple; cut extra short, like a stevedore, in solidarity with the dock strike in Tunis. Needless to say, the razor cut cost more than any stevedore earned in a week.

It did, however, suit her, now that a month of dieting had given

Zara back her cheekbones. And she understood the absurdity of her unstinting support for lost causes. Zara shrugged, then sighed, then shrugged again.

The final shrug was to annoy her mother.

Zara was dressed head-to-toe in a very grown-up *Atelier Azzedine* creation which revealed almost no flesh while clinging tightly to every curve. The gown had been worked up from a single sketch, then cut and corrected on the body of an appropriate house model. A notoriously slow and expensive way to work.

The honeymoon might not have happened, but Zara still appreciated her father letting her keep his present. Another of his surprises, altogether more unexpected, sat in her Gucci bag. The new Amex was not a top-up job, like the one which held her six-monthly allowance, nor a secondary card drawn against one of her father's banks. This was different, tied blind into a mega-interest account in Zurich. Just how mega only made sense once Zara had called Switzerland, read off the account number and had someone tell her just how many dollars sat with the gnomes.

So now she was both beautifully dressed and absolutely terrified. Because what her father had promised her, right after she nearly got murdered that evening in the warehouse, was her own flat . . . So she no longer had to live at Villa Hamzah.

Instead, he'd kept her at home and given her a one-off, nine-digit payment in US dollars, made to an account in a city where women having capital was obviously not against the law.

And for Zara, the real problem was not that her father had given her so much money, not even that he'd obviously changed his mind about letting her live alone, it was that she could no longer get close enough to him to find out why.

Later, was all he could say, *when things are sorted out*.

Taking a single caper from a nearby bowl, Zara sucked out the salt and reduced the flower bud to pulp with her tongue. She was reaching for another when a waiter materialized at her shoulder.

'Champagne?'

'Please.' Zara smiled and held up her glass, making someone at a table across the aisle snort with contempt. At the sight of a woman drinking, at the fact she'd lifted her own glass or just because she'd smiled at a waiter? It was hard to know and Zara told herself she didn't care. So she kept the smile in place and waited until her glass was full, then carefully thanked the man.

There was a Starbucks in New York at the intersection of Morningside and West 123rd, kitty corner to Central, where Zara had wasted every weekday evening for nine months waiting tables for basic plus tips rather than call home and admit the allowance she'd asked for wasn't enough to cover living in Manhattan, not even on a fifth floor walkup. The day she started being rude to waiters was the day she shot herself.

Still smiling, Zara looked across at the other table and raised her glass . . .

Millions had gone on Maxim's last refurbishment. Designers from Prague and Dublin had specified chairs that were, apparently, Arts and Crafts, ergonomically corrected to reflect modern requirements of comfort. The floor was smoked glass and the walls pale Burmese silk, taken from lava genetically fixed to excrete gossamer-thin strands of gold. Every painting was original, expertly provenanced. Mostly they were a mix of sombre Klee and Matisse, with the occasional August Macke. All this was the stuff of travel features.

What wasn't common knowledge was that a substantial proportion of the refurbishment costs went on bomb-proofing the restaurant car to US Army standards. Hamzah Effendi, however, knew the security specification exactly. SafetyUnlimited was a sub-division of Martini & Gattling, now a wholly-owned subsidiary of Quitrimala Enterprises.

Around the restaurant, interchangeable notables picked at roast turbot marinated in lime on a bed of cucumber, or prodded sautéed duck liver with fenugreek and Thai chilli. Maxim's was resolutely uncompromising in its allegiance to traditional fusion.

Personally, Hamzah would rather have been at home eating eggs fried with halumi but, as well as being *Ashura*, tonight was to celebrate Zara's escape from the clutches of a rogue *Thiergarten* assassin. That had been the idea anyway.

Only Zara sat gazing listlessly out of a window, Rahina was furious about something and their guest, a major who'd practically invited himself, was halfway through a boring description of the luxuries to be found aboard a liner called the *SS Jannah*.

'Do pay attention.'

Hamzah opened his eyes but Zara was the one being scolded. Somehow his wife's voice got the attention of everybody in the restaurant except her daughter.

'Zara, please pay attention.'

'To what exactly?' She smiled coldly at her mother.

'To what the major is telling you, darling.' The endearment was at odds with the anger in the dumpy woman's dark eyes.

'And what is the major telling me?' Zara asked, sweetly. She batted her eyelids at the man, who looked away, finally embarrassed. Quite at which of the many embarrassments on offer it was hard to say.

'Well?' Zara asked. When the major pretended not to hear her question, Zara went back to watching the shops go past.

According to the *Guide Michelin*, two Parisian chefs were first responsible for the idea of converting the tram into a moving restaurant. Where other entrepreneurs might have tried to cram in tables, they'd bought two wooden tramcars, linked them together and used the front car as a restaurant and the rear as offices and a kitchen. That had been 120 years before and, with only eight tables ever available, Maxim's had been booked solid for months ahead ever since.

'Just how did you get a reservation?' Zara asked suddenly.

The next table stopped talking. Maybe they were interested or maybe she'd just interrupted their idiot conversation, Zara didn't know and really didn't care.

'I mean,' she said bitterly, 'you couldn't know I was going to be *rescued* by Ashraf Bey, could you? And it wasn't like you knew he was going to turn out innocent.'

'I never believed that Raf . . .' began Madame Rahina.

Zara snorted.

Ignoring the look of outrage on her mother's face Zara turned to her father. 'The table,' she reminded him, just in case he'd forgotten.

'I never,' repeated her mother loudly, 'I never . . .' But she didn't get to finish that sentence either.

'You did,' said Zara. 'You told me execution was too good for him and that you knew, just as soon as you saw him, that he was an evil . . .'

'I got a list of everyone who had a table booked,' said Hamzah flatly, his voice cutting through the blossoming quarrel. Zara bet he pulled that trick at business meetings, not that he'd need to do it often. Most people he met owed him their living. 'Then I called them up in turn and made one of them an offer.'

'Which one?' The major's French carried a Cairene intonation that went with his hawk-like nose and high cheekbones. His skin was as honeyed as her own was dark and skilful tailoring on his dress uniform showed off his elegant figure. Zara reckoned she might even like him, if only he'd lighten up a bit.

'I mean,' he said, 'how did you choose?'

Hamzah laughed. 'Oh, that was easy. I told each one that I had every intention of eating here tonight and offered a token sum for his table to the one who sounded most horrified.'

Despite herself, Zara smiled, though it was obvious that the major was startled by the joke Hamzah made against himself. Which begged a big question, why was he really here? When she'd first walked into Maxim's and seen his name on a place card, Zara was sure he'd be her new suitor. Some well-born, near-bankrupt staff officer her mother had found to make her respectable . . . As if anything could make her respectable in Iskandryia's eyes after Raf had publicly jilted her.

Her father's money in return for social cachet. Class for cash, that was the deal Raf was offered. And it almost worked. Would have done in fact, if Raf's now-dead aunt and her own decidedly-undead mother had had anything to do with it. Only thing was, Raf had other ideas.

'Well,' said Zara, 'You got the table. So when do we actually get to eat?'

'There's plenty of time,' Hamzah said calmly.

'Really?' Zara her watch. 'Maybe my Rotary's fast.' She tapped the side, shrugged and went back to staring out of the tram. So what if she was behaving badly? She'd said the meal was a bad idea when he first suggested it and repeated herself when her father announced he'd booked a table. Nothing had happened since to make her change her mind.

The ornate offices of Thomas Cook and the Olympia building slid past, Café Athineos and the stuccoed Palais de Justice following after. Place Zaghloul let her look out over a dusty square to the dark sea beyond, until the view was cut off by a bus station. They were still headed west, one block back from the Corniche.

Coming next was the Tomb of the Unknown Soldier, where tramps slept against marble walls, tattered booths sold sticky almonds and foreign tourists walked hand in hand, seeing only beauty. Beyond that, the Corniche curved north towards the brooding weight of Fort Qaitbey.

Another road would herd the tram along the top of the promontory to Ras el-Tin, then steer south towards Maritime Station and the start of the old dockyards.

Seen on a map, the jutting promontory looked like a fat apple core. But the district's rock-like solidity was an illusion. Once, the area had been mostly underwater. Then a causeway joined an island to the shore. Eventually the causeway had been thickened, then thickened again with rubble until finally El Anfushi was created, with its narrow streets and weird, inward-looking Turko-Arabic houses. Houses that must be . . .

'Why couldn't you just invite Hani by herself?' Zara demanded suddenly. Hani might be nine but she could still date a building just by looking at it.

'Well?' Zara asked crossly.

'Perhaps she was the one who didn't want to come.' Madame

Rahina's words were brittle. Her anger at Raf's snub not quite offset by the pleasure she got from blaming Zara.

'You asked her?'

'No, of course I didn't *ask* her. You don't *ask* children. She was included on the invitation to Ashraf Bey.'

Terrific. Zara's glance slid to the empty chairs. Place names still showed who should have sat in them, though the maître d' had insisted on whisking away the table silver when he realized that Hamzah's missing guests were likely to remain that way.

'You didn't really expect him, did you?' Hamzah asked his daughter gently. There was no anger in his voice, no accusation. Just the acceptance of basic facts. Chief among them was that the last time Ashraf drove out to Villa Hamzah, she'd flatly refused to see him. Actually, Raf hadn't driven himself at all, Avatar was the one behind the wheel and she'd been cross about that too.

Expect him? She expected nothing.

That Av was missing was a given, Zara knew that. Her father only ever saw the kid if he knew her mother was busy elsewhere. And even that was a recent development, poor little bastard. Which was what Av was. In a city where polygamy was normal, to be illegitimate was by definition to be poor, one of the unwanted.

'Here,' said the major as he handed her a linen napkin, spotless and uncreased, 'you might want this . . .'

Zara looked at him blankly.

'You're crying,' he said.

She was too, which might explain the soft edges to the streets outside.

Chapter Ten

7th October

The girl at the window was unmistakable as the restaurant car trundled by. Her desolation so real that Raf could almost taste it through glass.

Been there, felt that.

He wore dark glasses from habit, a leather coat lined with spider's silk and boots with toecaps and black metal heels. Behind the Armani shades his eyes had four colour receptors, as they had done from birth, one more than strictly human. His fourth was in ultraviolet, though he could recalibrate across the entire spectrum.

Sound he adjusted by opening and closing his ears. So far, so predictable, if somewhat simplified. Unpredictability started with the fox, which now spat static, swore and raged inside his head.

The police bike on which Raf sat came with twin headlamps, featuring the very latest in multi-element cluster/light guide technology, but he'd disconnected them at the same time as he cut the wires to the brake light and both sets of indicators. The reflectors he'd ripped off by hand. Matt black alloys went with a racer-noir engine cage and a light-swallowing paint job. The whole bike was gloriously transparent to CCTV.

The paint job was fresh and done by a garage at cost. A lot of people in the city suddenly wanted to be friends with the new Chief of Detectives. As it was, Raf practically had to order his local store to start charging full price for groceries and only the threat of taking his business elsewhere had convinced the manager Raf was serious . . .

'You certain some fuckwit intends to snatch her?'

Raf wasn't sure whether to nod or cry, so he nodded. The fox might be back but it had rebooted to a default personality. And Raf had always thought the fox was the stable one while he suffered the glitches.

'*Says who?*' demanded the fox.

Said every snitch on the precinct's payroll, every cut-rate whore trying to cop a plea, even a few semi-honest members of the public too afraid to leave their names. Rumour had hit the streets on steroids and been breaking lap records ever since.

The *why* changed with every telling, but the *what* was rock solid, whispered from under veils and escaping like smoke in the cafés from between half-open lips; somehow, and it was a very indeterminate somehow, tables had been turned on Hamzah, the man himself had been made the proverbial offer that can't be . . . only he had, and as of now, Hamzah's kid was a walking target. Everybody but everybody who was anybody, who knew that kind of thing, already knew it. Hamzah included.

'*Daddy's rich?*'

'Come on,' Raf muttered crossly.

For a while the fox said little, so Raf went back to worrying about Hani, because some days that felt like what he did best.

Just before leaving home, Raf had asked the kid if there was anything she needed, meaning toast or hot chocolate before bed, and she'd looked at him, her arms like sticks and small face serious, flicked her dark fringe from darker eyes and said, '*more time.*'

So that was what he was trying to give her. Time and space. Life's great shortage for those who already had the luxury of water and food. Since the incident at the warehouse, Zara hated him, fair enough. Raf could live with that, but Hani's mistrust really hurt. He saw it in her every silence, her refusal to eat when he was in the madersa's huge kitchen, in sideways glances and half-conscious flickers of fear.

Most of the time Raf managed to convince himself that it was just his imagination. And then he'd come home to some unguarded look or catch a muttered reassurance from Donna to

Hani, as the kid was sent to kiss him goodnight before trundling off to bed.

Puddles, Hamzah had said, surprising Raf, the one time they talked. Adults might labour upstream against their grief but children step in and out of sadness, trailing it after them in damp footprints. Only to step back into misery when the ground behind them begins to look dry.

Chapter Eleven

7th October

'I'm fine,' Zara insisted.

'No, you're not.' There was a determined expression on her mother's face. 'Major Halim's absolutely right. What you need is some air.' Madame Rahina glanced at her husband for support but Hamzah was staring pointedly into the bottom of a brandy glass.

One of the advantages of dinner at Maxim's was that it held an international drinks licence. Alcohol might be frowned upon but it was not illegal.

'Air,' said Madame Rahina. 'A good idea . . . Don't you agree, my love?'

Hamzah pretended to wake with a start. He knew exactly what was going on and had done from the moment his wife first mentioned inviting the major, but he trusted his daughter to do only what she wanted.

'I think it's up to Zara,' Hamzah said carefully. 'Personally, I'm going to concentrate on pudding.' The thick-set man picked up a leather menu and held it in front of him like a shield.

Despite herself, Zara smiled.

The major smiled back and inside her head Zara shrugged. He was handsome in a flinty, movie-star kind of way, what with his granite jaw, brown eyes and hair just a little longer than Army regulations allowed. And he probably hadn't expected his off-the-cuff suggestion to be pounced on quite so hard by her mother.

Besides some problems were best got out of the way.

'Sure,' said Zara, pushing back her chair. 'Why not?' She waited for a second while the major tried to catch the attention of the maître d', then shrugged. 'No sweat,' Zara said. 'I can stop it myself.' And with that she reached for the emergency chain which looped its way down one wall and yanked.

Crockery hit the floor. Some from their table or others, but mostly from the arms of a stumbling waiter who'd been stacking plates in an opposite corner.

A woman screamed.

The tram stopped.

'Is there a problem?' The maître d' was white-faced with anxiety, his French accent as broken as the Limoges china around his feet.

'Of course there's a problem.' Zara grabbed the menu from her father. 'Look at this. You haven't even got chocolate ice cream . . .'

'Cut his engines now.'

'No.' Raf shook his head.

'Come on.' The fox sounded disgusted. *'It's a clean shot.'*

It was too. The man stepping down from the abruptly-stopped tram had paused to scan Ibrahim Square, one of his hands on Zara's shoulder, the other thrust deep in his jacket pocket. He said something to the girl and she nodded carefully, but moved away the moment he tried to take her arm.

What reassured Raf was that Zara looked irritated rather than afraid.

And yet Place Ibrahim Pasha was deserted, the restaurant car obviously planned to make good its escape and somewhere below Zara's feet were catacombs, cut into limestone a thousand years before the birth of the Prophet. Rumour said they spread beneath Pharos in endless dark passageways, rough-hewn chambers and deep oubliettes. Had Raf been Zara, he'd have been terrified.

'Just do it,' said the fox. *'Or maybe you're afraid?'*

Of killing if necessary? No, Raf shook his head. He didn't think so . . . If it wasn't necessary? Then yes, very. And something else was worrying Raf, worrying him enough to make him rewrite his plans on the fly.

'That uniform . . .'

'So?'

'You recognize?'

'Maybe it's fake,' suggested the fox.

'Yeah, that makes sense,' said Raf. Dress in the flashiest way possible. A bottle-green cavalry tunic with gold braid and sword knots to sleeves and collar. The kind of outfit guaranteed to make people look and remember. Rather than choose something anonymous like *sécurité*, whose black uniform made most people glance away, whether it was intended to or not.

Raf stood up, brushed dust from his knees and walked back to his bike.

'Where are you going?' the fox demanded.

'To talk to Zara.' Breaking stock from barrel, Raf folded his borrowed police-issue nightSniper in two, twisting off the tiny laser sight and dropping that in his pocket. The rest he clipped into place down one of the Honda's front forks.

'Very dinky . . .'

Ignoring the fox, Raf stalked across the square, a figure dressed in black moving across an expanses of unlit ground. He was impressed the major spotted him so quickly.

'Zara.'

She turned when he called, the smile freezing on her face. Her eyes raked over him, seeing nothing in the darkness but distant light reflecting off the emptiness of his shades.

'Still wearing disguises, I see.'

'You know him?' Major Halim took a hand from his pocket.

'Oh yes.' She turned to the watchful major, her eyes bitter. 'How could I possibly forget Ashraf al-Mansur . . .'

'The *bey?*'

Raf put out his hand and then lowered it again, unshaken. The police had a file on the General's *aide de camp*, but then they had a file on pretty much everyone. 'Whatever,' said Raf.

Major Halim had both hands clenched into fists, something Raf doubted the man even realized. And busy emotions worked their way across his movie-star face. Distrust battling doubt, caution fighting mistrust.

Caution lost.

Looking at the major's hand-made uniform, his immaculate leather boots, the careful disorder of his dark hair and a discreet signet ring on his left hand which signalled membership of a family known for its closeness to the Sultan in Stambul, Raf knew what was coming. He'd heard those rumours too . . .

'I have a brother at court,' said the major flatly.

'An elder brother,' Raf agreed, 'Faud Pasha.' Facts collected themselves for use, the structure of the Sublime Porte's directorate, the rank therein of Faud Pasha. 'Second Minister for Internal Affairs.'

'First Minister,' Major Halim corrected.

'Acting First Minister,' said Raf firmly. 'Married well. Trusted notary to His Sublime Majesty . . .' He could do this. He'd always had the skill, right back to when he was a kid. Every fact in his head was filed, cross-referenced, graded for likely importance. When he was seven Raf failed an exam. He did it to prove to himself that he could. There were other reasons too, but time was teaching Raf that it didn't pay to dwell on those.

He glared at the major. 'As for you . . . Unmarried, this year's mistress in Al Qahirah, last year's in Abukir, neither serious. An adequate trust fund but no capital and currently no way to pay your share of the extortionate repairs to the roof of Miclavez Court . . .'

Zara's eyes when Raf checked were wet. For a woman who'd once told him she never cried, she'd taken to doing a good imitation.

'. . . Oh yes, and you once shot an eleven-year-old *felaheen* rioter.'

'He was . . .'

'Holding an empty starting pistol,' said Raf. 'Something cheap, generic and Taiwanese.'

There were files on every member of Koenig Pasha's staff. Even one on the General, though the ex-Chief had drawn the line on keeping one on the Khedive himself. Either that, or it was so well hidden Raf had yet to find the thing.

Keeping those files up to date had turned out to be simplicity itself. All Raf had to do was nothing. The web of informers put in place by his predecessor, Felix Abrinsky, kept spinning, once they realized they'd continue to get paid for each snippet of information. 'Anything else you'd like to know about your friend?' Raf asked Zara, who promptly turned her back on him.

'What about you . . . ?' Raf asked the major. 'With me so far?' He watched uncertainty replace anger in the major's eyes. Rumour might hurt but hard information was actively dangerous and Raf tossed it around like a throwing knife.

'There's no record of . . .'

'Look,' said Raf, 'let's simplify things. Your brother checked me out in Stambul and found no record of my being an honorary attaché in Seattle . . .' He ticked points off on his fingers, trying not to miss any. 'No one in special forces has heard of me, Sandhurst say I'm not on their files, St Cyr ditto, I'm not on the Sultan's official payroll and so far as your brother can find out, I don't exist.'

Raf's cold smile was wasted in the darkness, but his voice carried enough ice to make even Zara shiver. 'Have you any idea of the level of security clearance that signifies?'

Slowly, reluctantly, Major Halim shook his head.

'Did you check me with my father?' Raf continued.

'The Emir?'

Yeah, the Emir of Tunis, apparently. That was what his aunt Nafisa had said, just before she got herself stabbed; Raf still didn't believe it, and it was hard to know in retrospect if she'd believed it or not. Whatever, no one had yet come out and said it wasn't true.

'Well? Did you?' said Zara, sounding suddenly interested.

'Yes, I did.' The major looked nervous. 'He wasn't able to answer.'

'Why not?' Raf asked, and knew he'd won when the major actually shuffled his feet, looking like the small boy he must once have been back before Zara was born.

'He was unwell.'

'You mean my father's mad,' said Raf. 'Stark raving.' That was what Iskandryian intelligence had down in their files. The Khedive's second cousin lived in a tent near Nefzaoua Oasis, surrounded by heavily-armed girls in green jumpsuits and guarded at all times by an elderly French woman. In private the Emir apparently favoured simple wool jebbas, but his public dress never changed from a striped jellaba, worn with a general's peaked hat.

He lived for hawks, grew generation after generation of saline-resistant grasses in a biodome on the edge of Chott el Jerid, Tunisia's salt-crusted inland sea, and had once hired a Soviet cryptographer and one of Cal-Tech's most brilliant geneticists, giving them orders to extract meaning from the randomness of junk DNA.

Political decisions the Emir made after consulting the heavens. Not listening to a pet astrologer, though that would have been bad enough, but asking questions of the constellations themselves. And when he spoke, in public or private, report had it that he spoke only in complex couplets, perfectly cadenced and delivered after long thought.

Among the Berber tribes, who still traversed the empty sands and rock seas with little care for international borders, he was regarded as North Africa's sole sane ruler. It was a minority opinion and one with which it was obvious Major Halim didn't agree.

'So tell me,' said Raf, 'who am I?'

The major looked at the young princeling in the black leather coat, the dark glasses and black gloves whose pale hair blew in the slight night breeze. 'The son of the Emir of Tunis,' he said without hesitation.

Raf nodded and offered his hand. This time they shook.

'Very touching,' said Zara. 'Now if you've both finished with the male-bonding shit perhaps Major Halim could escort me home. Of course,' she added crossly, 'if this wasn't El Isk I could get myself home. Since I'm perfectly capable of walking, chewing gum and looking where I'm going at the same time.

But since this *is* Iskandryia and any woman alone at night is *obviously* a prostitute . . .'

Raf grinned. Then smiled some more at Major Halim's discomfort. 'This is nothing,' he said, 'you wait until you know her better and she gets really cross.'

'*Better* . . . ?' The major executed a tiny bow in Zara's direction. 'Much as I'd welcome the chance to get to know Miss Quitrimala better, I'm afraid that's impossible.' His tone was genuinely regretful.

'Don't tell me,' said Zara, 'you couldn't cope with a third mistress.'

'It's not that,' the major said, looking shocked. 'I'm leaving for Berlin next week, on secondment to the *Thiergarten*. After that, if everything goes smoothly I hope to become Iskandryia's attaché to Stambul.' For a moment, admitting this, the major seemed almost bashful. But Zara was too cross to notice.

'Then what,' she asked furiously, 'was gate-crashing my supper about? All that sucking up to my mother. And the crap about me needing air and taking a walk . . .'

'This is difficult,' said the major and glanced at Raf. When it became obvious that Raf refused to take his cue to withdraw, Major Halim sighed. 'The Khedive intends to take a holiday . . . Well deserved obviously.'

Zara opened her mouth to speak and then closed it again. A sudden tension locked her shoulders, which refused to budge, even when she twisted her head from side to side. Zara had a nasty idea she knew exactly what was about to come next.

'His Highness was wondering if . . .'

'Have you talked to my parents about this?'

'Of course,' the major said nervously. 'Your father said it was your decision where you took your holidays and with whom. Which was not, to be honest, the reaction I was expecting. Your mother thinks it's an excellent idea.'

I bet she does, thought Zara. Somewhere in her mother's finely gradated misunderstanding of Iskandryian society, the woman undoubtedly believed that being mother to the

Khedive's mistress was even better than having a bey in the family.

Zara had been spot on about her mother's desperation that she take this walk, totally wrong about the motives. 'It's not going to happen,' she said calmly.

So calmly that even the major could hear her keep the anger in check.

'Tell the boy I'm not interested. Just that, nothing else. Don't make it polite, don't give my apologies or regrets because I'm not sending them . . .'

'You misunderstand,' the major said carefully. 'You misunderstand completely. The Khedive's intentions are entirely *honourable*.' He stumbled over the word, not certain how much he could actually say. In his own mind, before supper, when he'd been running through how to approach the coming evening, he'd seen them both taking a moonlit stroll through the terraces of the Palace Ras el-Tin while he proffered the Khedive's invitation and she accepted gratefully.

'He doesn't want to get me into bed?'

The major's lips twisted. 'Let me repeat myself. His intentions are strictly legitimate.'

Zara's eyes widened. Impossible visions of palaces, sleek yachts, long holidays aboard the *SS Jannah* opened like flowers before her.

'And if I go on this holiday?'

'Then he'll propose,' said Raf, 'won't he?'

Major Halim looked pained. 'You can't honestly expect me to comment.'

'God.' Raf laughed. 'Koenig Pasha must be climbing a wall . . . Only my cousin could decide he needed to marry a hard-line republican. Not to mention occasional communist.' They had files on Zara too, back at the precinct. Files he could recite from memory.

'Have you spoken to my parents about that bit as well?' Zara asked the major.

Major Halim shook his head. 'Only tentatively about the holiday. Enough to make clear that you would be an honoured . . .'

'Well don't,' Zara stressed. 'Speak to them, I mean. It's nothing they need to know.'

'They're your parents.'

'Talk to either of them about this,' said Zara, 'and I guarantee I won't go.'

'But the Khedive is determined to do this properly. By the book . . .'

'You do realize,' Zara interrupted crossly, 'that if the Prophet had been a woman there wouldn't even have been the Book, because no one would have listened, never mind written it down . . .'

Chapter Twelve

8th October

The first of that Friday's calls to prayer found Raf leant against a sea wall, watching smugglers run empty cigarette boats into Western Harbour under protection of both darkness, which came free, and the Commander of Ras el-Tin, whose protection came anything but . . .

And the Terbana Mosque's definition of dawn seemed open to debate. The Mufti had defined it as a point, not when light first touched the sky but when the absolute utterness of the night first lessened.

Raf thought the man was being unduly optimistic.

Hamzah's call came four hours later, just as Raf was about to shower away the black dog of his wasted night. Because even blasting his police Honda to Abu Sir and back, fifty clicks along the shore, had done nothing to improve Raf's mood, even though early mist had hung over the Mariout marshes and the Mediterranean had still worn her night colours.

'For you,' shouted Hani, her call echoing up the lift shaft from the haremlek below. 'It's Effendi.'

Raf had warned Hani not to call Hamzah that, but currently the child was paying zero attention to anything he said.

'Tell him I'll call back.'

'He says it's important.'

Sighing, Raf picked up his dressing gown from the floor and pulled on some old leather slippers which Khartoum insisted once belonged to Hani's grandfather. When Raf made some glib comment about dead men's shoes, the old porter had pulled deeply on the wrong end of a cigar and nodded like it was obvious.

'This alone is true,' he'd told Raf. 'This here, at this time, for this person.' Khartoum had announced it like that was also obvious. Three days later Raf was still puzzling over that one.

'Uncle Raf . . .' Hani's voice was tight with exasperation.

'I'm on my way.'

'. . . You could always get comms installed up there.'

Raf nodded and slid back the metal grille to step into the lift. He could indeed, but he wouldn't. His floor was the only level of the madersa not fitted with a screen and he liked it that way.

'. . . or you could try turning on your watch,' added Hani, when he finally reached her floor.

'But then you wouldn't have an excuse to complain, would you?' Raf said and punched a button to activate a screen. Hani stalked off in silence, chin up and shoulders rigid, and though Raf heard the slam of her bedroom door he didn't call her back.

Just after their Aunt Nafisa was murdered, Raf had made a promise to Hani not to send her away to school. Keeping his word was proving harder than he'd imagined. Particularly as everyone else seemed to think the girl would be better off living somewhere different, somewhere he wasn't. Until recently he'd have disagreed.

'Hamzah.'

'Your Excellency.'

'You don't need to call me . . .'

'This is official.' The industrialist's face was tight, with a greyness that suggested acute shock.

'Zara.'

'My daughter is here,' Hamzah said. 'And she's fine. Although for reasons I don't understand, I gather you met her early this morning.'

'Avatar?'

The man looked embarrassed. 'Avatar's gone,' he said simply. 'Kidnapped . . .'

'*Avatar?*'

Raf's explosion of anger brought Hani out of her room; or maybe it was the way he slammed the wall with the side of his fist. 'How do you know?'

'I've had a note.'

'Demanding what?'

The man on screen took a deep breath and then slowly released it. 'That doesn't matter.'

'I'll need to see the note.'

'It no longer exists,' said Hamzah, staring out at Raf. 'I burnt it . . .'

'So what do you want?' Raf asked tightly. 'Since you obviously don't consider you need police help to get Avatar back . . .'

'I want you to come out to the villa and take a look at something my gardener's just found . . .' With that, Hamzah fumbled at his end of the connection and the screen in the haremlek went dead.

Even ripped open and with her feet washed by the waves, the body might have shown signs of lividity had the girl been dead for much longer than a few hours. As it was, the skin was waxy and slightly warm, but gravity hadn't pooled blood along the underside of her legs. Both rigor and early, non-fixed lividity had yet to occur.

That gave Raf his time frame.

The killer had opened the blonde girl from pubis to sternum, then slashed again, straight across her ribcage, the cuts forming a cross. Smaller incisions, made at right angles, acted as stops to the cross. Her heart was missing, which was often the case in crimes of *mutilé*, so were both her lungs, and the killer had cut the initials *H.Q.* into her wrist.

Not a single print could be taken from her pale skin. Whoever had wielded the blade had worn surgical gloves and from the cleanness of the incisions Raf put odds on her killer using a scalpel or filleting knife.

Mind you, since what little Raf knew of forensics came from reading notebooks left by Felix Abrinsky, the previous Chief, and since the fat man's notes were often impossible to decipher, Raf fully accepted that the sooner he brought in professionals the better.

'Sir, you might want to take a look at this . . .' The young policewoman carrying a camera kept her voice level, almost businesslike. Raf hadn't met her before but she looked about twelve and wore a black *hijab*, the traditional headscarf, checked along its edge in the blue and white of the WPF.

Her boss, Madame Mila, coroner-magistrate for women and head of the WPF, had obviously already warned her in general against talking to other departments, and against talking to the Chief of Detectives in particular.

Raf's way round this prohibition had been to point out the obvious.

'*Touristica,*' he'd announced on seeing the body, mere seconds after arriving on Hamzah's beach. It didn't matter what sex tourists were, they still came under the *poliz touristica*, who reported to uniform; uniform automatically reported all unsolved serious to Raf.

'How do you know, Sir?' Stuck between a rock and the proverbial, Raf thought, looking at her heavy face. Upset Madame Mila or upset Iskandryia's new Chief of Detectives.

'What's your name?'

'Leila, Your Excellency.'

'Take a look at her breasts.'

The young woman blushed but did what she was told. The breasts in question were small and pale brown.

'What do you see?'

Leila stayed silent, staring desperately.

'It's okay,' said Raf, 'take a look at her . . . lower half.' The dead girl was completely naked, draped backwards across a rocky outcrop on Hamzah's beach. Her feet were underwater, the rest of her was beginning to mottle in the early morning light.

'What do you see?'

The police officer peered closely, looking for abrasions or thumb marks, something to say the woman had first been raped, but her flesh was unbruised and nothing obvious sprang to mind.

'She . . . has a tan line round her hips?'

Raf nodded and Leila almost sighed aloud with relief.

'What else?'

'That's the only tan line.'

'Neatly done.' Raf flicked on his Seiko and hot-keyed Champollion Precinct. Not bothering to announce himself, he rattled off time, place and crime code. 'The first official on the scene was Officer . . .' He glanced quickly at Leila.

'Durrell.'

'Officer Durrell from the Women's Police Force who recognized immediately, from the tan mark of a bikini bottom and a corresponding lack of a tan mark for the breasts, that the victim had to be a tourist. Accordingly the crime scene was handed over to me as the most senior detective present.'

Mind you, thought Raf, Officer Durrell was more impressed with his abilities than she need be. This was the second mutilated body to be found in a week. And since the first one was now on her way back to Austin in an ice box and the second was also blonde, young and obviously Western, it was difficult not to assume a pattern, albeit slightly unprofessional; since, having only two cases, the most Raf should be positing was a basic similarity.

Unfortunately, the police didn't know if the first victim had been raped. The pathologist had apparently forgotten to check.

In short, bleak sentences Raf ordered in a scene team and told the handler to notify Madame Mila's office of the change of responsibility. Only once did Raf's voice hesitate. Having just ordered that the tourist go to the nearest morgue, as soon as the site was swept and the crime scene shots completed, Raf had a change of mind.

'No,' he said, 'send it to Dr Kamila . . .' Kamila didn't work for his division but she could be persuaded, and she knew what she was doing. She was also a woman. In crimes like this that could count.

'Dr Kamila it is. The pick-up location. That's . . .'

Raf waited for the question which never came. Instead the handler muttered a hurried Ten4 and broke his connection. Within minutes the fact that a naked tourist had been found butchered in the grounds of Villa Hamzah would be round Police HQ. Within half an hour the outer precincts would know.

The fact Raf had called in the crime would only make the titbit more juicy.

Turning on his heel, Raf stamped up the salt grass which separated the rocky headland from the villa's terraces and entered Hamzah's study through its garden door, without knocking. There was a conversation that needed to be had and Raf wasn't looking forward to it.

The industrialist was sat at his desk, just as Raf expected. And he didn't even frown when Raf strode in from the garden.

'Where were you two hours ago?' Raf made little attempt to keep the anger out of his voice. This was the man who'd burnt the note sent by Avatar's kidnappers. The man who'd pimped his naked daughter the night Raf walked out of that door, who was now pimping her again to the Khedive.

'Still dining with my wife at Maxim's.'

With my wife . . . Raf looked for the slightest hint of irony in Hamzah's face but there was nothing. 'Can you prove that?'

Hamzah nodded. 'I think they'll remember us,' he said sourly.

'And this was a long-standing arrangement?'

'No,' said Hamzah, looking up. 'It was very last minute. Why?'

'Because there's a butchered girl in your garden, round about where your daughter usually swims and your initials are carved into her wrist. So what I want to know is the usual stuff . . . Who is she/where did she come from/who did it . . . ?'

'And if I tell you I have no idea?'

'No idea,' said Raf as he pulled a square of card from his pocket and tossed the Polaroid onto Hamzah's desk. 'No idea who did this?'

Hamzah Effendi picked up the photograph and began to tremble. The movement started in his fingers and spread like fever until his whole body shook. And his body kept shaking, even after he'd turned the photograph face down and pushed it away from him.

His body was still shaking when he pushed back his chair to rush to the lavatory. And it was doing the same when he came back after vomiting up his breakfast and what had remained of last night's meal.

'She was face down,' he said. 'When I saw her she was face down.'

Chapter Thirteen

8th October

'Eduardo?'

Eduardo nodded from instinct. It didn't matter that the person talking was half a city away and that Eduardo's watch wasn't toggled to visual. He still nodded.

'*Na'am* . . . This is me.' Eduardo folded his broadsheet and placed it carefully on the table. He would have preferred one of the Arabic-language tabloids but he had his position to consider, so he always downloaded *L'Iskandrian*.

The Frenchman and Frisco were watching him from the corners of their eye. They'd both decided his watch was a fake and his new job just empty words, but they were wrong. Instinctively, Eduardo straightened in his café chair and ran one hand though his thinning hair, then discreetly rubbed his fingers clean on the side of his black chinos.

He listened in silence, nodding seriously now and then like a man agreeing with a particularly pertinent point. Not everyone had an elegant Silver Seiko that double-encrypted conversation and screened itself from vanP hacking.

'*Na'am*, I understand.' Eduardo did too – really – but just to be sure he asked the man to repeat his instructions more slowly.

Eduardo liked his new job. He even had an office, a third-storey walk-up off Place Orabi, above a haberdasher's at the back of the bus depot. With the office and watch came new shoes, new trousers and a zip-up leather jacket that looked old and tatty unless you got really close, when it was possible to see that the scuff marks were printed onto the animal hide.

The man who gave Eduardo the jacket had pulled out a

gravity knife, dropped its blade and driven it hard into the leather. The sharp point of the blade hardly even left a mark.

'Mesh,' he told Eduardo, 'ultrafine, from spiders that shit steel.' Eduardo didn't know whether the man was making fun of him or not. All the same, Eduardo liked what he now did. Which was mostly sit in cafés and talk politics, something he wasn't sure he really understood. Listening to the counter-arguments, Eduardo had discovered a talent for separating half-truth from mere wish. A cast-iron, built-in bullshit detector, the man called it, speaking as if such a machine might actually exist.

Eduardo imagined it as small, with cog wheels that whirred and narrow brass pipes which grew hot from circulating water. When Eduardo was a child he lived in a small burg in Namibia and the local train, to Windhoek and back, had run on coal and wood, dried dung too when the shortages began, though dung didn't work that well.

'Mmm . . .' Eduardo said, nodding. 'Sure thing.' He tossed a handful of silver onto the table. Time to go. His watch didn't need him to shut down the connection, because it did that for itself. It did other things too, like bring him the latest football results and forecast that it was going to rain.

'Things to do,' he said to Frisco, speaking Ladino. 'Deals to make.' Iskandryia was a city with a number of languages that might claim to be the lingua franca, of which Spanish Hebrew was just one. The other man nodded. Frisco had told Eduardo his real name but Eduardo kept forgetting, though he remembered that the man claimed his forefathers were *moriscos*, expelled from Spain.

When Eduardo started coming to the café, he and Frisco had played a few games of chess but now the old man made excuses not to play, probably because Eduardo kept losing.

Inside Eduardo's office the air was cool, which was a miracle given his desk-fan had fused and the October sun beat direct on an outside wall; but the walls were thick, built decades before from limestone blocks stolen from a Coptic church three streets away. And anyway closed shutters kept out much of the brightness. There was also air-conditioning attached to one wall, a brown box that stuck its metal arse out into the street, as if threatening to shit on pedestrians beneath. Unfortunately that had been broken ever since someone hid a wank mag up the air outlet. When Eduardo first took the box apart to see if anything obvious was broken, he'd been left with frayed wires, rusting iron pipes and mildewed, disintegrating pictures of pale nipples and shaven pudenda.

So he'd put the casing back together and pushed the mags back where he found them, and now tiny mushrooms grew in clusters on the grey carpet, right below where the unit dripped water.

A Sony Eon3 sat on an otherwise clear desk. A simple Luxor terminal, he'd chosen it at random in a souk at the back of Rue Faransa. Glued to its side was an anonymizer, which had been given him by the man. On the 'mizer was a label, *Property of El Iskandryia Police Department: not to be removed from Champollion Precinct under any circumstances.*

Punching a key, Eduardo started random number software and waited. Without him having to ask, the terminal popped-up a comms screen and Eduardo keyed in the number he'd just been given. Then he did what the man had told him to do.

Eduardo didn't know that he was being re-routed or that, at the receiving end, his call was logged as having come direct from Fez; all Eduardo knew was that a tiny icon on the screen's task bar lit green and a connection got made.

The person who picked up at the other end said nothing to introduce himself, which was fine, because that was what Eduardo had been told to expect.

'I'm taking the contract.'

'Who gave you the details?' The voice was gruff.

'That doesn't matter.'

'What guarantees do I have that the job will be done?'

'None.'

'By the day after tomorrow or the line of credit closes.'

'Tomorrow night,' said Eduardo and broke the connection.

Chapter Fourteen

9th October

'Don't you like pastries?' Hani sounded puzzled instead of angry. She'd been ploughing her way through a dozen *basbousa*, stuffing them into her mouth with sticky fingers at the start, then eating more slowly and finally nibbling, mouse-like around the edge, once she realized Raf wasn't going to tell her to stop.

Her lunchtime vitamin stood untouched by her plate.

'What?'

Raf glanced up to find dark eyes staring at him from a pinched face. He tried to make sure he and Hani ate together at weekends, while Donna bustled around in the background, banging together pans and clattering knives into a double stone sink, each side large enough to be a horse trough.

The kitchen took up most of the ground floor of the al-Mansur madersa. Outside was a tiled courtyard with a fountain and beyond that a stone garden house and then a walled garden, roofed over with glass.

Above the kitchen was the *qaa*, where important guests were greeted. This had a large marble floor and smaller indoor fountain. The haremlek was a suite of rooms above the *qaa* and Raf's floor was at the top, above the haremlek.

The madersa was vast, old and badly in need of repair, but no other room was as large as Donna's kitchen, which seemed to spread in all directions.

It had taken Raf a while to realize that Donna's clattering wasn't irritation at finding him cluttering up her space, which was so big a crowd couldn't have cluttered it; she objected to his presence for different reasons. People like Hani and His

Excellency were meant to eat upstairs, at a marble table in the elegant *qaa*, waited on by others.

'You're not listening to me . . .' Hani said crossly.

'I'm sorry . . .' She was right. He wasn't.

There wasn't much else Raf could say. But Hani wanted more. Something dismissive of her concern, something adult. He could see that in her eyes, the wish for a fight so that she could stop being worried for him and go back to being angry.

'Look,' he said softly, 'Let it go, okay?'

By the time the noise of her falling chair had finished echoing round the kitchen, Hani was out of the room and racing up the outside steps to the *qaa*. Raf listened to her shoes slap the floor overhead and then heard Hani slam a hand against the button for the lift. Seconds later the madersa's ancient Orvis creaked into action.

Raf put his head in his hands. When he looked up again Donna was sat on the other side of the table and in front of him was a tiny cup of Turkish coffee. It was the old woman's cure for everything.

'The child's young, Your Excellency.'

Raf nodded.

'And she's scared.'

'That I will send her away?'

Donna shook her head and discreetly rubbed her crucifix. 'That you will die.' The old woman's voice was matter of fact. 'Since her aunt . . . She dreams all the time. That you die and she be left here alone.' Donna shrugged. 'They would not let people like me look after Lady Hana. They would not let me live here . . .'

Only Donna got away with calling the child by her real name. Everyone else had to use Hani. Named for the boy the child resented not being.

'Go to her, Excellency,' said Donna, 'and talk.'

'And say what?' His question sounded weak even to him.

The old woman shrugged. 'That you will not be going away. That you don't plan to die.' Her lips twisted into a sour smile at Raf's expression.

'Well, does Your Excellency?'

Raf shook his head.

'No,' said Donna, crossing herself. 'Somehow I didn't think so.'

'Go away.' Hani didn't bother looking up from her screen. On the floor beside her chair sat an untouched toy dog, still in its packaging. It was the most expensive model Raf had been able to afford.

'It smells in here,' said Raf.

She did look round at that.

'Old clothes,' he said, gesturing to a bundle on the floor. 'Old clothes and misery . . .' Raf pulled back the inner shutter of a mashrabiya and autumn sunlight washed into Hani's bedroom, through her balcony's ornately-carved screen.

'Now I can't see my monitor.'

'You can use it later,' Raf said, 'but first we need to talk.' He sat on the red-tiled floor, his spine hard against the edge of her metal bed. The springs were rusted and the mattress so old that horsehair poked through holes in its cover. Changing the thing was absolutely out of the question, apparently.

'Sit by me . . .'

Hani sighed and made a great show of turning off her machine, even through they both knew it would have gone to sleep at a simple voice command. Then, surprisingly, she did as he asked and parked herself next to Raf, her own back pressed into the side of her bed. Dust flecks danced in the afternoon sunlight in front of them. Their ersatz randomness actually the result of immutable laws of heat and motion.

'I saw a body yesterday morning.'

Hani grew still.

'It was at Zara's house. A stranger . . .' Raf added hurriedly.

'You've seen bodies before,' Hani said.

He nodded, they both had. Aunts Nafisa and Jalila. Those deaths were one of the things which bound them together.

'When you were an assassin . . .'

'Hani!' They'd been through this before. 'I was an attaché . . . Nothing more.'

'Attachés are spies. Spies kill people. Everyone knows that.' Raf sighed.

'Who was he?' Hani asked.

'*She*,' Raf corrected. 'And we haven't found out yet.' Obviously enough, he didn't mention the mutilation, which was actually a *cross potent* according to the pathologist, who'd looked it up.

Toxicology showed heavy traces of an mdma clone in the victim's blood and alcohol in her stomach. The girl had been alive and conscious from the start of the attack until near the end. And swabs taken from her oral, anal and vaginal mucosa indicated that she'd first been raped, then cut. So Raf now had a file to read on *crosses coupe*, which had apparently been the mutilation of choice during something called 'the little war'. There was one bite mark, below her right breast, but that was faded and the bruise yellow. So either it happened before she arrived in Isk, it was the result of a casual holiday romance or her boyfriend had come with her but had yet to step forward.

Which, at least, would give Raf one sensible suspect. Provided the boyfriend could be shown to have nerves of steel and a reasonable grasp of anatomy.

'The trouble,' Raf told Hani, 'is in realizing when facts aren't related . . .'

He halted himself there, wondering whether to begin again and decided not to bother with the talking. With luck, sitting next to Hani would be enough, because when he was a child, the point at which adults started in on explanations was the moment he stopped listening.

'Everything is related,' said Hani. And glancing sideways, Raf realized her face was screwed up in thought. 'That's what Khartoum says . . .'

The kid was nine, whipcord thin, with the body of a child younger still and eyes old before their time. Lack of sleep, bad dreams and night sweats, he remembered them all well. Although, these days, if Raf worked at it, he could go for months without recalling them once.

'Maybe he's right,' said Raf finally. 'Maybe everything does connect.'

'You don't know?' Hani looked interested.

'No.'

'I thought spies knew everything.'

'Not me.' Raf shook his head. 'Me, I know nothing, except that I'm not going to send you away, I'm not going to leave you and nobody is going to kill me . . .'

'Aunts Jalila and Nafisa were killed . . .' She waited for Raf to nod, which he did. 'But the reason's a secret . . .'

Raf nodded again.

'Why?'

'Because . . .' Raf stopped. 'Because that's the way things work in Iskandryia.' He ignored the doubtful expression on her face. 'What can I tell you? What the General says goes.'

'Koenig Pasha?' Hani looked suddenly relieved. 'Not Zara's idea? Not yours . . .'

Raf shook his head, his half-smile a reflection of hers.

Hani nodded. 'I was worried,' she said, 'that it was Zara. If it's Koenig Pasha who says we must lie, then that's different . . .' Her shrug was almost comically adult. 'Lying is his job.' For a second, she sounded almost exactly like her late unlamented Aunt Nafisa.

There were, it turned out, two entirely separate levels of morality in Hani's world. One occupied by those, like him, her and Zara, who weren't meant to lie, and another given over to those destined to massacre the truth.

Pushing himself to his feet, Raf wondered what would happen when the child finally realized that if he was a spy, then she'd got him filed under the wrong group.

'Where are you going?' Hani demanded.

'Out,' said Raf.

'The murder?'

Raf shook his head. 'Something else . . .'

Hani regarded him carefully. 'I thought you were going to leave finding Avatar to someone called Eduardo?'

'Hani!'

'So I listened,' said the child, 'Anyway . . . you need me to help with the search.'

'I don't.'

'Yes you do,' said Hani.

'There is no way,' said Raf, his voice firm. 'That you're coming with me.'

'Who wants to come with you?' Hani said dismissively. Scrambling to her feet, she waved one hand in front of her screen and watched it blink back to life. A pass of her thumb over a floating track ball and the active window closed, revealing an aerial shot of the city.

'He's locked in a cellar,' said Hani, voice casual. 'There's stale water outside.'

'What kind of stale water?'

'So you *do* want my help?'

Raf sighed.

'Ali Bey ordered the Mahmoudiya Canal built in 1817,' Hani said carefully. 'On the far side, a green tram comes towards the window, then turns left . . .'

'Anything else?' Raf didn't know what else to say.

Hani nodded. 'Turbini. No.' She stopped, correcting herself. 'Not turbini. Freight trains, long ones that rattle, somewhere behind the room. Which means he's . . .' She touched the picture, pulling up a tight lattice of streets, where tramlines ran south along Rue Amoud, before turning into Avenue Mahmoudiya. At the bottom of the picture, on the other side of the canal a fat ribbon of track ran towards a rail yard. 'Somewhere round here.'

'And you know this how?'

Hani nodded to a toy tortoise gathering dust in one corner of her bedroom. It was old, with over-rounded edges and what proved to be fractal patterns playing constantly across its shell, like swirling clouds. Someone had applied a sticker of a cartoon rabbit, then tried to peel it off sometime later, leaving a sticky patch and half a smug, buck-toothed face.

The tortoise was so ancient that it connected by cable to the wall feed, with another cable run round the edge of Hani's room to her screen.

'I used Herbert,' said Hani.

It was possible . . . In theory, CCTV cameras covered all the main streets in the city. Trams, trains, even licensed taxis carried vidcams by law. Face recognition software was notoriously flawed, but could probably just about pick a dreadlocked DJ with facial piercings from the crowd of suits or jellaba-clad market traders.

'Really?'

Hani turned away, killing her terminal with a snap of her fingers.

Conversation over.

'Hani,' Raf dropped to a crouch in front of the small girl, and she let him take her pointed chin in his hands and turn her face back, so they stared straight into each other's eyes. Dark brown and palest blue. Strange cousins.

'I need to know, honey. Please?' *Honey* was what Zara had taken to calling Hani, before Zara and Raf's quarrel meant Hani stopped seeing the older girl.

'Not fair,' said Hani, her voice suddenly cross. She shook free her head. 'Do I ask you about the fox? No, I don't. Ever . . .' The child was unmistakably upset.

'Sorry,' said Raf, backing away. It looked like an impasse, pure and simple, except that nothing would ever be pure in Hani's life, or simple. And they both knew she'd already answered him, in her own way. What Hani saw when she looked inside her head was not what he saw, obviously enough, but it was not what anyone else would expect to see either.

With one final apology, Raf left Hani to her tight and angry silence.

Chapter Fifteen

9th October

Eduardo was worried about his Vespa. It was genuine Italian and had belonged to his uncle. The torn seat had only just been replaced with a new one made from red leather, while the old two-stroke petrol motor had been swapped for a Sterling unit that ran on pretty much anything. Mostly, Eduardo had been feeding his Vespa with the cheapest grade of *jaz*, a brandy so rough that even Frisco refused to drink it, but the unit seemed happy to work with anything vaguely flammable.

He'd left his bike near the canal, watched over by an urchin in a blue jellaba who squinted badly and carried a stick too small to frighten away anyone. Five lila, the boy had asked. *Five*. Grandly Eduardo had offered him ten to keep an extra special watch and the small boy's smile had been vulpine, as if seeing straight through Eduardo's generosity.

This was the first time that Eduardo had visited a proper brothel and it wasn't nearly as grand as he'd been hoping. For a start, the huge entrance hall tickled his nose with dust and carpet cleaner, rather than with rose petals or expensive Parisian perfume. There were no chandeliers, few paintings and the Iskandryian rugs were old but not valuable. Though there were looking glasses, great big gilt ones on the walls, but these just showed Eduardo back to himself, a small man in a too-big leather coat.

At least the small cubicles above the bus station were easy to reach. Even if the beds were dirty and bare. Maison 52, Pascal Coste was so out of Eduardo's way that he'd got lost just getting there.

'Excellency.' The voice came from a narrow doorway, one

Eduardo had dismissed as belonging to a cupboard. In it stood a blonde woman with a face so white she could have walked out of one of those Japanese pantomimes. Her mouth was a slash of Chanel, red as a wound. Behind her shoulder bobbed other heads, fair haired and fair skinned and way, way younger.

'Our girls, Excellency.'

He wasn't an *excellency* and it seemed cruel to Eduardo to keep calling him one. True he wasn't exactly a *felaheen*, but neither was he rich or well connected. No one called on him for patronage. He was just some *pied noir* who'd recently found work and been told by the man to come to 52 Rue Pascal Coste.

'I'm due to meet . . .'

'All in good time, Excellency.' The old woman swayed into the room, her feet compressed into tight pumps and her body wrapped in a fringed cocktail dress nearly as old as she was. A matching shawl hid most of the crêpe lines that marked her shoulders, chest and neck. 'First you need to choose one of our delightful girls . . .'

They trooped silently into the hall. A few looked at him with vague curiosity but most just stared at the carpets or examined their nails. There were ten in total. Blonde or brunette. Two of his age and five somewhat younger. The last three were almost children and the prettiest had a dark frown on her face and a bruise across one soft cheek that no amount of make-up could hide.

All except the youngest were bare breasted, two of them completely naked, the rest wearing thin pants or white petticoats, mostly with tight elastic that cut into their middles. The youngest was dressed in a white nightgown with Maltese lace round the neck. Eduardo could recognize the stitching – his mother had worked in a sweatshop for most of his childhood. And when she wasn't at the machines, she sewed at home at a window until the light faded.

The young one in the nightdress glanced up, scowled at Eduardo and Eduardo quickly looked away. Straight into the resigned face of a brunette.

'That one,' said Eduardo and the chosen woman looked surprised at his choice. She was not quite the oldest, with heavy hips, small breasts and full derrière. A half-smoked Ziganov hung from between her fingers, its gold band stained pink from the lipstick she used. English, Eduardo decided, that was how she looked . . .

'I'm Rose,' said the woman.

Eduardo gave his card to the waiting Madame without being asked. The gold Amex was only to be used in emergencies or when so ordered by the man, like now.

He signed with a flourish, not bothering to look at the amount.

'Excellency.' There was new respect in the old woman's voice; and for the first time since she'd started using the honorific, it sounded like she might mean it.

Taking back his card, Eduardo smiled and started up the wide stairs. Then stopped to indicated that his choice should go first. He wanted to look at Rose's buttocks as she walked. She climbed slowly, well aware of his gaze. And at the top she paused to remember which chamber the Madame had wanted her to use. Although it wasn't exactly *her* the Madame had told. All the girls had been instructed in advance, hours before this excellency arrived.

'This room,' she said, opening a battered door.

'Eduardo,' said a voice Eduardo recognized. It was the man, dressed in black and wearing shades even though the chamber was shuttered against the evening light. Behind him sat a short-haired girl in a white shift. Her breasts full enough to be obvious beneath the cloth and tipped with nipples that showed like shadows.

'Boss.' Eduardo bowed, feeling stupid. Nothing about the man suggested he wanted Eduardo to shake hands, but bowing still didn't feel quite right.

'Come in and lock the door behind you,' ordered the man. He said something in a language Eduardo didn't understand and Rose went to sit quietly on a large *bateau lit* beside the other woman.

'You made it,' said Raf.

Eduardo looked puzzled. Of course he'd made it. 52 Pascal Coste was where the man had told him to come.

'And you bought the things I asked for?'

Eduardo nodded and pulled a heavy package from under his coat. For extra safety he'd tied it tight with string which suddenly seemed unwilling to untie.

'Later,' said Raf. 'Put it down there for now.' The chest of drawers he indicated was cracked on one side and scratched across the top. 'No, even better, put it in a drawer.'

Eduardo did what he was told.

The chamber was the largest in the brothel by far, with two leather divans and a big *bateau lit* filling most of its space. Most of the *maison*'s other rooms featured narrow single beds to discourage lingering. It had taken Raf nearly forty-five minutes of trawling the datacore at Police HQ before he finally found a brothel within easy distance of the corner of Mahmoudiya and Rue Amoud el-Sawari. Hani could undoubtedly have done it in a fraction of the time, Raf just hadn't felt right asking her.

This room had been the choice of visiting couples, back in the days before the General did his deal with the Mufti and the *morales* suddenly became a problem. It was somewhere wives could buy their jaded husbands a whore or two for their birthday, to do things that didn't get done at home. Most of the visiting women just watched, a few joined in. All were married, rich and decently connected. Respectable members of the kind of families who donated funds regularly to the police.

The *accord* had changed all that.

For the first time in a hundred years girls from poor families returned to wearing the *hijab*, while Iskandryia's *mesdames* made do with head-scarves and dark glasses, altogether more elegant and not remotely to the Mufti's liking. The property laws were revised to exclude female heirs, driving alone after dark became a criminal offence for women and to go out with bare arms was to invite some fanatic to scratch his disapproval into your skin with a metal comb . . .

Raf had heard Zara on the subject. She was old enough to

remember the city before it started to change. Felix too, the old Chief of Detectives, had been less than impressed with the General's decision to sign an *accord*.

All trades had been hit, brothels included. Not that they actually closed. The brothels of Iskandryia were both an institution and tourist attraction (which was altogether more important). Along the Corniche could be found several in the grander houses, where chambers were by the night, cash was forbidden and anything less than a gold card strongly discouraged.

Of course, visiting tourists were billed variously for cultural excursions, theatre groups or an art exhibition. That way everybody was kept happy, from the punters to the card companies and the brothels. Especially the brothels, because embarrassed punters had a habit of getting home, then denying they'd ever visited the place which billed them and that made the card companies very unhappy.

This *maison* was different, though . . . Somewhere for Iskandryia's own residents. It paid its local taxes, plus a little extra to Police HQ and in return found itself on the police database as an information source, which gave it some protection should the *morales* decide to call. The fat man had approved identical deals with brothels all across the city.

Raf and Eduardo were lovers, at least they were according to the Madame downstairs. That was how she'd explained Raf's request for a double chamber to her girls. Officially, of course, homosexuality didn't exist in Ottoman North Africa. In practice, it was almost universal, if staunchly illegal: because a society that placed a premium on female virginity, made pre-marital sex a killing matter and then made it too expensive for most men to get married before their mid twenties was bound to need an easy acceptance of the inevitable, whatever the law said. And that was quite apart from the one in five men born with little physical interest in women.

'What do we do now?' Eduardo asked.

'We fill the time,' said Raf. 'Until it gets dark.' Walking over to the window, he examined the chamber's mashrabiya which looked out over the canal, taking in its two sets of shutters. One set closed it off from the street directly below, the other closed off the actual balcony from the room in which he stood.

'You,' said Raf, pointing to the girl he'd selected at random when he first arrived. 'What did you say your name was?' She didn't, or he'd have remembered it.

'Justine.' It was meant to sound French, Raf guessed. From her skin and the black roots to her short hair, he'd have said *moriscos*, but he'd been in Isk less than four months and he wasn't Felix. His predecessor had been famed for his ability to read origins at a single glance.

'Can you get me a drink?'

She looked doubtful. 'What would Your Excellency like?'

'Wine,' said Raf, 'white and chilled, something dry.'

Justine looked more doubtful still.

'Anything you can find,' Raf said and she fumbled at the lock, then scurried from the room.

Raf sighed. He was tired of people being afraid of him. Maybe she was afraid because in her terms he was rich . . . To be honest, in Justine's terms he was probably beyond rich. Even though he could barely afford Donna and Khartoum's wages and repairs to the al-Mansur madersa were beyond his wallet. Maybe she realized he was police. Or perhaps it was just that he dressed in a suit and wore dark glasses indoors.

Probably it was all of those things. The girl was afraid of everything – of the punters, of her Madame and of time's winged chariot – he could see it in her eyes. If he asked, she'd say she was seventeen, but Justine had a good ten years on that. She was older than him by maybe three years, older than she could afford to be in her trade.

'Will this do?'

Justine held up a dusty bottle of Cru de Ptolémées, two tooth mugs and a handful of ice cubes. Her breathing was ragged from having run upstairs.

'Thank you.' Raf smiled at her and nodded towards the balcony. 'We're going out there,' he told Eduardo. 'I'll see you in an hour or so.'

'What do I do?'

Raf glanced round the chamber. 'Whatever.'

The wine tasted as sour as Raf expected, but all the same he smiled as he poured some for Justine.

'*Salut.*'

'I can try again?' Justine suggested, having tasted it.

'No.' Ice cubes clinked as Raf dropped a few into her glass. 'Who knows?' he said, giving her mug a quick swirl. 'This might help.' In fact, chilling it made no difference, but Raf finished his glass anyway and, when the sourness was gone, refilled. When that was done, he drank most of hers as well.

Sat back against a shutter, the one he'd told Eduardo to bolt from inside the chamber, Raf examined the balcony, as he examined everything . . .

Straight ahead, beyond an intricately carved screen could be seen fragments of the darkening city; while folded back, against the side walls of the mashrabiya were plain shutters that could be used to close off the screen against afternoon heat or cold night air.

He sat in a little world, boxed in on all sides.

'Your turn,' said Raf, handing back Justine's glass.

She drank a little and gave him back what was left. 'You can tell me,' she said finally, when the weight of his silence got too heavy for her to bear. 'Some men find it easier to talk.'

He was not *some men*, Raf wanted to tell her. He was *him*, however unsatisfactory that was. And there were days when he wasn't even sure he was that. When the noise inside his head reached out for the rest of him and his fingers froze and his neck ached and a knot that writhed like an injured snake appeared in the pit of his stomach, leaving him breathless and filled with dread.

Those were the days he needed the fox most. And now the fox was dying and it looked like for good this time.

'Tell me,' Justine said, taking the empty glass from his fingers to put it carefully on the floor. 'What's troubling you?' Her question was as practised as the butterfly touch of her fingers on his wrist. Even the slight tilt of her head looked like something she'd learnt. All the same, Raf felt a need to answer.

'I'm going to kill someone,' he said flatly.

'When?' Justine kept her expression masked and her question simple.

'Tonight,' said Raf.

'Me?'

He shook his head and felt a single tear slide under his shades. 'Not you, not me. Not those two.' He nodded his head backwards to the room behind. 'Just a man.'

'One man?'

'With luck . . .'

'Without luck?'

He thought about it. 'Several,' Raf said slowly, 'maybe more.'

Justine nodded as if this was to be expected. 'And this makes you sad?'

Raf shrugged.

Later, when he'd finished staring through the carved screen at the canal which ran wide and slow between concrete embankments, Justine helped him off with his jacket. And then, having folded that and placed it carefully beside his empty glass, she pulled up her slip and straddled him.

She turned away when he folded his fingers into her pinned-up hair to pull her forward into his kiss, then let him turn her back. They tasted the sourness on each others lips, their kiss slow, almost thoughtful. Not what she was expecting and not what Raf had intended. Putting up one hand to hold a breast, he felt Justine overflow his fingers.

A boat low in the water. A girl with her shirt undone. The salt of tears and the sea on her lips . . .

'Your Excellency's paid for me,' Justine said, seeing his sudden hesitation. 'You might as well have your money's worth.'

And he'd paid for Zara too. Or was it that her father had paid for him? Either way, breaking the deal had cost Raf almost as much as it had cost Zara. Which was too much. And how could he tell himself his choice of Justine was random? She had the same dark skin and eyes, the full breasts and smooth shoulders.

'Fuck me,' he said. So she did; her fingers reaching down to undo his old-fashioned fly. Over her shoulder, Raf could see a boy fishing in the shade of a felucca. A make-shift house had been built on the felucca's deck out of sheets of galvanized iron, laminated cardboard and what looked like the remains of a plywood tea-chest. A scar on the trunk of a squat palm nearby, where it had almost closed round the felucca's mooring rope said the boat had been there a lot longer than the boy.

Occasional barges piled high with hessian sacks slid in front of the felucca, obscuring it. Perhaps cotton from the fields or a date crop. Raf hadn't yet read up on the seasons in the Delta, what got gathered when.

'What's in the boats?'

Justine stopped moving on his lap.

'The barges,' Raf said, nodding towards the canal behind her.

'Cigarettes,' Justine said without looking. She named two brands of cheap cigarillo made from a dark locally-grown tobacco, then shrugged. 'Why sell to the kiosks when you can sell at three times the price to tourists?'

Wrapping her arms round Raf, she pulled him in close, so he could no longer see the canal over her shoulder. And rocking gently, she pushed down against him, and pushed and pushed, until she finally came, or at least pretended to . . . insides tightening as she ground her face into the side of his neck.

'Enough,' Raf slid hands under her buttocks to help her off him. She was breathing swiftly and he could hear her heart pound against her ribs. The sudden satiety seemed real enough. As did the musk-like stink of her body.

'What about you?' she asked eventually, sitting back on her heels.

'I'm okay.'

She smiled. 'You don't look like a man who lies.'

Raf's grin was fox-like. 'I seldom do anything else.'

Justine raised a carefully-painted eyebrow. 'As Your Excellency wishes.'

Bending forward, she took one of his nipples between her teeth and bit, then released it and backed away until she lay almost flat. After a while, Raf forgot everything except the ache in his groin and a building tightness as her mouth opened, swallowed him and withdrew, time and again. She was good, better than good. Experienced.

He came hard and fast, his fingers reaching out to grab her head as he emptied his fear into her mouth.

'Sorry,' he said, letting go.

Justine's shrug said it all. He wasn't the first to grab her like that and wouldn't be the last. He was a man, her expectations of the breed were no higher.

'I mean it,' said Raf. Over her shoulder, he could see that someone had lit a hurricane lamp aboard the felucca and that the boy with the fishing rod was gone.

Eduardo sprawled, snoring soundly while Rose stared at the cracked ceiling, her slip rucked up round her wide hips. She heard Raf use a knife to lift the bolt on the shutter and turned her head, but other than that she made no attempt to move.

He nodded and Rose nodded back. Watching as he walked slightly unsteadily across to the battered desk to take Eduardo's parcel from its top drawer. Cutting the string with a single swipe of a black glass knife, Raf returning the blade to the scabbard velcroed to his ankle and spread the contents on the nearest Ottoman.

One automatic, one spring-loaded cosh, one chilli spray, taken from a thin man with a head wound found floating in the hyacinth-infested shallows of Lake Mareotis. Also found on the man was a small pouch, impregnated with the residue of what looked like a dance drug, and a razor-sharp knife. The pouch was still with toxicology, but the knife was the black one Raf had just been using.

The pistol was a clone of a Sturm/Ruger KV95d, a ten-shot, 9mm double action with manual safety, weighing in at 27 oz and featuring a matt blued finish and black rubber grips. It had one bullet missing. The element that interested Raf was not that the KV's serial number had apparently been filed off, but that it had never been there in the first place, according to the armourer at Champollion. Best guess was that the gun had come out of a black weapons factory somewhere Soviet, without undergoing any of the internationally-prescribed security checks. Given this, it was no surprise that the history chip imbedded in the handle had never been initialized.

As for the cosh, it was a basic model of a type found in souks across North Africa, only this one had been machined with a titanium spring and shot-heavy neoprene head. The chilli spray was mass-produced in Morocco and sub-licensed from the US. It could have come from a corner shop almost anywhere.

The body itself had been dragged from Mareotis by a netsman, who dumped his unwelcome catch in the reeds on the bank rather than deal with the police. The old man had only retraced his steps after a local station reported that the German Consulate was offering a reward for information on a missing second secretary.

Sometime between then and the body being delivered in a handcart to the gates of the German compound every one of the dead man's possessions went missing. Raf knew this because a furious liaison officer had put a call through in person to find out what Ashraf Bey intended to do about the outrage.

Raf's promise to have a uniformed officer add the crime to that day's roster just as soon as someone came in from the Consulate to fill out the requisite forms didn't improve matters.

Eduardo had tracked down the old fisherman to a café at the end of a narrow main drag in a marsh village too poor to have more than one street anyway. Eduardo might have suggested he was from the police, though he never actually said so. He did, however, say there was a reward for the return of anything taken from the dead German's body. Since the sum Eduardo mentioned was significantly higher than any sum the fisherman might have got selling the dead man's possessions, the deal was swift and satisfactory on both sides.

Since then the package had been where Raf had told Eduardo to put it, sitting in a desk drawer in Eduardo's walk-up office above the haberdasher's, waiting for a use.

'How do I get onto the roof?'

'First left,' said Justine, 'then up the stairs.' She glanced at Rose, then at the sleeping Eduardo and back at Raf. 'What about him?'

'Let him be,' said Raf, and the woman beneath Eduardo nodded, like she expected no less.

'This is for you,' Raf said to Justine and peeled off twenty $100 notes. 'And this for Rose.' Raf handed across another ten. It was more money than either would earn in a year. When he turned back, the money had vanished from Justine's hand though she stood exactly where she'd been standing before. 'If I don't come back,' said Raf, 'then I threatened to kill you both if you dared tell the Madame I was gone . . . Which is what I will do,' he added, as an apparent afterthought. 'And if I return, then none of us ever left this chamber, understand?'

Both women nodded.

Justine did one final thing for Raf. She opened the chamber door, looked round to check that the passage really was empty and then walked to the women's bathroom, flipping the bolt on the roof door as she went past. She bolted it again on her way back, returned to the chamber and locked its door behind her. Then, job done, she lay back on one of the leather Ottomans and listened to the silence overhead that said His Excellency had already left the brothel roof.

Chapter Sixteen

9th October

Raf saw the grey kitten first. So he stopped, swaying slightly, and waited for the suddenly frozen animal to unarch its back and walk away. There were mice nesting in attics, geckoes so still they could be dead and desiccated and bats which spiralled like embers in the hot night, dancing through the air to a tune that only they and Raf could hear.

Bats liked old buildings and El Iskandryia was nearly as full of old buildings as it was of bats. It was one of the things that Raf . . .

Enough scribble, Raf told himself, *you need to concentrate.*

Crossing the darkened roofs without problem, Raf moved silently from one pool of shadow to another, until he was almost where he needed to be. Then he stopped and began the breathing.

He had a dozen triggers. Single words, snatches of song . . . But the long slow breath which emptied his head was the one he liked most. The facility was already there long before he first met I & I. And although the old Rasta had found it hard to believe how fast Raf picked up *rabo de arraira, querxada* and *esquiva*, killing moves disguised as Latin American dance, Raf never told him that he was designed to learn. He just left the old con where he'd found him, still in the yard at Remand3/Seattle.

Occasional cars prowled the street in front of the derelict house, fuelled by petrol, natural gas or alcohol. The signature from their exhausts mixing into a heavy soup of sugar and hydrocarbons that made his sinuses ache. And there were stronger smells, coming from somewhere closer. Food cooking, mixed with something raw and potent, like burning leaves, which is what it was . . .

Retracing his steps until he found a low wall that edged a roof terrace, Raf used this to clamber onto the tiles of a spice attic running the width of the next two houses. A couple of seconds of silence later, Raf was looking down on a thin man smoking in the shadow of a door, his hand curled round the end of his joint to hide its gleam. At the man's feet was a discarded copy of *Hustler*. Three cans of Diet Coke had been drunk and then crushed flat, before being lined up on the edge of a plastic table.

Careless, the fox would have said.

Beside the crushed cans was an empty automatic. Handle angled away from the man's reach, with its full clip resting alongside. The guy was standing guard because that's what he'd been told to do; not because he was expecting visitors.

'*Really careless*,' said Raf, dropping in from the low roof. And as the thin man spun round, Raf flipped out his cosh and tapped the side of his head, hard to medium. Catching the guy before he hit the tiles was the only difficult part.

A battered hiPower, an old Opinel lock-knife with a broken tip to its blade and a hand-made garrotte constructed from fishing line and toggle handles. Not exactly *Thiergarten*-issue. Raf still pocketed the lot, pushing the over-sized Browning through his belt. The unconscious body he rolled against the wall.

Braised mutton, Raf decided as he stood near an open doorway. Mutton, coriander and bread cooking on a skillet. Somewhere in the house a radio was tuned to a pirate station, raw *al-jeel* mixed with a thin synth loop that scratched at the back of Raf's mind. If there was anyone in the rooms directly below, then they were either very still or fast asleep.

No one was there, although Raf checked each room to make sure, finding them all empty. At the top of the next flight of stairs, he stopped to listen. The radio was closer this time and there were too many people for him to work in silence . . .

It was time to make another plan.

*   *   *

Up above the tiles, bats ran tight circles, losing their fear of the silent figure who stood frozen while they scooped insects from the warm wind.

Ten minutes was what Raf had allowed himself. Ten minutes of stilling his heart and breath and thoughts. Chasing away the sour fog in his head. And then, as one soft fragment of blackness lurched in too close, made clumsy by a struggling moth, Raf flipped out his hand and pulled the bat from the air. Breaking its wings, he tossed the animal down at his feet to watch it flap helplessly on the red tiles.

He was going to kill a human in a minute. Life's price for getting Avatar back. Both for the person who paid and the person who took. So it was, he realized, unutterably childish to be upset about hurting something with a brain the size of a grain of rice, especially something that made its living killing other things.

Red in tooth and claw, his mother would have said. It was humans who were unnatural, having placed themselves outside evolution from choice, which was bad for the world as a whole. He'd read her paper, *Restoring the Balance*. Pretty good for a woman who accepted cash from a Swiss multinational in return for stepping down as head of *NatureFirst*. Of course, they'd given her something extra as well, him . . .

Or perhaps it was the other way round. Maybe funding her films was extra and he was the deal. The fox was better at this kind of stuff. All Raf knew was he came with an 8,000-line guarantee from a company that went belly up after he was born.

So no one got to collect on anything.

'Hey.' Raf's whisper was low, but easily heard by a scrawny stray which watched him from the next roof, its back prickled with doubt as hunger fought its mistrust of Raf.

As ever, hunger won.

Raf knelt beside the twitching bat, watching the stray approach, its whiskers spread. Very slowly the small cat came within range. Not adult, but no longer really a kitten. The soft fur was gone and with it most of one ear.

And as the hungry stray shot forward to take the dying bat, Raf reached out and placed one finger on a broken wing, preventing the cat from dragging away its prey. 'Eat it here.'

The animal did so, killing the bat with a bite to the neck. By the time the cat realized Raf had released the wing, its meal was almost finished and all that remained was a smudge of soft leather dark against the cooling roof.

'I'd get you another,' Raf said, as he took the animal by the scruff of its neck, 'but we don't really have time.'

From the floor below came the sound of rats. Somewhere below that a water pipe banged and a conversation started up, then died as a door opened and shut. In the background a 3-chord special died mid-thrash, feeding into a jingle for Peugeot. All in all, it sounded like the backing track to utter normality.

'Okay,' said Raf, 'this is what we do . . .'

The cat landed at the bottom of the stairs, flipping itself over in midair to land on the bare boards. One glance said its route back to the roof was blocked so instead the animal ran towards an open door, stopped at the top of those stairs and froze as someone at the bottom looked up and swore.

'Ismail?' A gruff voice called up twice and, when hissing was the only answer, the questions turned to swearing. Raf heard the Arabic for *useless* and *idiot* several times. Confident steps on the stairs said the man expected no trouble and at the point he understood it was trouble that expected him, he was already heading for the floor.

'Two down,' said Raf to the cat, which did little but swish its tail in silent agreement.

Under his tatty jacket the unconscious man wore a shoulder holster and nestled inside that, still locked in place by a Velcro strap, was a snub-nosed revolver, with letters engraved along its chassis that read *genuine Colf, made in USA*. The fact that the engraving had sharp edges made it likely the actual place of origin was some local sweatshop.

Which worried Raf a lot.

That there were two sides to Hamzah Effendi was common

knowledge. The family man and the crime boss, Jekyll Effendi to Felaheen Hyde. Offend the first and he'd buy out your company and close it down. Offend the second and he'd slaughter your children, bulldoze your house into the ground and sew that ground with rock salt. There was something very biblical about some of those reports on file.

Kidnapping Hamzah's child, even a bastard born without property rights, was the crime world equivalent to standing on the rails at Masr Station and trying to hold back an incoming train. There might not be quicker ways to commit suicide but there were undoubtedly a dozen ways that were more pleasant.

So why do it? And why do it with cheap labour?

'Up you go.' Raf waved his hand at the cat, which had just taken to sharpening its claws on the edge of a bannister. The grey cat left via the roof stairs without a backward glance.

Raf telescoped the cosh and put it in his pocket. The fake Colt got stuffed into his belt. One cosh and three guns – his own, the Browning from the roof and now the fake – plus a black glass blade, its edge ground so sharp as to be almost fractal. That was what the advertising promised anyway. The fawn jacket he stripped off the unconscious man and shrugged his way into, feeling the cloth flop round his shoulders.

Holding a gun in each hand, Raf stamped his way down the flight of steps, pulling the clumsy tread of the other man from memory. He remembered in time to bang into the upright at the bottom and casually shoulder open the kitchen door rather than use its handle. Two men and a boy glanced up, boredom becoming alarm when they realized that whoever Raf was he wasn't one of them.

'No,' said Raf, twitching one gun, 'don't get up.' He spoke Arabic, his accent understandable if atrocious. 'And there's no need for anyone to die . . .' Just for a second the dark void of his gun's muzzle hovered over the heart of the boy.

'Unless that's your choice?'

They'd all shaken their heads before Raf had time to finish his question.

'Good,' said Raf, and found that he meant it. He also found he'd been wrong about them cooking. It was takeout he'd been able to smell.

In front of them, on a cracked pine table stood a foil plate filled with gristle and mutton bones, beside an even larger container that had held couscous. A half empty jar of harissa sat nearby. As did unleavened bread and a jar lid's worth of stubbed out roaches and twists of torn cardboard.

Carbohydrate and kif, two good ways to waste one's edge. Not that any of the three gave much sign of having had an edge to start with.

'Weapons on the table . . .'

A motley collection of go-faster revolvers and flashy switch-blades piled up next to the foil containers. All fake pearl handles and fuck-me electronic sights that looked great and did nothing constructive.

'All of them.'

A couple of boot knives and a pair of brass knuckledusters joined the growing pile. It reminded Raf of the trash that he used to take off teenagers at the door of BonBon, back in Seattle, in the days before Raf fell out with Hu San, leader of the local Triad and had to become someone else.

'And the rest . . .'

The middle one who Raf had figured for the boy's father and the old man's young brother pulled out a one-shot throw-down from the back of his belt and sullenly placed it next to his knife.

'Now put them into this,' said Raf, pushing across the foil container that had held couscous. Obediently, the three began piling up weapons, taking care not to point the guns anywhere near Raf.

Sit down, stand up, sit down . . . Every time they did what Raf ordered, the imprinting got stronger; that was how the human psyche worked . . . Had Raf been about to kill them, now would have been the right time. He assumed they were bright enough to understand that. And yet they were still way too casual.

'You do know who you've kidnapped?' Raf looked at the boy,

the one who'd shivered under the gaze of Raf's gun. Not only was he the youngest, he was also less obviously stoned. What Raf got by way of reply was a slight shake of the head. Though that turned out to be not in answer to the *who* part of Raf's question but the *what*. The kid was arguing definitions.

'We didn't kidnap anybody. We're just guarding him.'

'And that's meant to make a difference?'

The boy shrugged.

'It's DJ Avatar,' Raf said. 'Hamzah Effendi's kid.'

The kid looked suddenly shocked. But even that wasn't straightforward. It turned out he liked Avatar's music. Hamzah didn't figure.

'He's been fucking arrested,' said the old man. 'For torturing a *nasrani* to death.'

'Raped her first,' the boy's father added. 'He's in prison.'

'Really?' Raf asked. 'Who arrested him?'

'Ashraf-fucking-Bey. It happened yesterday.'

'No,' said Raf. 'That's not what happened. Believe me.'

'Yes it is . . .' The old man's pupils were dilated beyond their natural limit, expanded so much they looked like the eyes of someone with a fatal head wound, fixed at that point when the pupils explode. Whatever the man's poison, it was serious stuff.

'On his own beach,' added the boy, sounding suitably outraged.

They left via a back door into a rear alley, having collected both their lookout and Ismail, two men with evil headaches but no worse. The kind of small-time fry, all of them, evolved by every ghetto to fit the niches that others reject. Life's bottom feeders; too disorganized to mastermind their own events, at least not ones that worked, and not hard enough to handle real trouble. That they'd been hired to guard Avatar made no sense at all.

Pulling his automatic from its holster, Raf prowled the house, leaving the locked cellar until last. The roof was deserted and the attic empty. So Raf took the few remaining bulbs from their sockets and locked the roof door before sweeping the level below, where bedrooms had once been. Four empty rooms, filled with acrid dust and silence. Broken chairs filled the far corner of one. In another, some *clochard* had started a small fire on tiles which had cracked. A handful of Thunderbird cans lay blackened in the ashes. Taking each bulb in turn, Raf locked those doors too, using the iron mortice locks common to North Africa. Just to be on the safe side he pocketed the keys.

Empty houses were a familiar sight south of Mahmoudia. At least they were on that stretch west of Rue Menascae, where an area of almost sufficiency surrendered to the dank touch of institutionalized poverty. For streets to be derelict there was as normal as finding crack houses at crossroads, or over-crowded tenements which overlooked unsafe playgrounds, dead trees standing reminder to unmet aspirations.

Travel companies did a good line in offering the 'real Iskandryia' from the safety of air-conditioned coaches. As if the *arrondissement*'s simmering resentment somehow made it more real than the old wealth of the Greek District or the comfortable red-bricked mansion blocks near the fish market.

'Enough already,' said Raf, adding his varied collection of keys and bulbs to the weapons discarded by Avatar's guards. There was nothing he needed in the empty kitchen. It was time to find the cellar.

The Daimler-Benz which parked below the 'For Sale' sign had smoked windows and white-walled tyres, newish but dusty from trawling through too many back streets. The vehicle had *hire car* written all over it.

Seconds after its headlights died, the nearside rear door opened, briefly lighting the inside. What interested Raf was the woman who got out.

'You know her?' Raf asked, yanking Avatar to his feet and dragging him across to the cellar's high window. Had he had more time, Raf might have been kinder, gentler . . . The story of his life really.

'You're drunk!' Avatar said, belatedly realizing the obvious. He sounded surprisingly shocked.

'Not entirely,' said Raf, 'Now . . . you know her?'

Avatar shook his head.

'Well, I do. Last time I saw her she was stood behind your sister, waiting to climb onto a restaurant car.' The boy didn't ask what Raf was doing watching Maxim's. Which was a fair trade-off, because Raf didn't ask what made Avatar throw in his job as Raf's driver.

Zara had that effect on both of them.

'So what happens now?' whispered Avatar, watching the woman walk towards the house, her silhouette looming large above the bars of the cellar's only window. Behind her walked a driver.

'We dance,' said Raf. 'Then I go find whoever dumped a dead girl in your dad's garden.'

He saw surprise on Avatar's face. 'This is just the side-show,' Raf explained apologetically, looking at the drugged and swaying boy. 'Just a sideshow.' Quickly drawing the black blade from its sheath on his right ankle, Raf checked the point and tried out a couple of steps.

'Well,' he amended, 'I dance.'

Raf hauled Avatar over to a soiled mattress opposite the door. 'You lie down here and *pretend* to be ill.' Flipping round the blade so that it pointed upwards, Raf stood with his back to the door frame. All it took to embed the blade lightly in the wood was to flip up his hand and then step away, leaving the knife protruding from the frame behind him. There were probably better ways to guarantee having a blade ready for use while leaving both hands free, this just happened to be the one that I & I had taught him.

The next few minutes Raf reconstructed later from sounds alone, beginning with the scratch of a key. The Yale on the front door was oiled but even so the tumblers grated a little. There was the click of a light switch, followed immediately by a grunt of irritation. A snatch of Arabic fired into the darkness was repeated, louder this time. Irritation becoming anger as the woman caught her hip on the corner of a table in the hallway, scraping it across the tiles.

Already her breathing was less steady.

Raf caught the exact point her anger turned to worry. It came just after her driver banged open the kitchen door and found the room deserted, silent and dark. What little light came through the front door obviously revealed nothing except the fact her guards were gone.

'Fetch a torch.'

Heavy treads crossed the floor above Raf's head and then came the clash of metal heels on the front steps. The creak of a car door. A slam. Moments later the driver was back, his tone apologetic.

The woman swore, louder than was wise. And then Raf heard the click of a gas lighter, then heavy footsteps descending towards the cellar door.

'Fucking ragheads,' said the woman. 'You can't get them to do anything . . .'

The driver muttered something that might have been agreement. He was still muttering as he stepped through the door and dropped his lighter. Screaming was out of the question given that Raf's garrotte had already crushed the cartilage of his larynx, so the man gurgled instead.

'Come in,' Raf told the woman. 'Unless you want me to finish off your driver . . . ?'

It seemed she had other plans.

His fingers found her wrist in the darkness and pulled her hand, gun and all, from her side pocket. The weapon she held was tiny, impossibly elegant and looked very expensive. Twisting it from her shaking fingers, Raf tossed it into Avatar's slop bucket. Adding a splash and liquid clank to his collection of sounds.

Everybody did something well, that's what the fox used to insist when Raf was small. It was just that some people took longer than others to discover their real talent. And this, it turned out was his . . . Not caring about the doing until the doing was over. Of course, given his guarantee, Raf probably shouldn't have cared at all.

Blood had strung a necklace round the throat of the driver,

although Raf was the only person in the cellar who could see the dark pearls. And the wire was now too tight to be clearly visible even to him.

'Slip off your jacket,' Raf told the woman, 'then step away from it.' He waited while she shrugged off her dark coat and put it carefully on the damp tiles, folding it first. Did that signify strength or weakness? The fox would have known.

She was thin; dressed in a white silk blouse, thick black belt and a knee-length skirt that matched the folded jacket. As upscale and anonymous as the guards had been obvious and downmarket.

'Turn around.'

Tucked into a small holster on the back of her belt was a tiny Colt. While the almost invisible bulge on her thigh was undoubtedly something predictable like a derringer or throwing knife.

'Disarm,' Raf said simply.

The Colt she placed carefully on the floor. The bump remained where it was, which was her choice. Stupid, of course, but still her choice.

'This is where you tell me who you are,' said Raf.

The shake of the woman's head was so slight as to be almost subliminal.

'The alternative,' said Raf, yanking the garrotte, 'is that I finish strangling your driver.'

'Poor driver,' was all she said. And as the big man lurched in panic at the tightening of the wire, the woman dipped one hand towards her thigh, sliding back raw silk to reveal a razor-edged blade.

Now.

Without thought, without prior intention, Raf dropped the borrowed garrotte and reached up and back, his fingers folding around the handle of his own blade, which tumbled rapidly through the darkness; the woman's right eye empting onto her cheek like broken egg as vitreous humour slid down tight skin.

Stepping into her scream, Raf slammed palm against hilt

and drove the knife through the woman's parietal lobe and into her cerebellum. Somewhere in that sequence the woman's brainstem got sliced and she stopped being strictly human. Although the whimpering only stopped when Raf put thumb and first finger either side of her throat and squeezed.

He was in the process of lowering her to the ground when a mobile rang. Raf found it in the inside pocket of the woman's discarded jacket. The little phone was clumsier than he'd expected from someone of her erstwhile elegance.

'*Na'am?*'

Raf listened for few seconds and then shook his head.

'No,' he said, slightly breathless. 'Fraulein Lubeck can't come to the phone. Yes, I'll ask her to call you back . . .' He listened hard. 'No,' he said finally, 'I'm sure she's never heard of someone called Ashraf Bey.'

Chapter Seventeen

Sudan

Each Seraphim 4x4 had a blade at the front designed to dig into dunes and turn over sand, which is what they did. Within minutes the dead were ploughed under, enemy trucks torched and camera crews invited in.

Trucks burning weren't exactly hot news but new shots still got added to stale ones. And trustworthy faces in pale suits stood under the blistering sun and reassured the doubtful that after a bitter firefight rebel militia had been defeated with almost no loss of life to PaxForce.

'Zero loss of life . . .' corrected a voice in Ka's ear.

'Then why say almost?'

'What?' Sarah glanced round, then shrugged and turned her attention back to Saul. They were moored under an overhanging thorn which kept the afternoon at bay, while lapping water cooled their hiding place and tossed sunlight onto the underside of its spiky canopy.

Ka was ignoring all questions. He was getting good at that. Ignoring the others meant not facing questions he couldn't answer.

'Well?' Ka asked the voice.

'No dead would mean an unfair fight. Strong against weak. A few dead equals luck, skill, better weapons . . . It's about presentation.' The voice paused and, without asking for a change, Ka suddenly found himself looking down on a thorn bush rather than at a battlefield.

'Who are you?' the voice demanded.

Ka sighed. 'You've asked me this already . . .'

'Humour me,' said the voice. It didn't sound very humorous at all. 'That's a basic rule, okay?'

'Sergeant Ka,' said Ka. 'We were part of the Army.'

'Were?'

Ka thought of the ploughs turning over sand and blinked as his p.o.v. changed. The 4x4s were done now, even out at the edge of what had been Ka's camp. Some trucks were even leaving, helmeted troops waving to a blonde woman stood atop a dune, laden down with powerpack and portable satellite dish.

Ka turned off the radio. 'We can't go back,' he told the others, as if that was an end to the argument.

'Oh yes we fucking can.' Saul's voice was deeper than Ka's own. His superior age showing in its gruffness and the ease with which he dropped swearwords into his conversation. 'We just turn this shitty boat around.'

'They'd flog us publicly,' Sarah reminded him. 'Maybe shoot us.'

'Yeah.' Bec flicked her gaze from Sarah to Ka and then back again. 'We'll need an excuse.'

Lifting his shades, Ka stared at Bec. 'We can't go back,' he said slowly. 'You know why we can't go back? Because everyone's dead.'

Mouths dropped open and Zac instantly flung his hands over his ears, as if to block out Ka's lies. Both his sisters were in that camp, Ka realized; had been, rather . . .

'It was quick,' Ka insisted. 'Instant,' he added hurriedly. 'It was instant. A bomb made a small bang and everyone just fell over.'

'Yeah?' said Saul. 'And how do you know . . . ?'

'I just do. Then the 'copters came and trucks full of soldiers.'

'Why did they send soldiers?' Bec asked. 'If the bomb had already killed everyone?'

Ka didn't have an answer to that.

'Because the bomb doesn't exist,' said the voice in his ear.

'That's why . . . In a moment your radio is going to come on.
Talk to it direct.'

My radio is switched off, Ka wanted to say, but the blue box
was already noisily swooping hi-to-low at exactly sixty cycles
a minute, like a miniature police siren.

'Sergeant Ka,' said the boy, holding the radio to his ear and
feeling stupid.

'Lieutenant Ka,' corrected the voice. 'As of now. Lieutenant
Ka, Sergeant Sarah, Corporal Bec . . .'

'What about Saul and Zac?'

'Zac's a baby. And Saul . . .'

Ka waited.

'He's a spy, you understand?'

'I understand,' said Ka, sitting up so straight his hair almost
caught in down-hanging thorns.

'I understand, Sir.'

'Sir.'

'And you know who I am?'

Ka shook his head. Somehow that was enough.

'Colonel Abad,' said the Colonel, introducing himself. 'You've
heard of me?'

Oh yes. Ka grinned stupidly at the badge on his shirt. Those
shades, the cigar, that black beard. The Colonel.

'Where are you exactly?'

The boy looked round him. Cliffs tight on both sides of the
river and white-headed vultures overhead. But then there were
always vultures circling thermals over this stretch of the Nile.
Above the vultures, made smaller both by reality and distance,
hovered raptors. Black-winged kites, most probably.

Sarah's felucca was tied at the river's bend, on the side where
floodwater flowed less fast and silt almost buried rocks that
were pale and strangely square. Three thousand years earlier,
during the flood season, a cargo boat had run aground there.
Staying with his freshly-hewn sandstone, the captain had sent
slaves downriver to get help. He died in the night waiting for
their return, killed by an adder as he sat by a small fire lit to
keep jackals at bay.

Colonel Abad knew these things. The hieroglyphs of the pharaohs cartouched below their statues, the genera of birds and animals, even the molecular structure of each rock that made up the crumbling cliffs and temples, statues and ruins.

Ka could identify concrete, sandstone and polycrete, the frothy stuff that set hard and could be coated with sand or gravel, provided any covering was whacked on before the crete had time to dry. Both sides used it to make HQs that blended into any background.

'We're upriver from the camp,' Ka said, 'on a bend near low cliffs . . . And we haven't eaten all day,' he added as an afterthought.

'You got grenades?'

'Yes,' said Ka. At least Saul had. Zac, Sarah and Bec had two rifles, a knife and a pistol between them. He had the plastic gun. What his dead lieutenant called a doublePup. He didn't like it very much.

'Swap it,' said Colonel Abad. 'First chance you get. Right . . .' The radio crackled for a second. 'Listen up. Food first. That means losing a grenade to the river. Get Saul to throw and Bec and Zac to collect the fish . . . All of them.'

'Do we eat them raw?'

'Sushi.' The voice sounded amused. 'Only if you want. Personally I'd suggest a small fire and usually I'd recommend dry twigs, but today we want smoke, don't we?'

'Do we?'

'Oh yes,' said the voice, 'very definitely.'

Ka shuffled backwards, then stopped when his foot hit Sarah's shoulder. The girl didn't move but she did glare, waiting while Ka edged sideways to give her space. They were alone together in the desert, on an important mission . . . That was how Ka had explained it to the others.

'Accident,' said Ka.

Sarah nodded. Opened her mouth as if she was about to say something and then shut it. She had perfect teeth, Ka realized. Tourist's teeth. All in a neat line and with no chipped edges.

'How old are you?' He'd asked the question without thinking. 'I mean, really?' He knew Sarah said she was fourteen but then he said he was thirteen.

'Fifteen,' Sarah said firmly.

'Me too . . .' Ka smiled, then shrugged. Questions were never welcome, he should have known that. Ka just wanted to be the one who persuaded her to open up and talk. Already he could describe how she looked without looking. Hair as black as her eyes, braided into long plaits. Her skin somewhere between dark chocolate and purple, not café noir like his. She'd taken grief for that in the camp; grief, comments and idle slaps. Mostly from the older girls.

There were more girls than boys in the Ragged Army. That was because they fought better, according to Saul, having more to fear if captured. Although Saul was the only person Ka had ever heard say this and, besides, both sides chopped off the hands of those who wouldn't change and it was hard to think of much worse than that.

'What are you thinking?'

'About these,' said Ka and flexed his fingers. 'Sometimes . . . about being captured.'

Sarah nodded. 'Right,' she said. 'Scare yourself, why don't you?'

Sighting along the barrel of her rifle, she began to tighten her finger on the trigger.

'Not yet,' protested Ka. He had orders from Colonel Abad and he intended to obey them. 'I'll tell you when.'

'I can do it from here,' Sarah said crossly.

'I'm sure you can,' Ka agreed, 'but the Colonel . . .'

He'd told Sarah about Colonel Abad. He'd told them all. No one any of them knew had ever seen the man in the flesh, but even having talked to the Colonel by radio raised Ka's importance with the others.

'The Colonel?'

Ka had nodded.

'He spoke to you?' Zac's small face had been bright with wonder.

'Yes, he wants me to go on reconnaissance . . .' Ka stumbled over the word. 'After we've all eaten.' Ka gave them their new ranks, pretending not to see the anger in Saul's eyes. 'You,' he said to Saul, 'throw your grenade into the river and we'll grab the fish as they float to the surface.'

'It's my last one.' Saul's voice was suspicious.

'You were the person complaining you were hungry.' Which was true enough. He'd complained louder than anyone. 'Throw it into the middle,' Ka ordered.

'Wait.' That was Sarah.

Ka stared at her until she looked away, suddenly unsure. 'I mean,' she said quietly, 'perhaps you think he should throw it over there.' Sarah pointed to a gravel spit a hundred paces up river. 'So we can catch the fish as they float towards us.'

Agree with her, said a voice in his head.

'You're right,' said Ka. 'That's a much better idea.'

'Really?' Sarah suddenly looked more unsure than ever.

The explosion boiled the river and echoed off the cliff face, sending egrets skywards in a wheeling cloud. In total they collected fifty-three fish, with Ka just missing a log-like Nile catfish that came to the surface and then rolled over and sank. Most of the catch were fat perch sporting heavy lines like make-up around their eyes. And mixed in with the perch were a handful of deep blue talapia.

Sarah told the others that talapia collected a better price at market but, to Ka at least, both fish tasted equally good. In a flourish that surprised everyone, Bec ripped handfuls of leaves from a spindly bush and stuffed them inside the gutted perch before letting Sarah bake them on her smoking fire pit.

'Corporal Bec is in charge until I get back,' Ka announced when everyone had eaten more than they should. 'Sarah comes with me. The rest of you remain here.'

'Says who?'

He could pretend not to hear Saul or he could answer. And for once the truth was a better reply. 'Colonel Abad,' said Ka, 'those are his direct orders . . .' He turned to where Sarah was washing her fingers in the river.

'Sergeant . . .'

* * *

Ka had led the way up a wadi. Coarse gravel giving way to grit as rare grass scabs grew more spiky and then vanished altogether. Walking in the heat of the afternoon was insane but that was what the Colonel had wanted. And the man had been sympathetic, his voice understanding but firm as it crackled through the radio.

'I only ever ask for the necessary,' he had said. 'And you and Sergeant Sarah can do it. I'm certain you can.'

So Ka kept walking into the shimmering haze, with the low cliffs two hours behind him and miles of low slope ahead. Plus a dark line at the horizon which could have been mountains but was probably low cloud. And if not cloud, perhaps a trick of the heat haze. Whatever it was, that thin smudge of colour was further than either of them could walk.

'Give me the bottle . . .'

'No,' Ka shook his head and kept going. One foot in front of the other, his plastic rifle held firmly in front of him. They'd stopped twice already for water. If they finished their bottle now how could they manage the return?

'You don't even know where you're going . . .'

That was true.

'Colonel Abad will tell us,' said Ka. 'When he's ready.'

Sarah sucked at her teeth and pushed past Ka, forcing her aching legs to carry her over a crescent-shaped dune. Sweat had glued her vest to her back and drawn dark circles under her arms. Even her combats were sticky with perspiration and those were made from a special kind of cloth that breathed for itself. She knew that because it said so on the label.

Ka let her go on ahead. Sometimes when Sarah got angry it was best to leave her alone. But that wasn't the real reason Ka was happy to let her walk on. Ka liked watching the way her thin hips swung as she walked. And he liked the changing gap of nakedness between the top of her loose combats and the bottom of her vest. Also . . .

Any further thoughts were cut off by the crackle of his radio.

'Lieutenant Ka here.'

Ka noticed Sarah turn back but he was already intent on new orders that were simple and precise. Walk half a klick straight ahead, climb to the top of a vast mound and wait until their target was too close to miss. No more than fifty paces max . . .

'Load your rifle,' he told Sarah.

She shifted her Martini Henry so that it was angled across her body. 'It's already loaded,' Sarah said, as if she couldn't believe he'd say something that stupid.

'What about the sights?'

'What about them?

'Set them for fifty . . .'

Obediently Sarah adjusted for distance. Then she licked her finger and tested for wind, even though she knew there wasn't any. Satisfied that she was right, she made another slight adjustment and then worked the bolt, pulling a bullet into the gun's chamber.

'What now?' she asked.

'We wait . . .'

The truck looked like a child's toy. That might have been a side effect of a yellow paint-job that was intended to make it blend in with the desert but only made it look like a Tonka toy, or it might have been the balloon tyres which bulged with each jolt across the broken ground.

'The Colonel knew this was coming?' A look that Ka recognized began to creep across her face, smoothing away all expression. She didn't even glance over when she spoke. Instead she wriggled her body down into the sand, shuffling one knee outwards until it gripped the ground like a rider's leg locked tight to the side of a mount.

'Well?' she said.

'Yeah,' said Ka, 'undoubtedly.' Right on cue Ka heard his radio crackle to life. They both guessed what the orders would be but Ka told her anyway. 'Shoot the driver.'

Sarah wanted to suggest taking out a tyre instead. Only, so what if she killed the driver and the truck crashed? The hardest thing it could smack into was the side of a dune and besides, shooting people was her job. She never got the shakes, at least not in advance and she always held the moment.

Ice in the soul, her uncle had called it. The feeling had come after Kordofan; which was when she'd first been captured, towards the end of a battle with her brigade already retreating and the scrub full of bodies and abandoned weapons. One of Sarah's own officers had unwittingly provided camouflage and she'd almost got away with hiding in a ditch beneath him. And then the stripping crews had come and yanked away his body, intending to strip it of everything valuable and found Sarah crouched beneath.

Faced with five men who had wrists heavy with Rolexes and Tag Hauers worn like bracelets, she'd stood up, straightened her shirt and recited the first verse of the Holy Qur'an.

She'd been learning the words for weeks. Everyone she knew had been learning them in secret, when the officers weren't around; friends testing each other until their recitations were perfect.

The men still raped her, of course, but not that violently and when she crawled to her knees afterwards to find her clothes, she buttoned her shirt around a throat that was uncut and over a stomach that still had its guts where they should be, on the inside.

They'd taken nothing she couldn't afford to lose. At least that's what she told herself as she limped away towards her new camp. Equally it was nothing she'd wanted to give them either. And so the ice froze inside her and hardened around her like a shell, unnoticeable to everybody except those who got too close.

'Now,' Ka told her.

Close up it was possible to see blue lettering on the bonnet and a whip aerial that flew a blue pennant which cracked and flicked in the afternoon air. Two white men sat together up front, both wearing shades and talking to each other rather than keeping watch on the rough track.

North European or American. Or that other continent that

began with A. There were a lot of those. Pulling in a breath and holding it, Sarah aimed her rifle high, then slowly lowered the barrel and fired the moment she dropped through her target.

'Clean shot,' she said to no one.

Ka was already up and running. He rolled once at the bottom and came upright, then crashed forward, his double-Pup already sighting itself in . . . Not that Ka needed hi-tech to cut down the uniforms scrambling from the back of the truck. Those he missed with his first magazine were too stunned to do anything but panic as his next reduced them to non-combatant status.

Only one man, an elderly sergeant, hit the ground and racked back the slide on his own sub-machine-gun. Which was as far as he got. Ka's third magazine took off the top of the man's skull in a single burst.

'Got it.' It was the man's battered AK49 Ka wanted. A cookie-cutter buzz gun stamped out of cheap metal, idiot proof and unbreakable. Just getting that made his whole trip worthwhile.

'Lieutenant Ka,' he answered his radio without consciously realizing it had buzzed. The voice on the other end was quietly impressed. 'I knew you could do it. Heap sand over the bodies and then drive back to the river . . .'

'What about the cliffs?' Ka said.

'You can get to within 300 paces. Walk the rest. Now open the passenger door and check the glove compartment . . .'

Ka pulled the door open and yanked out both bodies. He must have missed hearing Sarah's second shot. The jelly splashes he wiped off everything with Kleenex taken from a pack on the dashboard. The blood puddles, urine and shit proved more difficult so Ka did what women used to do in his village and scrubbed handfuls of sand across the plastic seats and floor.

The tissues he burnt and the sand went back to join the other sand and the bodies Ka lost under the crusting edge of an overhang. It wasn't hard. Ka just dragged the dead over one at a time and then crumbled away the overhang by stamping along the sharp edge of its crust.

All the while, Sarah sat and watched and Ka let her, even though he was senior. She got like that after a firefight. Most of the time everyone else pretended not to notice. It was safer.

'Open the glove compartment,' said the Colonel. Ka could hear from his voice that he was preparing to be patient. 'It's that grey handle . . . That's right, on the dash . . .'

Inside was a map the Colonel obviously expected to be there, plus a big bar of chocolate and two cans of real Coke, both chilled.

'A map,' said Ka, 'sweets and two cans of Coke, they're still cold.'

'The compartment doubles as a chill cabinet,' the Colonel told him. 'What else?'

'Nothing.'

'Lift out the base.' There was additional static to the voice this time. A bigger distance.

'Tiny glass bottles,' Ka announced as he pulled out a handful of ampoules. 'With needles.' Each one was the length of his smallest finger, with a hollow needle the length of his thumbnail fixed at one end. The needles had plastic safety caps. Red lettering and a picture of two twisting snakes were printed on the side of each bottle.

'Well done,' said the Colonel. 'Now break a line of squares off the chocolate for Sarah and eat another yourself and then put the rest back in the cool compartment along with the ampoules . . . You can have the Cokes,' he added as an afterthought.

Chapter Eighteen

9th October

That Raf cried worried the cat not at all. Tears salt as blood ran into his neat beard and trickled across his chin. The cat would happily have dined on the puddle of fresh vomit between Raf's knees, but the tiny bats the man plucked out of the air were richer and warmer. And besides, they were *being offered*, the almost-kitten didn't even have to steal or beg. All it had to do was kill and eat.

Leaving Raf to his own memories . . .

'T-cells down fifteen per cent again.'

'Will he die?'

One could almost hear the shrug. Well, Raf could from where he sat in a window, staring out at the crooked tip of the Matterhorn. It was late spring and the lower meadow was alive with dog violet, speedwell and ladies smock. If he pushed his sight until his eyes hurt, he could just see a dark hawk frozen on the edge of the upper slopes, waiting to hit its prey.

'You know, Sir,' said the first voice, 'I'd really be tempted . . .'

'Would you?' The answering laugh was sour.

'Well, suppose . . .'

'Don't suppose,' the second voice was suddenly cross. 'Think instead. We can either carry over the costs or close the project and put the costs against this quarter's bottom line. Which one do you suggest?'

The other person thought about that.

'Fit one of the new synthetics,' said the cross voice. 'Ditto on the bone marrow.'

'Sir, we're already over budget.'

The senior man sighed, heavily. 'Take it off R&D. Slap a couple of new patent numbers on the chart. The usual . . .'

Twelve weeks followed in a blur of morphine until reality finally drip-fed its way into the analgesic fog and ruined the next three months of Raf's life. The three months when Raf didn't have to remind himself to eat or worry about whether or not he could get to sleep, because the snakes did that for him. They wove themselves under his skin and up his nose, into his throat and up his pee-pee. A fat one even came out of the side of his stomach.

One time when Raf grew bored exploring the walls inside his own head, he woke himself up to find a girl he didn't recognize sitting on the end of the bed, crying.

'What's wrong?'

She jumped and squeaked at the same time, and Raf smiled.

'You're awake . . .' The girl sounded shocked. She checked the readout from a grey box sitting on a bedside cabinet. 'It says you're asleep.' Her words were to herself.

'Look at this,' said Raf and jerked the dancing line so that it peaked right off the screen, then he levelled it out until it looked like the flat bit at a valley bottom. 'See, you just make it do what you want.'

The nurse looked at the small boy wired into the surgical slab. Her name was Anne Rigler and she was Scottish. The medical brokers were paying her less than nurses usually earned in Switzerland but much more than she could earn in Aberdeen now the oil was gone.

'It's a disgrace,' she said, sounding furious.

Raf stopped playing. 'I'm sorry. Does it break the machine?'

'No, no . . .' Pink fingers folded over his own, swallowing them. Her grip was so tight that it hurt. 'I don't mean what you're doing to their machine.' Anna's voice had a sob in it. 'This.' She jerked her chin towards the electronic bed, then round the small room. 'All of this.'

'They're mending me,' Raf explained patiently.

'Mending you?'

The boy nodded. 'New kidneys,' he said, 'improved breastbone and something to make my body mend faster when I get hurt. I don't mind, it's better than lessons.'

'Lessons?'

'I have to do lessons . . .'

She smiled. 'I wasn't mad about school either. Why don't you like yours?'

'Boring,' said Raf. '*Boring, boring, boring* . . . No one ever says anything new. It's just what's already in the textbooks.'

'You can read?'

He looked at Anne as if she was mad. 'Of course I can read,' he said. 'I'm five.'

The nurse thought about that for a while. As she did so, she jotted notes on a chart and swung her foot, so her sole scuffed the floor with each swing. Wherever the thoughts went, they didn't lead her anywhere she wanted to go.

'Do you like it here?'

Raf shrugged. 'It's okay. Better than the *Tigris* . . .'

Her look was a question.

'My mother's ship. It smells dirty and I get sick. All that static . . .'

'She's a sailor?'

'No,' Raf laughed. 'She saves whales . . .'

She did too. And cut together award-winning films from hours of footage taken with a tiny camera taped to the side of her mask. The whales were killers and ate seals like Scooby snacks. Raf often wondered why she didn't save the Scooby snacks instead.

Chapter Nineteen

9th October

'Enough,' Raf told the cat, wiping vomit from his shoes with a handkerchief taken from his jacket. Somehow a fresh one materialized in his top pocket every morning. Like eating lunch in the kitchen, it seemed ordinary tissues weren't for people like him.

Raf shrugged and screwed the soiled linen into a ball, pushing it deep into a trouser pocket. He was alone on the roof, Avatar having agreed to take the dusty hire car only after Raf marched him to the front door.

Av had been too weak to go, even after Raf had put back the lights, wiped down the door handles and carefully explained exactly why he should. So, to save time, Raf had cheated, ramping the kid up on a foil twist of speedballs taken from the driver's wallet.

'This will help you walk,' Raf told him. 'You want that, don't you?'

Avatar nodded, eyes huge.

'Yeah, figured.' Raf had dropped to a crouch beside Avatar's soiled mattress, with the driver's dropped lighter in one hand and the foil twist in his other. 'Suck the smoke,' said Raf and put a flame to the foil.

Avatar gagged.

'Slowly.' Raf's voice was soft, its tone soothing. He needed the boy out of the house and soon. Which bizarrely meant stopping Avatar from taking in too much smoke at once.

'Who are you?'

Raf stared at the boy, whose skin was as smooth as Italian leather in the overhead light. High cheekbones had become visible where there'd been adolescent softness only months before. The kid was Renaissance beautiful and part of that beauty was that Avatar didn't yet know it. To make matters more complicated, Avatar had his sister's eyes. Hurt and all.

Raf sighed. 'I'm your boss, remember . . .'

'You fired me!'

'You kind of fired yourself.'

'Well,' Avatar's smile was sad. 'Maybe.' He rolled sideways off his mattress and stood unsteadily. Around him the cellar rocked and then settled again. 'I could work for you again,' Avatar suggested.

'As of now, you do,' said Raf and turned the kid towards the door, watching him walk away, weak from hunger and dizzy with smoke.

'About Zara . . .' Avatar said over his shoulder.

'What about her?'

'She's . . .' Avatar searched in vain for the accurate word. 'Cool, I suppose.'

'So everyone keeps telling me.'

'She's also in love with you.'

Raf sighed and tossed Avatar the car keys. Adding an inevitable clang to his collection of sounds.

Chapter Twenty

Sudan

Ka could see Sarah's mouth open but her words were gone. Tears ebonied her cheeks and snot ran from her nose. His one attempt to put an arm round her had seen Sarah push him so hard that he almost fell over a small cliff.

It was Zac, Ka realized.

Tiny and doll-like in the river amid silver flashes.

Leaving Sarah where she stood, Ka ran through the wadi until, halfway down, rock crumbled under his feet and for a few blessed seconds all Ka's attention went on staying upright.

Then he was at the water's edge and reality came flooding in. Half-smoked perch were pegged out on twigs over the fire pit: but the real stink came from the humans, who had all been dead for hours by the look of it. Those bruises dead people get were already present wherever flesh touched ground.

Their fire pit was sodden with urine and Zac's ripped-open rucksack had been tossed on top of the cold embers. Everywhere had been searched and nothing found; because what the soldiers wanted still shaded Ka's eyes from the sun.

Bec had two bullet holes, one in her stomach and another below a breast. One shoe was missing and her rifle empty. Saul had a bullet through his good shoulder and another in his leg. He'd been finished with a rifle butt to the temple. Zac was a head shot, close up and through the back of his skull. The kid had fallen where he knelt.

90–2 ammo, UN-issue, meant nothing. All sides took weapons where they could capture them, ammo too. As for Sarah's felucca, a tossed grenade had reduced that to kindling, sending more dark-eyed perch to the surface.

'How did they get here?'

'Combat hovercraft, Thornycroft Mk 11, grade 5 stealth profile . . .'

Ka didn't listen. He'd been talking to himself anyway and since there weren't any track marks or, come to that, any tracks down which trucks could have come, he'd been on the point of working out that the enemy had used some kind of boat.

'We have to bury them.'

'No,' said Ka and held up one hand, as if that was enough to hold back her bubbling anger. 'The Colonel says we can't take that risk.'

Her answer was a glare.

'I want to,' said Ka, 'they were my friends too.' Which wasn't quite true. Saul was a bully and he'd never got to know Bec, but Ka knew the three of them had been together since Kordofan. And Zac . . . Zac had been Ka's responsibility. 'But what if the troops come back to make another search . . . ?'

Sarah said nothing.

'They'll know some of us are still alive and come looking with planes. What . . . ?' said Ka, seeing Sarah's face suddenly harden.

'You're afraid.'

'Afraid? I'm scared shitless. You, me . . . it's just a matter of time.'

'The will of God,' Sarah said.

'You believe that?'

She thought about it. 'I used to, kind of still do. Maybe I just want . . .'

'Yeah.' Ka put his arm round her shoulders and this time she didn't push him away . . .

In the back of the truck was a thermoflage net, fitted with a pocket at each corner that could be filled with stones or loaded with sand, for when the terrain was impossible to peg. As well as blanking out thermal signatures, the huge net stealthed radar. Or so the Colonel said and whatever that meant, it sounded good.

The smashed boat was far behind them and night had come

in. Heat still radiated from the sand but the temperature of the air was in free fall, latent heat losing out to the sprinkling of cold stars overhead.

'We'd be better sleeping inside . . .' Ka made it almost a question.

'Front seat?'

'That's still sticky. It should be the back.'

Sarah's grunt was doubtful.

'It's going to get colder,' warned Ka. Something experience had told Sarah already. Being out in the emptiness without a bag or fire was no joke and her survival blanket was back with the . . .

'Hey,' he reached out, 'it's okay.'

She cried when they lay side by side on folded matting in the back of the yellow Seraphim, hot tears for what she'd lost. Though crying made no real sense, because everything she'd ever had to lose, Sarah had long since thought gone. Except her life maybe, and she was finding that increasingly hard to care about.

And so Ka held her tight and muttered his desolate promises into her ear. That he would look after her and any soldiers who came after them were dead, that the war would stop once the river dried up . . .

And she let his words wash over her and by the time Ka stopped promising and climbed clumsily on top, she'd stopped crying. It was his tears that fell into her face and breasts as he moved slowly above her. His quiet sobs the last thing she heard before they both fell into sleep.

Chapter Twenty-one

10th October

'Present,' said Raf, tossing the scrawny animal at Hani so that it landed claws out and stuck to her bare shoulder. 'This one doesn't need batteries.'

'*Ouch.*' Grabbing the cat by the scruff of its neck, Hani yanked back its head and glared. The animal glared right back and five seconds into their staring contest it began to purr.

'The sound of nine lives,' said Raf.

Hani raised her dark eyebrows.

'Purring is a healing mechanism. 27-44Hz. That frequency helps bones mend and heals cuts. It works on humans too . . .'

Sunday morning, at a stone table in the madersa's walled courtyard, the splash of the marble fountain Raf had paid to be mended cutting through the clatter of Donna working nearby in her huge kitchen. Breakfast was spread out in front of them, almost untouched.

Coffee for Raf, orange juice for Hani.

Having drunk her juice, Hani had swallowed a token mouthful of balila and been on the point of getting down when Raf beat her to it and went to get his apology. Which was what the almost-cat was. For asking Hani how she found Avatar . . . Right question, wrong way.

'For me?'

Raf nodded.

'What does it eat?'

'Well . . .' He considered her question. 'Bats are its favourite . . . That's a joke,' Raf added hastily, when Hani started to look worried. 'Tell Donna to get it some meat.'

'What's it called?'

Raf shrugged.

'Uncle Ashraf,' Hani's voice was mock sweet. 'If it's a boy can he live in the haremlek?' Hani still had problems getting her head round the idea of anything male being allowed near the second floor of the madersa. Centuries of tradition were a hard mindset to break.

'It's a girl,' said Raf 'and she can't *live* there . . . but she can visit, all right? She lives in the courtyard . . .'

'. . . or the kitchens.'

Raf pretended to think about that, knowing already that he would let Hani have her way. 'Maybe,' he said. 'Provided you clean up any mess and Donna agrees.'

'She will,' said Hani, with the absolute certainty of a child who knows she has the winning hand in a particular relationship. With this, Hani slid from her seat, not to go ask Donna but to find Khartoum. She needed to have a serious discussion about a sensible name.

Having taken the dirty breakfast plates back to the kitchen, Raf stopped to check an update on the ISK rolling news channel which was all Donna ever watched. Bodies had been found in a derelict house near Mahmoudiya following a tip-off, and a nightclub called Sarahz, on the corner of Gumhuriya, had been firebombed, although the damage was less than it could have been.

According to Ferdie Abdullah, the channel's elegant if elderly anchorman, neither of these events were related.

Chapter Twenty-two

13th October

Changing down a gear, General Koenig Pasha slung his favourite car around a corner and glanced at his passenger. 'We got the murderer,' he said casually and smiled to see disbelief freeze the Senator's face.

'When?' Senator Liz was so shocked she forgot to be polite.

'A couple of days ago. My Chief of Detectives . . .' The call from Raf had come the previous evening. It seemed the killer had been killed. According to a cross-crime/evidence-sifting algorithm run that afternoon, seminal fluid taken from the girl butchered on Hamzah's beach gave an exact DNA match to a man found murdered in a deserted house in Mahmoudiya. Ashraf Bey proclaimed himself as surprised as the General.

'This man,' said the American. 'When will he stand trial?'

'Never,' the General announced airily.

'But surely . . .'

'I'm afraid not.'

If the black, box-like Bentley lacked the élan of the General's two-tone 1936 Rolls-Royce Phantom III or the racing lines of his green 1937 Hispano-Suiza it made up for that in raw power, being a two-handed broadsword to the others' rapier.

The General liked cars much more than he liked people. Most of whom lacked a quarter of the Bentley's character. And he decided that if Senator Liz Elsing had been a car, she'd have been a Ford, reliable, bland and irritating. He, however, would have been this Bentley.

'It seems the murderer died,' added the General. For propriety's sake, this was the point at which he should have said *under questioning*, because the woman would expect no less.

However, as her traditional Western prejudices could be relied upon to fill in that gap for herself, the General changed gear instead and heard the motor slow to a throaty, law-breaking roar. A roar that impressed him more than anything the American might say.

Originally made in 1931 and totally rebuilt in 1993 at the orders of a Sudanese drummer whose fingers could coax rhythms from goatskin that defied simple mathematical definition, the 8-litre vehicle had been presented to the General by Hamzah Quitrimala. A small token of the industrialist's appreciation at being given permission to build the Midas Refinery.

The red leather driver's seat on which Koenig Pasha sat was as battered and shiny as a club chair. The walnut trim on the dash was solid, not veneer, and years of careful hand-polishing had produced a patina that would enhance the most elegant antique.

Which it was, the General reminded himself. Though it was hard to remember that fact when the car's 7,983cc of in-line power could still accelerate its brick-like body to 110 mph. Only a hundred had been built and most of those with the 144-inch wheel base. The General's featured the 156.

And in fourth gear, the car could range from walking speed to the ton, vibrations kept to a minimum by rubber mountings to the engine and gear-box.

'What do you think?'

'Very colourful, Your Excellency,' said his passenger, watching as a small Citroen 3-wheeler laden with peppers pulled over to let the General pass. Her researchers informed Senator Liz that, unfortunately, the current vegetable crop would be bumper. Which gave her one less way to get leverage.

'I meant the car . . .'

'The car, Your Excellency?'

By now protocol demanded that Koenig Pasha ask the Senator to call him *General* or maybe even *Saeed*; at the very least it should have been *Sir* . . . General Saeed Koenig Pasha, however, had no intention of obliging. Senator Liz, as she insisted he call her, was known to the General as an international busybody so afraid of her own vices that she'd turned the magnifying glass of her insecurity on the virtues of everyone else.

He also doubted, strongly, that her fact-finding mission to El Iskandryia involved the finding out of any facts. In his long experience, special envoys from the White House or Berlin were only interested in trade, polishing their spheres of influence and issuing threats, usually disguised as a once-in-a-lifetime, one-off opportunity.

'Bentley, 8-litre, 1931 . . . Superb machine.'

The small woman looked embarrassed. Too clumsy to make small talk like the diplomat she was supposed to be and too worried about getting it wrong to pretend she knew about vintage cars, Senator Liz retreated into silence, which was something of a first.

Smiling grimly, Koenig Pasha put his foot to the floor and swung the heavy Bentley out into the middle of the road to over-take two army jeeps and a tractor which was the cause of their slowness. Let the soldiers catch up with him if they could.

Of course the Senator didn't like his car. Americans expected cruise control, air-conditioning and a basic AI, all of which the General regarded as utterly redundant. If the General got hot he opened a window and if that failed to work he just went faster . . .

As for directions, if he got lost he stopped and asked the *felaheen*. It was worth it for the shocked look when they realized to whom they were speaking.

'Finally,' said the General, 'we're here.' Stamping on the brakes, he swung his wooden steering wheel and aimed for a farm track, accelerating into the skid so that his rear barely missed shunting one side of a crumbling set of gate posts.

After that, the heavy car ate up the dirt road, bouncing in and out of potholes and past row after row of walled terraces cut into the sides of the hill, until the jeeps were just distant plumes of dust behind it.

His own trail would be visible for miles, an almost biblical column of smoke ascending to heaven. All the same, Hakim and

Ahmed would be worried, but then being his bodyguards that was their job, and his new *aide de camp* would be sweating blood and cursing under his breath. It had better be under his breath, because the General would hear about it if it wasn't.

'Here we go,' Koenig Pasha announced, skidding to a halt in a slick of gravel that popped like small-arms fire.

Here was a farmhouse cracked open like an egg. Red pantiles lay scattered across the earth, mostly in shards but with the occasional half tile. All the really good ones had been taken, then the not-so-good. What was left were discards, tiles too damaged to make stealing them worthwhile.

A single doorway stood doorless, while wooden shutters hung loose from shattered windows that had never known glass. And from inside came a scuttling like rats picking their way across broken crockery.

'Outside,' demanded the General. 'Out of there now.'

'Yes, Excellency . . .' The anxious voice probably called everyone *excellency*, just to be sure. But the General had to call again before its owner appeared.

'I'm coming, Excellency.' With his eyes blinking at the sudden glare, a moon-faced boy materialized in the dark doorway. His gaze slid to the old man's face and for a split second the young *fellah* didn't recognize who was standing there.

Then he did.

'Stand over there,' ordered Koenig Pasha, nodding towards an outhouse wall. The boy was almost drowning in fear and yet he did what he was told, moving dreamlike towards a point indicated, like a swimmer fighting the current. His feet were bare, just visible beneath an oversized jellaba, which sagged from narrow shoulders and scraped the ground.

'Your brother's clothes?'

The boy looked blank.

'The jellaba.'

'My father's old one, Excellency. I . . .' He stopped. 'I don't have a brother.'

The General nodded thoughtfully.

'And who else is in there?'

'In where, Excellency?' The voice was tight.

Koenig Pasha looked round at a row of ancient olive trees which time and war had reduced to splintered stumps. Once there'd been a retaining wall holding up their terracing, until its collapse had let red earth spill onto the level below. There'd been a well too, only that had been filled with rubble and capped off with polycrete. He'd given the order himself, years back.

'Where do you think I mean?' he asked.

'There's no . . .' The boy's voice slid an octave and halted.

'Come on,' said the General, directing his order to the empty door. 'It's not safe in there.'

A rat-like scuttle inside turned into a second face, dark skinned and broad cheeked. The girl was maybe thirteen, roughly the same age as the boy. Her black hair was pulled back under a *hijab* tied hastily round her head, so that only her face could be seen.

'We were looking for Hussein's goat.' Her words were a whisper she didn't really expect him to believe. Resignation and fear expanded eyes already darkened with charcoal. Red was smeared crudely across her lips. Pomegranate juice, probably. That was what girls used when he was young.

Koenig Pasha looked from one child to the other and then back again. 'No brother,' he said to the boy. 'But this is your sister, right?'

Puzzlement met hope in the boy's thin face. As if the child was watching for the catch, for a trap that would snap shut on his lies. He said nothing, not even when the General repeated his question.

The old man sighed. 'I thought so,' he said and waved them away.

Neither moved.

'Go,' Koenig Pasha ordered. 'Go now, before I change my mind . . .'

When they reached the edge of the ruined olive grove, the General suddenly stepped forward and shouted for the boy to stop. He did, as rooted to the dusty earth as the broken stump next to him.

'Good luck.'

Again those puzzled eyes, distant and uncertain.

'With finding your goat.'

The boy grinned fit to burst and snapped a ragged salute. Then, grabbing the girl's hand, he hurried her out of sight down a slope.

'Truants,' said the Senator.

'Who might have died,' the General agreed flatly. 'If their being alone up here was reported to the *morales* . . . Everything has a price,' he added, leaving blank which *everything* he had in mind.

'They die. That's the law?'

The old man shook his head. 'I am the law,' he said. It was a statement of fact, nothing more. 'The boy would have been badly beaten by his father. But the girl . . .' He shrugged. 'Locked in a cellar. Maybe even bricked in to starve or tossed in a ditch with her throat cut. Not stoned to death, not yet. Though that may come . . .'

If you don't support me. The Senator could read the General's subtext easily enough. *Stick with me because what comes next will be worse.* She'd heard it before. Hell, she'd heard it all over. Mostly in Central America. Half of her research staff agreed. She knew too that the other half thought she was breaking rule one of foreign affairs. *Never ask for what you know cannot be delivered.*

'What was it you wanted to tell me?' she asked the General.

'Tell you . . . ?'

'This is about achieving deniability, isn't it, Your Excellency?' Senator Liz indicated the empty terraces surrounding the sun-lit farmhouse. In the near distance dust plumed as a pair of jeeps juddered their way up the dirt track road towards the crown of the hill. The General and she had another two, maybe three minutes to themselves at the most.

'No.' The General shook his head and fished in his pocket, finding a box of Sobranie and his Zippo. Engraved on one side was an eagle over crossed thunderbolts, badge of the 5th French Foreign Legion. Koenig Pasha's capture of the lighter was a long story and he was resigned to no one ever getting it right.

'I didn't bring you here to talk,' said the General. 'I wanted to show you this . . .' He waved a hand at the ruined farmhouse and the terraces with their collapsing walls and uprooted vines. 'You know what this place is?'

He watched Senator Liz struggle to remember all she'd been told about the General's history, about Iskandryian politics. Sometime in the last week, before the woman landed at Ali Pasha, spooks from Langley would have briefed her. After the briefing, she'd brushed up on her protocol.

Those lessons had been only partly successful. At least that was the General's opinion. Her manners at the table were impeccable and practised. Small amounts of food got left at the side of her plate to acknowledge the richness of her hosts. She never showed the soles of her Manolos when she sat. Her right hand only was used to present her card and eat or drink, the unclean hand she kept to herself.

The Senator even kept eye contact longer than most Westerners and her handshake was gentle, lacking that bone-crunching grip most Americans believed indicated decisiveness or virility. But like most of her kind, her grasp on history was so slight as to be dangerous. And though she could *salaam* with grace, touching her hand to her breast and then forehead, before lifting it away, she lacked the wit to realize that in El Iskandryia no woman ever used that greeting.

Saeed Pasha sighed. He was prejudiced against Americans. Mind you, he wasn't that fond of the English either. The Germans and the French, now you knew where you were with them. The first were brutal, the second devious. He had the blood of both in his veins.

'This place,' said the General. 'You know where you are now?'

'No, I'm sorry . . . I don't.'

'They came up that track . . .' Koenig Pasha pointed to a strip of road. 'Wearing rags that had once been uniforms, their bare feet soled with tar from the desert road. Many of them were younger than your granddaughter.'

He'd been briefed too. On the woman's background and tastes, which were both predictably American.

The Senator knew what Koenig Pasha was talking about now. 'What did you do?' she asked; though she wasn't really sure she wanted to know.

'What could we do? We killed them. We gunned them down in their thousands as they shambled towards us. All the amulets in the world couldn't hold back our bullets, despite what the enemy had been told. They carried ancient kalashnikovs, spare magazines duct-taped together, pangas blunt with over-use, Martini Henrys . . .' The General stopped. '*Martini Henrys*. British revolvers taken by the Dinka, the barrels and cylinders drilled out to take current ammunition. It was a blood-bath.'

He could see it still in front of his eyes. A hot morning in early summer with the Nile only just on the rise. The mercury hitting 110F. No rain for six weeks.

Ten thousand strong they advanced up the desert highway with limp banners aloft in the hot and breezeless air. The dust from those in front had turned to khaki the ragged clothes of the ranks behind. Now, all that many of them had by way of uniform was a red ribbon tied to their upper arm. Behind them, at the rear, marched their officers, five hundred veterans of a ruthless campaign fought in the deserts around Meroe and the foothills of Abyssinia. They carried laser-sighted rifles, mortars and portable rocket launchers. Most wore lightweight body armour, air-conditioned helmets, earbeads and throat mikes. Men and women alike, their hair was cropped short and their eyes hard with satisfaction at how easily Al Qahirah had fallen.

Major Koenig Bey, as he was then, had three hundred men left from his regiment. Some had died but more had deserted in the face of assurances that to oppose this Ragged Army was to oppose the absolute will of God. In vain the local Mufti had insisted in proclamation after proclamation that this was untrue. The Sublime Porte, his imperial majesty Mehmet VII, in his role as religious leader of the Osmali empire issued an edict stigmatizing the Mahdi. No one paid any attention.

Winning was left to a twenty-eight-year-old sapper, a half-Egyptian, half-German who had reached regimental rank solely because every other officer had resigned, deserted or was already dead.

This was a man whose first action on arriving at his new HQ in a farmhouse overlooking the desert road was to send for a flame-thrower, have the pressure tank converted to take emulsion and order that the walls, floor and ceiling be sprayed white. While teenage officers advised by elder NCOs set up gun encampments and mortar pits, Major Koenig oversaw first the removal of all furniture from the downstairs of the farmhouse, then the removal of its two cheap overhead striplights and the light switches. Only then was the converted flame-thrower used to redecorate the rooms to suit the Major's taste.

Back in went a table and chairs, the overhead strips and a pot-bellied charcoal stove which the Major took everywhere, for when he wanted fresh bread or coffee.

People might mutter but not when he was within earshot. And besides, the Major knew exactly what he was doing as he stood in the middle of the redecorated room and told his officers not to bother setting up charts.

They were outnumbered and outgunned. All they had on their side was their command of a hill top. That and strategy. And in the end Major Saeed Koenig Bey won by retreating. Though first he shot his favourite brother through the head for refusing to follow an order.

Amil was young, handsome and the undisputed favourite of both his parents in the way that only youngest sons can be. Bizarrely, despite their difference in age, Major Koenig adored him.

With the Ragged Army marching uphill, into the fire of the Major's machine-guns and with every death being recorded by CNN drones hung high enough overhead to be out of rifle shot, Major Koenig ordered a retreat.

'Why?' Amil's question had been simple.

Because we're being filmed. Because we're turning ourselves into murderers. Because I won't order the deaths of a thousand twelve-year-olds who think that dirty feathers and dry twigs in a totem bag can stop bullets and that paradise waits with open gates for those who die, and see nothing contradictory in those two beliefs.

All of these would have been honest answers. But his senior sergeant and the other NCOs were watching the Major, their uncertainty as to the wisdom of his order curdling to doubt. And orders were orders, that was what he'd been taught. The rules of engagement demanded it.

'Because I say so . . .'

'But we command the hill.'

'Not any longer.'

Amil opened his mouth to protest and bit back the words as his brother pulled a Luger from his belt.

'We retreat now. Understand?' Major Koenig glanced round his command group, which comprised a couple of hardened NCOs and a dozen subalterns so young they hadn't yet had time to grow a first moustache. The Ragged Army advancing up the hill was forgotten momentarily. The crack of return fire from his own men outside the farmhouse gone from the Major's mind.

'We pull back to the crossroads and then stop.'

'Sir,' his senior sergeant had raised a hand.

'You have a problem, Sergeant?' Words sharper than flint and cold as ice. Disdain, derision, mounting disbelief that any NCO might dare question an order. All of those and more were in the five words.

The senior NCO swallowed a smile. He was old enough to know the voice of his old commander, the Major's father, a ruthless bastard but a highly efficient one. As commanding officers went he was good, but the sergeant wouldn't have wanted the man for his father.

'No, Sir. Absolutely not, Sir.' He snapped out a salute like the rawest, most frightened recruit and swung on his heels, the other NCOs straightening up, reassured now the decision had been taken.

And there matters would have ended if Amil hadn't insisted on taking a step forward to object. The rest had gone down in legend. Muttered by the General's enemies as proof of his ruthlessness and spoken openly by his friends as proof of the same. Amil died with a mocking smile on his face and a bullet from his brother's gun between the eyes.

Major Koenig left the body where it dropped.

By the time the Major returned to the farmhouse that evening, walking under a white flag of truce, Amil's body had been carried away and dumped with others in a pit dug into the terraces by a thin girl on a tractor. He came alone, unarmed, and stood silent and uncomplaining as rough hands searched him before letting him inside.

The ground floor of the farmhouse was crowded with the cream of the Ragged Army's generals, their own uniforms anything but that. Some of the junior officers wore battledress stripped from UN observers but most had uniforms cut and sewn by local tailors along the way.

A few were imported, bought via middlemen from military tailors in Algiers, Berlin or Stambul. Two officers were even dressed in the uniform of Major Koenig's regiment. One had, until that afternoon, been his *aide de camp* and the other the Major had thought dead. Certainly the man had never returned from the morning's reconnaissance.

Amused eyes watched him notice them.

A charcoal fire burned in the pot-bellied stove he'd been forced to abandon, heating a brass jug of fresh coffee. A hurricane lamp lit the room against advancing night.

Against centuries of tradition, Major Koeing was not offered a small cup of sweetened coffee or a brass sheesha filled with apple tobacco. He sat unasked on the only chair not in use and when he requested a glass of water to wet his throat this was refused. The Major was pleased. It made what came next easier.

He was there to negotiate the surrender of El Iskandryia to the Ragged Army. General Mahdi had not bothered to come in person. Rumour said the jihad leader was too busy imposing his rule on Al Qahirah, where cinema doors had been bolted tight, bars burnt and women whipped in public for going out with their heads uncovered. Schools for girls had been closed, female doctors banned from working and aid workers of both sexes given twenty-four hours to leave the country.

Berlin, Paris and Washington were too busy being outraged to have time for what was about to happen on a hill to the south of Iskandryia.

Camped on terraces that had been cut into the slope before Islam or Christianity even existed, the Ragged Army crouched round fires lit with dried dung or branches ripped from the ancient olive grove. Food had been plentiful in Al Qahirah and most were no longer hungry. But they lit fires and killed any goats they could scavenge because that was what they did. Habit can take only weeks to become tradition and they'd had years. First in the Sudan, then moving north.

'Tomorrow and the next day we march,' their leader told Major Koenig. 'The evening after that arrive at El Iskandryia. Friday we pray. Saturday you bring out the old man to make his surrender.'

Fat chance, thought the Major. The Khedive was too ill to leave his bed. Besides, he was Khedive, the old man would die rather than surrender his city. 'And the terms?' Major Koenig asked.

There were no terms. The city surrendered. That was all there was to it. Those whom the Ragged Army let live were those who would live. No promises would be made.

Same terms they gave Al Qahirah.

'I agree.' Major Koenig held out his hand and when this was not taken, bowed slightly and clicked his heels, Berlin style, purely for the pleasure of seeing hatred flood the faces of his enemy. 'The city will be ready for you,' he added.

Snapping a drill-perfect salute, he walked to the door, stopping only to reach into the emptiness where a light switch should be and touch together two wires.

The resulting blast broke the Major's right ulna in two places and dislocated his shoulder. Though what really hurt was the length of light fitting that scraped its way across his hip bone, fracturing his pelvis.

The bomb in the empty striplight was technologically primitive. All the same, it worked better than the Major had been expecting. And while the West had at its disposal numerous kinds of self-firing *plastique*, not to mention those little synthetic viruses they were so busy denying, he'd had to rely on a block of Semtex, a basic detonator, ball-bearings, batteries from a mobile and some recycled flex. All of it, excluding the ball-bearings obviously, well past its use-by date.

The light fitting killed everyone standing under it; just not all at the same time. The luckiest deaths were immediate. Necks snapped or skulls broken open, hearts pierced by shattered ribs. Under heavy fire from his own side, who'd advanced as ordered at the sound of the explosion, the Major got trucked to a camp in Al Qahirah, a shard of light fitting still embedded in his hip, his broken arm locked tight in a battle dressing. The *fellah* from the Ragged Army who'd pulled Major Koenig from the rubble thought the officer was one of her own.

'And General Mahdi. If I remember . . .' The Senator paused, wondering how she should put it delicately. 'Had his hands cut off . . .'

'Among other things.'

That was three weeks later, in Al Qahirah. By then the Ragged Army had mostly surrendered, its mercenary core either dead, under arrest or rapidly selling each other out in return for immunity. Major Koenig was right. Taking out the enemy's generals had been the solution.

And Senator Liz had finally remembered enough of the General's history to wish she was somewhere else. What type of man took visiting dignitaries to see where he'd shot his own brother? The answer was obvious. Someone like Koenig Pasha.

'They never did find who murdered General Mahdi, did they?'

'No,' said the General, his eyes holding those of the American woman, 'you're right. They never did . . .'

'And Colonel Abad?' She named Mahdi's infamous adviser, Washington's *bête noire*.

'In paradise, no doubt,' said Koenig Pasha. 'Or maybe hell.'

Chapter Twenty-three

14th October

'Hey,' Hani sounded so cross that Ifritah's ears flicked back and Hani had to stroke the cat to get her purring again. 'I was watching that . . .'

'Sorry,' said Raf, clicking his fingers to change channels. 'I need to see what other people are saying about what's happening . . .'

'Happening where?'

'Here.'

Hani raised her eyebrows but stayed put as Raf banged down his briefcase and turned his attention back to the screen. *Heute in Berlin* had nothing and neither did the US feeds, but that wasn't surprising, both countries were notoriously insular. And Iskandryia's own Ferdie Abdullah was concentrating on a second arson attack on a night club opposite Misr Station.

Raf found what he wanted on *Paris – la Ronde*, which segued straight from a snippet on the Prince Imperial's first term at St Andrews to a moderately gloating round-up of problems to be raised when representatives of the Kaiser and the Sublime Porte finally held separate meetings with a US arbitrator, to discuss renewing the Osmanli Accord, that treaty which defined spheres of economic influence in North Africa, the Middle East and the Balkans.

Berlin wanted the spheres expanded, as did Moscow. Paris was reserving its position. US Senator Elizabeth Elsing was on record as saying she thought spheres of influence were undemocratic. The French anchorman smirked when he reported this.

'Boring,' announced Hani, so Raf told the screen to find

another cartoon and soon a bug-eyed, yellow whatsit was bumbling round being kind to small animals. And while the whatsit ran rescue missions or fried scary monsters with its awesome magic power, Raf boned a leg of lamb, cubed the meat and braised it in a heavy pan.

'What are you making?' Hani asked in the ad break.

'*Hunkar begendi*, kind of . . .'

'Sultan's delight.' Having just discovered McDonald's, Hani's tastes had telescoped. Anything that failed to come between two bits of bun with reconstituted French fries didn't count.

For the sauce that gave its name to the dish, Raf needed to puncture tiny holes in four aubergines so they wouldn't burst when he grilled them in Donna's gas oven until their skins went black and blistered.

'You want to do this?' Raf picked up a fork and nodded to the uncooked aubergine.

Hani shook her head. So Raf punched holes in the purple skin instead.

'What *is* happening?' Hani asked. She was back with Ferdie Abdullah, who was running through the main headlines. Behind him a minor oil pipe bled crude onto gravel and hot sand while a huge billboard reading 'Midas Refinery' blazed like an advertisement for chaos. Before setting it on fire, the arsonists had taken time to stencil a row of red fists along the bottom of the sign.

Against a background of flames, impossibly young soldiers loaded two trespassing Ishies into a police van. With their faces hidden by goggles and belts studded with drives and umbrella modems, the freelance newshounds stumbled towards confinement like vintage astronauts traversing some monochrome lunar plain.

The masks were all affectation. A decent digital lens could be mounted onto the side of ordinary glasses and still be so small as to be almost invisible. As for the drives, anything bigger than a packet of Cleopatra was either outdated, third-world cheap or intentionally obvious.

On screen, Ferdie Abdullah was explaining that, according

to Iskandryia's bright new Chief of Detectives, the apparently-random, wide-ranging attacks of the previous week *were* connected after all, having been carried out by the Sword of God. Which was the first Raf had heard of it.

'*I never said that . . .*'

'What?'

'I never said the attacks weren't random.'

'No?' Hani looked up from stroking Ifritah. 'What does random mean?'

'Not related.'

Scooping the grilled aubergines out of their skins with a fork, Raf put the pulp to one side while he got butter from the fridge. Then all he needed was to add flour to the molten butter and beat hard as milk went into the mixture.

'So they are related?'

Raf stopped looking for a skillet. 'I don't know,' he said.

Hani sighed.

After he'd added mashed aubergine to his roux, Raf ground in a twist of pepper, a twist of sea salt and sprinkled on a handful of grated cheese. The lamb went onto the middle of an already-warmed serving plate, with the aubergine sauce swirled in an elegant circle round the outside.

'You hungry?'

Hani shook her head.

'No, me neither.' Raf passed the serving dish to Hani. 'See if Khartoum wants this, then I'll buy you a burger . . .'

'For you,' Hani announced from the doorway of the porter's quarters at the rear of the madersa's covered garden.

'For us?' Khartoum glanced up from his game of Go as did his opponent, the owner of a small stall in Rue Cif, which ran along the back of the madersa. 'You made this?' Khartoum looked surprised. Also disbelieving.

'No, Uncle Ashraf made it.'

'His Excellency . . .' the stall holder looked surprised. 'The bey cooks?'

Hani smiled at the man whose knee-length coat and white cap signified he'd made a *hajj*, the ritual pilgrimage to Mecca.

'His Excellency does a lot of strange things,' she said shortly and backed out of the room. If either man thought it strange that the child had a flea-bitten cat slung round her neck like a collar, they didn't mention it.

'You'll be fine,' promised Raf when Hani hesitated in the madersa's ornate marble hall. For reasons neither Khartoum nor Donna could properly explain, her late Aunt Nafisa had felt it necessary to keep the child indoors. Which meant the funeral of her aunt was the first time Hani got to leave the house.

'Of course I will,' Hani said and yanked open the front door. She smiled as she took Raf's hand, though her nails dug hard into his palm as they stepped from the quiet of the madersa into the noise of Rue Sherif.

Raf dug back and Hani's grin turned vulpine. When they reached the corner she was still grinning and still trying to dig her nails through his skin. They both knew she was only half joking . . .

That night, the fox came as clouds blocked off the stars and the sky moved closer to the earth, imposing an obvious but impressive boundary, like that loss of focus at the edge of a dream or the distant strangeness of the world beyond an aquarium as seen by some captive angel fish.

And as all this occurred, outside of the world outside the al-Mansur madersa, Raf sat on the edge of Hani's narrow bed and watched the small child sleep, badly . . . She mewled half-words and broken sentences that matched the fluttering behind her closed eyes. Panic glued strips of damp hair to her forehead and every so often she'd roll her shoulders as if fighting her way through a crowd. Raf watched and waited in what should have been darkness and would have been were he anyone else. At no point did he allow himself or the fox to sleep.

Chapter Twenty-four

Sudan

It was Sarah who taught Ka how to catch the birds that flocked south. While the ghosts of the others hunted lizards through the ruins of J'habite, she sat in the shade of the truck, sharing her pipe with Ka and refusing to talk.

Smoking always made Ka talkative. Sarah was the opposite. This was a month after Zac died and Ka was still afraid of Sarah's long silences and the sudden thunder bursts of her anger.

As she stared blankly at the blue sky, Ka risked an occasional sideways glance at where the top button of her shirt had come undone. Not her collar button which was missing, the one below that.

Through the slight gap he could see the start of a breast, shadow against shadow. And on the wrist of the hand holding her steel pipe, fine hairs lit in the light that dappled through the thermoflage covering their truck. His own skin had gone dark in the desert, yet hers was darker still. Almost purple, like al-badingan, a plant carried from Africa to al-Andalus by the army of Islam, though Ka didn't know that. He just knew his uncle had grown them one year. Soft fruit that spoiled easily and was eaten as a vegetable fried with mutton oil and salt.

The pipe was Sarah's own. Bent and scratched, it had been filthy when she took it off a dead nasrani photographer. Which meant Sarah had wasted hours meticulously scraping tar from the mouthpiece with a thorn stripped of its bark.

The last person to try taking the pipe from Sarah had ended up with two fingers of his right hand bound together for a month, to help his bones knit. But these last few weeks she'd taken to sharing her pipe with Ka and her food too, though only when there was enough to spare.

Everything about that afternoon was normal until a small dark bird swooped overhead and Sarah suddenly sat up straight. A minute later other birds followed, heading south.

'Netting,' Sarah demanded, her voice urgent.

Ka looked puzzled.

'Netting,' she repeated and pointed to an unused roll of thermoflage that still lay where they'd dumped it five days earlier. 'Hurry.' Sarah grabbed his hand and pulled Ka to his feet.

Ka knew better than to refuse. 'What are we hiding?' Ka asked. 'And what are we hiding it from?' Hiding themselves from the planes was the usual answer but the truck was already netted and the sky was free from silver specks.

'We're going to catch food,' she told Ka and the boy stopped fussing.

'Do what I do,' said Sarah. So Ka did.

Together they unrolled the net and laid it flat in the road. Then Sarah cut two long lengths of electrical flex from a cardboard roll in the back of the truck and gave one to Ka.

'The net goes there,' Sarah said, indicating a dark slit of alley between two broken houses. 'You take the one on this side and I'll take the other.'

Reaching the roof on his side of the alley was easier than Ka expected, mainly because the stairs were in place and neither floor had fallen in. Sarah's climb took longer and when she finally appeared on the roof opposite, sweat had fastened her shirt tight against her back.

'Broken stairs.'

Ka nodded, silently threading one end of his wire through a gap in the parapet when he saw Sarah do the same. When she tied one end tight, he did that too and obediently tossed the rest of his flex over the edge, watching as it fell into the street below.

'Okay,' said Sarah. 'Now we do the netting.' She disappeared from view and it took Ka a moment to realize she'd started the return climb. Although he still made it down before she did.

'Stairs,' Sarah said.

Ka nodded guiltily.

'Some people . . .' Crouched back on her heels, mouth slightly open and face fierce with concentration, Sarah carefully tied her wire to a corner of the net and then waited for Ka do the same. After that, all they had to do was climb back to the top and haul on their wires until the net was in position.

She smelt of kif, as always, but beneath the smoke Ka could smell sweat as it dried into her shirt and a feral stink that he also carried, but mostly forgot to notice. All of the other girls he'd met had washed with sand, disappearing behind a wall or bush to scrub it into their skin. Sarah was different. If the river was nearby she used that; otherwise she used nothing.

'Why are you sniffing?'

'I'm not.'

Sarah looked at him.

'The pipe,' said Ka, 'I like it.'

Sarah nodded, like she understood. But a few minutes later she got up to make a hard-to-see adjustment to one corner of the trap and when she came back, she sat somewhere else.

Later on, the blue sky turned pink along its edge. Pink turned to purple and purple to a blue so deep it was almost black. And stars hung silent as Sarah lay back and tried to imagine the unimaginable distances.

Sat on the other side of the fire, Ka held a spit-roasted bird, one of a dozen that he'd eaten as the evening wore on and the flames burned low. Two more tiny birds cooled on a length of aerial near his feet. The wings he'd taken to discarding as hardly worth the bother, throwing them back to sizzle in the fire while he concentrated instead on pinching strips of hot meat from the tiny carcass.

When the fire was done and the night turned colder, they

retreated to the back of the truck, Sarah to clean her pipe and Ka to talk to the Colonel. He was still talking when Sarah fell asleep. Though she woke once, later on, to remove his hand from inside her shirt.

Chapter Twenty-five

15th October

It was a job and someone had to do it. Shutting his eyes briefly against a flickering beam of red laser, the man calling himself Mike Estelle opened them again, then smiled through the yellow afterglow at a young American dancing opposite.

Wide face, fair hair, a turned-up nose that looked natural; sweat darkening the valley between her breasts and beading her throat like glitter dust. Trousers slung low enough at the back to expose the black waistband of a thong.

Her name was Dawn, apparently.

'Okay?'

She grinned back and danced closer.

And closer.

When Mike jerked his head at an exit, she nodded. And when he put one arm round her shoulder to steer her towards the door, she smiled and let his hand slip forward until it hovered above her shiny bra. With a sideways glance, he grabbed a handful, ready to make a joke of it if she protested but Dawn just giggled and turned her head, mouth opening as she raised her face for a kiss.

A crowd of students pushed past on both sides, jeering at the thirty-something man with his arms locked round a teenager, though no one actually seemed to mind that he blocked the door between the main dance floor and the loos at Neutropic. The last of the students, a kid with a magenta dread wig, silver contacts and a vest that read 'deep and tribal' glanced back, noticed that the girl now had one breast completely out of her bra and grinned. So Mike twisted his lips into a smile and nodded to the student, an ubiquitous knowing nod which the *Thiergarten* agent hoped said *sorted*.

From the floor came the gut-crunching, ear-bleeding thud of bass bins overlaid with a wasp-like electronic loop that wound itself up and up but went nowhere, endlessly . . .

Mike hated the noise but then, he hated nightclubs, which was why he'd been so happy to firebomb the last one. To really like the music, he'd decided, you had to be out of your head and Mike was teetotal everything. Unlike the Friday night crowd around him.

That any clubs opened on a holy day upset the mullahs; so those which did made sure their licences were up to date, closing times were met and the local uniforms paid off. The *morales* themselves were mostly beyond bribery, though black-mail could work.

The other thing Neutropic did was weed out locals at the door. Anyone who didn't do a convincing impression of a well-dressed foreigner got bounced by the fashion police. Letting in Iskandryia's own just wasn't worth the grief.

Which was fine with Mike Estelle. The last thing he needed was to hook up with some local kid who had an angry elder brother and five uncles.

'You know what I like about this place?'

He didn't.

'Everyone's always off their heads.'

Yeah, he liked that too. Mind you . . . 'You know, it's a bit noisy . . .'

'What?'

He started to repeat himself and then realized she was grinning, so he grinned back and gently steered her through the door and towards some fire doors.

'Wait.'

He looked at her.

'Rehydration,' she said, pulling three tiny pink hearts from the pocket of her white jeans. 'Need a bottle for these.' Actually they weren't jeans, they were some kind of paper-thin trouser, bias-cut from acetate, belted with a silver sheriff's star on a leather throng threaded through loops. And she didn't need water . . .

'You ever tried a kite?' He dipped his own hand inside his shirt, reaching for a small pouch that hung on a silver chain round his neck. Shaking out a tiny purple lozenge, he dropped it into her open hand.

'No need for water with these,' he said. 'They just melt in your mouth.'

'What's in them?'

He smiled and named a cat valium analogue mentioned earlier at the bar by some girl he'd bought a drink. She had been older than this one, not yet close to being drunk and there was a hardness to her, a neurotic edge that made him nod politely, knock back his Diet Coke and disengage. Places like Neutropic didn't exist for people like her to waste his time. Besides, she'd been Swiss and he needed a Yank . . . Or at the very least some Yank wanabee from the American university.

What he actually fed the kid was something else, obviously; but the chemical formula would mean nothing to her and no one had bothered to name this drug something snappy. She didn't yet know it but she was about to be reeled in on something none of her friends even knew existed.

'They're great,' said Mike, closing her hand around the lozenge, the chemical formula of which was just one molecule off an anaesthetic that had been briefly popular fifty years earlier. This version had remained on paper – well, disk – in a Swiss lab until a May evening three years earlier when a Sudanese research student working up something for the weekend had screwed over one of her sequences.

Asked later that night at Zurich's Apocalypso if she was carrying drugs, the research student said, *yes, lots*. Ordered to empty her bag, she laboriously took out everything. Credit chips, tram tickets, vapour-thin condoms, a tampon, loose change, the fluff in the bottom . . .

Standing in the queue watching all this happen was a very junior opportunities exec from the research division of Bayer-Rochelle. A thousand US dollars to the largest of the door staff saw the girl, plus her emptied bag, in a taxi headed out of Zurich towards an elegantly-landscaped campus beside Lake Lucerne.

They talked, at least she did. About everything she'd ever done that had embarrassed her. They ate supper at the campus canteen and then, much later, after a romantic walk beside the lake they went to bed via a quick detour to his open-plan office. She remembered nothing of the chocolate torte or Wiener Schnitzel, the moon glistening on cold water or the sex but she woke bandy-legged and raw, having signed a contract relinquishing any intellectual rights she might possess in whatever chemical had induced such a chronic attack of honesty and obedience.

It was a good story, true or not. And amnesia was one of the more useful side effects of the drug. Amnesia, anaesthesia and obedience. What more could any person want?

At the moment nothing. That would come later.

'Real rush,' said the man, mouthing his words over the background noise.

'If you say so.' Dawn shrugged, smiled and put the lozenge on her tongue, looking like a child with a sweet. Within seconds her smile had become a grin and then her personality imploded, her pupils widening into vast black circles through which she fell.

3.45 a.m. Exactly one hour and forty-five minutes after he walked through the door. With a satisfied smile, Mike reset the alarm on his Rolex and checked that it was offline for all functions. It would be extremely inconvenient if some over-zealous Iskandryian cop was to use station switching to check Mike's progress across the city at a later date.

'This way.'

She nodded, her face so unguarded as to be almost infantile. Wrapping his arm tight around her shoulders, Mike steered her through the emergency door at the back of Neutropic and into a parking lot packed with cars but empty of people.

'Which one do you like?'

Dark eyes regarded him gravely.

'Tell me.' It was an order.

'That one,' said the girl without hesitation. The red Mazda to which she pointed was exactly what he'd have expected of her.

Flash without being that well made. This was the difference between him and an American. He'd have gone for something expensive but understated. Which, obviously enough, was why he'd got her to make the choice. That way police had a harder time trying to construct a profile.

Pulling a thin grey card from the pocket of his trousers, he rested it against the lock of the little Mazda and let the internal electronics do their magic. Commercial versions of the universal key did stupid things like ping when the right combination was found or have diodes that flashed up the side in sequence, as if part of some scanning routine.

His version had no diodes and made no noise. So the only way to know if the lock was disengaged and the alarm disabled was to listen very carefully to the tumblers.

'Get in.'

Without waiting to see if the girl would do what she was told – she would – Mike climbed into the driver's seat and slid his card into the key slot. Lights lit on the faux-metal dash and the engine fired up. So did the sound system which the owner had left tuned to some shit station that pumped dance.

'Find something you like.'

'I like this,' said the girl, nodding towards a speaker.

He sighed. 'Something else,' Mike said and waited while she found some woman singing about the taste on her tongue.

Whatever . . . First gear meshed into third, then fifth, as he skipped second and fourth. From where they were to where he needed to be was next to no distance. Except that it would be best if the clock showed he'd driven somewhere else first, especially if he hadn't . . . Or at least nowhere that mattered.

A rip out along the Corniche added some distance, the little Mazda nipping in and out of the sparse traffic, hugging in behind trucks or bigger cars every time a camera came into view. One of them might actually have picked out his licence plate but, chances were, it wouldn't matter. He'd be gone and the car dumped.

As for her . . .

'Enjoying yourself?'

The girl nodded. She had goose bumps on her bare arms and her slight tummy pushed its way over the waist of trousers not really designed for sitting, but her smile was still happy and he believed her.

'Good.' He flipped the Mazda off the Corniche and down a side street, overtaking a VW camper. The traffic was thinning to non-existent and the sky looked less dark than it had.

'We've arrived,' he told the girl, parking alongside a metal gate set in a heavy-duty fence. A rusty iron padlock hung from the bolt. 'Time to get out . . .'

Obediently she climbed from her seat and stood beside the car.

'In here.'

The padlock looked tight but since it only shut on itself and the casino's rear gate was actually closed off with a twist of wire, that didn't matter. Only one security light lit the gate and that badly; the other two lights having been vandalized. But then everything in life was down to pre-planning and, before he'd retired, the man calling himself Mike Estelle had been extremely good at that.

The best in fact. Most controls were pure amateurs when it came to setting the stage and arranging the props. Both of those he could do without thinking. It was the wet work he didn't usually handle.

'Where are we?'

The man glanced round at the smiling girl, noticing again her pale hair and the wide face of someone whose ancestors farmed a bleak edge of the fjords. She shouldn't have been asking him questions, only answering those he asked and doing exactly what she was told . . . Which, pretty soon, was going to involve taking off that silver bra and climbing out of those stupid trousers.

'We're at another club,' he told her. 'A different kind.' Which was the truth but wasn't about to set her free. 'Here,' he added, pulling a second purple kite from his pouch. 'Take this, you'll like it.'

She looked at him, puzzled, her eyes trying to look past something inside her head.

'Go on.'

Obediently, she swallowed the kite without waiting to let it dissolve on her tongue. Again that grin. And anyone inside her head who might still have been at home switched off the last of the lights and moved out.

'This way.' He snipped the wire holding shut the gate with tiny, orange-handled clippers and discarded them on the gravel, secure in the knowledge that the latex gloves he wore were surgical specials. In the ordinary run of things, his prints might still have been visible to forensics, but each fingerprint had been softened earlier that evening, using a simple solution of household bleach.

Just inside the gate stood a security hut, mirrored glass in its only window, looking out at a road that led from the gates to a loading bay, where a pull-down shutter was locked to a clasp set in concrete. The loading bay clasp was properly padlocked.

Mike shrugged. The key would be where those keys always were. Hung on a board inside the hut, should he need it, which was unlikely. So far so predictable . . .

The grey card he'd used on the little Mazda also worked for the door of the security hut. Whoever had decided to replace a standard Chubb with a Japanese box had made a bad mistake. It was still way harder to pick an old-fashioned mortice than jazz some chip, probably always would be.

Inside, the hut was the usual clutter: a microwave, so old its inside was enamelled with fat, a stained Braun coffee maker, five mugs, none of them matching, no saucers and more discarded packaging around the plastic swing bin than inside it.

The man sighed. This was why he'd never taken to fieldwork . . .

'Clean the mess up,' he told the girl and she nodded.

'All done now.' Her voice was matter of fact, as if she found nothing odd in having happily picked up someone else's rubbish, scrubbed down all the work surfaces and cleaned out the inside of an old microwave; but then the drugs ensured there was nothing odd about the situation for her to find.

'Good girl.'

Closing his borrowed copy of *Hustler*, illegal in all of North Africa, if slightly less illegal in El Isk than most other cities, Mike stretched, pushed himself up from where he sat and walked across to where the American girl stood smiling.

5.49 a.m. Saturday morning. The Quitrimala Casino. The call to prayer had come and gone. It was time, more or less.

Chapter Twenty-six

16th October

Dawn had broken by the time he locked the hut door behind him.

Dawn had . . .

Mike smiled tightly at his own joke and stretched the fingers of one hand, like a concert pianist doing post-performance exercises. Then he turned his head from side to side, trying to reach the pain in his neck.

In his other hand he carried a heart and two dripping lungs; they weighed more than he expected.

'Hey, dipshit . . .' The insult was light, contemptuous. The accent a mix of street rough and faux polite. What was most unnerving was that the boy behind him chose German, Mike's original language.

Slowly, very slowly, Mike turned. As he did so, his free hand swung down, reaching for a holster hidden on the back of his belt.

'I don't think so . . .' The boy with the magenta dreads jerked his own automatic and Mike's hand froze. He was remembering.

'The club,' said the boy with the noisy gold earbead. 'In the corridor.'

The man remembered. The group of students, with one lagging at the end. Their eyes meeting, that knowing nod. It hadn't been about the girl, or rather it had, just not in the way he'd thought.

'And before that,' said Avatar. He popped silver contacts from his pupils and dumped them and the magenta wig onto the tarmac, then decided to play safe and scooped up the jelly-like

158

disposables, pushing them into his shirt pocket. 'On a roof at Sarahz, remember? You were pretending to be English.'

Adjusting his earbead, Avatar faded out some weirdshit track about dogs, boats and guns.

'You're not police?' Mike's eyes widened.

'*Les merde?* You'd be so lucky. . .' Avatar's smile was grim. 'I command the *RustNeverSleeps* brigade of *Action Directe* . . .'

'You're military . . . ?'

Avatar sneered, with all the arrogance of someone whose fourteen years had seen things that made growing up fast the only safe thing to do. 'Anarcho-Marxist-Syndicalist. If anyone strips this city back to its machine code it's going to be us . . .'

'You're too late,' said Mike. 'Another dead American. Another burst of outrage.'

Avatar's gaze flicked towards the gristly relics in the man's hand. He'd been working on the assumption that rape would precede killing, probably carried out slowly and methodically given the almost feline cruelty of the man's earlier behaviour.

Making a wrong call wasn't something Avatar liked.

'Drop the offal and empty your pockets.'

Avatar waited while the man took out a disposable camera, cigarettes, the flat electronic key, a cheap lighter and a small Japanese sushi knife that looked just like a child's chopper.

'And the rest . . .'

'That's it,' said the man, pulling his coat pockets inside out. 'Travel light, don't you?'

Action Directe approved of travelling light. No baggage, emotional, literal or political; because all three were known to slow down the response time between opportunity and action. And yet, personal was political, according to Zara.

How was Avatar to know if his decision to act owed its driving force to the fact this man was obviously *Thiergarten*, and thus an enemy of progress, or to the fact that the girl butchered on the beach at Villa Hamzah had, in some way, been a warning to Avatar's father, whose politics were definitely not Avatar's own?

And then there was Raf, who was *merde* himself but who had saved Avatar's life, something Avatar hadn't yet admitted to the old man.

The boy shook his head.

'Just give me the pills,' said Avatar and waited for Mike to unbutton the first two buttons of his shirt. They both noticed that Mike's hands trembled as he handed over his pouch.

'Open wide.' Avatar held out a tiny purple kite and raised his gun until it touched the underneath of Mike's chin. The metal was cool against the German's early-morning stubble.

The man swallowed his fate.

'Pick up the offal and walk,' said the boy.

The door to the cargo bay opened easily, though the man no longer had the capacity to be surprised when the boy produced a spare key from his own pocket and unclicked the padlock, sending the metal shutter scrolling skywards in a rattle of metal machine music.

'My My, Hey Hey . . .'

Avatar had named his brigade after an ancient CD found in a market. Weird shit, of the best kind. He'd sampled the tracks he wanted and given the CD to Zara. She'd said nothing about it since, so he figured it just wasn't her taste.

'Hey Hey, My My . . .'

It took Avatar and the man more than ten minutes to find spare cylinders of butano and drag them from the kitchens up to the loading bay. There were seven in total. Each one large, orange and as heavy as Avatar, maybe heavier. After that came huge blocks of lard to be smeared around the casino, vats of margarine and a couple of industrial-sized containers of ghee. Then methylated spirits on the stairs, used to fuel fondue heaters, the flashy old-fashioned kind.

'You see those?' Avatar pointed to cans stacked against a kitchen wall, each one full of maize oil. The casino might boast two world-class chefs, poached from the *SS Jannah*, but half of the visiting punters still stuffed themselves with freshly-cooked chips sprinkled with paprika. The Soviet half . . .

The German nodded.

'Pour them on the hall carpets and come back here when you're finished.'

Avatar's first idea had been to let the man do all the work but carrying the butano had been a job for two and time was running out . . . For himself and the city, for his father, even for the General if the word in the alleys was true. And Avatar trusted what he heard in the souks and cafés because they were where he belonged. No matter how much Zara wished it otherwise.

As for this casino. He didn't approve of casinos or the people they attracted. And he didn't want it.

'. . . Finished now.'

Avatar smiled at the German and beckoned him closer. Child-like eyes looked into his as the man smiled back. He'd just gutted a girl, Avatar had to remind himself. A girl whose ripped open corpse was in a hut not fifty paces from where he stood, probably with his father's initials cut into her wrist.

'Here,' said Avatar as he passed over a bottle of cooking brandy. The name was French, the label printed in Isk and the grapes grown in Algiers. Ersatz identity. Coming from nowhere. As fucked up as the city. 'Take a drink.'

The man did, gagging on the raw spirit.

'And again.'

When the bottle was almost empty, Avatar walked the man up the darkened stairs to the loading bay and stood him in the middle of a concrete floor that was now awash with spilt oil, methylated spirits and smashed bottles of brandy. The gas cylinders stood like sentries around the edge.

Using coins, Avatar jammed open the butano valves and, as soon as the smell of gas was strong enough to overpower the stink of evaporating alcohol, he told the man to count down from a hundred and then, when he reached zero light himself a cigarette. The other thing Avatar did before he slammed the bay doors and hiked the volume on his earbead was skim the sushi knife across concrete so it came to a halt beside the bloody relics at the man's feet.

It was only later, when Avatar was driving his camper van

back to Club Neutropic, alibis already building in his mind, that he realized he should have questioned the German before killing him. Direct action was fine, but some answers might have been better.

Chapter Twenty-seven

17th October

If anybody else in the computer room had been stuffing their face with a Big Mac and large fries, chocolate shake and a side dish of onion rings, Madame Roden would have thrown them out, if not banned them altogether.

Because it was Hani, who'd knocked first, asked if she might come in and then smilingly thrust a carton of fries at the fastidious systems manager for the night shift, Madame Roden had politely taken a luke-warm reconstituted fry and chewed it as if sampling a priceless Perigord black truffle.

'Shouldn't you be at home asleep?' No sooner was the comment made than Madame Roden winced at her own lack of tact. If she'd been recently orphaned like that, she'd have wanted to follow her new uncle everywhere too.

'Uncle Ashraf came back to get some papers,' said Hani, apparently oblivious to the woman's *faux pas*. They weren't really papers, of course. Most of Raf's day-to-day files downloaded direct to his watch. But a few, the really important ones, he had to sign for with a handprint before collecting them from the precinct's central datacore.

Madame Roden was responsible for the night running of the core, but it more or less ran itself and most of her shift was spent stopping uniforms from slopping coffee on their keyboards and preventing them from trying to reach unsuitable photographs archived by the *morales*.

Pictures snatched by police photographers played a big part in most immorality cases. Though, of course, to the *morales* the grabs were just evidence. Well, to most of them.

Madame Roden shook her head. She shouldn't even be thinking such stuff with a small child around.

'Could I use a terminal?'

The elderly woman looked doubtful. Nothing in police regulations actually forbade it, but then, nothing said it was all right either. As for previous precedents, nine-year-olds wanting to use her computer room were a novelty. Come to that, civilians this side of the front desk were a novelty, full stop. Children or not.

'I saw Kamila on the way in,' Hani said suddenly. 'I told her I was coming up here and she said to say hello . . .' Hani grinned. 'Hello.'

Madame Roden smiled. She could remember when Kamila was this age. More than ten years ago, though it seemed for less. These days her daughter was a pathologist, reporting *direct* to Madame Mila, unbelievable though this was.

'Can I?'

Madame Roden blinked. 'Yes, of course,' she said, sounding slightly bemused. Hani had that effect on her. Actually Madame Roden had noticed the child had that effect on most people.

'Thank you,' said Hani and scrambled up onto a seat to tap the space bar in front of her, waking the terminal.

'Do you want me to help you find something to play with?'

Hani shook her head. She liked the neatly-dressed elderly woman but that didn't mean she felt guilty about tricking her. Life had long since taught her that all adults existed to be tricked, except maybe Ashraf, but her uncle was different.

'No, thank you,' Hani said politely. 'I'm going to write another fairy tale.'

'Another?'

Hani smiled. 'About Suliman the Magnificent and the angry Djinn . . .'

As soon as she had the screen to herself, Hani went to her post-box, grabbed a half-finished story she'd started months before and pasted it into the precinct's basic word-processing package over a scuzzy parchment background. Rubbish page texture and rubbish font. At home she had fifty-three kinds of illuminated capital alone, most of them lifted from a university archive in Al Qahirah.

Minimizing *Suliman's Dream, trope III* and twisting her screen slightly so that it was no longer overlooked, Hani did a double log-in, remaining as a guest but adding a window that knew her as Mushin Bey, husband to her dead aunt Jalila, not to mention Minister of Police and thus Ashraf's theoretical boss.

One rumour said Uncle Mushin was at home, sat in darkness grieving for his dead wife, another had him in a clinic getting over a long-term alcohol habit. Hani preferred the second theory.

No one had thought to cancel Mushin Bey's network access. No one had even changed his password, which inevitably was *Jalila*.

Top access, obviously. Super-user status. Hani doubted her uncle even knew what that meant or entailed. Flicking her fingers from key to key, Hani called up a current crime list and highlighted only the ones that had been mentioned on the news by Ferdie Abdullah.

Then she decided to read about the girl found on Hamzah's beach and changed her mind two paragraphs in. A lot of the medical words were strange to her, but enough of the others made sense enough for her to close the file.

'I wonder,' said Raf, 'have you seen . . .'

'In the computer room, Ya Bey.' Madame Roden never quite knew whether or not to smile when she met Ashraf al-Mansur. True, he was her husband's boss, which meant she should. But then there was all that sad stuff with his dead aunt. And Kamila's boss Madame Mila apparently hated him. And it was said poor Mushin Bey couldn't hear the name al-Mansur without falling into a rage . . . Though that was unfair. As if the bey could have saved everyone from those terrible assassins.

His Excellency looked positively ill with exhaustion, poor man.

'I should thank you,' Raf said. 'For letting Hani use a machine.'

'A pleasure.' The small woman blushed.

'Do you know what she's doing?'

'Writing another story, Your Excellency, so she says . . .'

'That sounds about right.' Raf nodded to Madame Roden and returned to his office, where a black bakelite phone was trying to wake the dead. The telephone had to be some kind of joke. At least, Raf assumed it was. Felix had definitely been making a statement of some kind.

Raf had moved straight into the fat man's office. Not bothering to get the place redecorated first. Claimed the man's desk too. In the bottom right drawer, behind a box of nanopore gloves, was a bottle of Jack Daniels, more than half full. Four empty bottles occupied the drawer on the left. That seemed to be about the extent of the old Chief's filing skills.

Raf was about to pick up the receiver when the phone went dead and a bulb lit, signifying that his assistant had finally arrived. He checked his Seiko. 8.30 a.m., Sunday morning. Raf sighed.

'Caffeine,' he demanded, punching a button on a bulky office intercom. Another of Felix's joke purchases, presumably. 'Please,' Raf added as a belated afterthought.

'Your coffee, Excellency . . .' The thin girl put down a tray and straightened it, so that the marquetry along one rim aligned exactly with the edge of his huge desk. 'And you have . . .' Her voice was nervous. 'You have three calls to return.'

'It that all?' Most days, even Sundays, he had several dozen backed up and waiting not to be answered.

'Three you need to deal with, Excellency,' said the girl, as she carefully poured a tiny brass cup of coffee. He thought her name was Natacha Something. The fox had spotted her coming out of an interview room carrying papers and got Raf to ask someone her name.

Quite why, Raf still wasn't sure; except that the girl had deep eyes, skin the colour of dry chamois and a body toned from evenings spent in an expensive gym. But what both he and the fox had really noticed, on their first glance down the corridor, was long dark hair, falling to her narrow hips. Utterly straight and midnight black.

Next time Raf had seen her, the girl was opening the door of his office for him and handing him a coffee and that morning's crime sheet. Someone, somewhere in the precinct had translated his casual enquiry into the fact he wanted the girl as his new PA. So now she handled his post, made him coffee, kept his diary and did other stuff he knew less than nothing about, all the while watching him nervously from the corner of her eye.

Wondering when I'm going to proposition her probably, Raf thought with a sigh.

'Trouble, Your Excellency?'

Raf looked up. She was . . .

'How old are you?'

Natacha blushed. 'Eighteen, Excellency.'

And now working for the new Chief of Detectives, even if she had fallen into that job by accident. No doubt she dressed carefully outside the office, but in here she wore black jeans and a white cotton blouse, black leather shoes with lowish heels and matching belt. The neck button of her blouse was unfastened and her sleeves folded back, like in the magazines, to make it obvious that she was ready to work hard.

A year ago, from what Raf gathered, those bare wrists would have been fine. Now they were only just acceptable. A year from now, dressed like that, she might well be breaking some official code. Of course, a year from now she could be unemployable in any office in the city, just on the basis of her gender.

'What are the important calls?' Raf's voice was more abrupt than he intended and he could see the girl try to work out exactly what she'd done to offend him.

'Hamzah Effendi was the first. Then his daughter Zara.' The girl paused. 'She left a new number. Apparently she'd had the old one changed and forgotten to tell you.' Was there an element of disapproval in that face?

Raf thought that, on balance, there might be . . .

'And the third?' he asked gently.

'The General.'

Just what he needed. Raf glanced at the report open on his screen. Stomach ripped, heart and lungs missing, slashed stops to the long strokes of the cross, the initials *H.Q.* cut into her wrist . . . It was getting so Raf could recite the litany of wounds in his sleep. Only sleep wasn't currently an option. Not if it meant letting the fox disappear again.

'Tell them all I've gone to breakfast,' said Raf. 'That is, should they call back.'

Natacha's shock almost made him smile. Hamzah Quitrimala was rich and everyone in Iskandryia knew Raf had been meant to marry Zara. But the girl's horror was reserved for the fact that he might refuse to jump when the General ordered. Koenig Pasha's main advantage was that no one dared underestimate his power; with the result that the old man barely had to use it.

'Just tell them,' said Raf.

Felix's old Cadillac sat in the fat man's bay. That is, the sign still read *Felix Abrinsky, Chief of Detectives* because the paperwork needed to change the sign was sitting on Raf's desk awaiting his signature. Since Raf wasn't too sure about sticking with the job, he'd been ignoring the forms. And besides, he got some weird kick out of seeing the sign still there. Like the fat man was about to come shambling out of the lift onto the garage level and head for his car, trailing whisky fumes, litter and bad advice.

Chapter Twenty-eight

17th October

The arms were those of El Iskandryia, their use on a pennant restricted to the governor, though almost anyone on Rue Missala would have announced confidently that the flag was that of Koenig Pasha himself, such was the immutable link in most people's minds between the General and their city.

And the last time Raf had seen the young officer at the Bentley's wheel was months back, the day Raf arrived at Iskandryia's airport. At the time, Raf was being bumped up a chain of command like the problem he was.

'. . . *sef,*' said a whisper in Raf's head.

'Captain Yousef,' Raf offered his hand.

The man looked pleased to be remembered but slightly embarrassed all the same. 'Major Yousef, Excellency. I've been promoted.'

'Congratulations. For services rendered . . . ?'

Major Yousef looked more embarrassed still. It didn't seem appropriate to explain that he'd come to the General's attention by refusing to take responsibility for deporting His Excellency as an undesirable, or that he'd been promoted because this turned out to be a wise decision . . . And the fact this promotion had been over the head of older men, including a senior captain the General disliked intensely was, of course, not to be mentioned.

'Coffee?' Raf asked, as Le Trianon's head waiter materialized from within the café. 'Or perhaps mint tea?'

'Neither, I'm afraid, Your Excellency.' The Major nodded towards the waiting Bentley. 'You're expected.'

'The General . . . ?' Raf did his best to look surprised.

Major Yousef nodded. 'There's been another murder. A dead American. But apparently Your Excellency already knows that . . .' Gesturing towards Raf's Cadillac, parked on the pavement where the fat man used to park, he added, 'I'll have someone bring your car.'

At the oak door to the mansion in Shallalat Gardens, Raf was met by a young boy who glanced once at the Chief of Detectives' haggard face, raised his eyebrows and nodded towards a door behind him.

'He's in there . . .'

The boy paused, as if he intended saying more, and then shrugged, mostly it seemed to himself.

'I know,' said Raf tiredly, 'he's upset.'

'*Upset.*' His Highness Mohammed Tewfik Pasha, Khedive of El Iskandryia and also ruler of Egypt, at least in name, stopped dead. 'Upset,' he said, staring at Raf with large eyes. 'Upset doesn't cover half of it . . . Oh yes.' The boy paused, remembering something else. 'And apparently he knows the truth about your origins.'

Raf hammered on the study door, waited for a couple of seconds and then hammered again. Instead of hitting it a third time, he straightened his shoulders and walked into the governor's office, only to find the small room deserted.

Panelling, mirrors and a floor of white marble, all that came as no surprise. Every high-ranking office in El Iskandryia seemed kitted out with variations on ersatz European, although Islamicist mosaic did at least replace wood panelling in some. What was surprising was a new oil painting taking up most of one wall, its brushwork bright and its heavy gilt frame positively pristine.

In it, the boy who'd met Raf at the front door wore a bottle-green uniform with three gold loops of braid knotted around each wrist. Other than that, and a thin gold stripe down each side of his trousers, the uniform was bare apart from star and crescent badges either side of its high collar.

At the boy's side hung a simple sabre, with a single gold

knot on a double length of braid. On his head was a red fez.

'Dressed like some *mutahfiz* . . .'

Which wasn't a word Raf recognized, though it was obvious from the voice behind him that it wasn't a compliment.

'. . . and now apparently you want to lose him his city.' The old man stood swaying at the French windows, white knuckles gripping the top of a Malacca cane. Over his shoulder Raf could see a preternaturally green garden of monkey puzzle, rhododendron, bronze statues and tightly-clipped box hedges.

'Having a bad day?' Raf asked.

Eyes dark as any storm glared back at him.

Olive trees. Red earth. A boy falling backwards, face shocked. The hurt in his eyes mental not physical, despite the venous blood that ran from one side of his mouth.

Raf blinked.

'Afraid?' demanded the General.

'Always,' said Raf.

The old man looked surprised at that. 'Of what . . . Me?'

Raf shook his head. 'Not just of you, of everything. Waking up/falling asleep. Looking in the mirror. Losing a bit of me I'm not even sure exists.'

'The usual . . .' The old man nodded and absent-mindedly put his brandy balloon on the immaculately-polished surface of an antique desk, creating a ring. That was how Raf knew Iskandryia's most famous teetotaller really was drunk. 'The condition of life,' said the General. 'We live, we die. In between we're afraid to admit we're afraid. You know the real definition of courage?'

'There are dozens,' said Raf, picking up the General's glass and wiping the desk with his sleeve. 'Most of them contradictory.' He swirled the cognac until it coated the inside and then watched its pale liquid break into rivulets.

'. . . *egs,* said the fox. '. . . *gn of a good VSOP.'* Raf could remember being told about *legs* by one of his mother's lovers, the Animal Channel producer probably. Speaking to the boy about brandy while really trying to impress a drunk obsessive, being too stupid to realize the only thing likely to impress Raf's mother was money to fund her films.

'What . . . ?' Raf looked at the General who stood waiting.

'My definition of courage,' said the old man. 'You know it?'

'Dying well?'

'Acting as if you believe, even when you don't.'

'Same thing,' said Raf as he put down the General's glass, this time on top of a folded paper that sat on the desk between them.

A fuzzy picture showed a missing teenager, her long blonde hair uncovered as she stood grinning on a street corner in some city that wasn't El Iskandryia . . . Paris, maybe, judging from a sugary white basilica behind her.

What little text there was screamed its certainty that this girl was the butcher's most recent victim. No underlined links pretended to go somewhere, because *Saiyidi* wasn't downloaded from a news vendor. It was run off an old-fashioned press in a cellar somewhere in Karmous and read by those without paid access to newsfeeds or money for vendors. The same kind of urban poor who listened to pirate stations and recognized souk rumour for the truth it was.

'You promised me the killer was already dead.'

'She is . . .'

'*She?*' Koening Pasha raised his eyebrows at the pronoun. 'Whoever told you that was wrong. Sack your informant.'

'No one told me,' Raf said crossly. 'The woman's dead. I killed her.'

'So who did it this time?' demanded the General. 'Her ghost?' His laugh was bitter, tired also. 'Drink,' he said.

Raf shook his head, then realized that wasn't an invitation but an order. Glancing round, he found a large bottle of Hine sat on a semi-circular marble table, balanced on top of a fat pile of intelligence reports.

Half the cognac was gone and its cork was missing. Raf was still looking round for a glass when the General grunted with irritation.

'Not you, idiot, me . . .' He held out his brandy balloon while

Raf filled it halfway to the top. Then, turning unsteadily towards the French windows, the old man stamped back into his garden, not bothering to check that Raf was ready to follow.

Which he very definitely wasn't. Raf was too busy skimming an intelligence report, the one under the bottle. It was concise, factual and loaded. According to some second attaché at the temporary Consulate in Seattle, the Five Winds Triad, represented by a button man named Wild Boy, was offering $1,000,000 for news of someone known as ZeeZee. The man had been tracked to an Ottoman Airways flight bound for Zanzibar. Unfortunately, enquiries at the Ottoman Airways office in SeaTac/Seattle had failed to identify the name under which ZeeZee had travelled or whether his journey had been broken en route.

What was known, was that the man had travelled on a diplomatic passport, probably issued by Stambul. Though, regretfully, the woman on the check-in desk had not actually looked inside.

'Remind you of anyone?'

Raf looked up to find the Khedive stood in the hall doorway, face quizzical.

'No,' said Raf. 'Afraid not.'

The boy smiled. 'Me neither.'

Under the biggest cypress tree was an ornate bench. Between the cast-iron bench and a nearby oak stood a rain-streaked statue slightly taller than Raf. The statue showed a rudimentary metal tree with a naked girl falling headlong between its stark branches.

'*Pike sverer mellom grenene,*' said the General. '1907. Gustav Vigeland. You know what it represents?'

Eyes wide, mouth open, small fists clenched. Raf could take a reasonable guess. But the General got there first, answering his own question as if he'd been the one asked.

'Whatever you want it to represent . . . So the next question,' said the General, 'is who decides exactly what *we* represent . . . ?'

He didn't wait for the answer to that either.

'Because I don't and you sure as hell don't . . .' The old man raised his brandy balloon and suddenly the dark eyes that stared at Raf over the top of the glass were anything but drunk.

'The city decides.'

Raf thought he should do something about now, so he nodded.

'You've probably heard them all. Isk the whore and Isk the virgin. The city of glass. Solid and ephemeral, transient and timeless. The city within the city. Every cliché from every guide book. The old man used the analogy of a card house as belief . . .'

Koenig Pasha was talking about the Khedive's father, Raf realized. The man who sat for fifteen years in a small tea house on an island off El Muntaza, which was how long it took him to die. The tea house became his bed, the island his ward and the Haremlik across its narrow bridge became his hospital, filled with specialists from around the world.

'And he stole the card-as-belief metaphor from his father . . . An old-fashioned, out-dated man.' The General's voice was uncharacteristically bitter. 'But one who was none the less intelligent.'

Seeing the blank look on Raf's thin face, the General began to explain himself, his long fingers and narrow wrists twitching as he mimicked adding and subtracting playing cards to a card house that wasn't there.

'Knock down a couple of cards at the top and only the top rocks. Maybe the top falls, maybe it stands. And if that level falls it can be rebuilt, using the same cards if you must. But take a card from the bottom and the whole edifice is in danger. No matter how secure the top. Once the lowest level goes, everything goes. The old man knew this. I know this. Felix knew this. Even the boy in there knows this. It seems you don't . . .'

'Iskandryia isn't a pack of cards,' said Raf.

'No, it's myth layered with history, so stiff with legacy code that life barely runs. A free city that half the free world would like to see abolished. Berlin mistrusts us, Paris too . . .

Washington. Well, Washington hates us. The only thing still keeping us standing is that we're too stupid to know we're dead. You know what our Unique Selling Point is?'

Raf shook his head.

'Inertia. Iskandryia's been a free city for so long no one can quite imagine how North Africa might operate if we weren't. Well, take a look at the newsfeeds. People out there are beginning to imagine it . . .' The General swallowed back the last of his cognac and breathed in, inhaling the fumes. By the time he'd finished coughing he'd apparently reached a decision.

'So far as I can see,' said the General, 'as Chief you have three main problems.'

'I have?'

'The first,' said the General, 'is personal. The way life works is public virtue, private vice. You keep doing it the wrong way round. The remaining two problems are more serious . . .' Koenig Pasha's voice was harsh but thin. Its determination at odds with an old man's frailty. 'One big problem, one slightly smaller. First, find out why tourists are being butchered.'

'We think . . .'

The old man sighed heavily. 'The problem,' he said, 'is that you don't . . . You're going to tell me the killer's dead, again. Burned up in that fire. You think I don't get reports from your office? Forget finding out who carried out the latest atrocity. I told you to find out *why* it happened.'

'And how do you suggest I do that?'

'Break heads. Use the Army. Take whatever you need from the treasury . . .' The old man looked for a moment as if he might be about to rescind that last suggestion, but instead he shrugged. 'Just find out. And keep it out of the papers and off the newsfeeds.'

'That's the big problem, right?'

The general's smile was wintry. Flicking a curled leaf from the arm of the bench, he followed its brief and twisting fall. Then he told Raf what Senator Liz really wanted and exactly why he, the General, couldn't give it to her.

*   *   *

With trembling hand, the General took a crisp sheet of paper from his desk drawer and reached for a fountain pen, the black Mont Blanc inlaid with a silver cartouche bearing the arms of Prussia. The pen had been a present from his father.

The old man was still writing laboriously when a knock came at the door. A second knock followed and when the General didn't answer it was Raf who said *enter* and watched the door open a little. The boy who'd let Raf into the gubernatorial mansion slid sideways through the narrow gap, only to stop and glance anxiously between Raf and the General.

'Excellency . . .'

The old man nodded but kept writing.

If the Khedive minded his chief minister sitting while he himself stood it didn't show. In fact, nothing about the boy suggested he found the situation in any way odd, and only a glance at the ornately-framed painting on the wall convinced Raf that he stood opposite El Iskandryia's absolute ruler.

'. . . The newsfeeds.'

Without looking up, the General tapped one corner of his desk and a long glass with a opalescent Murano frame lit to reveal a worried woman standing outside an old-fashioned mansion, built in an early-twentieth-century style dismissed as High Arabesque. In an open sub-frame in one corner, fire engines hosed down the broken shell of something sheet glass and concrete.

Raf caught the words *casino, firebomb* and *US negotiator*. And then the main picture flicked to a woman in a black suit behind a large desk. On the front of the desk was a large seal displaying the American eagle. *Chaos, lawlessness* and *organized crime* cropped up in almost every other sentence. Just in case Senator Liz's disgust wasn't obvious enough, C3N had thoughtfully run Arabic subtitles along the bottom of the screen.

'She flew UN 'copters,' the General said, 'back in the little war.' He reached for another sheet of paper and scrawled two lines across its china-clay surface then signed the sheet with spidery handwriting and pushed it across the desk towards the Khedive, his fingers shaking. 'All I need now is your signature for these . . .'

The boy signed without dragging his attention away from the news, which showed a crime team sifting the wreckage of the smouldering casino. A voice-over was talking, guardedly, about rumours of a dead girl found nearby. Raf got the feeling that more was intentionally being said with the gaps than with the words.

'Enough,' said the General, tapping his table to blank the screen. 'We need to concentrate on getting His Highness out of here . . .'

'I'm sorry?' The Khedive looked startled, then stubborn. 'No,' he said. 'I can't possibly . . . Not now.'

'Your holiday,' said Koenig Pasha. 'What time's your flight?' The voice was little more than a cross whisper from an old man. And he did look old, if one looked past his immaculate uniform to the liver spots speckling his trembling wrists or the carcinoma scars that puckered one side of his neck, below his sunken jaw.

'Fik, what time . . . ?'

Mohammed Tewfik Pasha blinked, tears prickling up until he had to look away. He couldn't quite remember the last time the old man had used his pet name. Maybe when he was ten, that time he caught scarlet fever and was confined for days to a darkened room with curtains soaked in vinegar, much to the disgust of the palace's English doctor . . .

'Early evening,' said the boy. 'The flight's collecting me at 7 p.m.'

'And you *are* going alone?'

The Khedive shook his head.

'She's the wrong choice,' said the General tiredly. 'You know that.' He stared at the boy, seeing anxiety turn to stubbornness, and sighed. 'Do what you have to do . . . Just remember, your job is to be on that flight. And yours,' he said turning to Raf, 'is to make sure His Highness goes.'

Folding his resignation into three, Koenig Pasha gave the sheet of paper to Khedive Mohammed with a slight bow. The letter to Raf, the General folded just the once and handed over with a nod. Then the old man waited until they'd both read and then re-read what he'd written.

Chapter Twenty-nine

17th October

Nothing so slight as a mere ring. Instead, long bursts of increasing frustration filled the large hall.

Raf had been ignoring the bell for a while.

Sighing, he looked round for someone to answer the General's front door and realized there was no one but him. So he went to answer it himself.

Another bad mistake.

While he and Zara stood, staring in disbelief at each other, the study door swung back and the young Khedive stormed out, tears of frustration streaming down his soft face.

Whatever final retort the boy was about to make died when he spotted Zara, with her cases. For a moment, it looked like the boy might walk across to where Zara stood, but then he shot Raf a bitter scowl, turned away and ran up the stairs. Somewhere a door slammed and then there was silence.

And as Zara stared between her suitcases and the emptiness on the landing above, Raf glanced into the study, his eyes meeting those of the General. What Raf got was an abrupt nod and an amused if wintry smile. And then the old man stretched, stood up from his desk and walked resolutely to the door, which he closed. The General didn't even pretend to need his cane.

'What are you doing here?' Zara's query was curt.

'Leaving,' said Raf. 'To visit a crime scene.' He looked at her. 'Oh, yeah, and trying to keep your father from being arrested for murder . . . Take your pick.'

Zara practically threw her suitcases into the boot of Raf's

Cadillac, stamped round to the passenger side and climbed in, shutting the door with a slam. As an afterthought, she reached behind her for a seat belt and found nothing. The fat man had never got round to having them fitted and Raf hadn't bothered to make good their lack.

Still seething about this stupidity, Zara stared resolutely ahead.

Which was how she missed seeing Raf clamber into the driver's seat of the big Bentley, ram the huge car into reverse and spin it round on protesting tyres until it faced the mansion's wrought-iron gates.

'What the . . .'

Zara never got to finish her question because Raf was already gone, all eight cylinders powering the Bentley out into traffic that skidded and stalled rather than risk scratching the General's car.

My car, Raf corrected himself, watching his gubernatorial pennant crack in the afternoon wind. My car, my city, my problem. My world coming down around my ears. And Hani's too, if he wasn't careful.

The Bentley's bolt-on GPS was so ancient the map flickered every time the screen changed streets, which was pretty migraine inducing. Though that might just be the day. Raf shrugged. Up ahead was where Zara's club had briefly been. Now CdeH was gone, and the venue had reverted to its original existence as a deserted cistern beneath a rain-stained, multistorey car park; the famous arrest and bust being relegated to part of Iskandryia's rapidly-receding good times.

The number of clubbers who now swore they'd been there that night would fill the third-class stands at Iskandryia stadium.

He could have taken a direct route, east onto Faud Premier and then cut south, just before Shallalat Gardens, but instead Raf concentrated on working the big car round narrow back streets marked on the GPS in red, too narrow for the vehicle in which he drove.

So far he'd done little more than scrape one fender on a wall.

Although this changed once he reached the car park at Casino Quitrimala. Of course, if he hadn't spotted Madame Mila's blue government Renault on his way in, he probably would have missed that concrete gate post as well.

Madame Mila stood next to her car, back straight and eyes fixed firmly on the Bentley. Exactly a pace behind her, at a distance obviously laid down in regulations, stood two officers from the women's police, both wearing the familiar police-issue *hijab*. Madame Mila, while obviously the most senior, was also by far the youngest. In place of her *hijab* she wore a simple blue scarf.

'General . . .' Her voice faltered as Raf climbed from the huge car, and Raf decided that maybe his morning wasn't going to be so bad after all. Unfortunately, his optimism lasted only as long as it took him to reach the crime scene.

Right in the middle of the sodden wreckage of what had once been a casino stood a handful of uniforms, including a grey-haired lieutenant, a crime-locale technician in whites, two members of the *morales* made obvious by their bottle-green jackets, and three plain-clothes in matching black jeans, blue shirts and long leather coats. From what Raf could see, it was a typical Iskandryian crime scene, five times as many officers as needed, with inter-departmental rivalries and demarcation disputes guaranteeing that no one was doing anything useful.

'Boss.' An elderly plain-clothes stepped forward, all heavy moustache and combed-over greying hair.

'You've got something?'

'Looks like it.'

Beside him, the uniformed lieutenant snorted. The hyena-like grin on his youthful face didn't even pretend to reach his eyes. 'I think you'll find *we've* got something.' There was an unsubtle stress to his words.

Raf raised one hand to chop dead an immediate protest from his own man and saw hurt pride and irritation swamp the old detective's heavy face, only to be wiped. It was a reaction Raf had begun to recognize.

'What's your name?'

The detective looked at him, judging the danger inherent in the question, while knowing he'd answer it anyway. 'Osman, Sir . . . Ibrahim Osman.'

'And what's your job?'

Ibrahim Osman looked at him. 'I'm your deputy.'

Raf sighed.

'What,' Raf asked the uniform, 'makes you think this man was the butcher?'

The young lieutenant frowned. 'We got his murder weapon,' he said defensively and reached into his pocket, pulling out a blackened hunk of metal he'd probably trampled all over a crime scene to find.

'. . . fic,' whispered the fox. '. . . taminated evidence . . . ow original.'

Raf beckoned for the two *morales*. 'There's nothing for you here,' he told them. 'You can go too,' he said to the lieutenant. 'Take your men and leave the blade . . . In an evidence bag,' he added tiredly. Not waiting for the man's reply, Raf turned on his heels and headed back to Madame Mila.

Inside his head, the fox's grin was thin and mostly invisible. While in the world outside, slight rain began, threatening to make life a misery for everyone who'd dressed expecting sun.

'Excellency . . .'

Heavy clouds crowded the horizon and according to Raf's watch the temperature had fallen to 53° Fahrenheit, making it the coldest October for eighty-seven years. Mind you, according to his watch, he'd also missed three calls from Zara, who apparently needed to talk to him about her father. And one from Hani, which Raf found infinitely more worrying. .

Toggling his Seiko to sound/vision, Raf added vibrate for any call coming in from the kid, while beside him the officers waited expectantly. Way too expectantly.

When Raf looked up from resetting his watch the coroner-magistrate was stood directly in front of him. A small and intense woman with braided black hair, minimal jewellery and shoes that were immaculately polished, for all that they were obviously cheap, she was, as Felix had once said, probably the most beautiful female in the city and the most implacable. She wore her disapproval of Raf like cheap cologne, flooding the moist air between them, colouring her every emotion.

'Madame Mila . . .'

It was obvious from her eyes what she saw when she looked at Ráf. A rich, spoilt and over-privileged young notable who'd fallen into the job of Chief of Detectives. The dark glasses he wore permanently glued to his face she took as affectation, the rumours of his combat skills, exaggeration, nothing else. Which was true enough, they were exaggeration. But the ever-present shades were down to retinal intolerance and rich was the last thing he was. As for over-privileged . . . He could argue that definition with her all day.

'Well?' The woman was waiting for some response from him. So was the tight little group of uniforms, gathered on the edge of Madame Mila's conversation.

'I'm sorry,' said Raf tiredly, 'what was your question?' Behind him, one of his own men sniggered and Madame Mila's scowl grew, her face darkening and perfect lips setting into a bitter line.

'A whole day's been and gone,' she said finally.

'And your point is?' said Raf, then realized what she meant. They were back to Sharia law. 'You want proof the dead girl wasn't local . . .' He was talking to himself but a plain-clothes stood nearby took it as a question and nodded, careful not to meet Raf's eye. Which meant that was undoubtedly *exactly* what Madame Mila had just told Raf.

'Where's the body now?'

'Still on ice.' It was Madame Mila who answered. 'She'd been spring cleaning a guard hut when she died, apparently . . .' Her voice made it silkily obvious she wasn't about to accept that fact without further proof.

'Wearing what?' He saw the sudden tension in Madame Mila's face and qualified his question. 'Before she was murdered,' he said, gently enough to surprise himself. 'I've read the preliminary report. I know she was naked when found.'

'White trousers,' said Madame Mila stiffly. 'Thin, like silk. And a silver . . .' Her hands sketched a slight, embarrassed double-circle, well away from her own body. 'A metal brassiere . . .'

'Friday night. Wearing almost nothing. You think someone from this city would behave like that?'

Madame Mila thought about it. 'No,' she admitted finally. 'Probably not.'

Raf did, but he wasn't about to say so. 'And the wounds,' he said, 'no change at all?'

A blank look.

'Upward slash from pubis to throat, a right to left across the rib cage, entrails disturbed . . .' And if ever there was an appropriate word *disturbed* was it. Three psy-profilers had been busy from the start trying to explain exactly what that shit with the ripped guts might signify. So far, their sole conclusion was that the mutilation was historically interesting.

Madame Mila nodded, tight lipped.

'You took a close look?'

Another nod.

Which probably explained the tightness in her eyes, thought Raf. She had slight sweat marks under her arms and tiny beads of perspiration, where her dark hair was pulled into a shape nature never meant it to hold. By anyone else's standards Madame Mila still looked immaculate: judged by her own, the woman was a wreck.

'Go on,' said Raf. 'Get out of here.' He meant it kindly but that wasn't how his comment was taken.

Instead Madame Mila bridled. She actually pulled herself up to her full height, slight though that was.

'Out,' Raf said, finally losing his patience. 'I want all of you out of here . . . Except for you,' he added and pointed to a uniform at random. 'You get to finish taping off the crime scene and chase sightseers away.'

The uniform glanced at his young lieutenant, who glared at Raf, caught between outrage and a growing unease. Madame Mila just felt the outrage, which was how she got her question in first.

'Just who do . . .'

'. . . *oes he think he is? . . . nteresting question.*' The fox had Raf take out his two-line letter and hand it to the furious woman. '. . . *erson giving orders, like it or not.*'

Raf shut his eyes.

He was stood, dead on his feet, in an almost deserted car park, outside a firebombed casino, in a city undergoing meltdown, with five different flavours of police, none of whom knew his real name, his record or that he was meant to be serving time for . . .

Well, welcome to the Apocalypso . . .

Except that was a club, wasn't it? Somewhere in downtown Zurich. He used to be driven past it on his way from the airport to school.

'. . . *ap out of it,*' hissed the fox.

'Why?'

Madame Mila stared at him. 'Why what?' Somehow she managed to added *your excellency* to the end of that sentence, as she handed back his letter. Though she did it through gritted teeth.

Raf ignored her. 'Why?' he demanded, only this time when he spoke it was inside his own head.

'. . . *ause you need to sleep and I've got to go.*'

'No.' Raf's silent refusal was loud enough to set his own teeth on edge. 'You can't go.'

'. . . *y to stop me,*' the fox whispered, its voice fading. And Raf wasn't sure if that was a threat, a plea or a simple suggestion. Whatever, he had to try.

'You,' Raf said, turning to the lieutenant. 'You carrying any meth?'

'No, Sir.' The shake of the head was emphatic.

No use asking her.

Stamping past Madame Mila as if she didn't exist, Raf reached one of the cherry tops just as its driver slid into gear. The crime-scene tech pulled back into neutral when Raf rapped on the glass. A whir of electrics and cigarette smoke billowed from a suddenly open window. Smoking was illegal on duty for all ranks in all departments, but neither of them bothered with that.

'Meth, got any?'

Dark eyes looked at Raf from behind dark glasses. If the tech thought Raf couldn't see his expression then he hadn't allowed for the Chief recalibrating his vision.

'Me, personally, Your Excellency?'

'Evidence, stuff on the way to a lab?'

'I'm not . . .'

'Redeem yourself,' said Raf and held out his hand. Sometime or other, he was going to have to find out their names, what jobs they did, official shit like that.

Raf weighed the evidence bag, appreciatively. Fifty ready-made-up origamis of . . .

'What is it?'

'Dunno, Your Excel . . . Boss.' The techie shrugged. 'We haven't taken it to the labs.'

'You mean,' said Raf, 'you haven't taken it to the labs *yet*.'

The techie nodded.

Ripping open a fold, Raf tasted the earth-grey powder and felt the tip of his tongue disappear. 'Ice,' he told the tech, 'about sixty per cent pure . . .' Raf debated cutting out a line and finding himself a clean note to roll but that seemed too much like hard work. So he just tipped the entire origami into his mouth and chewed, crunching crystals like sherbet. There was a synthetic sweetness that said someone had cut the dose with sorbitol.

Great, so tomorrow or the next day he was going to get the runs as well as suffer some hideous come down . . . Or maybe not. There was enough in that bag to keep him up for . . .

Lights wrote themselves round fire-twisted trees. Broken casino walls suddenly became brighter, almost fluorescent. The slow sweep of the revolving cherry top looked positively alive, lambent. Even the rain fell like music.

Raf took a look at the plastic bag he was holding. There had to be enough ice in there to keep him up until the end of the world, which, according to Koenig Pasha, came the Tuesday after next, or somesuch. Raf still needed to get to the bottom of that one.

'You know Kamila?' Raf pulled the name from memory. 'Works at the mortuary.' They had to know her, the woman's father was one of them. A uniform. That was what Felix had said.

He took their silence for assent.

'Tell her to expect a couple of bodies. Tell her not to start without me.'

Chapter Thirty

19th October

Avatar slid his finger under the flap and ripped.

He wasn't sure what he anticipated from the envelope addressed to his sister on the cabin's dressing table . . . Not a love letter from the Khedive, because even the Khedive wasn't that stupid. Maybe an invitation to something aboard the *SS Jannah* that Zara would now miss.

Which would worry her no more than it would worry Avatar, so long as the Khedive didn't expect him to attend instead. It was bad enough that Zara had suggested that Avatar take her place aboard.

And she was wrong to try to remake him; to force on him the opportunities she felt he needed. Avatar belonged where he belonged, he knew that. And he was much too proud of what he'd learnt in his fourteen years to change.

Shaking the contents of the envelope out onto his cabin's pink bedspread, Avatar's eyes widened. Whatever else he'd expected Zara to be sent, an engraving of a naked, full-breasted woman bent backwards, scuttling across the dirt on limbs that turned to those of a spider was not on his list. On the back in elegant copperplate pen was the word *Judecca*. Beneath this, *Welcome to limbo*.

Nothing else whatsoever.

With a shrug, Avatar screwed up the envelope and tossed it out of a porthole, watching the wind that caught his crumpled offering and kept it for a few seconds from the embrace of the waves.

Maybe he should do the same with the naked spider? Avatar had dismissed the possibility before he'd finished thinking it.

He was going to send the pervy engraving to Zara. As her just reward for getting Hamzah to agree he should take her place.

Avatar sighed heavily, and wished he was somewhere else. The palm in the corner of his cabin was hideous. The size of a child and planted in a Chinese container which was painted with a ridiculous number of waterfalls and colts kicking their heels on a mountain side.

Pot or palm by itself would have been bad enough, but together they constituted an insult. It was all Avatar could do not to tip the plant, pot and all, after the envelope into the Mediterranean below.

Avatar was pretty sure Zara would have loathed the palm, not to mention the cabin's kitsch Victorian screen plastered with pictures of children cut from old magazines; both of which had been meant for Zara, because this was to have been her cabin. And Avatar had been assured, by a very shocked steward, that everything in the suite had been selected personally by the Khedive himself.

If so, the Khedive had even less idea of what made his sister tick than Avatar imagined. And that included sending her a naked spider.

Avatar looked round his cabin for a scanner, realized there wasn't one and took a lift down to the bleached-blond retro of the *SS Jannah*'s business suite. After he'd got over his shock at being told everything was free to a guest of the Khedive, he found and made do with a fax.

Chapter Thirty-one

20th–21st October

Hell was a circle with bars and walkways, guards and unseen voices; level after level of honesty. Each level more brutal that the last. Endless faces that Raf knew intimately and had never before seen. A cold that filled his mind and chilled the inside of his bones.

'Ice,' he heard someone say. 'A massive dose of methamphetamine. Close to fatal.'

'And the voices?'

'Cerebrospinal tests show viral RNA associated with schizophrenia.'

'He's caught a virus?'

The voice was amused. 'Someone did. Twenty million years ago. All we've got are molecular footprints.' And then the voice and the white coat it wore went away and the darkness came back in.

Sometime later, a small hand slapped Raf back to life, then cross fingers swung his head from side to side, like a physiotherapist checking mobility.

'*Come on*,' demanded Hani.

She sat perched on top of his quilt, knees bent either side of his chest, her face almost touching Raf's own. The blur of movement Raf saw when he finally opened his eyes was Hani moving away, shifting backwards.

For a fleeting second she looked relieved, but when Raf checked again that expression was gone. 'About time,' Hani said, scrambling off his chest. 'You won't believe the trouble you're in.'

'I can't be in trouble,' said Raf, 'I'm . . .'

'. . . the new governor.' Hani rolled her eyes, 'I wouldn't try that one on Zara.'

Over Hani's shoulder Raf could see a distant blue sky, small white clouds and rays of golden sun that reflected on the skin of flying babies. Next to a cluster of pink cherubs floated an even pinker woman dressed in a strategically-placed whip of cloud.

The room in which he lay must have been thirty feet high, maybe more. Its ceiling was domed, the dome supported on marble pillars that, when he looked closer, turned out to be painted onto plastered walls.

'Late Victorian, trompe l'oeil,' Hani told him, following his gaze. 'The dome's earlier. You should see my room.'

The child slid off the bed and onto the floor. 'I brought you coffee,' she said. 'Proper coffee.' She indicated a cafetière and a china cup resting on a salver. The small tray was silver, a length of gold twisted like rope along its edge. Next to the salver was a sprig of bougainvillea stuffed into a tooth mug, the French kind with slab-like base and heavy sides.

Its smell was sickly.

'I picked it in the garden.' Hani's eyes were open wide. 'You should see the statues,' she said, 'they're all . . .'

'Naked.'

She nodded. Then carefully put the cup on its saucer . . . The thing that really worried Raf was just how hard Hani was trying to pretend that everything was normal.

'Why are they naked?' Hani asked, as if an afterthought

'Perhaps it was warmer in the old days.'

'Yeah, right. But what about . . . ?'

'Coffee,' suggested Raf and Hani smiled.

Pushing hard, she managed to wrestle the plunger to the bottom without spilling any onto the tray. Equally carefully, she poured Raf half a cupful, and then her face came apart and tears overflowed her eyes.

'Milk,' she said, between sobs. 'I forgot the . . .'

Raf let Hani pour him a second cup of black coffee. Her tears over and not to be mentioned. At least not yet.

'You blacked out,' said Hani. She used the term confidently, something overheard and assimilated. She seemed about to say more but instead lapsed into thoughtful silence, glancing at Raf when she imagined he wasn't looking. Whatever she saw reassured her.

'Here.' She passed him the cup but he was already asleep. He slept for another day.

'Excellency . . .' Khartoum stood in the open doorway, the chewed stub of a cheroot in one hand and a tea glass in the other. It took Raf a few seconds to work out that the old man was waiting for permission to enter.

Permission given, Khartoum shuffled past Raf's bed to put his tea glass on the floor in front of a huge sash window. Yanking back the velvet curtains and throwing up the bottom sash, Khartoum carefully repositioned the glass, until it stood in the centre of a patch of brightness.

'Sunlight increases strength,' he told Raf, as the Bey scrabbled for his dark glasses. 'And green glass is good for added serenity.' The man paused. 'As for fresh air . . .'

'What about air?'

Cupping his hands, Khartoum indicated the empty space within. 'This one handful contains more power than every single substation in El Iskandryia . . . No, in the whole of North Africa.'

'Nice idea,' said Raf.

'One person's mysticism is another's zero point energy.' The old man shrugged. 'I have a message for you from Koenig Pasha in America.'

'You?' Raf said it without thinking.

'Donna was scared to take the call and Hani is too young . . .' An element of disapproval tinted Khartoum's voice. 'So I talked to him. Ya Pasha says three things. The first is that next time you are to take his calls. The second is that he hopes you found your picture instructive . . .'

The old man nodded to Raf's bedside table and the yellowing engraving ripped from Dante's *Inferno*, with its naked man clutching at his slashed-open chest. It took Raf another few seconds to remember the solemn *aide de camp* who'd delivered it to him outside Le Trianon, the night his fox finally died.

'The third and final thing,' said Khartoum, 'is that His Excellency is most impressed.' A smile crossed the old man's face. 'The networks are waiting. The UN is waiting. Senator Liz is going insane. C3N has started talking about you as a new force in North Africa.'

'Why?' Raf pushed himself up on his pillows.

'You've kept them all waiting for three days.'

'I've . . .'

'That's how long you've been . . . asleep.' Scooping the tea glass from the floor, Khartoum carried it across the room and offered it to Raf. Black slivers of bark floated in water thick with sediment, some of which had settled at the bottom of the glass.

'Take it,' Khartoum said. It wasn't a suggestion.

Raf did. At least he took the tea glass, but that was all. 'Is this going to make me sleep again?'

The skeletal man snorted. 'You've slept enough,' he said. 'It's time you woke up . . .' He paused on the edge of saying something, glanced at Raf huddled under a thin quilt and said it anyway.

'Demons are useful,' said Khartoum. 'They keep us respectful of the dark. But you let yours ride you like djinn.' He stared long and hard. 'I see them look out of your eyes. You think we don't know why you always wear those dark things?'

Walking over to the window, the old man stared out at the mansion's famous garden. From behind, he looked as fragile as a dying tree and as solid as rock. 'Hani's asleep outside your door,' he said, tossing his words over one thin shoulder. 'That's where she's slept since she got here, but you know that, don't you?'

Raf didn't, although something in Khartoum's voice warned him he should have done. 'Three nights she's slept there. Her and that cat. She thought you were dying . . . Ya Pasha thinks you're being clever. Hani thinks you're going to die. The noisy American thinks you're refusing to see her out of spite. But God knows the truth. You been hiding. Most of your life has been hiding.'

'And you are who?' asked Raf.

'Who's anyone?' said Khartoum. 'So much dust. There are people in this city who would give all of what they own to see you dead . . .'

'Me?'

'Iskandryia's governor,' said Khartoum. 'That's you, isn't it?'

'And you represent them?'

'No,' said Khartoum, 'I represent the woollen cloak.' He shook his head at the boast, amending his words. 'No,' he said. 'Not true. No one represents anyone, other than themselves and the will of God.'

The taste of Khartoum's medicine was bitter, somewhere between burnt earth and crushed aniseed; but it flowed down Raf's throat and spread through his veins like creeping light, as the headache he forgot having lifted like burning mist.

'Good,' said Khartoum, and nodded grimly. 'Now you eat . . . I'd bring you something myself but then Hani would be upset.'

'Bagels,' announced Hani. 'And I remembered milk for the coffee . . .' There were three already-split bagels, untoasted and minus schmeer piled into a mound on a plate so fine that Raf could see Hani's fingers through the bone china. The coffee was the colour of dishwater, its cup narrow at the base and wide at the top, so that tiny globules of goat's milk floated slick-like on the surface.

'This is what they eat in Seattle . . .' said Hani.

It was a question, Raf realized, not the statement he'd thought it was.

'You're right,' he said.

'I looked it up,' she explained defensively. 'Bagels and milky coffee, it's traditional.'

Raf nodded.

'And I downloaded you some papers to read with your break-fast.' Hani paused. 'I'm not sure you'll want them,' she added, resting her bagel plate on the side of his bed and taking a huge bundle of papers from under her arm.

They were worse than Raf expected. Monday's *Die Berliner*

dealt with leaked documents suggesting that out-going governor Koenig Pasha had once taken a $5,000,000 bribe from El Iskandryia's beleaguered industrialist, Hamazah Effendi. Nowhere was it mentioned that this was for facilitating Raf's marriage to Zara, the one that didn't happen.

The word *anarchy* featured heavily in the leader column. Questions were apparently being asked in Geneva, forcing Berlin, however reluctantly, to agree with the position of France and America . . . El Iskandryia had become a liability.

City in chaos, he'd read that one already

Koenig Pasha rushed to New York hospital . . . That was new. Raf skimmed Tuesday's *Times* and grinned. So the old man had got himself out of the country, strapped to a stretcher and wired in to more machines than looked strictly necessary. In the picture his eyes were closed, his face even more sepulchral than usual.

Raf wouldn't put it past the old bastard to have starved himself for a day or two, just to make it look more convincing.

The General's arrival at Mount Olive Hospital in New York was as low-key as any arrival could be which was greeted by a hundred chanting, placard-waving protesters. An old man, frail as melting snow, in a borrowed wheelchair, being pushed up a ramp by a young staff nurse.

'Is Koenig Pasha really dying?' Hani asked.

Raf shook his head. 'Doubt it,' he said. 'I doubt if he's even really ill.'

'A trick,' she said, smiling. Hani could appreciate that.

Wednesday's *New York Times*, *Le Monde*, *Frankfurter*, *El Pais*, *Herald Tribune* . . . Hani had downloaded the lot and the story they told was the same. The General was ill, El Isk was in chaos, no one knew anything significant about the new governor.

There was, Raf was sorry to say, very little significant to know.

'You had a call from Zara,' said Hani. 'And from . . . Kamila.'

It took Raf a moment to pull the name from memory. Kamila was the young coroner he'd told not to go ahead until he was there. That was what, four days ago?

*　　*　　*

Hani caught up with Raf after he'd shaved and dressed and was preparing to go tour the city. Although the words *fiddling, Nero* and *burns* came to his mind.

'I need to show you something,' she said

'Later.'

'No,' Hani insisted, 'Now.'

Her fingers grabbed the pocket of his jacket and held fast. One of the guards by the front door looked as if he didn't know whether to be amused or appalled. A glance at Raf's face convinced him to be neither.

'What is it?' said Raf with a sigh.

Hani squinted at the guard, then at Raf. 'It's a secret,' she said. 'You'd better come with me.' The room she led Raf to smelled of dust and damp, of rotting wall hangings and ancient books going musty on oak shelves. But the data port in the wall by the window was working.

'Should it be able to do this?' asked Raf, watching figures scroll lightning-fast down the screen of a toy computer shaped like a sea shell.

Hani shrugged.

'I made some changes,' she said, then went back to her screen. Figure followed figure, ever faster as Hani's fingers danced over keys, never quite touching.

'Okay,' she said, 'here we go.'

They were in Tiny Tina zone, apparently. Occupying an impossibly frilly bedroom constructed from wavy planes and pastel colours. Stuffed toys sat on the fat bed. In one corner of the virtual room sat a pink chest of drawers, decorated with stuck-on pictures of Hani's cat Ifritah.

Making some kind of pass over her keyboard, Hani popped out one of the drawers and clicked on the emptiness. Instantly the childish bedroom was gone, replaced by thumbnail pix of five wrecked buildings.

'See,' she said, 'they're not *random* at all.'

Lines radiated from thumbnails to various logos, from those logos to offshore shells, back to different logos. All the lines eventually ended in the same place, with one logo, that of Hamzah Enterprises GmB.

'They've all been burnt,' said Raf.

'And every burnt building belongs to Effendi,' stressed Hani. 'All five.' She was grinning at her own cleverness.

That was when Raf realized something. Usually his ideas came fast, pulled from memory in a flurry of facts, with the connections ready made; but this came slowly, like a fish rising to the bait, and it came not formed but uncertain. Becoming certain only when he thought about it.

Over and over again, Hamzah's refinery had also been attacked and each time the harm was minimal. Highly visible, usually photogenic, but not even close to serious damage. Someone badly wanted the Midas Refinery kept in the news but not broken.

That ruled out the Sword of God, who abhorred Hamzah's links with St Cloud. One of the ironies of the Midas Refinery being that Europe saw St Cloud as the refinery's acceptable face, while the fundamentalists, regarded him as degenerate. And if SoG weren't really behind the attacks on the refinery then Raf found it hard to believe they'd bothered to burn Hamzah's other buildings.

On the way out of the first floor room, Hani dragged Raf over to a long fly-specked looking glass. 'Are you meant to be dressed like that?' she asked.

Raf took a look and saw a pale man in a high-necked suit, wearing Armani shades and carrying a silver-topped Malacca cane in one hand. A bit thinner than before he iced himself, but otherwise not that different. Swept back blond hair, neat beard, high cheekbones, drop-pearl earring. He saw the person he expected to see, people mostly did; until the day they looked in the mirror and saw somebody else.

'You're dressed like the General,' Hani said patiently.

'That's the plan,' said Raf. 'If I dress like the General, then maybe people will treat me like the General.'

'Yeah, right,' said Hani, 'they'll probably try to shoot you.'

Chapter Thirty-two

22nd October

Next morning, a couple of hours before dawn, Khartoum woke himself and went to fetch Raf. He waited in silence while the surprised bey sat on the edge of his bed and pulled on a pair of trousers, buttoned his shirt and slid into a black coat.

Sitting to dress was ordained. Something the bey had not understood until Khartoum explained this. Dressing in the pitch dark was the bey's own choice.

Khartoum had nodded to a Sudanese guard standing outside Raf's room on his way in, and when he nodded again on his way out, the guard fell into step behind them. Two more soldiers fell into step at the front door. They were five minutes from the sleeping mansion before Khartoum saw Raf realize that not one of his escort carried a weapon.

South through the sodium of Rue Ptolomies, across Faud Premier's hard neon and into a darkened alley little wider than a shop doorway, one city giving way to another as Khartoum knew it would. Some people thought it was the *arrondissements* which mattered, because those were what got shown on maps. It was a simple enough mistake to make. The same people divided their lives. This is my job, this is my wife, my friends from the market, my other friends, my family, this is the emptiness which should be occupied by my God.

Life didn't work like that. It was layered, not separate. Woven together into a hidden script that few knew existed and fewer still ever got to read.

Wood smoke drifted from mean doorways. There was a whining of sleepy children. A thrown-open wooden shutter swung so hard it bounced off the wall. Someone hawked and spat noisily in a room nearby. The further into the alley they walked, the sourer the air and the more battered the front doors. Until finally beaten-earth walls, stripped of their render by time or rain, framed doorways closed only by blankets. Beneath Raf's feet, shattered tarmac scabbed the damp earth like broken skin.

Khartoum was watching him in the near darkness.

'Where are we?' Raf asked.

'Undoubtedly almost here,' said Khartoum and kept walking.

There were others in the darkened alley. Figures slipping from the curtained doorways, their jellabas poor, their faces sunken with hunger. Scars went uncorrected and poor eyesight unimproved. They had the dark skin of those who had migrated from where the rivers met. They were the city's incomers. The city's invisibles.

Lacking shoes, history, a voice.

For most of those who joined Khartoum, Raf's escort were invisible. Although at least one man did hesitate, seeing uniforms lit from an open door. And two or three slunk back into darkness and safety.

A few of the men smiled at Khartoum, most just nodded a simple *marhaba*. One or two, mainly the older ones, gave the *salaam*, right hands sweeping up to touch their heart and then that little finger-flick out from the head. To those alone Khartoum replied formally, *wa 'alaykum assalam*.

One of the smallest boys reached out to touch Khartoum's robe and was instantly yanked away by his father. Khartoum appeared not to hear the slap which followed or the muffled protests which followed that. In total there were no more than fifty people, all men and mostly young.

Occasionally, when light spilled out from a high window some of them would stare at Raf when they thought he wouldn't notice. Mostly they just trudged in silence, until the narrow cut ended, opening onto a gloomy scar of scrubland and railway track.

Away to their right, arc lights bathed the vast neo-baroque

business that was Misr Station, its exuberance curtailed only by distance and intervening darkness. And somewhere nearby was a lorry park, where a diesel crunched its gears, but other than this, the only sound was of feet shuffling over gravel as the group left the tracks behind to slip through a hole cut in a link fence.

An unbroken line of blank-faced, five-storey tenements faced them across a deserted road, all that now separated them from a small *zawiya* built in the courtyard of the tenement opposite. The *zawiya*'s minaret was little more than a squat tower. And Khartoum's voice, when it echoed from the top, was thin and quavering against the amplified magnificence coming from grander minarets across the waking city.

The small mosque looked out of place but that was just appearance, reality was the other way round. The mosque had been there first. Once, in fact, it had been a Coptic church, home to a famous Gnostic, but that was before the armies of God burst out of the desert, bringing blood, coffee, decent cooking and the truth.

'In the name of God, the Merciful, the Compassionate . . .'

The *Fatiha* gave way to other prayers, then a Bible story that Raf didn't recognize from Sunday services at school. One in which Satan was cast out for refusing to bow down before Adam and in which Adam repented of eating the Apple.

Original sin did not exist.

Vicarious atonement was not required.

To find the law, logic had only to be systematically applied to situations not explicitly mentioned in the Holy Qu'ran . . . *Hadith* and *Ijma'*. Raf pulled the terms from memory and meaning came tumbling after. *Hadith* was a database of oral law, second only to the Book and more important than *Ijma'*, agreed precedents. Together, with logic, they made up the four classical roots of jurisprudence, which all rulers must use . . .

Hunched on his heels at the back of the crowd, Raf understood instantly why he'd been brought. Why Khartoum was so insistent.

Raf dragged his eyes away from the cracked dome overhead

with its constellation of tessera broken by the tiny darkness of fallen stars. Stained glass filled with morning light at one end of the mosque and below the window was a wooden minbar, a kind of carved pulpit in which Khartoum now stood. To one side was a niche, richly decorated with polychrome marble and painted tiles. At the top of the niche were carved stones of alternate colours, dark red and pale sandstone. It was an ancient technique known as . . .

Ablaq, Raf said to himself.

Next to him, a middle-aged man frowned, suddenly recognized Raf as the new governor and looked hurriedly away.

'This is the truth.'

Now Khartoum was sat facing the crowd, telling them the story of a famous mystic who challenged a Caliph and was crucified, his ashes thrown into the Tigris. Somehow the tale of al-Hallaj developed into one about a mullah who rode his donkey backwards, waving a lighter and a mug of water. When asked why, he announced that it was to ignite heaven and put out the flames of hell.

After that the stories became lighter. The poor mullah and the rich beggar. The night the mullah fell down a well. The time he announced, when presented with a pregnant woman, whose husband had died falling off a cart five years before, that the fault lay with the lazy foetus who'd been sleeping, not the mother. And then, while the men were still thinking about that, the stories ended . . .

'They are the city,' Khartoum said to Raf later. 'You forget this at your peril. And besides,' he smiled, 'what's that phrase *nasranis* have . . . ? *Seeing is believing . . .*'

'You wanted me to believe in them?'

Khartoum looked at Raf as if he was a complete idiot. 'No,' he said heavily, 'I want them to believe in you.'

Chapter Thirty-three

22nd October

She wasn't the first person to decide that Raf had engineered the departure of Koenig Pasha . . . Dr Kamila was just more obvious about her suspicions than most.

'A poison-induced heart attack?' Raf raised his eyebrows. 'Who said anything about a heart attack?'

'The local news. Were they wrong?' Kamila kept her tone several degrees below comfortable. One degree above the autopsy suite.

'Yes,' said Raf, 'undoubtedly . . . For a start, to have a heart attack you need a heart.'

Behind him a man snorted, but when Raf glanced round the General's old bodyguard, Hakim, was busy staring straight ahead.

'I'll be with you when this is done,' Kamila said stiffly and returned to her scalpel and a plump woman largely hidden under a green sheet.

It was three months since Raf had been in Kamila's autopsy suite. Then there'd been two bodies, one of them a stranger unrelated to his own narrative, the other the woman he was meant to have murdered. Now there were half a dozen. In El Iskandryia these days, even death was suffering from inflation.

'That man I sent . . .'

'In a minute,' said Kamila crossly, turning back to where the plump woman's scalp had been sliced around the hair line and pulled forward, so it hid her face. A section of yellow bone beneath had been cut away. Whatever was in the stainless steel dish beside the half-empty skull might look like minced jelly but was, Raf decided, undoubtedly something nastier.

'Now,' said Raf.

'As soon as this is finished.'

Raf clicked his fingers and pointed to the electric scalpel. 'Take that toy away from Ms Kamila.'

'Sure, Boss.' Hakim squeezed between two trolleys and held out a meaty hand. 'If you would, Miss . . .'

Very carefully, Kamila put the bowl and her scalpel on the nearest table, the double clink of metal on metal momentarily drowning out Raf's sigh. She obviously hadn't forgiven him the last time they'd met.

'The scalpel . . .' Hakim's hand was still outstretched.

'Let it go,' said Raf and the sergeant padded silently back to his place. Ahmed, Raf's other bodyguard, waited at ground level, at the top of the stairs. In the street outside, his official driver stood by the Bentley. It seemed that the only place Raf was to be free of guards was on the loo. And even that had been a battle.

At the mansion itself, he had anxious secretaries, keen assistants, more staff than hours in the day and all awaiting orders, with only Hani willing to disagree with him if she thought his ideas were bad. Raf seriously doubted if an idiot supported by a nine-year-old was what the General had in mind when he resigned and appointed Raf in his place. So far, it seemed, his greatest successes had come from doing nothing . . . Zero input shadow play.

'Hakim,' Raf said. 'Go join Ahmed. Understand?' The big man nodded doubtfully, then looked at Raf and shrugged.

'Is that an order, Boss?'

'Whatever it takes,' said Raf.

Hakim gone, Raf turned his full attention to Kamila. He was pretty sure the pathologist's face showed open contempt, though that could have been his imagination, given that she wore a green surgical mask over her nose and mouth.

'You know why the General appointed me governor?'

The shake of her head was quick, abrupt.

'You want to know?'

She thought about that. Her face tilted slightly to one side. Dark eyes flicked over his shoulder to the shut door beyond. No, she shook her head again, she didn't . . .

'Good,' said Raf, 'because I haven't a fucking clue.'

'*That makes two of us.*' He wasn't meant to hear her aside, but he did. Just as he heard a raggedness in her heartbeat, the rush of her breath and the crackle of paper as she pushed her hand through a slit in the side of her surgical gown, searching for a cigarette.

Ignoring a dozen 'No Smoking' signs, Kamila tapped a Cleopatra straight from its packet to her mouth and zapped the end, tugging smoke down into her lungs. She put the crumpled packet back without offering a cigarette to Raf.

Nicotine-heavy and carcinogen-free, the smoke mixed with formaldehyde and almost swamped the underlying signature of slowly decaying meat. And while a clock on the wall ticked off the seconds, an air purifier scrubbed at the smoke and a humming wall unit kept the tiled room not far above zero.

The morgue was fifteen feet below the sidewalk, sound proof, cut out of solid rock. Back times, before it was used for dead bodies, it had been a prison for live ones. Then the sound proofing had been more useful. Before this it was a charnel house for dry bones. Earlier still, Gnostic heretics had hidden there from the might of Byzantium.

History backed up inside Raf's head like memory, ghost after ghost, silent and hopeless. Some days he could almost taste it.

'Ever read any Ibsen?' Raf asked.

She hadn't.

'Small town gets poisoned, everybody wants to keep it quiet. I've forgotten the end . . .' Behind her mask, the girl's face remained impassive.

Raf sighed. 'Show me the bodies,' he said.

Kamila nodded. They were back to a relationship she understood. He gave orders, she quietly resented them. 'This way,' she said, walking across to a trolley that was on its own. 'This is the man you insisted we take . . .' Pulling back a body cloth, she indicated something with the stink of stale embers and the consistency of twisted bog oak.

Clothes had fused in places to flesh, where flesh was left, legs were bent at the knees, the body angled forwards, fists raised, as if fighting an invisible enemy . . .

Occasional flakes of bark-like flesh dotted onto the trolley's top but mostly what remained of the man was polished anthracite. The thread of a toe-tag had been looped round one ankle, the actual toes having fused together.

'PA,' said Kamila, indicating the twisted limbs. '*Pugilistic attitude*, it happens when strong muscles cook in the heat. Muscles tighten, spine expands, head goes back. You find it in everything from house fires to the dead at Pompeii. He got caught in a fireball and then fell beneath the worst of the flames. You got lucky.'

Raf looked at her.

'If the heat's intense enough, the brain boils and the skull explodes . . . looks like a gun shot. Well, if you don't know what you're looking at. Instead,' said Kamila, 'the skull's in one piece and X-rays show not all of the fillings melted. And he did have fillings, rather than replacements. Which makes him a traditionalist.'

Or an idiot.

'And fillings will tell me what?'

'Country of origin, if God wills . . .' She shrugged. 'I'll take a look as soon as the surface work is complete.' Kamila stubbed out the remains of her cigarette and picked up a UV rod, flicking its switch.

'Forget that,' said Raf, quietly taking the rod from her hand. 'I need his nationality now. Anything that's not now is already too late.'

'Okay, you're the boss,' Kamila said. The tightness around her eyes contradicting the politeness of her words. Picking up a scalpel, she hacked open one blacked cheek, swapped instruments and reached in with a pair of tiny snub-nosed pliers. 'Already heat cracked,' she said to herself. To Raf, she said, 'We can do this professionally or we can do it fast.'

Not waiting for his answer, Kamila crushed the tooth and used the pliers to extract a minute shard of amalgam from deep inside. The fragment went into a glass dish, the dish into a little spectrometer and Kamila punched a button. Behind smoked glass, a laser vaporized the amalgam and data began to scroll down a tiny flat screen.

'Austro-Hungarian,' she said, 'maybe German. Could be American, just about, though slightly wrong composition for US amalgam.'

'So he's not Iskandryian?'

'I'm talking about the fillings,' said Kamila.

'I'm not,' said Raf. 'What about the girl?'

'That's all you want on this one?'

'It's enough.'

It was too. *Tourists butchered by tourist.* The dead man was a foreigner. If necessary, he could be made into a tourist. That gave him something to give the newsfeeds. And the earlier deaths could also be put down to this man. Raf was still writing headlines in his head when Kamila walked over to another trolley and pulled back the sheet, exposing the face and shoulders of a blonde teenager.

She treated this corpse with more respect. Maybe because the victim was female or this was a victim not a killer. Perhaps just because the body was more obviously human. A jigsaw of a human, true enough, with some pieces missing, but still more obviously like her, even when dead.

The dead girl looked unnaturally thin beneath the cloth, and then Raf realized why. Both her large and small intestine were already in a surgical chill bucket beneath the trolley. The bucket tagged and numbered. The more Raf looked at the corpse the more it reminded Raf of himself. He could swear there'd been one time he was across the other side of an operating theatre looking at his body as it lay on a table, figures in white coats standing around it.

'She's American,' said Raf. 'Nineteen, a politics major, doing well at university. Originally from Kansas City. Her father works for Hallmark . . .' Raf caught the pathologist's look and held it. 'I was talking to the poor bastard half an hour ago.'

And saying nothing of any consequence, obviously enough, the meeting brief and painful. A jowly middle-aged man, still jet-lagged and pale with shock, accompanied by a vodka-sodden woman whose anger was barely in check. First they learn their kid is missing and then – once they arrive where she's meant to be – no one in authority will even take their calls. And then twenty-four hours later, just as they're ready to flip, Iskandryia's chief muckety-muck turns up at their hotel, accompanied by three armed guards.

In the end, Raf had apologized to the Haugers and left, trailing his guards behind him. And the parting glare from the dead girl's mother made it obvious she held him personally responsible for every injury inflicted on her child.

Only manners and being in a foreign city made Mrs Hauger swallow her words. On his way out of the hotel, Raf had met Senator Liz coming in. From the look on her face she also held Raf accountable.

All he'd learnt from his uncomfortable encounter with the Haugers was that their daughter Dawn didn't drink, didn't do drugs and wasn't interested in boys . . .

Pulling the modesty cloth back to her hips, Raf looked down at what was left of their daughter. She'd been beautiful in an ordinary sort of way and she was someone's child. And those someones were trying to hold their life together in a Hyatt hotel room, in a city so alien it might as well have been on another planet.

He tried to see Dawn as her parents would remember her, if they got lucky. Not as this emptiness with its faint tinge of decay, but as she'd been: blonde, pretty, with high cheeks and eyes of speedwell blue.

'Talk me through the injuries,' said Raf, folding the modesty cloth into a strip and positioning it carefully. His attempt not to offend Kamila more than circumstances required. 'How much preliminary work have you done?'

'None,' the pathologist said flatly, 'apart from X-rays. Those were your orders, apparently . . . Hold everything until you were here in person.'

'Yeah, I know. Sorry . . .'

Not the response Kamila had been expecting but then, in part, that was Raf's intention. The fox had a tag from Machiavelli covering emotional sleight-of-hand, but unfortunately the fox was missing, assumed dead.

'Well,' said Kamila, more embarrassed than mollified. 'You're here now.'

'True enough,' Raf said and wondered why he shivered. Then he remembered that he'd thought a lot about such places when he was a child, around the time he got his second kidney replacement.

Speed had been essential according to his doctor. And it had been this time constraint that made the clinic go through an organ broker. Searching for a matching kidney from someone dying or freshly dead. Of course, going this route was cheaper than growing a new one, but they'd assured his mother that wasn't an issue.

Raf had given up trying to remember which bits of him were retreads. Although, occasionally, he'd catch a slight seam of scar where he didn't expect to see one. Across his ribs or down one arm, and think, *what's that?*

Shadow memories.

'You all right?'

Raf glanced up to find Kamila staring at him, eyes anxious.

'I'm Iskandryia's new can carrier,' he said. 'What do you think?'

'I don't,' said Kamila. 'I'm not that stupid.' Reaching into her pocket, she produced a floating camera which she tossed into the air, waiting while it ran self diagnostics.

'Friday, 22nd October, 2.38 p.m.,' she announced once a diode lit green. 'I am Kamila bint-Abdullah, city pathologist, second grade.' Kamila's tone made clear what she thought about that. 'Also present at the autopsy is His Excellency, Ashraf . . .' She cleared her throat. 'Delete that . . . is His Excellency, the Governor of El Iskandryia.'

'This is case number 49–3957, Jane Doe . . .' Kamila's smile was almost apologetic and Raf realized she'd need a formal identification before the corpse earned itself a name. 'The body is that of an apparently healthy, well-nourished female, Caucasian, late teens/early twenties. The body is sixty-four inches long and in total, but minus lungs and heart, weighs . . .'

Taking a read-out from the autopsy table and the bucket which held the girl's intestines, Kamila added the two figures together in her head. '. . . 115 pounds. Blonde hair, blue eyes . . . The skin is of normal texture. There are no scars, moles, sub-dermal chips or tattoos.'

'Preliminary X-rays and scans reveal no bone fragments, fractures, bullet tracks, knife wounds, needles or objects embedded beyond point of entry. No foreign objects in throat, anus or vagina.'

Kamila lifted Dawn Hauger's right hand and examined each finger. 'Nails painted, neatly filed and unbroken, no indication of embedded foreign material. No defensive cuts to palm, dorsal side of arm, no damage to webbing between fingers . . .

'Which should suggest suicide,' Kamila tossed the comment over her shoulder. 'At least it should according to the textbooks.' Her voice was darkly ironic, animosity briefly forgotten. She was good at the job, Raf realized. Her manner professional and assured.

'Initials *H.Q.* inscribed on inside of left wrist,' Kamila announced, finishing up the other hand.

A quick sweep with a UV rod produced no significant areas of flare, though Kamila still took swabs from one corner of the dead girl's mouth, her nasal area and just outside the vagina. She also swept the pubic area for foreign body hair, despite the fact this had already been done once at the crime scene.

Using a plastic ruler, Kamila began to measure the wounds, her voice emotionless. The longest cut ran from throat to pubis, the second longest traversed the ribs, just below heavy breasts. Together the gashes formed a cross potent. And it was a cross potent rather than a mere cross, because once again wounds showed short lines cut at either end of each slash. The top one conveniently opened the girl's throat and the bottom one bisected her pudenda, the other two scored down both sides of her ribs. Though the terms Kamila used to describe their position were *cephalic, caudal* and *lateral.*

'This is too neat,' Kamila said. 'Much too neat . . .' The pause which followed was to let Raf ask a question.

'I had a look at the crime scene report,' she added into his silence.

'How did . . . ?' Of course, her father, sat at his front desk, proud of how well his only daughter was doing. 'What did it tell you?'

Kamila hesitated, replying with a question of her own. 'Wouldn't you expect increased disorganization?'

'Expect what?'

Kamila shrugged. 'This is the third death. Personally, at this point, I'd be looking for proof of greater risks run, not enough time allowed, less safe crime scenes, fewer escape routes . . .' She ticked the points off in her head. 'Yet, if anything, this killing is more meticulous than the last, which had inherent differences in MO to the one before.'

'You're absolutely certain?'

'Sure.' Kamila nodded. 'I pulled out all the files,' she said, pointing to a distant wall screen. 'Examined the earlier crime shots. Identical wounds, different MOs. The discrepancy just didn't get logged.'

'Why not?'

Her shrug was expressive. In it was everything Kamila felt about her opposite number at the *polizia touristica.* But what she said was, 'Maybe he's overworked . . .'

On average one per cent of a city dies each year. Iskandryia had four million people. Which meant 40,000 deaths, a quarter of which might merit investigation. Setting aside the poor and the unimportant reduced that figure to 3,000, the vast majority of whom had to be buried by noon (if they died in the previous twenty-four hours), or by the following noon (if they died at noon or after).

So far this year *polizia touristica* had dealt with seven bodies.

Four drownings and the three butchered tourists, on the last of which she was doing the work for them.

'My unofficial opinion,' Kamila said hesitantly, 'based on observation and on having sight of the autopsy reports of the earlier killings . . .' She was picking her words with care. 'Despite obvious similarities, my unofficial belief is that victim three was not killed by the same person as victim two, because, in the case I've examined, the positioning of each cut is more, not less, precise.'

Kamila nodded to the dead girl's opened throat, then indicated the matching cross-wound at other end of the upright. 'Exact,' she said reaching for her ruler. 'Exactly halfway between chin and breast bone, exactly halfway down the length of the genitals. And again, the ribs . . . Identical length of cut, identical positioning. Of course,' she said, 'I'm not in a position to refute that murders one and two were committed by the same killer.'

'What are you trying to tell me?' Raf asked, it seemed a fair enough question.

'On the record,' said Kamila, 'I'm highlighting disquieting aspects of a crime. More than that it's impossible to say without further work.' Her smile was bleak. 'Off the record, I reckon Dawn Hauger was bled to death, then mutilated by someone who lacked the nerve required to butcher her while alive . . .'

'You're saying,' said Raf, 'that we've got a series of copy-cat killings . . .'

Kamila looked at him. 'You disagree?'

'Yes,' said Raf, nodding. 'I think what we've got is atrocity by numbers.'

Chapter Thirty-four

22nd October

What was it with the missing mirrors? The last time Senator Elsing had been invited to meet Iskandryia's governor, half a dozen ornate Murano looking glasses had covered the walls, making a large room look even larger. Now the old man and his mirrors were gone, their memory etched in lighter patches on age-darkened silk. So what was that about, and was it safe to ask?

Was it even safe to be alone with this man?

In front of her sat a killer. Senator Liz couldn't get that fact out of her head. Not a killer like the General, when war or political expediency dictated, but the real thing. Ashraf Bey had put a revolver to the head of the previous Chief of Detectives and pulled the trigger, claiming humanitarian reasons. And the really weird bit was, no one in the city seemed to find that remotely odd.

But then that was Iskandryia for you.

It seemed the bey might also be behind the assassination in Kabul of Sheik el-Halana, the man who authorized the bombing of the Ottoman Consulate in Seattle. Then there was the death of a *Thiergarten* agent. And the bey's rumoured links with the Sultan himself.

As far as Senator Liz was concerned, the sooner a deal was done and she was out of his company the better. Her only problem, and it was a big one, was that the ostensibly polite young man sat opposite was obviously not listening to a word she said. And she really did need him to get behind the plan.

'Your Excellency . . .'

Twin ovals of dark glass. Somewhere behind those lenses was

the man himself, whoever he was. And White House opinion was divided on that.

'Tell me,' said Raf, 'Do you like our wallpaper?

'Do I . . .' Senator Liz looked as put out as she felt.

'It's Turkish,' said Raf, 'I was thinking of having it painted. Only that's going to take gallons of emulsion and I can't decide on a colour.' He lapsed back into silence, leaving Senator Liz to look around while she decided what, if anything, his comment actually meant.

Added to the main building in 1803, the chamber they used was too large for a withdrawing room, too small to qualify as a proper ballroom. And at exactly one and a half times the height of every other room on the ground floor, it guaranteed that the roof space above was so cramped as to be useless for anything but storage, but Raf still liked it more than any other room in the mansion.

Somewhere, hidden beneath its floor covering were marble tiles, hacked from a quarry by slaves. But, none of the tiles could actually be seen, because most of the space was taken by two vast Chinese silk carpets, with Bokhara runners and Isphahan rugs filling in the gaps.

'It's very nice wallpaper,' Senator Liz said carefully.

'You're right.' The man sitting opposite her nodded. 'The question is, would it look better painted? And if so, should that paint be white?'

Senator Liz swallowed a sigh. Pashazade Ashraf al-Mansur looked frighteningly like his father, the Emir of Tunis, and it appeared the similarity went more than skin deep. The last time the Senator had been allowed into the Emir's presence, the man had been camped deep on Jubal Dahar, guarded by dark-eyed girls carrying snubPups. His Highness had taken all of thirty seconds out of that evening's routine to tell Senator Liz that the answer was *no*, whatever her query was, except for those bits to which his answer was *yes* . . .

Behind the Senator stood an interpreter, redundant from the moment she'd discovered that Ashraf Bey spoke English. Since the interpreter's day job was actually second intelligence attaché at the US Embassy in El Qahirah, Senator Liz had intended to get on-the-hoof briefings as her meeting with the bey progressed. Now, of course, that was impossible.

The Senator would have felt much happier if the impressively-bulky file in front of her had contained even one sheet of usable information on the man sat opposite. But he had no vices, apparently. Having saved the life of the Quitrimala girl, he took no reward, though the sum offered had been vast, astronomical . . . He'd turned down a marriage worth billions, because he wasn't in love with the girl. He belonged to no clique, no cabal.

And he was unquestionably insane.

Three days he'd kept the world waiting. The President in Washington, the Kaiser . . . Hell, even his own Sultan in Stambul.

'Your Excellency . . .' The entreaty stuck in Senator Liz's throat. But she had a job to do, even if that job wasn't easy. 'Iskandryia . . .'

'. . . is fucked,' Raf didn't even let her finish the sentence. 'You hear that . . . ?' He cocked one ear to the sound of a cherry top blasting past the grounds of the mansion. 'Riots in Karmous. One of the co-op banks has folded.'

'Bad news, nothing but bad news,' said Senator Liz, her voice mournful. It was a sadness that didn't reach her pale eyes.

'Not necessarily,' Raf said lightly. 'For example, we've established beyond doubt that Hamzah Effendi is not implicated in the murder of the second girl, the one found on his beach. Unfortunately, the real murderer was killed . . .'

By me, added Raf, under his breath, in the basement of a deserted house in Moharrem Bey. But he didn't say that aloud, obviously enough.

'We also know that the murderer of the first girl shot himself at Lake Mareotis . . .'

Raf didn't know that at all, but a chemical residue impregnating the pouch found with that man apparently matched the drug used to sedate Dawn Hauger at Casino Quitrimala. So it was a reasonable guess.

'Which means,' said Raf, 'three murders, three butchers, each carrying out a near-identical crime to order. Of course, now the third one is also out of action . . .'

Elizabeth Elsing blinked, but it was the reaction of her man stood behind her that interested Raf. 'You have him under arrest?' he asked, before he could stop himself.

Raf stared at the interpreter, who looked very much as if he'd like to take back the question, but when Raf answered, he took care to address his words to the Senator.

'Unfortunately,' said Raf as he put down his coffee cup and leant back, 'he also died . . .'

'He died?' So intent was the small woman that she almost fell off the sofa from bending too far forward.

'Sad, isn't it?' said Raf. 'I can, however, tell you that he was German.' Raf flicked open a leather notebook and hit resume, watching as words scrolled up the page. Yet another message from Hani by the look of it and two missed calls from Zara.

'We'll be releasing his name later . . .' Raf flicked shut the notebook and put it back on the table.

'Advance notification of which,' Senator Liz began to say, 'would be very . . .'

'*Useful.* Yes,' said Raf, 'I'm sure it would.' Whatever froideur might be about to fall ended as double doors crashed open and Khartoum staggered in, carrying a heavy silver tray.

Double loops of gold tied themselves in knots up the front of his frock coat. A cravat of yellowing Maltese lace frothed from his neck. And beneath the large silver buckles of his shiny shoes, grey showed against black, where Khartoum had missed patches of dust on their freshly-cleaned patent leather.

'Fresh coffee, Your Excellency.'

Raf took one look at the old man's face and swallowed his smile. If Khartoum was dressed like that then there was a reason. Just as there had to be a reason for the parable Khartoum had told Raf before the meeting began. It had begun by Khartoum asking him if he'd read any of Hani's stories.

The answer to that had been *no*. Although he'd had some read to him.

'Good,' Khartoum smiled. 'Here's another. A thief creeps into the enclosure of a Sufi master and finds nothing there but sand and dry crusts. As he leaves, understanding his disappointment, the Sufi tosses the thief the tattered blanket from his bed, so that he should not go back into the street empty handed.'

'That's one of Hani's tales?'

'No.' The old man had said. 'Not yet . . .'

Raf watched in fascination as the old man lowered his heavy tray carefully onto the table. A small gilt jug was accompanied by two tiny gilt cups, a Limoges platter of rose-water Turkish delight, dusted with sugar, and a smaller plate, piled high with tiny crescents of pastry. An open cigarette box, made from beaten silver but lined with rosewood, was filled with Balkan cigarillos.

'I trust Your Excellency needs nothing.' Khartoum gave the tiniest bow and walked backwards from the chamber, as if he'd been a major-domo all his life.

Coffee, tiny croissants, Turkish delight . . . Limoges dishes and an *English silver tray*. Somewhere in there, sure as mathematical certainty, was an answer to their sum. Concentrate, the fox would have said. So Raf did, starting with the 'nothing' that Khartoum considered he needed.

Zero had been an Arabic understanding. The *nasrani* who came with their heavy mail and what passed for cooking grasped the numerical concept of *something* plus *something*, but zero, the addition, subtraction and definition of nothing, had to be explained.

The French, the English, the Germans, now the Americans. And before that the Mamelukes and the Arab invaders. He had it! What Khartoum was saying was, given the chance, Isk would again recreate itself. No one ever truly conquered this city . . . They either passed through or were adopted by the city they thought had fallen to them.

'What do you want from us?' Raf demanded.

'Us?'

'With the city, with me . . .'

He faced her across a low table and both of them understood that they'd finally arrived at the real reason why they were there.

'Iskandryia . . .' said the Senator.

'Is in chaos,' Raf shrugged. 'We've had this conversation. What matters is . . . Why are you here?'

'To offer help.' The Senator sat back, forcing herself to relax. Unfortunately, Raf saw her do it. Which just made her stressed again.

'Help?' Right, thought Raf. Obvious really. 'And in return?'

For a second it looked as if Senator Liz was about to say, *there is no in return.* But something in Raf's smile stopped her. 'The situation is tricky.' She began again . . .

Your carpet is moth-eaten, hardly worth buying, the quality is poor, besides it is too small, too expensive and I don't need a carpet anyway . . . Raf had heard it often, that opening position. The one which said, *out of the goodness of my heart I'm going to agree to rob you blind.*

Tuning out the low drone of the Senator's explanation, Raf traced the Doppler spore of a cherry top as it raced down Fuad Premier, passed through Shallalat Gardens and vanished along Avenue Horreya. Orders had gone out that afternoon locking down the city. Leave had been cancelled across all divisions of the police, even the *morales.* The military were on standby, confined to barracks but ready. His Sudanese guard patrolled the streets around the mansion.

Raf could imagine tomorrow's headlines.

'. . . does that sound acceptable?'

Yanking his attention back to the chamber, Raf smiled at the American woman sat opposite. 'Run through that last part again,' he said. 'I think I might have missed something . . .'

Unsweetened by its sugar coating the pill was bitter. On behalf of PaxForce – read Washington, Berlin and Paris – Senator Liz demanded the right to station armed observers within the city to keep the peace. But there was worse, infinitely worse. And finally Raf understood why Hamzah had been desperate to see his daughter safely married, so desperate that he'd been prepared to bribe Lady Nafisa to achieve it.

'We have evidence,' the Senator was saying. Flipping open her old-fashioned file, she pulled out a stack of 10x4s, all of them copyrighted to 'Jean René' and dated decades earlier.

The photographs might have been arranged in chronological order, or by level of atrocity, or maybe the order was as random as the place names printed on the back and war really was God's way of teaching geography.

Mostly the dead were children, some almost old enough to count as adults, if that threshold was sufficiently flexible. They varied in race, skin colour, age and sex. And the only thing they had in common beside a gaping cross cut into each chest was the bareness of their feet and the raggedness of ripped uniforms . . . In as much as tee-shirts and cargo pants could count as uniform. Most of the dead also wore amulets, small leather bags, metal charms and badges, lots and lots of badges.

Cheap and plastic, black on red. The eyes of a saint above the beard of a prophet.

'Colonel Abad,' Senator Liz said redundantly.

Raf already knew that. He'd had a tri-D of the man on his study wall at school. Between the plastic badges, dark poppies blossomed against dark skin, wounds from the bullets those amulets were meant to stop. Flies hovered frozen around faces which stared blindly into a sky that time had long since left behind.

'Hamzah was involved in this?' Raf's question was hesitant. As if he couldn't quite believe his own suspicion, but the crosses that disfigured each corpse were unmistakable.

'No,' said Senator Liz, 'this was done by Ras Michael's Church Militant. Those responsible were tried and executed or jailed. These are Hamzah's responsibility . . .' She took the remaining photographs from Raf and discarded the top third, handing back the rest.

They were no less ugly. Children still lay face up to the sky, their feather and bone amulets as impotent as the combat patches tacked to their shirts. 'God Rules,' read one tee-shirt. Below the slogan someone had sewn a star, cut from red cloth.

'Don't tell me,' said Raf, reaching for the original photographs. 'This is one side.' He flipped over a photograph. 'And this is the other . . .' Side by side on the table, a dead girl and a ripped-open boy stared back at him.

Senator Liz nodded.

'So why go for Hamzah rather than Colonel Abad?'

'Because we know where Hamzah is. Anyway,' she said, 'our best intelligence suggests Abad's already dead.'

'Already . . .' Raf tossed down his photographs. 'If you'll excuse me.' He didn't wait for her answer, just stood up and stormed out of the chamber. On his way through the door, he flicked off the lights. Something about that woman irritated him to hell.

Raf had an office full of researchers back at Third Circle, an Intelligence Department based out of the barracks at Ras el-Tin and a dozen detectives, one or two of whom might even be able to do their job; but he found the information he needed in the kitchens, holding a skillet in one hand and a wooden spatula in his other. Flames roared from a gas ring as the gaunt man shuffled coffee beans backwards and forwards, like a skeleton mixing concrete.

'There was a war,' said Raf. 'When Hamzah Effendi was a child.'

'Before *you* were born?' Khartoum sounded amused by his own question. 'Yes, there were many wars. All unnecessary. What of it?'

What indeed?

'Who was in the right?' The question sounded stupid even as Raf asked it; but sometimes questions need to be asked, even stupid ones. And he knew the Sufi's answer would be honest, no matter that the old man was partisan.

'No one was in the right,' said Khartoum.

'Then who was in the wrong?'

'No one.' Dark eyes regarded Raf, as piercing as those of a hawk. 'They were children,' said Khartoum. 'Not men, not women . . . You should ask who armed them. Who had an interest in seeing them fight? Or maybe this is a question you too think best left unasked . . .'

The skeletal man turned away and tossed the charred contents of his skillet straight into a waste bin. Then he wiped down the inside of his pan with an old rag and scooped up a fistful of arabica beans. He still wore the ridiculous uniform.

Chapter Thirty-five

22nd October

'Hey you . . .' Hani grabbed Ifritah by the scruff of the neck and pulled so that the cat's head yanked back and its purr stopped as rapidly as if somebody had flicked a switch. 'That's better,' the girl whispered, hugging the cat to her chest. Immediately the scraggy animal started to purr again.

Hani sighed.

One of her arms ached from holding Ifritah, her foot had pins and needles and the narrowness of the window ledge on which she perched had sent her behind to sleep. The long velvet curtain she hid behind was both old and dusty, so half the time Hani had to hold the bridge of her nose just to concentrate on not sneezing because sneezing would ruin everything. Besides, as it was, her own breathing was almost too loud to let her hear what was being said by the cross American woman.

It should have been easy. But something in one of the woman's pockets was interfering with the tiny microphone Hani had stuck to the bottom of the table. Or maybe the microphone was broken. After all, it came from a Tina Tears whose head she'd cracked open with a paperweight, when the plastic proved too tough to cut using a kitchen knife.

Hani knew she shouldn't be there. Just as she knew she was in trouble if Ashraf found out. And he probably didn't even want her help. She was a child, as everybody from Zara to Khartoum kept telling her. But she also had an IQ of 160 for real, could do crosswords in French, English and Arabic and had forgotten more about computers than Raf knew, even if she couldn't see in the dark.

Hani wasn't meant to know about his night vision or maybe

she was meant to have forgotten – but she did know. She knew other things too, dark swirling facts that waited at the edges of her mind, wanting to come to her if only she'd let them.

On the other side of the curtain, the small woman was arguing again. She'd been angry since Raf came back, only this was worse. She wanted Raf to give up Effendi, that was how she put it . . . Effendi had to be given up, like cigarettes.

Ashraf refused, of course, and Hani hoped he'd go on refusing. She liked Zara and Effendi was Zara's father. Hani didn't like Zara's mother, but then Zara didn't like Zara's mother so the American could have her if she wanted.

'I'll leave the photographs,' the woman said crossly, climbing to her feet. Hani knew that was what she was doing by the creak of a sofa. Footsteps padded across carpet and then stopped. The Senator was turning in the doorway, wanting to say something. Only the threat or retort never came. Instead the woman and her interpreter let themselves out of the governor's chambers.

That was bad. Khartoum should have been there to let her out. Hani knew this from living with her Aunt Nafisa, notables never opened their own doors. A creak from the other sofa told her that Raf was leaving. After the creak and steps came the slam of a door and then nothing.

'You can go now,' said Hani, yanking open her nearest window to release the struggling cat. With Ifritah gone the room became more silent still. So Hani padded across the silence and picked up one of the famous photographs. The gutted boy was little older than she was, though his skin was darker and his black hair scraped back into a fat ponytail. The two girls in the next photograph were about Hani's age. One of them was missing her hands.

Looking down, it wasn't the boy's face which gripped Hani's attention but that of the bearded man on the badge pinned to his dirty shirt. Except for a beret and a small cigar clamped between his teeth, the man could have been the *nasrani* God, the one who got himself killed.

'Abad,' Hani said to herself and picked up the photograph, tucking it down the side of her jeans and smoothing her tee-shirt back into place. No one stopped her as she left the chamber or saw her in the corridor outside. All the same, as Raf sometimes said, better safe than sorry when being sorry wasn't an option.

The girl blanked her screen. 'It's nothing,' she said hurriedly.

Raf glanced from Hani's face to the photograph she was trying to slide into a open drawer. She had it turned upside down, but he could still see some of the caption. *Kordofan, 30th March. Investigators* . . .

Inside his head Raf swore.

'You got that from downstairs?'

Hani nodded. 'I'm sorry.' There was a haunted look on her face and she'd chewed one corner of her lip until it was raw. What upset Raf most was the way she leant away from him, hunching her shoulders without realizing it, in preparation for the slap that would never come.

'No,' said Raf, stepping back. 'My fault. I apologize . . .'

'Why?' The small girl asked suspiciously.

'Because I shouldn't have left those out for you to find.' Raf wanted to add, because this is a world from which I can't protect you, a world that may get worse. Instead, he scooped up the child and carried her over to her bedroom window.

Standing there, they looked out at the darkened city. As ever, her legs were bony against his arms, her wrists round his neck as thin as sticks.

'You need feeding up,' said Raf and the next question asked itself. 'Where's Donna?'

'At home.' There was a smile, fleeting and slightly exasperated. 'She won't sleep here,' said Hani. 'Apparently someone has to look after the madersa, but really she's afraid.' Hani indicated her new bedroom, the gesture taking in oil paintings, Chinese vases and a bronze dryad whose verdigrised shoulders and upturned breasts carried a faint sheen of dust.

Hani was right of course. The mansion would have frightened Donna even if it hadn't belonged to the General.

'So who feeds you while I'm working?' Raf asked.

'Me,' said Hani crossly. 'I can cook.'

'And when did you last eat?'

'I've had breakfast.' Hani scrambled out of his arms but stayed close. Away from the desk and her pink plastic laptop.

'Today?'

The child looked at him.

'You had breakfast today?'

The eyes opposite suddenly bruised with tears. 'Leave me alone, all right . . . And take your stupid photograph.' She left the room without looking back, slamming the door for good measure. As always, adults got it wrong. It wasn't the photograph she'd needed. Hani had wanted the face on the badge.

And besides, all that look-at-me-I'm-hiding-something routine was to stop Uncle Ashraf noticing what she really had in the drawer. The Doré engraving, the one of hell she'd borrowed from his office.

Chapter Thirty-six

23rd October

Outside on the beach, *Zara's beach*, October waves exploded against the headland and draped dark rocks with seaweed. And on the French windows to her father's study, a stray leaf trapped in a dying spider's web released its ribbon of rainbow down the glass as gasoline or herbicide slowly leached from its pores.

Zara saw neither, because the curtains were firmly drawn. She wore a nightdress, dressing gown and fur slippers. The warmth of those nursery clothes at odds with the arctic cold in her heart.

'Tell me it's not true . . .'

She wasn't meant to shout at her father. She wasn't even meant to swear either, but the rules were gone, left in a corridor along with her wailing mother and a discarded copy of the iniquitous *New York Times*. And all her father could do was huddle in his leather chair, a tumbler of whisky beside him and an old-fashioned revolver lying on a weird etching on his lap. The glass was Soviet crystal. Zara didn't recognize the weapon – revolvers weren't her thing. Come the revolution, she'd always seen herself using *plastique*.

Shutting her eyes to block out the world, Zara nursed the darkness until she could hold on to it no longer. Needless to say, when she looked again nothing in the study had changed, but then it never used to work for her as a child either.

'So it's true?' Zara said.

Of course it was. Her father wore his guilt like cheap cologne. And even the smell of fresh vomit couldn't hide the whisky fumes. A whole bottle was gone. Enough to reduce him to childish tears without lifting the horror from his eyes.

Top Industrialist Charged With Genocide . . .

He should have warned her. Before the American papers and the downloads and rolling newsfeeds began, before Trustafarian Ishies with their headsets and cameras started churning the lawns to mud. She could almost feel the hunger out there, calling its questions and tapping at windows, hammering on the big brass knocker and ringing the bell. News was a commodity to the soi-disant Free World, not a duty. And the bear-pit growl of its news gatherers could be heard through the study's double glazing, through windows closed and locked, curtains drawn and shutters bolted.

'Dad, come on . . .' Dropping to a crouch in front of his chair, Zara rested her forearms on his knees and felt her father flinch. That was all it took to turn anger to tears. Zara began crying then, sorrow rolling down her cheeks. Somewhere she had a tissue, but couldn't remember which pocket and it didn't seem to matter.

They cried in silence together.

She'd taken to asking herself a question a few years back. What was the worst it could be, the secret of her father's rise from nothing? She'd searched for clues to the answer. Once, aged fifteen, she'd riffled through his desk, using a key taken from his jacket. All she'd found was a small leather case containing pornographic photographs of a young man and two girls even younger . . . Apart from a wood-handled knife, a handful of Sudanese coins and a bone crucifix, that had been the sum total of her find.

She hadn't been able to look him in the face for weeks afterwards.

The worst she could say, until recently, was that he kept Western erotica in a drawer in his study. Now he was less than that, a man diminished. Except that Zara was rapidly coming to realize that, just maybe, she'd never actually known who he was, not really. Her father, the industrialist Hamzah Effendi.

He broke the law for a living, she accepted that. Only he broke it less than he used to do and nothing like as much as when he was young. And anyway the free market was a crime in itself. As a good Marxist she did believe that. Of course, he also killed, or had done, at least once . . .

When she was nine she had overheard two servants discussing this and been proud. The dead man had been bad, obviously. Someone who attacked her father, forcing him to defend himself. It was all so clear in Zara's head. Only when she tried asking her ma about it she'd been slapped for her pains. By the next morning both her nanny and the maid were gone.

Now nothing she could say to her father would change what was about to happen. PaxForce wanted him to stand trial and, according to the *New York Times*, Iskandryia's new governor had agreed to hand over Hamzah, subject to agreeing a timetable.

What more was there to say?

Plenty. And such was the shallowness of the Western press that *how* it was said would be as important as *what* was said. Picking up his revolver, weird-shit etching and whisky bottle, Zara slammed Hamzah's study door behind her and went to get changed. Already she was rewriting elements of her plan.

'Zara . . .' The voice that met her on the landing was angry and bitter, but then it would be, it belonged to her mother.

'What?' Zara demanded.

It had been a joke among Zara's friends that they could hear Madame Rahina long before they could see her, such was the clatter of gold from her wrists. Noisy bangles and an almost permanent scowl were Zara's memories of her mother. Sometimes the gold had been so loud Zara hadn't been able to hear the coming slap.

'How could he . . . ?'

'I thought you knew everything there was to know about him,' Zara said, her voice contemptuous. 'Wasn't that what you told everyone? Soulmates. Apart from his endless mistresses, your tranquillizers and the whisky . . .'

'*Zara* . . .'

Zara covered the outraged face with the spread fingers of one hand and pushed. Which was all it took to throw the woman backwards. Zara didn't bother to check how she landed.

*   *   *

Some of the men even had little ladders so they could peer over the heads of other photographers in front. Many wore pale safari suits of the kind carried at airports by ignorant *nasrani* journalists, who expected to land somewhere blisteringly hot. Only now their suits were dark with rain and hung with all the elegance of rags on a line.

'Miss Zara . . .'

She turned, saw Alex and sighed. The huge Soviet bodyguard stood like a scolded child, head down and fists clenched so hard that veins made freeways along his wrists. An hour earlier, while her father was still drinking himself into a stupor, Alex had been faced with a highly tenacious member of the press, who took bolt cutters to the gates and challenged Alex to shoot him. Without orders, Alex had retreated.

'You took the correct action,' Zara said, for about the third time.

Alex looked doubtful.

'Examine the options,' she said. 'You think you should have shot him?' He did too, Zara could see it in his broad face. 'Sometimes retreat is necessary,' Zara told Alex carefully. 'But now someone must guard the front door. And that must be you.'

Zara watched the cogs whir as Alex glanced from her to the heavy wooden door and then back again. He was nice in his way, but monolithically slow. Still, each according to his talents . . .

'The door, right.' He nodded agreement and turned away, shoulders straightening.

'Comrade . . .'

'Yes, Miss Zara . . . ?' He paused, shoulders broad, back straight, a Makarov 9mm bulging under one arm.

She smiled. 'Nothing.'

Nothing will come of nothing, that was a line from a play she was in, back when she went to college in New York . . . A city of high-rise boxes where girls her age fucked anything with a pulse and a penis and quality control seemed to be a contradiction in terms. But something always did come from nothing. The universe, for a start. Time itself. All that other shit Raf talked about that one night on the boat, stuff she didn't understand and guessed he didn't either, not really . . .

Zara sighed and went back to working on her plan.

The bell was made from beaten silver and had an ivory handle. Its clapper was a narrow twist of iron that ended with a small ball of soft metal the size of a pea. For as long as Zara could remember, the bell had been used by her mother to summon the nearest maid. Her father thought the bell unnecessary, he just shouted.

'Come on.' Zara rang the bell until the first maid appeared and then kept going until she had every member of staff mustered in the hall. There were seven in total. Five housemaids, a French chef and a Sudanese gardener. A surprisingly small number for a house the size of Villa Hamzah.

'I want coffee,' she told the chef. 'A large pot.'

'Of course, Miss Zara.' The little man nodded. 'I'll have Maryam bring it to the back drawing room.'

'No,' said Zara. 'You're missing the point. I want a *lot* of coffee.'

The chef blinked. 'How much?' he asked, his voice neutral.

'Jugs of the stuff. Enough for 200 people. And *semit* . . .' Zara named the soft sesame-covered pretzels sold everywhere in the city. 'Can we do that?'

'Of course I can.'

Zara smiled. The Parisian would be baking all afternoon, mixing dough and waiting anxiously for his yeast to rise. 'Make the coffee first,' she suggested. 'I'll take it outside myself.'

That got their attention.

'Ridiculous,' said the chef. 'It'll be far too heavy. Maryam and Lisa can carry it.'

'All right,' said Zara. 'We also need as many umbrellas as you can find . . . Start with my mother's dressing room,' she suggested, remembering a line of them hanging in a row along the back of a cupboard.

'Oh . . . and Alex,' She left out her usual *comrade*, not wanting to embarrass the big Russian in front of the others. 'Order me a marquee. Something large, but without sides . . . We don't want to overdo it.'

Chapter Thirty-seven

23rd October

The air was warm, the afternoon sun a haze of ultraviolet through cloud. The heavy rain didn't bother him. Not like back in Seattle.

'Ashraf Bey . . .'

Raf kept going, while behind him Hakim took it upon himself to punch the photographer to the ground. Providing the world with another picture.

The new governor's face already fronted *Time, Paris Match* and *Newsweek*. Cheeks hollow, eyes hard behind dark glasses, hair swept back. It was a face that Raf didn't recognize, even when he stared hard in the mirror.

As to why a mere handful of journalists clustered around the mansion in Shallalat Gardens . . . That was easy to answer. The rest were camped out on the lawns at Villa Hamzah, from where talking heads currently reported seriously on nothing very much.

Zara's offer of coffee and *semit* had been a flash of brilliance, but ordering a marquee and then staying outside to watch while a hundred journalists struggled with poles and wet ropes was beyond genius. And as they struggled, Zara had watched, not offering to help or saying anything, just standing on the lawn of Villa Hamzah, while photographers captured her guarded amusement at the chaos.

When the marquee was finally up and the journalists were out of the rain, Zara had walked into the middle of their group, without a bodyguard, without having to ask anyone to move out of her way. And then she stopped, watching them as they watched her. Meeting their lenses and the bursts of flash without blinking or looking away . . .

'Where to, Boss?'

Raf came awake in the back of his Bentley.

'Villa Hamzah.' Same as it ever was.

Then Zara had spun in a slow circle, meeting their eyes, one person at a time. At least that's what they thought; but really she'd been looking for a single logo among dozens.

Raf knew that now without doubt.

The journalists might have thought Zara was there to talk to them, only they were wrong. She'd stopped turning, stopped smiling the moment she saw someone from a local newsfeed. After that, her words had been for Raf alone.

'I am waiting to hear back from the governor. I'm sorry, but until then there is nothing more I can say . . .'

So now the governor was on his way, through a city that flickered by like the backdrop to some film he vaguely remembered preferring the first time round. The statue of Mehmet V which once seemed so impressive now looked tatty and grandiose, more parks than ever looked empty, windows to shops were unlit or shuttered tight with steel grilles: the rococo mansions of the Corniche that once seemed so magnificent behind their wrought-iron gates now looked defeated, held prisoner by their own defences.

We define ourselves by our own limitations. The fox had said that to him once, in Seattle, shortly before it pointed out that on this basis Raf should be very defined indeed.

But am I? Raf wanted to ask, only the voice in his head refused to answer and the voice in his heart that Khartoum talked about was missing, absent without leave. So maybe he was just the sum of his parts, few though those were. A face that looked like someone else, a fake identity and a job he hadn't asked for . . .

'Ahmed, you know who you are?'

The bigger of his two gun-toting bodyguards turned his head, while the driver and Hakim kept staring straight on: watching the Corniche unravel through the car's ancient windscreen. 'You what, Boss?'

'You know who you are?'

Ahmed nodded.

'You ever think you might be somebody else . . . ?'

Raf saw the answer written in the other man's puzzled frown. 'Doesn't matter,' he said flatly. 'Just forget it.'

There was silence in the Bentley after that as the driver concentrated on the road and Hakim and Ahmed eyeballed the sidewalk and beach respectively, their fingers never leaving the triggers of their H&K5s.

'Your Excellency . . .' It was the driver. 'Five and counting.'

Koenig Pasha was the one who'd originally demanded five minutes advance warning of when he was due to arrive. And there was a hierarchy of address too. Apparently Ahmed and Hakim got to call him Boss, while the driver was required to be more formal. It was a city of rules, from opaque to transparent. Every city was.

Opening his eyes, Raf sat up and watched the coast become familiar. That café, a swimming hut on stilts and then the beach where . . . a galaxy of stars had skimmed across bare shoulders to be swallowed into darkness between perfect breasts. The hunger brought on by the memory corroded what was left of his pride.

He was no use to Zara as he was, that much Raf understood. No use to anyone; not even himself. Certainly not to the city or to Hani, which was what he mostly cared about these days.

And that meant it was time to change.

'We're here, Boss.'

They were too, passing through heavy wrought-iron gates that had been yanked open and pushed back. Lawns which had been immaculate the last time Raf saw them were crude scars of dark earth, trampled to mud by the same journalists who now rushed the huge Bentley. Already photographers were scuffling for the best shot as a 'copter overhead suddenly dropped height, its specially-adapted gun pod swinging a long lens in Raf's direction.

'Take it down,' Raf ordered.

Ahmed looked doubtful but wound down his side window and started to unsling his machine-gun all at the same time. Instantly the camera crews moved closer, unleashing a firestorm of flashguns and shouted questions.

'Not like that,' Raf said as he slapped down the gun. 'Get on the wire and ground that piece of shit.'

'Sure thing,' said Ahmed, tapping his throat mike. 'What do I tell them, Boss?'

'Tell them that, as of now, airspace over El Iskandryia is a no-fly zone. No overflights, nothing. Tell the pilot if he's not landed in one minute we'll blast him out of the sky. Final warning.'

'No overflights . . . What about the airport?'

'Close it.'

The flash and arc lights didn't bother Raf, he just recalibrated his vision and kept walking towards the blank-eyed cameras. *Reptiles* was what the General called Ishies, that and other things. Watching them watch him reminded Raf of his mother's early films; not the cuddly shit she shot for money, the tooth and claw stuff that made her name. He couldn't remember their titles now, but all those films had blood in them. Red blood on white snow. Zhivago shots, she called them, she was big on those.

'Governor . . .' A thin woman thrust a microphone in his direction and a dozen shouted questions cancelled each other out, leaving only babble.

Raf waited. And when one photographer came in too close, Raf just stared until the man took a step backwards.

'Ashraf Bey . . .'

'Excellency . . .'

The shouts kept coming until everyone finally realized that Raf still hadn't said a word. And then came silence. It stretched out, distorted by the crowd's expectation and broken only by the rhythmic thud of a grounded Sikorsky chopping to a halt on the Corniche behind him. He milked the silence, because that was exactly what the General would have done: and at the point their expectation was about to curdle into anger, Raf pointed at random to three people near the front, snapping out the order . . .

'One, two, three . . . Okay, your name, your station, then the question.'

As it turned out, number one was a good choice. She was American, on staff, not a freelancer, and represented C3N, biggest of the news channels. Or so Raf gathered from the gabble with which Helen Giles introduced herself.

'Excellence . . . Will you agree to hand over Hamad Quitrimala?' She managed to trip over both Raf's honorific and Hamzah's name.

'So that he can be tried in America and jailed?'

She nodded.

'Why would I do that?' Raf asked, his voice clear but cool.

'But PaxForce . . .'

'Are you saying we don't have courts in El Iskandryia?'

That got another babble of questions, which ended the moment Raf chopped at the air for silence. He was beginning to enjoy this, Raf realized with something approaching shock.

'Well?'

The woman's worry lines deepened.

'If Hamzah is to be tried,' said Raf. 'He'll be tried here in Iskandryia. And if the evidence goes against him, he will be found guilty . . . and shot.'

Raf walked through their shocked silence, while behind him Ahmed and Hakim ported their H&K5s and glared at anyone who got too close. As they approached the villa's heavy front door it swung back and Raf found himself staring at the girl he should have married.

Flashguns fire-stormed.

'Excellency.' Zara stepped back to let him pass through into the hall.

'Zara . . .'

'Yes, Your Excellency?' She stood ramrod straight, chin up. Only the rawness that rimmed her grey eyes spoke of privately-spilt tears. And one look into their cold depths was enough to tell him that the tears had been dried by hatred.

'Feeding them was a good idea.'

She said nothing in reply. Just waited, unmoving, for Raf to announce why he was there. Except that they both knew he was there because she'd said she wanted to talk to him – and now it seemed she didn't.

'I'll go,' said Raf and turned for the door, Hakim and Ahmed falling into position behind him. It was strange how quickly one could become used to having a shadow.

'Do you really intend to . . . ?'

'Intend to what?' Raf asked, one hand on the door handle. He knew exactly what Zara was asking but he made her ask it all the same.

'Execute him . . .'

Not if I can help it, but somehow that didn't seem the appropriate thing to say.

'If they extradite him,' said Raf, 'you'll never get your father back. You know that, don't you?'

'At least they won't kill him . . .'

'No,' Raf said, 'they'll just lock him up until he dies. Surround him with guards 24/seven. Dismantle Hamzah Enterprises and break-up the Midas Refinery to pay for court costs and reparations. You think that's what he wants? Your father knew this was coming . . .'

'I'd worked that out,' said Zara, tears starting up in her eyes. 'That's why he wanted you to marry me.'

Raf nodded.

'The Khedive,' her voice was a whisper, 'that meal.'

'He was trying to protect you in the only way he knew how,' said Raf, his smile rueful. 'He even tried sending you back to America, he told me you refused . . .'

Her shoulders beneath his fingers were bony and she wore a scent he didn't recognize and undoubtedly wouldn't have been able to afford, had he wanted to buy her some more. And up close, with her arms tight round his neck and her face buried wetly in his shoulder, Raf could tell that Zara wasn't wearing a bra. It was a shit time to notice something like that, but where Zara was concerned he always seemed to notice things like that at the wrong time. Like now was a really lousy time to realize that he loved her.

Raf pushed Zara away, very slowly, until they stood a hand's breadth apart, facing each other, their eyes locked. There was something she wanted to say.

'Anything you want,' said Zara. 'I'll give you anything you want, if you can save him.'

Chapter Thirty-eight

Sudan

'Safety off,' said the gun.

Lying beside Lieutenant Ka, the ghost of Bec's little sister said nothing. She'd taken to appearing at odd moments when Sarah wasn't around, but now Sarah was gone and so Bec's sister was smiling but silent. In fact, the whole world was silent except for a couple of green parakeets that squawked from a telegraph wire overhead, pretty much right above where he'd set up the thermoflage netting.

Of course, Ka knew what Bec's sister wanted to say. What she'd been saying every night in his dreams, before she did what she once did, stood up from a long-dead fire and shuffled out beyond the big camp's pickets to find a thorn bush. Only it wasn't her bowels she needed to empty but her head, which she did by sucking on a revolver.

They weren't going to reach the source of the river. Nobody was going to turn off the Nile. The war and the river would keep flowing: the river wherever geography took it, the war wherever it wanted to go.

'Distance?'

'Five klicks and closing . . .'

Status and range. That was about all the H&K/cw could ever manage. And Ka really didn't know why the manufacturer had bothered. Ka had a feeling he might have got cross about that before. He was finding it increasingly hard to remember.

The Nile was out of sight, across rock and thorn. Last time he'd seen it, the river had still been grand even though Ka was now south of Omdurman City, where the Bahr el-Abiad and Bahr el-Azrak joined to become the life-giver everybody knew.

Somewhere still further south, the river split again but either Ka hadn't reached that point or he was past it.

The Colonel could have told him, only Ka wouldn't ask. The last time he'd wanted an answer was half an hour before, when something dark had moved in the tall rushes of the river bank. A simple question had elicited a long lecture on the habitat of the marabou stork.

Elaborate canals had once fed the area's rich cotton fields but the narrow canals were mostly cracked open or filled with dirt, their bottoms broken and dry.

Ahead of him, when he'd first arrived, had been mud-brick ruins and beyond those foothills, backdropped by faded and cloud-covered mountains. Now the foothills were at his back and the enemy ahead.

The ruined houses behind Ka were all that remained of a town to which a handful of nineteenth-century Mamelukes had retreated, to live under the protection of Mek Nimr, Leopard King of Shendi, after their defeat by the Albanian warlord Khedive Mohammed.

But Mohammed Ali sent his son Ismail south to subdue Nubia. And in October 1822 Ismail demanded as tribute from Mek Nimr thirty thousand Maria Theresa dollars, six thousand slaves and food for his army, all to be delivered within two days.

And when Mek Nimr protested that the Sudan already faced famine, Ismail struck him in the face. The Leopard King's reply came that evening during banquet, when his followers set fire to Ismail's house, incinerating the prince, who died in the flames rather than be cut down like his fleeing bodyguard.

Word of this reached the Defterdar, Ismail's brother-in-law. First the Defterdar burnt Metemma and Damer and then every village along the Nile from Sennar to Berber. Finally he reached Shendi, where his troops threw down the walls and raped and impaled its inhabitants . . . But he failed to capture Mek Nimr or his family.

Fifty thousand died.

Next the Defterdar chased Mek Nimr south along the Blue

River, torturing everyone he suspected of helping the fleeing king. Men were castrated, the breasts of the women were sliced away and every wound was sealed with molten pitch . . . Ka's uncle had always insisted that things were better in the old days. But to Ka, from what the Colonel said, it just sounded like more of the same.

Ka needed to eat, only that wasn't possible. The food was gone and so was most of his water. Actually, it was all the water, if he didn't count a half litre sloshing round in Sarah's old flask, the one with the cap jammed solid. He'd tried wrenching off the top and, when that failed, had tried punching a hole in the flask with his knife, but the mesh was too hard or he was too weak, one of the two, it didn't matter much which.

'Weapons check . . .'

Whatever. Ka did a count in his head . . . twenty-one grenades, two Heckler&Koch OI/cw, an HK21e machine-gun heavy enough to require a tripod, five assorted side arms plus a dozen boxes of bullets, some of which might actually fit, plus a fat slab of ganja and a Seraphim 4x4, minus gas. Unfortunately, since there was only one of him, most of his riches were wasted.

The other thing he had, of course, were his spectacles and his radio. The radio and the spectacles would only work together, although it had taken Ka days to figure this out. In fact, he wasn't entirely sure he had figured it out; he had a feeling the radio might have told him. Sometimes Colonel Abad spoke through the radio and other times he showed Ka things through the spectacles.

As for the ganja, that was some good shit, as Sergeant Sarah would say. He wore her bone cross now, along with both of Saul's amulets and that bundle of feathers Zac kept pinned to his shirt. Taking Sarah's luck had been theft but he did it to protect her. She shouldn't have been wearing a cross in the first place and Ka didn't know on which side the doctors would be. So he'd taken her luck just to be safe and borrowed her gun because it was so much better than his.

The doctors would make her well again and that was more than the Colonel could manage. Maybe it had been the river water or perhaps too much sun . . . Whatever it was, she'd taken to greeting each new day on her knees, vomiting. And she wouldn't talk to Ka or even look at him, though he gave her all the food and kept every watch himself.

Now she was in a camp and he was here, staring down on a road with ruins behind him, a jagged rock off to one side, sticking up through the earth like a broken shoulder blade, and a long line of enemy trucks directly ahead.

'Approaching,' said a voice in his ear.

'Yeah, the gun's already told me,' Ka said crossly. It wasn't exactly news: the Colonel had first warned him an hour ago that troops were due. He'd also informed Ka that he must stop the troops in their tracks. Those were the Colonel's words . . . Looking at the converted 4x4s and purpose-built half-tracks coming down the road towards him, Ka decided that was meant to be some kind of joke.

'You know what you have to do?'

Yeah, he knew. First he had to fit a feldlafetten to the HK21e, which was its tripod, and then fit a Zeiss scope, after that he had to lift the safety gate or whatever it was called and slot in a new belt of 7.62/51. (What Colonel Abad always called point three-eight.)

The HK21e took either a 20-round mag, which was plain stupid, or a 110-round belt box. Only Ka wasn't planning to use either of those. He had been busy knitting together a couple of belts at a time, until he had a mountain of brass all ready for the HK21e's roller-locked bolt.

They skinned people alive, the enemy. Ate them alive too, if Bec was to be believed. Raped the youngest prisoners to ward off wasting sickness. Mind you, that happened everywhere. But eating human flesh, that was part of a fire ritual: brain for intelligence, heart for courage, liver for cunning. Bec had told them all about it, one night months back round the camp fire.

'Establish . . .'

Yeah, right. Establish a position. Ka shifted the heavy gun across to a gap between two rocks and then crawled back for the long, snaking belts. To win he had to keep under the protection of the thermoflage nets, Colonel Abad was very definite about that. After the belts, Ka unwrapped a HK/cw. This was really two weapons in one and could be broken into an upper section that fired air-burst munitions, colour-coded for convenience, and a lower pull-away section which functioned as a basic light machine-gun.

'Distance,' Ka demanded.

Reading this off from the HK21e would have been easy enough, but Colonel Abad judged distances better. Besides Ka liked to make the Colonel work.

'Half a click,' said the voice in his ear. 'You should be fitting the belts now.'

With trembling fingers, Ka fed the first of the bullets into the HK21e, checking again that the belt could feed in smoothly. A single kink might jam the machine-gun and bring the ambush to an early end. The Colonel would hate that.

Then Ka reached for the HK/cw and slid a mag's worth of 5.56 kinetic into a narrow slot on its underside, following this with a fat clip of bursters. Except, the first burster he fed to the upper slot wasn't a blue meanie, it was orange with a red tip, wizz bang rather than air burst.

'Take out the . . .'

He knew, God knows. The Colonel had already been over this more times than Ka could stand. 'I know. All right?' Ka said flatly.

Absence whispered down the static. A silence as impossibly distant as it was brief. And then Colonel Abad was back, sounding concerned. 'You'll be all right,' he promised. 'You'll come out of this a hero.'

Ka didn't want to be a hero and anyway . . . For a moment Ka considered pointing out that he'd rather be alive. Instead he shrugged and raised the heavy HK/cw.

'Hold it . . .'

He held. And kept holding as ants became beetles and his spectacles adjusted for focus. There were three half-tracks and two converted Seraphim followed by a solid mass that moved across the gravel like a stain. Ka had taken a while to work out that the half-tracks growled along in second gear because the officers inside were afraid, rather than kind. Afraid to be separated from the children who followed after them.

Ka knew which truck to take out first because it was suddenly circled in green. Fat neon hairs bisecting the circle. He pulled the trigger when circle and cross hairs flipped from green to red, like they always did.

The first truck disintegrated in a crunch of fire as flame punched its way through broken windows, and every single one of the remaining trucks ignored standing orders and slammed to a halt.

Idiots.

Doors swung open and uniforms tumbled out, guns unslung. Instinct made Ka duck as bees began to spit above his head but it was not necessary. The enemy's return fire was both sporadic and random, raking into scrub, rocks and trees alike and lifting a flock of parakeets into hysterical green protest.

The officers were mostly reloading when Ka slammed off four rounds of air burst in quick succession, exploding each directly above a vehicle. Flesh shredded from bone and suddenly dying uniforms found themselves forced to their knees. The fifth and final airburst Ka expended on a lieutenant too broken to realize she couldn't swim away to safety across the pock-marked dirt.

Officers down, Ka burnt out a mag's worth of kinetic on a red-circled movement off to his right and then rolled across to the waiting machine-gun. All he was required to do then was pull the trigger and keep it pulled while the HK21e ate up the snake belt in three-bullet bursts.

Green.

Red.

Fire.

He kept the stutter going for as long as the coloured circles kept blossoming, which seemed forever. Maybe the enemy were just crazed by the heat, or maybe the green foothills behind him exerted too strong a pull after the bleakness through which they'd marched. There were no officers left to make anyone *advance and yet, every time Ka cleared a gap it filled instantly, until the mass marching towards him grew smaller and the gaps began to grow.*

Soon there was more gap than mass and finally there was only gap. Not silence, because what had become one with the ground kept quivering and moaning until Ka emptied all of his fat clips of air-burst over its head . . .

Chapter Thirty-nine

24th October

'And then? Raf asked, glancing at a low coffee table. A small police-issue recorder sat in the middle, green light lit and numbers counting down what time was left. They were sat in an elegant club room usually reserved for senior officers. The club room was on the third floor of Champollion Precinct, next door to the general canteen. It had a fountain, leather chairs and bomb-proof windows.

The General, of course, would have put Hamzah in the cells. Raf had decided to do things differently.

'Then?' Hamzah thought about it. 'I walked down the slope towards the first half-track.'

'You were looking for survivors?'

'No,' Hamzah shook his head, 'I was after water. And then.'

'Then what . . . ?'

Hamzah let himself remember. 'The Red Cross came . . .' He nodded towards Hakim, who stood at Raf's shoulder. 'Any chance of someone finding a drink?'

'Check the evidence cupboards,' Raf told his bodyguard. 'Whisky if we've got any.'

What Hakim found was Spanish brandy, confiscated from an illegal club at Maritime Station, and Raf let Hamzah pour himself a drink, a heavy slug of the Carlos V mixed with Canada Dry.

Instead of drinking it straight down, Hamzah sat in his chair and stared into the glass, watching bubbles break for the surface. He looked, despite his age, exactly like Hani when she watched static on her screen. Intent on imposing meaning onto chaos. Maybe, thought Raf, everyone is trying to find a world behind the world. As if that world might somehow make more sense or, at the very least, be more real . . .

'Tell me about when the Red Cross arrived . . .'

'I was searching among the bodies for Sarah.'

Raf looked at him.

'We changed sides now and then,' Hamzah explained. 'We all knew soldiers who'd been raped or mutilated after a battle, but if you could get through that . . .' He picked up his glass and drank from it. 'If you could do that. If you were one of the ones left alive at the end . . . Colonel Abad said the field hospital where I left Sarah had been overrun. So I thought . . .'

'Did you find her?'

'No. Though I thought I had. You know, her skin was . . .' Hamzah opened the collar of his shirt to reveal skin the colour of old leather. 'Darker than this . . . Purple like the night. Bitter like chocolate. It shone.'

He was crying, slow tears that trickled down jowly cheeks and vanished into stubble. There was no self-pity in his eyes and precious little guilt or fear of what might come next, just grief.

'I thought I would recognize her,' said Hamzah. 'But I didn't, I couldn't. Some of the bodies were faceless and broken, but it wasn't that. In the end there were just too many for me to search. When the Red Cross landed their first helicopter I was pulling a Dinka girl from under a pile.'

'What did they say?'

'To me? They said nothing. But then, they didn't know I spoke their language. To each other . . . ? A thin woman turned to a small man and said, *At least one of them survived.*'

Hamzah finished his drink in a single gulp and banged down his glass.

'They gave me vitamins, an injection against retrovirus and water in a silver pouch with a thin straw that stopped me drinking it too fast. After that, they photographed me, took my fingerprints, swabbed my mouth for a DNA sample and air-lifted me to an American aircraft carrier off Massaua. They gave me a Gap tee-shirt, black Levis and a pair of silver Nikes.

All donations from a charity appeal. They offered to replace my radio and cracked dark glasses, but I said I still liked them. Maybe I should have given them up . . .'

Hamzah shrugged.

'Only, I didn't, because that wasn't what Colonel Abad wanted.'

'What the Colonel wanted?' Raf raised his eyebrows. 'What happened to Colonel Abad . . . ?'

'Koenig Pasha stole him.'

That was the point Raf turned off the police-issue recorder, thought about his options for all of thirty seconds and hit *delete/all/confirm.*

It took another brandy and the rest of that Sunday morning for Raf to get from Hamzah a collection of facts that the drink-sodden industrialist thought obvious. Chief among them was that the Arab-speaking, Ottoman-appointed liaison officer aboard the *USS Richmond* had been a certain Major Koenig Bey.

So impressed was he by the boy's tragedy that he insisted on finding a children's home for the boy and personally escorting him to El Iskandryia, cracked radio, spectacles and all.

'And Sarah,' asked Raf, 'you ever find out what happened to her?'

'Oh yes,' said Hamzah. 'She died.'

'You eventually traced her records then?'

'No,' said Hamzah, 'But her daughter found me . . .' he added bleakly. 'Avatar's mother.'

'I thought Avatar was your son?' Raf said, sounding genuinely puzzled.

Hamzah nodded. 'That too.'

Chapter Forty

25th October

Hamzah Effendi came down the Precinct steps into a storm of flashguns. Behind him walked Raf with one hand heavy on the industrialist's shoulder. In that gesture was ownership and authority. That was what the cameras were meant to catch and that was what they reported, streaming the Monday evening press conference live to newsfeeds around the world.

Behind Raf came his bodyguards. And to one side of the front steps, watching them intently, stood Zara, her face a mask of misery.

'*Excellency . . .*'

Raf spotted the questioner in the middle of the scrum and nodded. 'In the red, blonde hair . . .'

'Claude duBois, Television 5. Is Hamzah Effendi under arrest?'

'He has put himself into police custody.'

'Yes, but . . .' The rest of her reply got drowned beneath a wave of competing questions. So Raf waited for the storm to still and then pointed to a man from C3N.

'Nick Richardson, C3N. Do you expect to allow Hamzah's extradition?'

'As you unquestionably know,' said Raf, looking round at the cameras, 'PaxForce has issued a warrant for Hamzah Effendi's arrest on the charge of crimes against humanity . . .' Out of the corner of his eye, Raf spotted the limousine used by Senator Liz slide itself into a parking bay reserved for the Minister of Police.

'Excellency?'

'*Wait.*' One by one the Ishies and journalists turned to see what His Excellency was watching. Which was why most of the newsfeeds ended up featuring the face of Senator Liz Elsing when the first bomb exploded.

It was nothing spectacular, just a rattling crump and a burst of static that drizzled snow across a dozen different camera screens.

'What was that?' The accent was English, the speaker a crook-backed little man with bad hair and worse dress sense.

Raf shrugged. 'Sword of God, I imagine.' His gaze as it took in the journalists was cool, almost amused. He smiled sourly and flicked blond hair back from the shades he wore to keep flashguns at bay. 'This is Iskandryia, bombs happen . . .'

'What about the extradition?' The man from C3N refused to let go of his question.

'What about it . . . ?'

Raf was being watched by the Senator, who was being watched by about a third of the press corps, mostly those from American channels. All of them looked anxious, torn between chasing down the distant bomb and sticking with the news happening in front of them.

'You accept the need for a trial?'

'If a Grand Jury so decides,' said Raf.

'And where would this trial be, *if the Grand Jury so decides . . .*' The speaker was Austrian, the humour heavy.

'Iskandryia,' said Raf. 'However, I will not be a judge.' He paused to let them consider that. 'And the rules of evidence will be those used by The Hague.'

'And the judges?'

'Three,' Raf said. 'French, German and American . . .' He was selecting the nationalities as he went along. Raf wondered if any of them realized that. And if the Grand Jury did decide Hamzah had a case to answer, then they'd automatically become his judges. Though Raf didn't think he'd mention that fact just then.

'Excuse me . . .' Raf touched his earbead and took a call, nodding rapidly. 'I have to go,' he told the crowd. 'My men have found a second bomb outside a children's home in Kharmous.'

Pushing Hamzah slightly, Raf steered the industrialist towards the waiting Bentley and saw the man from C3N materialize beside him, persistent as a shadow.

'Will you be acting as prosecutor?'

Raf turned back and smiled in admiration. There was a lot to recommend sheer bloody-mindedness when it came to a job. 'No,' he said. 'One of the judges will be chosen as prosecuting judge. And I won't be acting for the defence either . . . She will.' Raf jerked his thumb backwards and heard Zara gasp.

Which was around the point the second EMF bomb exploded, followed by a third and a fourth, so those watching newsfeeds in other countries never knew if Zara's shock was at being named defender or the fact that El Iskandryia had begun to shut down around her.

'Boss.' Bodyguards closed in on both sides, obviously anxious but still functioning. 'We've got to get you back inside.'

Overhead, bright stars blossomed between clouds as the lights of the city began to flicker, its sodium halo fading from orange through palest yellow to perfect night. Somewhere far distant a dog began to bark.

Chapter Forty-one

26th October

'I shouldn't be here,' said Zara, 'you know that . . .'

Here was Raf's bedroom, with its domed roof and high windows, naked babies staring down from the painted ceiling and the air rich with the scent of orchids. A newly-cut bunch stood in a Lalique vase beside the bed. Where Khartoum had found tiger orchids, Raf couldn't begin to imagine. A smaller vase was thick with lilies and a silver bowl on his glass-topped dressing table contained pot pourri. Neither flowers nor bowl had been there when they finally fell asleep.

But Raf's smile was at the memory of warm skin and the smell of lapsang suchong, mixed with something citrus, labelled for an American/Japanese designer and bottled in Frankfurt. The tiny scent flask was on his dressing table along with the rest of Zara's cosmetics. And, actually, that hadn't been there either . . .

'Maybe I'm the one who should be somewhere else,' said Raf and Zara smiled, rolling over with a linen sheet tucked around her. The night before she'd had darkness to hide behind and only a candle flame to let them see each other. Now the sun streamed in through high windows, turning the white marble floor to a sheet of glistening ice, and the sea breeze tasted of iodine. Outside, the whole city was silent, with Rue Riyad Pasha devoid of cars. Or at least of cars that moved.

'Let it go,' said Raf, giving the sheet a small tug.

Zara shook her head.

'Please,' he said and so she did, at least partly. Letting him unwrap her shoulders to reveal full breasts and the start of a soft stomach. Her skin was honey, her nipples dark walnut.

The rest she kept hidden, one hand holding her modesty in place.

'Marry me,' Raf said.

She pulled a face and grinned, but her smile died the second she realized Raf's suggestion was serious. 'Last night you wanted to have me arrested.'

'That was last night.'

Zara nodded. 'Yeah,' she said, 'that makes sense.'

It did too, at least to him. To be honest, Raf didn't know the reason he'd shot the question. Being institutionalized did that to you. Half the time you didn't really know the reason for most things. Time was, as the fox would say . . . time was he could blame what he did on the fox. Now he had no one to blame but himself and he was, if not white-knuckle sober then, at the very least, white-knuckle sane. Some time or other, when he was feeling braver, he'd try to explain that to Zara.

Try to explain it and fail, most probably, but he'd still try. This too was coded into that famous 8,000-line guarantee.

'What will happen to my father . . .'

'You'll marry me if I get him off?'

'Is that your price?'

Raf sighed. 'Is it yours?'

'No,' Zara said shakily. 'I just need to know. Will he be executed?' She would have cried, except she was all cried out. The first part of last night she'd spent wrapped tight in Raf's arms, sometimes angry and occasionally scared, but mostly just crying silently into his shoulder. The second part . . . For all that nothing really happened, that was somewhere they'd both need to go.

'Look,' said Raf, 'he may actually be innocent.'

Zara looked at him. 'I can't stand up there and defend him you know . . .'

'It's your choice,' Raf said. Meaning that it wasn't, not really.

'No,' Zara sat up, taking the sheet with her. 'You're missing the point. I refuse to defend him if he won't defend himself.'

Raf understood how she felt. Her father had killed 183 people, all but 12 of them children. What Hamzah Effendi did was, almost literally, indefensible. And yet . . . Sat beside her, in a sun-lit bedroom thick with the scent of hot-house flowers, Raf told Zara the story as Hamzah had told it to him, about Ka, Sarah and the Colonel . . .

The evening before had begun very differently. In the light of an emergency lamp, seven people had watched Zara hit Raf and only one, a female clerk from the technical section, had made any move to stop Zara from taking a second shot. Which told Raf something he didn't like about Hakim, Ahmed and the rest of his officers.

Although maybe such a reaction was inevitable in a city where crimes by or against women got dealt with by a separate force. And if any of them really thought women were incapable of being deeply dangerous, they should meet Hu San, leader of Seattle's Five Winds Society. Compared to her, Iskandryia's Dons were amateurs, which they mostly were. The only real professional among them was the man Raf had just arrested, and that was for something else.

'*You poisonous . . .*'

Raf had watched Zara fail to find the right word.

'*Putain de merde?*' he suggested.

She didn't even pause. 'How could you?'

'Arrest him? Easily, I just pulled out a card and read the words.' Which wasn't true because, for a start, Raf didn't carry a Miranda card and secondly, he had uniforms to do that shit, but he was playing to an audience and she knew it. That was one of the things making her so angry.

'You . . . I thought you liked him.'

Better than me, that was the subtext, or maybe not. Perhaps he was misreading the feeling that hung sour as ghost's breath in the air between them. Chances were, she was just scared.

Raf sighed and cleared his head of the Huntsville psychotrash that flooded it every time he tried to think about what he felt.

Other people's feeling he could do. His own . . . He'd been analysed so many times by Dr Millbank that he could no longer distinguish what was emotionally real from what he'd been told were his feelings. Which was weird because, and the fox always used to agree with this, half the time Raf was sure he felt nothing at all.

'Are you listening to me?' That was the point at which Zara pushed her face in close.

No, thought Raf, *not really*. And before he could stop himself, he leant forward and kissed her, very lightly.

He apologized on the drive back to the governor's mansion. A drive so short that he and Zara could have walked it in the time it took Hakim and Ahmed to safety-check the Bentley.

Of course, before he apologized he had to get his breath back.

'Columbia,' she told him. 'Power-punching exercises.'

She'd been reluctant to get into the Bentley until Raf explained that her alternative was to wait for a horse-drawn calèche to take her out to Villa Hamzah to be with her mother. Whatever her decision, Hamzah Effendi would remain under guard at the precinct.

Hakim and Ahmed he'd made walk back to the gubernatorial mansion. Punishment for grinning when she punched him in the stomach.

'Why all the play acting?'

'Because that's my job,' said Raf. 'And the best way to fake something, is to pretend to be what you already are . . .' Catching Zara's appalled glance, he shrugged and yanked at the wheel, suddenly dragging the Bentley round a bend into a side street. The car had no power steering, that was its beauty and Raf strongly suspected the absence was intentional.

He wouldn't put it past Koenig Pasha to drive a telemetrics-free vehicle precisely *because* it lacked assisted steering, voice-activated starting, electronic locks or air-conditioning, not to mention adaptive cruise control. In fact, the only bit of the Bentley not working was a now-defunct, self-powered GPS unit bolted to the dashboard. Even the engine could be hand-cranked, though it was hard to know if that was special or had once come as standard.

The point was, while almost every other vehicle in the city had seen its electronics go belly up in the blasts, the governor's Bentley still functioned. Which was how Raf ended up with a dusty square to himself. And it was obvious from the way pedestrians turned to watch the unlit Bentley slide slowly round Place al-Mansur, its pennant fluttering in the darkness, that they expected no less.

The city had a confidence in its new governor that Raf had never had in himself, that no one on the right side of sanity could ever have.

'Remember that lunch?' Raf asked. 'When we met officially? Your father told me you never cried.'

'That was then,' said Zara crossly. 'Things change.'

'Either that, or we change them,' Raf replied. 'Sometimes surviving is all it takes.'

'And that's what you do, is it? Survive . . .'

Raf nodded.

Sitting there beside him, her hands clasped tight between stockinged knees and her shoulders hunched forward like a frightened child, Zara took a deep breath and slowly willed herself back under control as a familiar street slipped by and the dark gateposts of the mansion came forward to meet her.

The fact Raf was right didn't make her like him any more.

'I took a detour,' Raf told Hakim, seeing him stood by the gate, and with that Raf edged the Bentley into a courtyard lit by coal-filled oil drums.

'The master arrives . . .' Khartoum was no longer dressed in his ornate livery. Instead, the old man wore a pale grey souf so long its rough edges dragged on damp cobbles. Around him stood soldiers, plus a thin clerk in a flapping suit. The old man looked amused.

'Your office is worried.' The Sufi practically had to push the clerk towards the car window. 'Tell him then.'

'Excellency . . . Ambassador Graf von Bismarck demands an immediate audience.'

Did he now?

'And the one from Paris?'

The man nodded.

'London, Washington, Vienna?'

A quick nod greeted each capital in its turn.

'And Stambul?'

'The red phone . . .' The man was embarrassed. 'It rang, Excellency, but when I finally answered it the line was dead. Perhaps the main exchange . . .'

'It's been fried,' said Raf. 'Along with the relay stations. Please tell the Graf that I'll see him for ten minutes, an hour from now, in the council chamber.'

'Your Excellency . . . The ambassador was hoping . . .'

'That I'd go there. Too bad.' Raf watched the clerk debate with himself which it would be most dangerous to offend, the Germans or Iskandryia's new governor. His decision quickly became clear when the man snapped off a smart salute and stepped back from the car.

'You scare them, don't you?' Zara's smile was thin.

'It's the aftertaste of the General.'

Zara shook her head. 'It's you,' she said. 'Take a good look at yourself in the mirror.'

'I don't do mirrors,' said Raf.

'That's what I mean.'

There didn't seem to be much to say after that so, once Khartoum had opened Raf's door, Raf walked round to the other side of the car and opened the door for Zara.

'And I wish you'd stop that,' Zara said with a scowl. 'All this heel-clicking shit.' Her scowl lasted until she reached the mansion's steps, at which point Hani came bundling out of the big front door.

'Zara!'

'Hello honey.'

Hani grinned. 'How are you?' she added as an afterthought; visibly remembering her manners.

'Okay, I suppose. And you?'

'Terrific.' Hani suddenly opened both arms to embrace the ink-black sky. 'Someone's killed the lights. All of them. You can see what's happened better from the roof.' Hani turned to go, then swung back, remembering something. 'You and I,' said the child, looking serious. 'We need to talk . . .'

Chapter Forty-two

25th October

'You know Colonel Abad stole someone else's face?'

Zara didn't.

'On the badges,' said Hani. 'It's not him. The face belongs to someone who died years and years ago. You know what that means? It means he kept himself to himself, or people would have noticed he wasn't the same as his picture . . .'

Hani nodded. 'I'm right, aren't I?' She looked at the older girl, then frowned. 'Don't you like clues?'

Zara stared round at the governor's study, her face doubtful. Official papers were piled in untidy heaps, encyclopedias, old history books, ancient maps of the Sudan. A book case along one wall had half the volumes pulled out and dumped on the floor. It looked like a whirlwind had hit the place. And the whirlwind was about four paces away, laying a fire and asking riddles.

'Honey, we really shouldn't be in here.'

'You *want* to save your father?'

Did she . . . ? Zara stared at the child, throat tight.

'Thought so.' Hani walked over to Zara, gave her a quick hug and went back to work, crunching old financial reports into tight balls and pushing them under kindling.

'Clues,' Hani said firmly, putting a match to a computer printout. 'Crosswords, logic puzzles, number grids, those stupid MENSA things in the papers . . . Do you like them?'

'Sometimes.'

Hani sighed. It was late. Raf was still furious about something, and Zara was so busy trying not to get upset in front of her that she wasn't really listening to a thing Hani said. Even

Khartoum was useless. She'd tried to talk to him but he'd just excused himself, then come back later with matches and a jug of water from the kitchens.

Which was less than no help.

It was hard being the only one who could think properly. Especially if you were nine. 'In a moment,' said Hani, 'I'll make you some cocoa.' She blew on the flames until the kindling caught, added a couple of wooden candleholders from the mantelpiece and all the pencils from the General's desk tidy.

Uncle Ashraf's desk tidy, Hani corrected herself. Taking a half-eaten bar of Fry's chocolate from her pocket – it was possible for a human to last a week on a single bar, she'd read it in some magazine – Hani broke cubes off the chocolate and dropped five or six into the water jug. She should probably have heated the water first, she realized, looking at the lumps lying there at the bottom.

Still, it was a bit late to decide that now. Pushing the copper jug into the middle of the flames, Hani sucked her fingers where they'd got singed and went back to the real problem.

'Did you bring your weird picture?'

'Did I . . . ?' Zara was shocked. 'Honey, how did you know about that?'

'It must have been sent to you,' Hani said firmly. 'I've asked everyone else. The General sent you something from Dante's *Purgatorio* . . . A Doré engraving. Am I right?'

Hani pulled a yellowing page from her jeans pocket and smoothed it out on the desk. 'He sent this one to Raf. It's from *Inferno*.'

The engraving showed the man with his chest sliced open. His hands gripping the edges of the wound, not to close it but to pull it apart. From her other pocket, she extracted what Zara thought was a photocopy but then realized was a printout of a low-rez scan. The last time she'd seen the bare-breasted angel had been in her father's study. That time, he'd had a revolver resting on top of it.

'I couldn't get the original,' said Hani, 'because that's locked away. But Uncle Ashraf had this copy on computer in an evidence file. When he still had a working computer,' she added thoughtfully.

'It was the General who sent this to my father?'

'That's Koenig Pasha's writing,' said Hani, turning over the printout to show Zara the handwriting script on the other side. 'So I guess so . . . In Raf's file it says Effendi asked the General for help.'

'For help!' Zara's laugh was hollow. 'How do we know that's the General's writing?'

Hani shrugged. 'I had a look at his diary,' she said, pulling a notebook from a desk drawer and handing it to Zara, who shook her head and gave it straight back.

'You read his diary?'

'No. It's in German,' said Hani. 'I don't know German . . .'

Zara did, but she didn't mention that. This was where the conversation paused, while Hani kicked off one silver Nike, pulled off the sock underneath and used it as an oven-glove to lift the copper jug from the fire. The jug she put on the hearth to cool and the sock got tossed in the fire. It had started to smoulder anyway. When they drank the cocoa, it tasted more of water than chocolate, but neither Zara nor Hani mentioned the fact.

'You got a Doré engraving from the General?'

Zara shook her head, so Hani started again.

'You got an engraving?'

Zara nodded.

'Are you sure the General didn't give it to you?'

'It was sent by fax,' said Zara. 'from the *SS Jannah*.'

'Jannah,' said Hani. 'What does that mean?'

'It means garden,' Zara said, sounding puzzled. Hani had to know that.

'Garden.' Hani wrote the word in pen on a clean piece of paper. 'So who do you think sent the picture?' She sounded like Raf, Zara realized, at his most serious.

Zara blushed. 'I thought it was the Khedive . . . But it could have been Avatar. I let him go in my place.' Which couldn't have been popular with His Highness, except that the boy was much too polite ever to mention that fact.

'Have you got the engraving?'

Zara nodded.

'Can I have a look?' Hani asked, once it became obvious that Zara intended to leave it at that. 'It would be useful . . .'

'It's . . .' Zara hunted for the right word. 'Very rude.'

'So's the angel,' said Hani, nodding to the bare-breasted woman with wings and a discreet drape of cloth across her broad, Victorian hips.

'This is ruder,' Zara said, but she went to get the picture anyway . . .

'Mmm,' said Hani. She did her best to sound grown up, but the slight widening of her eyes and a growing grin gave away her shock. 'She's a spider.'

'That's right.'

'A woman spider, bent over backwards . . .' Hani flipped to the sheet underneath, nodding to herself; it showed the back, on which the General had written a brief note, plus the word *Judecca*.

Next Hani re-checked the titles of the books from which the pictures had been ripped.

'*Paradiso, Purgatorio, Inferno* . . .' The words went down on her sheet of paper one under the other. As an afterthought, Hani numbered them. She'd already found a book called *Inferno* on the shelves by the door. Sure enough, it had the fly-leaf ripped out. Hani was as certain as anything that she'd also find vandalized books called *Paradiso* and *Purgatorio*, once she bothered to check.

'*Only here will you find peace.*' That was what the General had written on the back of the first picture. Paradise. Only here will you . . . It made sense. Hani copied the words onto her bit of paper and numbered it.

Taking Zara's spider woman, she turned the weird picture over and wrote down '*Welcome to limbo*'. Having numbered this to match *Purgatorio*, she put '*At its centre hell is not hot*' directly underneath and numbered that as well.

Apollyon, Judecca and *Cocytus* came last.

She thought of drawing different coloured lines to link the General's comments to the names of the books, but it didn't seem necessary. Instead, she drew a big exclamation mark under the list.

'Do you actually know what any of this means?' asked Zara.

'Not yet,' Hani admitted. 'But I'll let you know when I do.' Pushing the paper to one side, Hani scraped back her chair and tiptoed to the door, which she opened a fraction. Sudanese soldiers were coming and going in the hall. Mostly they seemed to be Raf's guard. 'The German's arriving,' she told Zara. 'He looks cross.'

Zara peered over Hani's shoulder at the young German ambassador. 'No,' she said, 'what he looks is nervous . . .' Just then, Khartoum came into the hall and bowed to the visitor, ushering him through an open door. 'That's not the audience chamber,' said Zara.

'No,' said Hani, 'it's a waiting room. *Now* he'll look cross.'

Chapter Forty-three

25th October

'Coffee,' Raf suggested and the German youth in front of him winced; as Raf suspected he might. According to his file, the ambassador from Berlin loathed the stuff.

'In Iskandryia it's traditional,' said Raf.

'Isn't everything?' The ambassador's voice was resigned. According to Koenig Pasha's notes His Excellency Graf von Bismarck was nineteen. He looked younger, fourteen going on twelve, with the faintest trace of a blond moustache and long hair that flopped over one eye. The unflopped eye, startlingly blue, stared nervously at Raf whenever the ambassador thought Raf wasn't looking.

Iskandryia was one of the most career-destroying posts on offer, particularly for someone who hated intrigue and coffee. And from what Raf could gather, Ernst von Bismarck had taken it only because his other alternative was marriage to some Schleswig-Holstein. It seemed the Graf wasn't the marrying type.

'If not coffee,' said Raf, voice suddenly sympathetic, 'then what?'

'Orange juice . . . If that's possible.'

A clap of Raf's hands brought not Khartoum but Hani. She'd changed from jeans into a dress at least one size too big. Unfortunately, she'd retained the silver Nike trainers.

'I'm Hani al-Mansur,' Hani announced, thrusting her hand at the startled ambassador. 'He's my uncle.'

'Where's . . . ?' Raf began.

'Doing something,' said Hani firmly. 'Whatever you want – I'll get it.'

When the orange juice arrived it came on a tray complete with a silver bowl of pistachios, soft skinned and bright green on the inside, two small brass pipes and a fingertip of sticky resin.

The German ambassador and Raf waited while Hani withdrew. Only then did Raf notice a note folded neatly on the tray under his glass.

'A sweet child,' said the Graf.

Raf re-read Hani's scrawl, nodded doubtfully and pushed the note deep into his pocket. 'Endlessly surprising,' he said and changed the subject. 'You demanded a meeting . . . ?'

It seemed preposterous to call what was happening an audience, so Raf didn't.

'Berlin wants . . .'

'I'm sure it does,' said Raf. 'But first explain why your intelligence service has been waging war against Hamzah Effendi.' He stared at the boy, who put down his glass and went deep red.

Personally, Raf lacked the capacity for visible embarrassment, but then he'd had a lung deflated when he was six and a very minor blood-supply nerve to his face snipped where it ran between his second and third ribs. The surgeon went after the nerve through a tiny incision in his armpit.

'They haven't . . .'

'Are you telling me the man pulled out of Lake Mareotis wasn't *Thiergarten* . . . ?'

'You don't know that he killed the first girl,' Ernst von B said hotly. 'Whatever you've been saying.'

'What about the attack on the Casino Quitrimala?' said Raf. 'Are you telling me the *Thiergarten* didn't organize that?'

'That had nothing to do with us.'

'And I'm supposed to believe this?'

'You have my word,' Graf von Bismarck said stiffly. He looked as if he was getting ready to cry.

'But the man who died in the fire *was* German?'

The nod was slight enough to be almost invisible.

'Okay,' said Raf. 'Just suppose some of your men have been turned . . . Who corrupted them?'

Needless to say, the Graf had no idea, although he immediately suggested Paris because Berlin always blamed Paris for everything.

'And the bomb?'

'My intelligence officers suggest the mujahadeen.' Von Bismarck looked hesitant. 'But I'm not convinced the rebels have that level of sophistication.'

Raf reached behind his chair for a cardboard box and pulled out a thin tube the length of his arm, attached to a small wooden base. 'Sophisticated it's not,' he said, voice grim. 'Effective, yes. You can buy most of the components from the nearest souk.'

Circling the thin tube he held, but not touching it, was a spiral of bare copper wire, with a metal clothes hanger looped at the top, like a makeshift replacement for a vandalized car aerial.

The object looked like something from sculpture 101 at St Mark's.

'Detonator,' said Raf, pointing to a cigarette-sized tube rammed into the underside of the weird exhibit. Copper wire, aluminium stuffed with cheap explosive, aerial loop, battery pack.

'To create a magnetic field between copper coil and tube,' Raf added, when the German ambassador looked blank. He didn't mention that he'd spent the last few minutes before the Graf arrived checking a pencil-sketched schematic for a flux-generator, as e-bombs were apparently called.

'Detonate the charge,' said Raf.

'. . . and the whole thing blows up.' Graf von Bismarck finished the sentence for him.

'You got it.' Raf took a brass pipe from the tray and gave it to the young German, who absent-mindedly inhaled.

'As it blows,' said Raf, 'the blast rips up the tube at 6,000 metres a second or something, the exploding tube flares out to touch the wire and power gets diverted into the undamaged coil ahead . . .'

Absolute incomprehension closed down the Graf's boyish face.

'You didn't do physics, did you?'

The German shook his head. 'It wasn't an option. I took philosophy, politics and history at Heidelberg.'

Yeah, exactly as recorded in Koenig Pasha's file.

'It works like this,' said Raf patiently. 'The magnetic force gets squeezed as the tube behind it explodes. That creates a huge rise in current in the coil ahead. When the current finally hits the loop antenna it sprays out a *terawatt* of electromagnetic energy . . . From detonation to destruction takes less than . . .'

He clicked his fingers. 'A hundredth of that, probably less. There were seven of these spread across the city . . . Six went off.'

'But the worst is now over . . .'

'I wish,' said Raf, meaning it. 'The worst is only just beginning.'

'Then even more reason . . .' The Graf put down his little pipe. 'This trial . . .' He stopped and pursed his lips. 'The thing is,' he said, 'Berlin are . . .' The Graf shrugged and reached again for the pipe. 'My problem is . . .'

'Berlin are worried,' said Raf. 'Who wouldn't be?' He picked up his own pipe but didn't actually inhale, merely watched thin strands of pungent smoke spiral away into what the Graf saw as darkness and Raf knew to be a different density of light.

By now Astolphe de St Cloud, France's ambassador to El Iskandryia, would have heard that Ashraf Bey was locked in a meeting with the ambassador from Berlin and would be at the mansion's gates demanding admittance. Raf was depending on it.

'The trial . . . ?' Raf prodded gently.

'We want it in Berlin,' said the Graf.

'No,' Raf shook his head, 'Absolutely impossible.'

'You misunderstand,' the Graf said, sounding nervous. 'We demand it be held in Berlin.'

'As I said, impossible.'

Something flitted across the young man's face that looked to Raf remarkably like relief. 'We will be making an official protest . . .'

'I'm sure you will,' said Raf gently. 'But the trial will be held in Iskandryia. Not in The Hague or Paris or Berlin. And I'm relying on you to be a judge . . . The court will be calling Jean René . . .'

Ernst von Bismarck nodded knowledgeably.

'The photographer who filmed the aftermath of the massacre,' Raf explained. 'I should also inform you,' he added, pulling Hani's scribbled note from his pocket, 'that my intelligence officers tell me Hamzah Effendi may call a character witness from his own brigade.'

'Impossible,' the Graf said. 'Every one of them died except Hamzah. I've read the report.'

'If that's true,' said Raf with a smile, 'it should make for an interesting trial.'

The Graf frowned. 'I will inform Berlin of the situation.'

'How?' Raf asked and watched the Graf realize that doing so would be less simple than he'd imagined. 'How will you go about informing Berlin?'

'By letter. There's a passenger service to Syracuse . . .'

'If it runs.'

Both ferries would run, Raf already knew that, because one of the first things he'd done was send Hakim to Maritime Station to find out which of the regular boats had been caught in the blast and which, if any, had been lucky enough to be at sea.

They were currently two Soviet liners without electricity, a worthless aircraft carrier, and half a dozen expensive yachts that now needed a partial refit. The people who owned those could afford the damage. It was worse for the fishing boats. Almost all of those had lost their navigation systems and sonar. They also had engines that now wouldn't start.

'Oh,' said Raf, 'if you do write, be sure to tell Berlin that I'm closing the city. A total curfew is being imposed. Other than mine, all cars are banned, assuming any still work. No one comes in or leaves without my written permission . . . My hand-written permission,' he added grimly. 'Except for those travelling under a diplomatic passport or a *carte blanche*, obviously enough. And the accredited press. They can come in. They can even bring cameras. Leaving, of course, is another matter.'

'How long . . . ?'

'Until we catch the bombers.' Raf rose from his chair, waited until the Graf realized his meeting was over and then walked the young German to the chamber door.

'I have a city in meltdown,' he told the boy, 'a natural gas plant that can't pump natural gas, a petroleum refinery that isn't refining crude, no electricity, no telephones. The few computers that still work are dying by the minute. Most cars don't run, garages can't dispense gas . . . You know what that means? No working hospitals, no schools. Think about it.'

Raf ushered the Graf through the hall and out into the rain. Goodbyes said, he went back into the darkened chamber and listened.

'You can come out now,' he said.

Very slowly, Zara appeared. 'You knew I was here.' It was half question, half statement.

'I heard you.'

'Across that distance?' She stared in disbelief from where she stood to where Raf and von Bismarck had been sat.

'I can hear the heartbeat of a bat,' he told her simply, 'and see a hunting cat across Zaghloul Square at the dead of night. Everything that has ever happened to me I remember. Everything . . .'

I can't die, he added in his head. *I can only be killed.* But he kept those words where they belonged because her smile was already gone, shocked out of being by his honesty, her shock coloured round the edges with unease, even fright.

'You mean it, don't you?' said Zara.

Did he? Raf nodded. 'Yes,' he said. 'I'm afraid I do.' He didn't mention that he could smell expensive scent oxidizing on the inside of her wrist, an overlay of white willow extract from her shampoo and something underneath all that, much more animal.

'You remember everything?' Zara asked in disbelief.

'Exactly as it happened.' Raf stopped opposite the girl and caught the point at which her eyes widened and she remembered that night they'd spent on her father's boat. Her mouth had tasted of olives and her breasts had rested heavy in his hands, salt with the memory of a wine-dark sea and blood from where she'd bitten his lip.

There had been more, but not much, not as much as he wanted. Now things between them were broken and the memory was what he had left.

'I'd better get off to bed,' said Raf.

'What about me?'

'Choose a room, use it. Call it protective custody,' Raf suggested. 'Find Khartoum,' he added when Zara looked blank. 'Tell him to find you something or else share Hani's room. She'd like that . . .' Raf paused, took a deep breath. 'Alternatively, there's always mine . . .'

'What about seeing the French ambassador?' Zara asked. Which wasn't exactly what Raf expected her to say.

'What about him?'

'Isn't he waiting . . . ?'

'Undoubtedly.' Raf shrugged. 'I don't want to see the man,' he said. 'And besides, St Cloud hired a man to have me killed.'

Raf smiled at her surprise.

'The night I first arrived,' he said. 'Someone tried to knife me . . . I told Felix. It was one of the things the fat man was investigating when he died . . .'

'What happened to the someone?'

'He attacked me, so I killed him.'

'And that's the scar?' Zara said when Raf had finished hanging his jacket in an old rosewood cupboard. In her hand was a wine glass, still half-full of white Rioja. It was Raf's glass. Her own was long since empty.

She pointed to a seam visible along his wrist.

'No,' said Raf, pulling off his shirt. 'This is the scar.' He traced a line across his ribs with one finger and felt the faintest echo of hardened tissue. 'It was only a flesh wound, nothing more . . .'

'What?' he asked when Zara smiled, a little sadly.

The room was lit by a single candle that sat, fat and pale in a dish turned from a single section of monkey puzzle, the ancient wood so thin that the candle's dancing flame made it translucent. The monkey-puzzle dish sat on an oak table beside a metal bed so old that its horse-hair mattress rested on wire mesh. Since the room Raf had chosen was originally meant for the General's personal use, the choice of bed undoubtedly held some special significance.

Raf had selected the room because Hani had one next door. A small dark space that might once have been a dressing room to this, though the entrance between rooms had been bricked up long enough for the Persian wallpaper that covered it to have faded to faint horsemen who hunted in shadow.

'Blow out the candle.'

'I can see in the dark,' Raf warned Zara.

'Maybe,' she said, 'but I can't.' And so Raf blew out the single candle and the room's cool air flooded with acrid smoke.

'How?' Zara demanded suddenly. 'How do you see in the dark?'

'My eyes adjust . . .' Raf thought about it. 'No,' he said, 'I adjust my eyes. There's a difference.'

'Then don't.'

Raf looked at her.

'Stay blind.'

'If that's what you want.' The last thing Raf saw before he tuned the room into darkness was Zara unbuttoning the front of her short dress. She wore no bra and her body was as perfect as his memory of it.

He met her clumsily in space that waited between them, neither one quite certain of where the other stood in the darkness. Zara felt his hands reach up to grip her naked shoulders and he felt her fingers brush against his face. And this time their kiss was slower, much less frenzied than that time when they were drunk and tired and on her father's boat.

Zara's breath tasted of wine and her throat of salt. He got colours and memories with each kiss, though they might have been imagined. Putting both hands around her, Raf followed her spine with his fingers, pausing only when he reached the silk of her thong.

He smiled.

'No.' The command was simple, far simpler than the mix of emotions encoded in her suddenly-breaking voice. Sheer nervousness Raf could have understood. His own body was almost vibrating with tension. And fear of what might come next was possible. As was worry that she'd let things get this far . . .

But this was anger.

Raf just wasn't sure it was directed at him.

He stepped back just enough to put a slight distance between them. 'You okay?'

Zara nodded, realized Raf couldn't see and so leant her head against his neck and nodded again, feeling his answering smile. There was a neat scar under his jaw, the one half the city assumed was *RenSchmiss*. And another on his shoulder, so ugly that no one in their right mind could have assumed it resulted from a formal duel.

'Seattle . . . ?' Zara asked, running her fingers across ridged skin. Something else he didn't talk about, the bombing of the Consulate in Seattle.

'A fox cub,' said Raf lightly, 'when I was a child.' He touched her face and let his hands rest there before dropping them to cup breasts that were full and high, with nipples that hardened beneath his touch. They both shivered, but he did so first.

'You like?' Zara's voice was low, almost mocking.

In answer, Raf shifted one hand to the back of her head, feeling her lips silence and her mouth open wider.

'Of course I like.' His right hand found a pressure point between her third and fourth vertebrae and he pushed, so that her chin came up and her neck exposed itself. Her pulse beneath his lips was as loud as a bass loop.

Somewhere, in the hollow where the fox should have been, Raf knew this was merely an act of mutual empathy, the grown-up equivalent of the intimate attunement of infant to mother, mere parasympathetic arousal. Everything that wasn't the fox-shaped void didn't mind about that. It welcomed the night outside and the faint pricks of light glimpsed through a badly-drawn curtain. And it bathed in the sound of gulls riding salt winds over a city struck into near darkness for the first time in centuries.

'Open the curtains and shutters,' demanded Zara suddenly. 'It'll let in the stars.'

'That much I can cope with,' she said in a voice as bitter sweet as black chocolate. 'Probably . . .'

When Raf turned round from pulling back the double shutters which usually closed off each of the room's five, floor-to-ceiling windows, Zara was in bed, safely tucked under a linen sheet.

The first thing she said when he joined her there was, 'I won't have sex with you . . .'

'So how old were you when it happened?'

'Seven, maybe eight . . . At an age you don't really realize what's being done. Maybe that helps.' Zara sounded doubtful, like she was trying to convince herself.

Raf's answer was non-committal.

'You know,' Zara added, 'I forgot all about it for years. I just thought it was normal.'

'What changed?'

She was lying beside Raf in the darkness with a late October wind rattling the sash windows and a quilt pulled up so tight around her it almost hid her face. One of Raf's arms held her shoulder as she lay on her side, facing him, and when she spoke it was in a monotone so soft and so quiet that Raf doubted if anyone but him could have heard even half of what she said.

Sometimes she spoke and sometimes there was silence. When the silence grew too strong, Raf asked another question. Zara had been talking for hours, her voice never raised nor showing any emotion Raf could recognize. Except its very emptiness told Raf more than her answers to half a dozen of his questions.

Zara had, so far as he could tell, long since forgotten he was there. He didn't know who she thought he was . . . Maybe some part of herself.

'What changed? Raf asked again.

'Schools changed. My mother refused but I kept insisting.

And eventually Dad agreed I could go to the American High. They did a medical.'

'With a male doctor?'

'Of course not! The nurse was French. Probably not much more than five or six years older than me. She did a blood test. Asked for a sample of urine. Cut a strand of my hair and took a swab from my mouth . . . Drugs and DNA profile,' Zara added, as if Raf couldn't work that out for himself.

'She listened to my heart and lungs, took my blood pressure and did a quick CAT scan with a hand-held. Then she asked about periods. Only I didn't know what those were, so she explained and I said they hadn't started. Which was when she asked me to get back on the couch.'

Zara sighed.

'I don't think she'd ever seen a female circumcision before. When she came back she had Sister Angelica, our school doctor, in tow. She was maybe thirty-five, though she seemed much older to me.' Zara spoke as if this had all happened decades earlier, rather than just five years before. 'It was the first time I heard a woman swear . . .

'Apparently, because there were now laws against female circumcision, Sister Angelica thought it didn't happen.'

'What did she do?'

Zara's laugh was a bitter bark. 'After she'd slammed the phone down on my mother, she went to see my father at his office. It's probably the only time he's stood there, utterly speechless while a woman shouted at him.'

'And then?'

Silence was Zara's answer. An absence which stretched so thin that Raf finally decided Zara must have fallen asleep, but he was wrong. She was busy remembering the bits she didn't usually allow herself to remember.

'They cut the stitches,' she announced flatly. 'Sister Angelica did it herself. There were five in total, each separate, transparent and beautifully neat, pulling together the sides of my . . .'

Zara stopped, starting up again, minutes later, as if she'd never paused.

'Sister Angelica cleaned the area where the inner labia should have been and removed an oval of surgical plastic designed to create enough space for urination . . . It had been done in a hospital, you see. A good hospital with qualified doctors and a resident anaesthetist. And that was the problem. Because if it had been done by a jobbing midwife with a piece of broken glass in a backroom then I'd have struggled, which would have made it hard to cut away as much as my mother wanted.

'You know what Sister Angelica did after that? She bought me a German porn mag . . .'

'She . . .'

'I knew it was German because I'd started learning German the year before. Every spread had women naked with other women . . . I remember the Sister gave me a large cup of coffee and left me with the magazine and a mirror. By the time she came back I'd worked out the differences for myself. But Sister Angelica slipped up with the magazine because it wasn't until later, when I was sharing a shower with another girl that I discovered that some girls have this . . .'

Zara slid her hand across Raf's hip and touched the very edge of his pubic hair.

'I don't, you see. Also I don't have small labia, a clitoral hood or the top of my clitoris. But apparently I got lucky.' Her voice was hard. 'They could have done a full Pharaonic instead of a Sunna. You know what that is?'

Raf knew, but he shook his head. 'Tell me,' he said.

'The first thing you'd have had to do, come our wedding night, was slice through scar tissue. But even with all Dad's money at her disposal, my mother couldn't get the hospital at El Qahirah to go that far. So, you see . . .'

Raf did. Like most things in life, luck was subjective.

Chapter Forty-four

26th October

Hani dreamt of gardens. This wasn't unusual, gardens figured heavily in her stories and in most of the computer games she liked. In fact, *Rashid III* took place entirely in a nest of walled gardens, complete with fountains, djinn, houris and tiny gazelle. Only, her own computer was now dead and, anyway, she'd finished all the levels of *Rashid III* months ago. All levels/all difficulties/all characters. It hadn't been a very hard game.

The software was cheap, though. And that was probably the reason Aunt Nafisa had let her have it.

When Hani woke, at the first call to prayer, she lay there under the covers, which she wasn't meant to do, and thought about gardens. Then she thought about God. After that she thought about gardens and God. And then she got up, wrapped herself tightly in her dressing gown and went to find Raf.

'Jannah means garden or heaven,' Hani told herself as she opened her door. 'And paradiso also means heaven. So paradiso means jannah. *SS Jannah*. And I've got a list of other clues.'

She was talking to herself because Ifritah wasn't there. Raf had said Hani could come to the mansion with him and Khartoum but the grey cat had to stay with Donna at the madersa. This was because Ifritah was a wild cat and no one had taught her to do her business outside.

Hani had been planning to look up on the web how to house-train a cat which was already mostly grown up, but now she couldn't do that either. So Ifritah had to stay where she was.

The man who stood guard outside Raf's door was called

Ahmed. Hani knew this because she'd asked him earlier. He was big and dark and sometimes he looked at her and shrugged to the others when he thought she wasn't looking.

Ahmed said nothing, not even when Hani shone a torch in his face. Just raised his eyebrows and turned the handle for her. Hani realized what the raised eyebrows meant when she saw a lump in the bed next to Uncle Ashraf. The lump was sleeping, safely tucked under a sheet, but Hani could see Zara's hair poking out at the top.

Hani tried very hard not to be shocked.

After a little while, she decided that she *was* shocked and went back to her room. Ahmed said nothing to Hani on her way out either. Instead of going back to bed Hani got dressed, wrote Zara a note which she left with Ahmed and then went down to the kitchens to find Khartoum.

The rest of the day, while Ashraf worked at the Precinct and Zara walked, ghost-like and silent, through the formal gardens at the mansion, looking at statues without seeing them, Hani sat at a kitchen table with an Italian dictionary, three volumes of Dante and a notepad. After a while she decided it might be easier if she just concentrated on the pictures.

The volumes of the *Divina Commedia* came from the General's study, as did the notepad and fountain pen. So too did a list of all the working computers in the city that still had functioning modems/lines/firewire. The list was handwritten, distressingly brief and the original was meant for Ashraf's eyes only. Which was why Hani kept the copy she'd made in her pocket.

Ashraf came back as Tuesday evening began its slide into darkness, trailing his shadows behind him; although Hakim and Ahmed didn't go with Raf when he walked out into the garden to talk to Zara. Whatever he said to her, they slept in different rooms that night.

Chapter Forty-five

27th October

Astolphe, Marquis de St Cloud was enjoying himself. Unfortunately for Raf it was mostly at his expense, though the real target of the Frenchman's quiet vitriol was Elizabeth Elsing, as St Cloud insisted on calling Senator Liz.

Following yesterday's decision by the Grand Jury that Hamzah should indeed face charges, Senator Liz seemed unusually keen that the defendant be tried immediately, found guilty by lunchtime and executed before tea.

Which was fine, except for the fact that Hamzah Effendi had yet to be formally arraigned. And the reason this had been delayed was that it took until noon for the American woman to agree that St Cloud should hold the chair. Senator Liz also seemed slightly put out by the number of explosions happening across the city.

'Bring in the prisoner.'

'Bring in the prisoner . . .'

The courtroom was small but it was in the nature of ushers everywhere to shout. Raf heard his demand echo down a corridor outside and then heard an answering tramp of feet. The first argument of the day, long before the scrap for precedence between St Cloud and Senator Liz, had been about the suitability of the room itself.

Surprisingly, it was the young German Graf who objected most violently to the meagreness of the room on offer. Stating that its size was an affront to the seriousness of the case. His other complaint, that Hamzah Quitrimala's arraignment should have been thrown open to the press, drew a snort of laughter from St Cloud. Berlin wasn't known for the transparency of its legal process.

El Iskandryia's law courts were in Place Orabi, almost directly opposite the tomb of the unknown warrior and occupying what had once been the Italian Consulate. At ground level, the central Hall of Justice was three times the size of the courtroom Raf had chosen, and came replete with gilded chairs set out like small thrones for five judges, a seal of the Khedival arms hung behind the central chair and, above these, carved from Lebanese cedar and gilded with beaten gold, a *tugra*, the imperial monogram of the Ottoman Porte himself.

It was, Raf agreed, an altogether more imposing setting. It was also accessible from Place Orabi on one side and Rue el Tigarya on another, making it simple to attack and complex to defend.

'Defend from whom?' the Graf had demanded.

'You tell me,' had been Raf's answer and he made the Graf, Senator Liz and St Cloud, plus the ushers, the court stenographer and Zara climb three flights of marble stairs to a smaller courtroom usually used for family disputes.

At the top, just before he went into the room, Raf halted to yank open a steel fire escape. A helmeted Hakim stood on metal steps outside, clutching an old-fashioned Lee Enfield. Next to Hakim was Ahmed, a Soviet machine-gun resting heavy in the crook of his arm. The gun was chopped from sheet steel and finished on a lathe. It had the advantage of having only five moving parts, none of them involving electronics.

'If shit happens,' Raf said, 'this is the way we leave. Don't look back and don't stop to help anybody else, just move . . .'

As Raf turned to go, an explosion ruptured the city's nervous silence and flames boiled into the air from the deserted railyard at Kharmous.

'What perfect timing,' said a voice in Raf's ear. It was St Cloud, a smile on the old man's weather-beaten face as he watched smoke stain the sky. 'Almost too perfect,' he added.

Since then the Marquis had been watching Raf. That Cheshire

cat smile coming and going, but never quite vanishing from the old roué's face. Now St Cloud had the defendant standing in the dock in front of him.

'Your name?'

Hamzah Quitrimala gave no answer.

'You will give the court your name.'

Eyes expressionless and mouth slack, the thick-set industrialist looked as if St Cloud's order carried no weight against whatever was happening inside his head.

'Has this man been tested for mental competence?' the Marquis asked Raf.

'He has been examined by a doctor . . .'

'That wasn't quite what I asked,' St Cloud's voice was silky. 'Has he undergone the usual tests?'

'Obviously not,' said Raf. 'Since we don't have access to the usual machines.'

'All the more reason to hold the trial in Washington,' insisted the Senator and St Cloud sat back with a smile. Winding up Elizabeth Elsing and letting her go was about as subtle as winding up an old clockwork toy and twice as amusing.

'That question has already been debated and decided,' Raf said flatly. 'The trial takes place here.'

'Decided by you,' said St Cloud.

'Yes,' said Raf, 'decided by me.'

'In your capacity as governor of the city.'

Raf nodded.

'As is your right?'

Raf nodded once more.

'Remind me,' said the Frenchman politely. 'In which of your capacities are you now answering my question about the defendant's mental capacity?'

'As *magister*.'

The elderly Frenchman nodded and turned his attention back to the man in the dock. 'We need your name,' said the Marquis. 'We need to know that you understand our questions . . .'

Hamzah opened his mouth but no words came to carry his

answer to the waiting court and seconds later the light went out of his eyes.

St Cloud shrugged.

'Is there any man here who speaks for the defendant?'

'Yes,' came a voice from the back. 'I do . . .'

Heads twisted but Raf didn't need to look. It was his turn to smile.

'I said any man,' St Cloud said gently.

'Whatever,' Zara walked to the front and stopped beside her father. 'Let me speak for him,' she said. 'God knows, he needs somebody.'

'The weight of a woman's word is a third of that given to the words of a man . . . Isn't that now the law in El Iskandryia? Come to think of it,' the Frenchman added softly, 'I seem to remember that being the law across most of North Africa.'

'This court operates under the rules of The Hague,' said Raf firmly. 'As you well know.'

St Cloud nodded. 'So you allow this girl to speak for her father?'

'Yes,' said Raf, without looking at Zara, 'I allow it.'

'Remind me,' said the Frenchman with a sly smile, 'in exactly which capacity did you make that decision?'

'A Grand Jury, having unanimously decided that probable cause and sufficient reason exist to bring this case to trial, it is my duty as senior judge to appraise you of the formal charges . . .'

Pausing, St Cloud reached for a glass and sipped, very slowly. The tumbler was smeared and the water it held tasted stale. Chances were, the water had been brought in a jug from a stand-pipe hastily erected in the square outside.

It was interesting just how much the people of any city relied on electricity without really realizing that fact. At least St Cloud found it interesting; but then he found almost everything interesting, which had proved a salvation in his long and sometimes difficult life.

What interested him most, at least most for now, was how ready both the German boy and that irritating American were to agree that Hamzah Effendi was faking illness, when it was blindingly obvious that the defendant was crippled by despair. Not guilt, despair . . . The Marquis had been around enough of both to be able to tell the difference.

Also interesting was that the dutiful daughter who now stood beside the defendant spent more time watching Ashraf Bey than she did looking at her father or the judges. And that for his part, the young Berber princeling worked hard to do the opposite. So far he hadn't looked at her once.

'The charge,' said St Cloud as he carefully put down his glass, 'is murder in the first degree, murder in the second degree and culpable homicide. The prosecution will bring a *representative* case for each of these charges. If all three charges are found then a fourth charge will be considered to have been brought against you . . . That of a Section 3 crime against humanity . . .

'Under The Hague Convention you have a constitutional right to be represented. But I see that no law firm has been appointed.' The Frenchman made a show of consulting documents, if handwritten scrawls on cheap lined paper could so be called. 'Do you wish me to appoint counsel?'

St Cloud took another slow sip from his glass. He'd first learnt of the trick as a young lawyer, watching an elderly judge in Marseilles. Every few minutes, the woman would stop to sip from a small glass of iced Evian. Rumour said the glass contained vodka but rumour lied. Water was all it ever was. The sipping existed to create natural breaks that let her words trickle into the bedrock of everyone's thought. Faced with inexorable evidence and enough silence, defendants had been known to change their pleas mid-trial, without consulting their lawyers and to their lawyers' considerable horror. It had taken the Marquis months of watching the judge to work out how the old woman stage-managed it.

Of course, sometimes it didn't work.

'Very well then,' St Cloud said with a sigh. 'This court orders that a public defender be appointed by the city.'

'*No*.' It was the first word Hamzah Effendi had uttered since being led into the room, the first word from the man in two days. 'No attorney, no public defender.'

St Cloud shrugged. 'If that's what you want . . . Do you wish to apply for bail?' He looked at the silent man but it was Zara who answered.

'Yes,' she said defiantly, 'We do . . . I do. And I ask that my father be released on his own recognizance.'

'Completely impossible.' Senator Liz spoke without bothering to defer to the chair. On the other side of St Cloud, the young Graf nodded frantic agreement.

'Bail, even with a bond, would be unusual in a case like this,' St Cloud said softly. 'But it might be possible, if the bond is set high enough and you, personally, give your word not to attempt to help your father leave the city.'

Her word.

The Marquis smiled at the outrage on the face of the ushers and court stenographer; even Hamzah looked momentarily shocked.

'You have my word,' said Zara. 'Now how much do you want?'

'For myself,' said the Marquis, 'I want nothing.' She had the grace to blush, though her chin came up and she refused to look away. 'The sum is a matter for the court,' he added, 'though I suggest not less than . . .'

'No bail,' announced Raf from his seat to one side of the judges. He stood up slowly and stepped into the empty area between the judges and the dock, feeling very alone. Turning to Zara, he spread his hands in apology.

'I cannot allow bail,' he said flatly. 'And that decision is taken in my capacity as governor of this city.' He stared at St Cloud. 'You know as well as I do that if bail is granted I cannot guarantee his safety . . .'

'In that case . . . Request for bail dismissed. All that remains,' said St Cloud, 'is for the court to set a date for trial. Since it seems the case *will*, after all, be tried in Iskandryia.' He smiled sweetly at the Senator. 'And since the defendant has refused counsel I would suggest to the other judges that we begin first thing tomorrow . . .'

'Too soon,' said Raf. 'Make it Saturday . . . Iskandryian airspace will need to be opened to fly in Jean René, the photographer who took the shots already seen by the Grand Jury.'

'Saturday it is.'

'No.' This time it was Zara who objected. 'That doesn't give my father time to find a character witness.'

'For a murder charge?' St Cloud scanned his handwritten notes. There was nothing about a character witness in there.

'One only,' Zara said. 'We're also in the process of organizing travel arrangements.'

'You have until Sunday,' St Cloud said firmly. 'After that, the trial takes place, whether you have your witness or not.' He glanced at Raf and frowned. 'And that decision is taken in my capacity as senior judge.'

Chapter Forty-six

27th October

'Hani al-Mansur . . .' The child answered her mobile at the first ring, voice extra polite. 'Can I ask who's calling . . . ?'

Her Nokia was one of only a dozen let into El Iskandryia on special licence from the governor, who turned out to be the person on the other end of the call. She had to ask who it was because these cell phones were analogue, very stupid ones without the option of vision.

For some reason, Ashraf had been most insistent about the analogue bit.

Their conversation was short. 'Yes,' said Hani, 'Ifritah's fine. She's here with me and I'm really pleased to see her.'

She listened to Uncle Ashraf's next question and sucked her teeth, but not that crossly. 'Yes . . . I've had supper and I'm ready for bed. No, you don't need to collect me in the morning. Donna's going to the market. I'll walk in with her . . .'

At the next question, Hani groaned theatrically. 'Yes,' she said. 'You are fussing. That's your job.' She listened to Uncle Ashraf's goodnights, added her own and went back to the keyboard of the *bibliotheka*'s only working web connection.

'I'm back,' she announced quietly.

'About time,' said Avatar.

He owed Raf a life. Hani hadn't needed to remind him of that but she did anyway . . . Then apologized. Only to decide that she didn't need to apologize because it was true. After that, she asked him some weird questions about whether Zara now wanted to marry Raf. Avatar was beginning to think the kid was as fucked over as he was.

The rest of it, Avatar didn't understand and Hani had given

up trying to explain. He got the bit about him forwarding on the spider fax to Zara. Things imploded at the point when Hani added the spider fax to an angel and a wounded man and came up with the fact that hell was cold, purgatory was water-bound and he knew heaven better as the *SS Jannah*.

It was only the fact that Hani swore she'd been told this by the General that made Avatar believe any of it was true. So now, at Hani's insistence, he was looking for the ninth level of hell, otherwise known as *Cocytus*.

Needless to say, it wasn't on any of the numerous wall maps dotted around the corridors and stairways of the *SS Jannah* . . .

The rucksack slung on Avatar's shoulder was heavy and awkward. What was worse, it clanked every time he brushed against a wall, which was often. Those were its bad points. On the plus side, it contained rope, pepper spray and several cans of Coke.

'Guard.' Hani's voice in his earbead was matter of fact, unhurried.

'Yeah, seen him.' Avatar stepped backwards into a recess, out of the guard's line of sight and out of his line of fire as well. There were two men, one in a suit, the other dressed in bell bottoms and white top, a black silk folded neatly around his muscular neck. Avatar knew this was a guard, not a crewman, by the gun he carried.

Dminus4 was off limits to civilians; guests in the parlance of the *SS Jannah*. The official reason was that Dminus4 housed the vaults of Hong Kong Suisse, the liner's official bank. *Welcome Aboard*, the induction film for the *SS Jannah*, described the vault as made from weapons-grade steel with a single time-coded, iris-specific door and reassuringly thick walls. From what Hani had said, it was a perfectly ordinary floor-to-ceiling blockhouse with a boringly ordinary lock.

But then why not? Everything except gambling chips for the casino was included in the overall and frighteningly-extortionate price and the only real valuables brought on board by guests, their papers and jewellery, were kept secure in individual safes that came with each cabin. The heist-proof vault was a sop to tradition, only there by repute.

'Clear now.'

'Yeah.'

Avatar stepped out of his hiding place and checked both ways along the corridor. He was in plain sight of at least three CCTV cameras but those didn't worry him, everywhere on board was in sight of cameras. Nothing obvious, mind you. At least not on the guest levels. No little robot lenses to twist their heads as one walked from room to room. Most of the guest-level cameras used little pin lenses embedded into the walls and linked to some gizmo running visual-recognition software.

Quite how Hani had spliced herself in to them Avatar had no idea. Something to do with a handshake, according to the kid. And it was a clean connection, although there was a tiny time lag between them, defined not by the miles between *SS Jannah* and El Iskandryia but by how long it took to bounce data packets off a comsat slung somewhere over Sao Tomé.

'How long we got left?'

'About thirty minutes,' said Hani.

'There wasn't another battery?'

'Dead.' The kid's voice was resigned. So resigned that Avatar had trouble working out if Hani was seriously chilled or just having trouble getting her head round how bad things actually were.

When Hani had first called Avatar, she asked if he wanted her to fix a voice connection to Zara, so he could check what Hani said. He'd thought about it for all of a second and rejected the idea. He believed what she'd told him about how bad things were looking for his old man.

'There should be a door at the end of this corridor . . .'

'Locked,' said Avatar.

'How do you know?'

'I'm guessing.'

'Try it anyway.'

Sighing, Avatar crab-walked swiftly towards the heavy door,

his back to the wall and the revolver he'd stolen from the Khedive's cabin held upright, combat style.

Avatar was doing his very best not to rush things but there was an ache behind his eyes and a hollow in his gut where his stomach should be. Since he regularly went a week on two kebabs and three lines of sulphate, the hollowness had to be fear rather than hunger. Not a good feeling.

The door wasn't just locked. Someone had welded it shut with a splatter gun. Cold drops of solder beading the edge of its frame like metal tears.

'They're coming back!' Hani's warning came seconds ahead of footsteps echoing along a corridor.

'Come on,' Hani said. 'Hide . . .'

Avatar shook his head, then realized the kid wouldn't pick up his gesture on her monitor. She'd be too busy watching the guards. 'Which way are they headed?'

'Towards the lifts,' said Hani, her voice tight.

'Good.' Avatar meant the comment for himself, but the kid picked it up anyway from one of the wall mics or something equally scary. Avatar's relationship with machines was confined to his mixing decks, and he liked those dumb and pliable.

'Avatar . . .'

'Yeah, okay, I can see them now.'

They were jiving between themselves, some joke about a v' Actor on the third deck. Their laughter was not cruel, just barbed, the armour that those who lack wear against those who have. Except that in this case *lack* was relative. The crew aboard the SS *Jannah* earned more in a month than Avatar scratched together in a year.

Pulling back the hammer on his borrowed Taurus, Avatar muffled the click it made by folding his fingers over the top. Then he pressed himself back flat against the corridor wall, putting a fat down-pipe between himself and the approaching pair.

They did what Avatar expected them to do, which was head straight past, still deep in conversation.

Very gently, Avatar touched his revolver to the side of the guard's hair and watched irritation turn to fear, as the hand that flicked up to brush away whatever it was met the cold ceramic of Avatar's weapon.

'Make a noise,' growled Avatar, 'and say goodbye to your head.' The threat came out exactly as he'd imagined and Avatar felt unreasonably proud. It was, he hoped, exactly the kind of thing Raf might say.

'You . . .' The suit not suffering a gun to his head spun round and found himself face to face with a dread-locked stowaway wearing a 'God Speed You Black Emperor' tee-shirt. It made the suit even more unhappy. 'You won't get . . .'

'I just did.' Avatar gestured towards the lift. 'That way,' he said, herding them towards a waiting Orvis. 'Now,' said Avatar when they were both safely inside. 'How do I reach the floors below this?'

At this level the lifts didn't thank you for travelling or hope you enjoyed the rest of your day, they were blind and dumb, with buttons that needed pushing. And the lowest level on the small array of buttons in front of him was Dminus4, this one.

'There isn't a floor below this,' the suit said through gritted teeth. 'This is as low as it gets . . . And how did you get aboard anyway?' His eyes took in Avatar's black combats, the tee-shirt and the strands of black glitter threaded into his dreads. Nike sneakers completed the outfit.

The *SS Jannah* had no second or third class cabins. Come to that, it didn't even have first-class accommodation. Everything was executive or above, running all the way up to the Imperial Suite, where Mohammed Tewfik Pasha, Khedive of what remained of El Iskandryia, currently occupied the whole seventh floor. No more than 200 guests were ever on board at any one time. And it was the ship's proud boast that guests were outnumbered three to one by hotel staff. That was before one even considered whatever crew were actually needed to run the ship.

'The floor below this,' Avatar said crossly. 'How do I get to it?'

The two crew members looked at each other, and the suit raised his eyes to heaven. 'Look kid,' he said, 'there isn't . . .'

Avatar shot him through the leg, just above the knee. By the time the slug exited the man's quadriceps and flattened itself against the steel wall of the lift, the suit's lungs were dragging in mountains of air.

'Don't even think about screaming,' Avatar advised him. 'Now, let's try again, how do I . . . ?'

'Okay, okay . . .' the unharmed guard had one hand out, as if to ward off bullets from the gun Avatar began to raise. 'So far as I know,' he said slowly, 'this is the ship's lowest level. Everything else below this is buoyancy tanks, turbines or ballast.'

'What about servicing the engines?'

'It's a self-functioning sealed unit. Right . . . ?' He glanced to the man on the floor for confirmation. 'It's sealed.'

'There must be hatches.'

'Yes and no,' said the guard nervously. 'They're welded shut.'

'Too bad.' Avatar looked at the puddle of red spreading itself across the lift's grey floor and pointed his gun at the injured suit's other leg.

'It's true, I promise you . . .' The man nodded his head like a frantic puppet, as if his frenzy alone could convince Avatar. 'There is no way down . . .'

'Find me one,' Avatar demanded, but he was talking to Hani.

Chapter Forty-seven

28th October

'I shouldn't . . .

'Yeah, so you keep saying,' said Raf. 'You shouldn't be here, you shouldn't have done that . . .' He was grinning like an idiot, he couldn't help it. Beside him, Zara lay curled tight, with one of her arms thrown across his stomach and tiny beads of sweat tangled in her short dark hair, at the point where it brushed back from her forehead. Quick breaths flexed the cage of her ribs.

'You okay?'

'What do you think?' Zara untangled her legs from his and rolled away. This time round she didn't bother to pull up a sheet, merely sprawled on Raf's bed with one arm up over her grey eyes, revealing dark-tipped breasts that were high and perfect and honey-sweet in the early daylight that crept through the windows from the garden outside.

'Do you think they heard?'

Raf listened to the crunch of heels on gravel below, the unmistakable squeal of boots as a soldier executed a perfect about-turn at the end of the path, swivelling on the spot.

'I would imagine so,' he said, straight-faced, only to shake his head when Zara sat up and stared across, eyes wide.

He'd done only what she allowed. Which was more than Zara intended and less than he wanted. She was working to rules, though even Zara wasn't quite sure whose rules those were.

'How about you,' she asked, 'you okay?'

'Sure,' Raf shrugged. 'I'm fine.'

'Right.' Her smile was lopsided. 'Of course you are.' Zara yanked back his covers. 'Anyone can see that.'

Somewhere in the hinterland between midnight and early

morning, as the stubborn darkness finally diluted, Raf had first struggled out of his shirt and then his pants, stripping himself bare. Neither of them had suggested Zara might want to do the same. But his hands had caressed her beneath her nightdress and found answering movement from her body. Movement that built slowly until she took his hand and almost pushed it into her pants.

'Stand over there,' said Zara and pointed to a patch of sun that lit the room's white floor. So Raf did what she asked, aware that she watched as he climbed naked out of the bed and walked across the tiles. When he stood where she wanted, he turned to face her and saw her blush.

'Now what . . . ?'

She knelt with marble tiles cold and hard against her bare knees. There were a dozen good reasons why she shouldn't be kneeling there. Some personal, some cultural, a few of them even political.

'What?' Raf asked, seeing her shoulders shrug.

'Nothing,' said Zara and then could say no more. She felt his hips tense under her grip and heard him begin to swear softly as his back arched and every muscle in his legs seemed to lock.

She was a republican and Marxist, he was an Ottoman bey. She was new money and he was wealth inherited. No, she scrubbed that, Raf had little money, either way. He was police and her father was a criminal. Iskandryia's establishment had adopted him and that too made him her enemy. Her father was on trial and he controlled the court. If it was in her power, she would overthrow everything he represented and the order to which he belonged.

And here she was on her knees before a man, something she'd promised herself would never happen. It didn't matter if it was sex, money, violence or necessity that put a woman there, once there the weight of history made it hard to get back up again.

Zara could feel Raf's fingers hard on the side of her head, so she took her right hand and wrapped it round him and moved her mouth in time to his need.

And later, with his taste still in her mouth, she led Raf back to the bed and sat beside him while he curled into a foetal ball and slept like the child she guessed he'd never been.

It was impossible that he knew how much she loved him, how much his vulnerability made her afraid.

Chapter Forty-eight

28th October

Avatar wasn't sure what he'd expected. Maybe a whole deck given over to the Colonel's quarters. PaxForce guards doubling as prison officers. Certainly daylight-perfect lighting tied to a season-specific 24/seven clock, some trees, birdsong and an artificial stream; even the most basic clubs had those these days. At least they did in the circadian/chill-out zones.

And if not warders, then exile in splendid isolation. Imposing state rooms run to seed and ruin. Once fabulous tapestries grimed with dust. Avatar imagined it like something from a newsfeed novella. *Golden Youth*, *In Place of Trust*, *Forbidden Fortune* . . . Somewhere suited to murderous fathers, flirtatious mothers, drug-addled uncles and teenage schemers who usually wanted either their parents or siblings dead, if not both.

He didn't think of Hamzah like this. Hamzah was a villain, not pure but pretty simple, and his money wasn't knotted up in trusts and he had only one heir, Zara.

Avatar had no illusions about that. No real problems with it either.

All the same, he'd been expecting more from the Colonel's lair. Actually, even that wasn't accurate, he hadn't so much been expecting more as been expecting *something*. Something other than a vast hangar-like emptiness, filled with acrid dust and lit by distant portholes that lined the gloom on either side of him, like tiny holes punched out into the real world.

His feet left tracks on the carpet in dust that was undisturbed by any other sign of human passage. Just because something made no sense didn't make it untrue, however; Avatar knew that. Knew too that he needed to find a way down to the deck below, where there would be no portholes at all, unless the liner had a level designed to look out underwater. Which was possible.

'Lights . . .'

The futile command echoed back from steel walls, making him feel more alone than ever. Avatar's problem was that silence irritated him and always had done. It scared him, if he was being honest. From the grinding of gears in the narrow street outside his children's home and the jewels of music heard through other people's windows to the hammering of water pipes each night in the dorm, noise had been his comfort from the start.

'Fuck it all . . .' Avatar pulled a twist of paper from his pocket and crunched the crystals. He'd have snorted the pinch, like snuff, but his nostrils were still recovering from a batch of ice that had given him twenty-four hours' worth of paranoia and a week of nose bleeds.

The sulphate tasted sour as vomit but it did its job. Melting into his saliva and sending shivers down his neck. Life improved in a rush.

'Hani?'

There was no answer. But then there'd been no answer last time he asked either, or the time before that. No answer, no sounds . . . Sound was what he needed. It fed his sense of time and place and himself, it threaded through his unconscious. Put him down in any back street in the city and, chances were, he could navigate his way to a café in Shatby blindfold, just by listening to the noise from different souks and the rattle of trams.

Here there was only the engine's slow heartbeat beneath his feet, which he felt rather than heard, like being in the belly of a whale. This was more Raf's territory than his, Avatar decided as he took another few crystals, just to be safe. That was the obvious difference between them. The only dark Avatar liked came wrapped up with neon, sound systems and strobes. For the rest, he'd take daylight and warmth every time . . .

*   *   *

Moving through the cold aquarium gloom, Avatar made for a distant strip of colour that turned out, minutes later, to be one long, elaborate, stained-glass window spanning the whole width of the liner's stern. On it, heroic miners swung glass pickaxes at coal seams of purple glass, fishermen pulled elaborate nets loaded with cod from dark glass waves and a plump girl with blonde hair and impossibly-blue eyes stood dead centre with a glass sun behind her, a sickle at her bare feet and a sheaf of wheat held proudly above her head. She looked as warm and happy as Avatar was cold and miserable.

Agitprop meets Chartres. That had been a quip from Mapplethorpe, the first American to photograph the window for a Sunday supplement, back before President Maxudov lost the liner to Prime Minister Moro as part reparation at the end of the third Russo-Japanese War.

Avatar was too young to know any of this. He just nodded at the glass girl and figured she'd look fit on a club flyer.

Beneath the wide window, an ornate sweep of double stairs led into even deeper gloom below, looking as if it had been ripped from a New York hotel — brass stair-rods and all — and bolted between decks. A long Art Nouveau rail, verdigrised with age and missing an occasional banister, had been fixed around the edge of the drop to protect Avatar and the ghosts of passengers long dead from falling to the deck below.

Beyond the dim pool of light at the foot of the stairs stretched icy blackness, growing colder and more ink-like the further in Avatar went. He already knew, from having walked the full length of the deck overhead, that the gloom extended for more than a kilometre in front of him. Somewhere in the emptiness would be a door leading down to a level below this. All Avatar had to do was find the right door.

Whether the door Avatar found was right or not was hard to guess. True enough, it opened and had stairs leading down. Those were both plus points. Unfortunately it was also two hundred paces after where Hani had told him it should be and on the wrong side of the ship. Avatar was still worrying about these discrepancies when he came out onto the deck below and stumbled upon his first freezer pipe, promptly tripping over it.

'Oh f—' Picking himself off carpet tiles so chilled their nap was brittle with ice, Avatar let his long low variation on the theme of *fuck* segue slowly into silence.

Not his day.

Having adjusted the rucksack on his shoulder, he headed on, moving towards a point in the far distance that might as well have been hidden behind his eyes for all Avatar could really see it. And a hundred or so paces later, he tripped over his second pipe.

Fucking . . .

Echoes of swearing gave way to silence and an awareness that both shins now hurt so badly he was moving beyond the ability to curse. Tentatively, Avatar wrapped one hand around his ankle, half from gut instinct/half to check for real damage and felt warmth ooze from beneath frozen skin. Somehow, finding blood returned his ability to swear.

'You could always try turning on the lights,' said a voice behind him.

Ankle bleeding or not, Avatar spun on the spot and flipped his gun to firing position, thumb already ratcheting back its hammer. The only thing that stopped Avatar from doing what he intended, which was ram the barrel into the gut of whoever stood directly behind, was that no one stood directly behind. The darkness was empty.

'To your left,' said the voice. 'Over near the wall . . . Follow the pipe until you hit a pillar. The control is on the nearest side . . . Oh,' it sounded darkly amused, 'and try not to trip over anything else.'

The switch was where the voice said it would be. A simple square of cracked white plastic that, once clicked, lit a single bank of strips from one side of the low ceiling to the other, leaving Avatar stood in a dimly-lit hold. At his feet, a frosted pipe vanished through the floor. There was a new pipe every hundred paces or so, rising out of the deck on one side of the hangar-like space, crossing the floor and then disappearing again. Most of the pipes were frosted for their entire length with ice.

'It was cheap,' said the voice. 'From a decommissioned power station outside Helsinki. You're probably wondering why the Soviets didn't use something better suited.'

Avatar wasn't. He could honestly say the question had never occurred to him.

'Inefficiency. Plus they had to take what they could get at the time. That's a good maxim for politics, you know. Take what you can. Let free what you can't . . .'

'Sounds like shit to me, man,' said Avatar.

'Oh.' The voice sounded puzzled, the puzzlement breeding a long pause that left Avatar time to look round the hold. And Avatar remained there, hung inside that pause, until he grew bored with waiting and decided to demand a few answers of his own. Get the basics, Raf had once said. Most people didn't, but then, as Raf pointed out, most people were dead.

'Where am I?'

'Where . . . ?'

'Yes,' said Avatar. 'That's what I said. Where am I, exactly . . . ?'

The voice thought about that. 'You're on Dminus7, a third of the way into krill processing. Well, what used to be processing before the partitions were bulldozed and the vats dismantled.'

'Right,' Avatar said flatly, 'and where are you?'

'Exactly?'

'Yeah, exactly.'

'I'm exactly close enough to make contact.'

Avatar smiled, despite himself and in spite of air so cold that it leached heat from his arms and dragged the questions from his mouth in wisps of smoke.

'You can do better than that.'

'And if I can't?'

'I'll leave you face down with a bullet through the back of your head.'

'You're not Ka, are you?'

'No,' Avatar said slowly. 'You can safely assume I'm not Ka.'

'But you are armed?'

'Oh yes.' Avatar waved his borrowed Taurus in the air, so whichever camera was watching though the gloom could get a clear view. 'That's me. Always ready. Armed to the teeth.'

'Good,' said the voice. 'Though personally I'd recommend an HK/cw, double-loaded with kinetics and 20mm fatboys, explosive and air-burst.'

Silence.

'Looks like a pig and weighs like one too,' added the voice. 'Heckler and Koch, plastic and ceramic job. Kill anything. Really useful if you're an amateur.'

'If I'm an . . .' Avatar snapped off a shot in the direction of the insult, then ducked as sound waves swamped the low hold, deafening him.

'Are you sure you're not Ka?' The voice sounded amused.

'No,' said Avatar. 'I'm, um, Kamil ben-Hamzah . . . More famous as DJ Avatar,' he added quickly, refusing to compromise totally.

'Kamil . . . eh? Tell me, not Ka, why exactly are you here?'

'To claim a debt.' That seemed to be the only way to put it.

'You mean to kill me?'

Avatar took a deep breath. Every hour since Hani first called him up he'd spent riffing this moment. He'd done what a lifetime of street smarts suggested he do, which was introduce himself. Only now Avatar couldn't remember in which order he was supposed to make his points.

'My father's on trial . . .'

No, Avatar shook his head, that wasn't where he was meant to start.

'My name is Kamil. My father's name is Hamzah Quitrimala. I've come to . . .'

'How old are you?' demanded the voice.

'Old enough,' said Avatar.

'I had tank commanders younger than that.' The voice sounded almost regretful, as if the man speaking wished Avatar was less than his fourteen years. 'Hell, by your age most of my tank commanders . . .'

'Were dead.' Relief cascaded over the boy as he realized that he'd done it right and found the Colonel; but all he said was, 'Yeah, I heard.'

If silence could have shrugged, it did.

'Everybody dies,' said the Colonel. 'Well, almost everybody.'

'You're alive . . .'

'And so, it seems, is little Ka.'

'Ka?'

'Kamil. The boy who hated war so much he gunned down everyone who wanted to take part, including the whole of his own platoon, if you believe the reports. And officially I always make a point of believing official reports . . .'

'He actually killed all those people?'

Avatar lowered his revolver and shook off his rucksack. He felt sick, sick and empty, like someone had ripped open his stomach and taken his guts when he wasn't looking. 'I thought you were meant to be Dad's alibi . . .'

'I think,' said Colonel Abad carefully, 'you'll find I'm meant to tell the truth.'

'You'll do it?' Avatar sounded shocked. 'You'll stand up in court?'

The way Hani explained it, the *SS Jannah* functioned as an autonomous micro-nation. That was, so long as the liner stayed within international waters it ran to its own laws. So why would someone like Colonel Abad put himself in danger by offering to come ashore?

'You thought you'd have to kidnap me?' The Colonel's voice was sour. 'No chance. This is my Elba. You remember Napoleon needing to be forced off that island at gun point?'

Avatar didn't remember anything about Napoleon at all. Zara was the one with the expensive education.

'You'll find me on Dminus9, right at the bottom of the pit. You do know that the last and deepest circle of hell is ice cold, don't you? In the fourth round, *Judecca*. And the ninth circle, *Cocytus*. That's the problem with being captured by someone with a classical education. They want to get all clever on your arse.'

As there wasn't an answer to that, Avatar turned his attention to reaching the far end of the hangar, though now the Taurus was heavy in his combats pocket and most of his attention went on not tripping over the trip-wire pipes.

'How do I get through this?' Avatar asked, when he hit a steel wall thrown across the point of the liner. In it was a door, also steel, with three heavy, old-fashioned locks. Since this was the first door he'd seen on the entire level, apart from the one he'd used to get in, Avatar figured it had to be right.

'Try opening it . . .'

Avatar did, and the heavy door swung open in a cascade of metal dandruff as its hinges creaked and popped fat flakes of rust. A twist of riveted steps fed down to the coldness below and then kept on going to the level below that, by-passing the turbine rooms.

Old-fashioned switches waited for Avatar at every landing but the bulkhead lights were empty of bulbs, so he felt his way through the darkness, until the fingers following the icy rail ceased to be his and vanished into a dull ache.

The deeper Avatar went, the colder it became until every inward breath froze in his throat or plated the inside of his nostrils and every outward breath condensed at his lips. The cold had a physicality which was new to him. And with the cold came a tiredness and the need for sleep.

Heat he'd lived with all his life. It arrived with late spring, sometimes earlier if a *khamsin* hit, with its fifty days of hot dry wind, and trickled away into the end of autumn. With it came cat-like lassitude and pointless quarrels. But this was more than heat's opposite. Every twist of stair Avatar descended took him further inside himself, folding him into lethargy.

'What's the temperature?' Avatar demanded.

'Cold,' said the voice. 'Cold enough to shut down your core.'

'And you live in this?'

'It makes no difference to me,' the voice said. 'And Saeed Koenig wanted to discourage sightseers.'

*　　*　　*

His teeth chattered uncontrollably and his feet were a memory beyond feeling. The black tee-shirt and combats he'd put on that morning now seemed less of a fashion statement and more of an absent-mindedly written suicide note.

'Where now?' Avatar asked, knowing he'd been followed on camera every step of his descent.

'Straight ahead. Use the door . . .'

Still cursing the lack of a flashlight, Avatar inched through the darkness until his outstretched hand found a handle, low down and on the right. He gripped it tight with shaking fingers and everything started to go wrong. Disbelief giving way to panic as he tried to yank free his hand and heard skin rip. What panicked Avatar wasn't pain but its complete absence.

He was frozen fast to a sub-zero metal door handle.

'Piss on it,' said the Colonel.

Avatar ignored the comment and tugged again.

'*Piss on it,*' Colonel Abad ordered crossly, his voice echoing from two places at once. 'Go on. Do it now.'

The man meant it, Avatar realized. Using his good hand, Avatar fumbled at the nylon zip of his combats.

'Now piss on the other hand. Get some warmth into those bones.'

Avatar did as Colonel Abad ordered, fastened his fly and stepped through to the Colonel's quarters, fingers still dripping. He didn't imagine the Colonel would want to shake hands.

The room was in darkness.

'Lights,' said the Colonel, and a strip lit overheard. What it revealed was an empty space like all the others Avatar had passed through; just smaller, narrower and less high. The walls which curved on both sides were blasted back to bare steel and riveted plate. Obviously enough, there were no portholes. Also no furniture, apart from a low metal table, and no cooking equipment. No sign of human habitation and no Colonel.

As jokes went, it was a bad one.

'How are the fingers?' asked a voice behind him. 'I've just checked my libraries and you may need a skin graft, when we get ashore . . . *If we get ashore,*' the voice amended, as if suddenly concerned not to push the bounds of accuracy.

'What the fuck?' Avatar looked round until he spotted a speaker, attached to the ceiling over in the corner of the room. It was so out of date that its grille was cloth, set into a case that looked like it might actually be wood. Soviet-made, from the look of things.

'I'm the housekeeping routine on the table.'

'You're what?' Avatar looked across to see a small radio wired into a feed socket on the wall. At first glance the radio looked to be covered with grey suede, but that was just dust fallen from the ceiling or carried in through a ventilation duct on the Arctic wind. Beside it, by themselves, stood an ugly-looking pair of spectacles.

'Yeah,' said the Colonel, 'that's me.' A CCTV camera on the wall swung slowly between Avatar and the table. It looked like nothing so much as a duck shaking its head. 'Not what you expected, huh?'

Avatar shook his head in turn. 'No, it's not.' All the same, he felt he needed to clarify the position. 'You're my dad's boss? Colonel Abad?'

'"But in the Greek tongue hath his name Apollyon. That is, destroyer. Angel of the abyss, he that brings God's woes upon his enemies . . ."'

'Revelation,' added the voice, when Avatar looked blank. 'I'm either the true angel of God or his deadly enemy. Unfortunately, no one can decide which, though theologians once wasted a lot of time trying.' The Colonel's tone made clear what he thought of that.

Revelation? That was the *nasrani* political endgame, at least Avatar thought it was. He wasn't big on politics. 'You believe this stuff . . .'

'What do you think?'

He thought not.

'Either it was a geek joke,' explained the Colonel, 'or they needed to find a framework in a hurry . . . Lash-ups are always easier than starting from scratch, take a look at religion or computer games. My guess is the shapers fed in a couple of terabytes of world myth plus Jung. It didn't worry them if the deep background was sub-optimal. I was only there for the duration of the war. And that was only meant to last a few months.'

'I'm dying of cold,' said Avatar, 'and you're talking shit . . .'

Chapter Forty-nine

28th October

Mohammed Tewfik Pasha, Khedive of El Iskandryia, rolled over in his huge waterbed and opened one eye at the sound of knocking. The bed in which he woke was larger than king sized, obviously enough, since this was the Imperial Suite.

It was also empty apart from him, and that choice was his. He'd seen how he was watched by the daughters of other guests, their eyes tracking him as he walked down the ornate stairs into the dining room to take his place at the captain's table. And he knew too that the Van der Bilt girl had dined alone in her cabin every night, until he'd taken to eating his supper in public.

El Iskandryia was widely expected to lose its status as a free city. And the shallow end of the gene pool was preparing itself for the Khedive's new role as romantic but tragic hero (with looks, money and title).

His face was on this week's *Time*, but for all the wrong reasons. *Cosmo Girl* had even produced a poster showing him in shorts and tee-shirt, standing barefoot on the deck of a yacht and staring moodily out to sea, or so he'd read. He'd never actually seen the poster and couldn't remember having been allowed to go barefoot anywhere. Just getting permission from the General to appear out of uniform usually took a tantrum.

Any one of the young mothers who promenaded their children through the upper deck's Palm Garden each morning would go to bed with him. He'd had sly smiles, batted eyelashes, even a handwritten note folded and slipped into his trouser pocket by a mother of twins. Then there was that Australian woman, her smile anything but innocent, asking him how many slaves he had in his harem . . . And would he like one more?

Yet the only girl he wanted, the one he'd actually invited, had sent her bastard half-brother instead.

'*Rotate.*' Across the suite on a white ash sideboard (so retro-Cunard), a silver photo frame started to flick from picture to picture. It showed what the Khedive's guests expected it to show. The General and Tewfik Pasha standing together in the throne room. Tewfik Pasha silhouetted against the sun in the luxuriant green of the General's garden. A winter sunset over the Corniche. And, as a default setting, elegant hand-drawn calligraphy showing the name of God.

They were all an irrelevance . . . Except for the name of God, obviously. The Khedive's correction was heartfelt and instant, but all the same he felt sick at the thought of his unintended blasphemy. And yet, the fact remained that the only picture which really mattered to him was a tattered clipping, tucked away in the back of his wallet.

It was taken in the early dawn outside an illegal cellar club and showed Zara naked except for a tight faux-fur coat. The grainy shadow between her half-seen breasts bothered him more than any of the pink Renoir nudes so carefully collected by his grandfather and great grandfather.

'*Your Highness . . .*'

He'd forgotten about the earlier knock at his bedroom door.

'Yes,' said the Khedive and watched a heavy door swing open to reveal the captain, looking every inch the master of the world's largest sea-going liner. One thick and three lesser rings circled the cuffs of Captain Bruford's immaculate jacket. Her trousers had razor-sharp creases at the front and a heavy gold stripe down each outer seam. She seemed slightly embarrassed to see the Khedive, which puzzled Tewfik Pasha until he realized it might be because he was wearing nothing, at least nothing visible.

'Can I help you?'

'Yes, Sir.' With an effort, Captain Bruford shook her gaze from the half-naked boy. 'You know we pride ourselves on how seriously we take the safety of our important guests. All our guests,' she corrected herself.

The Khedive nodded. It seemed unlikely that she'd come up to the Imperial Suite to make a mission statement on behalf of her company, much less discuss its core values or whatever buzz word best described the clichés he'd already heard on the induction film. All the same, the captain seemed to be having trouble coming to the point.

'Yes?'

'Helicopter . . .'

He looked at her in blank amazement.

'On the edge of our systems,' she said. 'Approaching the *SS Jannah*.'

'And that's a problem?' Guests came and went by helicopter all the time: that was the whole point of being aboard the *SS Jannah*; it never docked, anywhere, ever. The only time it left international waters, and that time was covered by special treaty, was when the liner passed through the Panama Canal or the Pillars of Hercules.

'They're shielded,' said Captain Bruford. 'And we can't get a handshake. Believe me, we've tried.' The middle-aged English woman looked something between irritated and anxious.

'I think it would be safer,' she added, 'if we were to get Your Highness off the ship. We have three high-speed VSVs available, Thornycroft-built and with submersible capacities . . .'

She just couldn't help it, the Khedive realized. Every statement she made about Utopia Lines came out sounding like an advertisement. It had to be something the company burned into their brains at training school.

'You think I'd be safer aboard the VSV?'

'No.' The captain looked at him, her mind already made up. 'I think everybody else would be safer. My chief of security has spent the last ten minutes running a risk analysis and you're the obvious target.'

Tewfik Pasha nodded. In all probability that was true.

Climbing out of bed without thinking about how that might appear to his visitor, he collected a towel from the back of a chair, only to drop it on the tiles when he reached the cubicle.

One month each year was what he got. Time off for good behaviour, that was how he thought of the *SS Jannah*. One month away from lessons, from his staff, from protocol, from the General . . .

Four weeks in which he could do what he wanted. Sleep, eat, watch old Beat Takahashi vids, if that was what took his fancy. And then it was back to the uniforms, to living in a goldfish bowl, to being immensely rich but having no money. He owned palaces and slept for eleven months of the year in a small room without either air-conditioning or heating. A room where the basin ran only cold water and his antique Chinese carpet was worn to the thinness of tapestry, its holes and stains covered by a rug, thrown down in the strategic place. Living like that was supposed to teach him humility.

Tewfik Pasha wasn't an idiot. He wasn't even a child. He knew there were whole districts of his city which had no water for drinking, washing or anything else, *arrondissements* where houses had no glass in the windows and sewage ran untreated in the gutters, alleys where raggeds slept at night, curled against walls or under benches, hiding from the police or their families, or from both – violence came in many guises.

Ten years back, when he was small, death squads had cleared the streets of raggeds and kinderwhores, dumping childish bodies by the lorry load into the weed-heavy waters of Lake Mareotis. As July had slid into August and the temperatures soared and foreign film crews began to descend on the city, the entourage around the young Khedive spoke of little else. Normal gossip ceased, as did back-biting and the daily jostle for position. A horrified fascination took hold of the palace from which the Khedive had to be protected.

Rooms stilled when he walked into them, conversations died, no one would talk if he was there. Which made it twice as hard to work out exactly what was going on. It was weeks before he discovered the rubbish being removed from the souks and alleys was human.

Almost everyone the Khedive overheard approved of what was being done. So much so that in the kitchens and sculleries, hard-worked porters cursed each other for not having had the idea first.

The one person not impressed was Koenig Pasha.

With the arrival of autumn came the executions. An army major, two detective sergeants, a colonel in the *morales* and a uniformed police officer. After that, the street cleaning stopped and the only thing left to drive raggeds from their narrow alleys was that winter's lashing rain.

Shaking water from his long dark hair, Tewfik Pasha stepped out of his shower and blinked, surprised to find Captain Bruford waiting impatiently in the doorway to his bedroom. He hadn't actually asked the woman in, Tewfik Pasha remembered with a sigh. Unidentified helicopter or no, punctilious courtesy had kept the Utopia Line's captain where she stood.

'Come in,' he suggested and turned away to slip his arms through the sleeves of a dressing gown. 'Can I offer you coffee?'

His sudden smile dazzled Captain Bruford so much that she accepted, without stopping to remember that it was almost noon and her own breakfast had been eaten hours before. Coffee and toast, served on the bridge; which was what a few of her older officers still called the computer room.

'That helicopter . . .'

The Khedive handed her coffee in a bone-china cup with matching saucer. Both items featured a discreet Utopia Lines logo. 'Do you want me to order some croissant?'

She refused the croissant, only too aware that eyes of darkest brown watched her from a face that was perfectly symmetrical, perfectly proportioned . . . just perfect really.

Captain Bruford shook her head and glanced back to find the eyes still watching her. 'The VSV,' she said. 'You really . . .'

'I am afraid I can't.' The Khedive's shrug was apologetic. Almost as apologetic as his voice. 'You see,' he said as he spread both hands to indicate his helplessness, 'I can't be seen to run away.'

'But the other passengers . . .'

'You have an on-board defence system,' said the Khedive. He nodded to a complimentary notebook resting on his bedside table. It was that year's Toshiba, an update of the model with the lizard-skin cover and silver corners. In it was everything a guest might want to know about the *SS Jannah*.

'Somewhere in the small print,' said the Khedive, 'it mentions that you carry ship-to-air defences. However, my own intelligence digests confirm that you have functioning PCB.'

'We've got what?' The captain's voice was hollow.

'Lightning throwers, three of them, LockMart-made, second generation.' The boy wriggled the fingers of one hand. 'I've got some too. They look like black metal spiders.'

They weren't exactly his intelligence digests, of course. They'd been delivered to the General, restricted to a reading list of one, his Excellency General Saeed Koenig Pasha. The Khedive had never been able to work out if the General left them open on his own desk because he expected His Highness to read them or because the old man thought he wouldn't dare.

'If they attack you,' said the Khedive, 'attack back. If they don't, then let them land on the 'copter deck. If there's a problem, I and my bodyguards will deal with it.'

'*Bodyguards?*'

'Well, bodyguard,' the Khedive admitted. 'Sort of . . .'

'And where is this bodyguard?' asked the captain, still cross at being blackmailed over the particle beam weapons. It was blackmail, because PCBs were illegal under an anti-proliferation treaty signed eighteen months earlier. Added to which, bodyguards were strictly forbidden aboard the *SS Jannah*. That was condition one of being accepted aboard.

'Where's Avatar?' The Khedive glanced round his suite and then at the sun-lit balcony beyond. 'Now there's a question.' Dropping his silk dressing gown to the floor, Tewfik Pasha hunted for some trousers. 'To be honest, I haven't a clue . . .'

He was still looking for something to wear when Captain Bruford let herself out. In total, she'd been in his suite for less than ten minutes. And he was, she told herself, irritating, difficult and over-privileged even by the standards of guests on the *SS Jannah*. He was also undeniably beautiful, with a charisma that made Hollywood replicas look shallow and contrived.

She considered briefly the possibility that he really was the General's lover. And then her watch chimed and she took the first available Orvis, overriding its programming so that it took her straight down to the ops room. She might be the captain, but this was a civilized ship and she didn't want to keep her chief of security waiting any longer than was necessary.

Chapter Fifty

28th October

Café Le Trianon was closed. That meant the private lift which went straight up to the floor above and the offices of the Third Circle was out of action. And that meant Hani had to use the stairs from Rue Sa'ad Zaghloul. She didn't mind; in fact, things were much quieter in the HQ of Iskandryia's civil service now that the lift and the telephones had stopped working.

Unfortunately, people still kept interrupting her.

Hani hit a hot key and her list of satellites vanished. Although the sub-routine that was supposed to be making contact with Avatar kept running in the background, without success.

'Hani. What are you doing here?'

The severe-looking Swede, the one in a dark suit with her pale hair pulled back into a bun, saw the young girl's face freeze and stepped back, forcing a smile.

Life at the Third Circle had been difficult these last few days. There was no real work for her to give the staff when they came in, but equally no one had given her permission to let them stay away.

Ingrid Nordstrom sighed.

None of this was the child's fault and actually Ingrid liked Hani. Much more than she usually liked children, or most other adults, come to that. The bey's young niece was the politest child Ingrid had ever met and the quietest. And if not for the child's obsession with computers, no one would have noticed she was here at all: but with just two machines working in the whole office, it was inconvenient if Lady Hani decided to monopolize one of them.

'I'm halfway through a story,' said Hani. 'I'm good at stories.'

She was too.

Raf thought she was with Khartoum, who thought she was at the madersa with Donna. And Donna thought she was shopping with Zara. Whereas, in fact, she'd walked from Shallalat Gardens to Le Trianon by herself. Later she'd say sorry, if she got found out, but at the moment things were much too critical to explain.

'It's a fairy story,' said Hani, 'sort of . . .'

This time Ingrid's smile was genuine. She'd been obsessed like this when she was a child. Her face always buried in Tove Janssen or Joan Lingard. And while it was true she'd never written a story herself, because her mother was too ill with nerves and sadness to be able to bear the tap of a keyboard, Ingrid had always had stories running in her head.

'What's it about?'

Hani's face creased in concentration, one finger hammering at the *page up* key until she found the passage she wanted.

'And lo as dusk fell over the stony desert, a son of Lilith came out of the night wrapped in a mantle of darkness. Across his chest he wore a necklace of human teeth and in his hand he carried a staff carved from the wing-bone of a djinn . . .'

Out of the corner of her eye Hani could see the woman frown so she skipped down a few paragraphs.

'. . . and when the sun rose over the rose-hued walls of Al Qahirah, the son of Lilith hid in the shadow of a house and wrapped darkness tight around his thin body. And this day passed as days always pass, slowly for those who labour and more swiftly for those to whom life is joy.

'Women came with water jugs to the stand-pipe as did a slave leading a thirsty donkey. For though Needle Alley was too narrow for a camel to pass, the donkey was thin and the carpets it carried were loaded on its back rather than in panniers as we do now . . .'

Hani stopped. 'There's more,' she said politely. 'If you'd like me to read it.'

Ingrid Nordstrom shook her head. 'I need to go.' She seemed

to be about to say something else but hesitated on the edge of speaking.

It would be about the son of Lilith, Hani imagined. Most of the people Hani had talked to about this, which admittedly was very few, were unsettled by the idea of djinn and vampyres. 'This vampyre's good,' explained Hani, her voice firm. 'You do get good ones . . .'

The woman looked surprised.

'It's true,' Hani insisted. 'I've checked it in a book. If a son of Lilith survives seven years undetected, he can travel to a land where a different language is spoken and become human. He can even marry and have children. Although,' Hani paused and her face grew serious, 'the children will still be sons and daughters of Lilith.'

'How fascinating.'

'And I won't be much longer,' Hani promised. 'As soon as I've finished here I'm going to the library.'

'Take your time,' said Madame Ingrid, and was surprised to discover that she meant it. Hani had become such a regular at the Third Circle it was hard to remember she was there on sufferance . . . That was what the bey had said the first time he brought her in, on sufferance. Ingrid wasn't to let Hani become a problem.

He'd been staring at Hani when he said it.

Ingrid decided to leave the child to her story. These were difficult times for everyone. And getting more difficult. She just hoped the bey wasn't being too strict with the girl.

Chapter Fifty-one

28th October

A window opened in the air in front of Avatar: a sleek black
'copter, blades chopping to a deep bass beat, smoked-glass
windscreen and not a decal in sight to say where it came from
or who might be inside.

'Floating focus,' said the Colonel. He was talking about the
spectacles.

'And the 'copter . . . ?'

'Mi-24x Hind gunship, adapted for three 20mm cannon with
Hellmouth, Rattlesnake and Quickdraw rockets. $189.3 million,
plus $1.6m per missile. Old model.'

'No,' Avatar said crossly. 'I mean, who does it belong to?'

'No idea,' said Colonel Abad. 'It won't tell me. Didn't want to
tell me its model number or price range until I told it you were
in the market to buy one. Then the imprinted sales coding took
over, always does . . .'

Avatar looked at the tiny machine that floated in front of his
eyes. Watching as toy-sized doors blew back and even smaller
figures tumbled out, guns ready. Somewhere just above his
hearing, sirens wailed and a gun spat, distant as the echo of
yesterday's fire-crackers. The black-suited figures were firing
over the heads of an unseen crowd.

'I'm in trouble, aren't I?'

The Colonel thought about this for a split second. 'As much
as you want and more.' His voice was apologetic. 'It was the
hidden door,' he explained. 'Not an original idea but effective.
One of the Medicis did something similar at the Pitti Palace. Of
course, the difference is, this one had a silent alarm.'

Even Hani had been impressed. Solder shut every normal

door on level Dminus4 and then leave an exit through the back wall of a strong room. The safe's entrance had featured antique defences: fear gas between inner and outer layers, tasers positioned down both sides of the frame, all the stuff that putting a gun to the wounded suit's head had miraculously disabled. But the trap door at the back, that had tripped an alarm satellite in low earth orbit. And half the intelligence agencies in Europe were busy going apeshit . . .

It looked like one of them had arrived.

Climbing the first twist of stairs was easy. More so, since Colonel Abad showed Avatar how to adjust the spectacles to infrared. The cold the Colonel could do nothing about, except get Avatar back to the warmth of an upper deck as soon as possible. Although, at Colonel Abad's suggestion, Avatar did empty his rucksack of its handcuffs, pepper gas and rope, and slice a hole in the bottom and another on either side, then invert the bag to wear as a tunic.

'Protect your core temperature,' the Colonel advised him, 'if you want to stop your brain from shutting down.' Avatar was slightly surprised to learn his brain could shut down, but he did what Colonel Abad suggested, mainly because he'd been doing pretty much everything the Colonel said since it first suggested he turn on those lights.

'You're manipulating me,' Avatar said, stopping dead at the thought.

'That's my job.' The familiar bearded figure smiled sadly, having first popped into floating focus. 'Only in the specifications it's called functional motivation.' With an apologetic shrug, Colonel Abad vanished and Avatar was left staring at riveted steps lit by a dull red gloom.

His skull ached as if someone had nail-gunned a metal band around his head and the only proof Avatar had that his hands were still attached to his wrists was that he could see one of them in the half gloom, wrapped dead and pale round the handle and trigger of his Taurus.

Another endless twist of stairs and then another, and still

Avatar was waiting to recognize the door that led through to
the ripped-out deck with the frozen pipes. So he kept climbing,
breath ragged in this throat and his jaw too numb to do more
than mangle his words.

'Sweet fuck . . .'

He was swearing for the sake of it, for the company. Because
every time he said something the Colonel flicked into focus at
the edge of his vision. Avatar's serious, sympathetic new friend,
iconic with history.

'Sweet, sweet . . .'

'Door's ahead,' said the Colonel. 'But first stop and listen
to me.'

'No,' said Avatar, shivering. 'Won't be able to start again.'

'The enemy eat children.'

Avatar nodded. Quite probably. There were some weird
fuckers around. One of them had left a dead body on his
dad's beach.

'You need to listen. I mean it.'

Avatar tried.

'Better,' said the voice. 'Look, I don't have time to make you
me . . . Tempting though it is.'

'You?' Avatar muttered. 'Why the fuck would I want to
be you?'

'Then who do you want to be?'

'Me,' said Avatar, 'DJ Avatar.'

Colonel Abad sighed. 'Failing that,' he said, 'and it will fail,
who else?'

It seemed an odd question. No, Avatar decided, fighting the
cold for long enough to reach a conclusion, it *was* an odd
question. 'Raf,' he said, not having to over-think his answer.
In the past he'd always dreamed of being Hamzah, but not
since that night with the kidnappers, when Raf appeared.
Raf was different. Raf was . . . Everyone else thought the bey
was a trained killer, one of the Sultan's best, but Avatar knew
different . . .

Raf was weirder than that. Way weirder.

'You know about Lilith?'

Adam's first wife had been bounced from Eden for refusing Adam. Well, for refusing his suggestion that she spread them. When Adam got bounced in turn, Lilith fucked him against Eden's outer wall and got pregnant, while Eve was still sulking (this was before Adam repented). After Adam got Eden back, Lilith fucked the snake and gave birth to the djinn.

Like her, not having eaten of the fruit, her children never died.

Avatar had seen the vid nasty several times.

'He really is . . .' Avatar felt the need to stress that, just in case Colonel Abad thought he meant Raf was one of those kindergoths and candyravers who haunted the clubs behind Place Orabi, where the dress options were sun-sucking black or ghetto ghastly.

'Really?'

'Too right,' said Avatar. 'Raf can see in the dark and hear things better than a bat. Kills like an animal when necessary, without conscience . . .'

'You like this man?'

'Oh yeah.' Avatar nodded his head, heavy though it was. 'He was meant to marry my half-sister . . . They'd have been perfect.' Realizing what he'd just said, the boy laughed but didn't quite recognize the croak that forced its painful way between his teeth.

'So what would this . . . *son of Lilith* do?'

'With the enemy? Take no prisoners.' Avatar could see it in his head, the way Raf would slide up to the door ahead, all set to kill the lot of them, never putting a footstep wrong. Except, of course, Raf was some place unhelpful, trapped in El Iskandryia. A city without . . .

'Turn off the ship's lights,' Avatar demanded.

'There's a problem with that suggestion,' said the Colonel. 'I can only override components of the electrical infrastructure in an emergency . . .'

'*This is an emergency*,' Avatar said, putting a space between each word. 'Anyway, I thought you ran this ship?'

'Routine tasks only. Engine maintenance and supply systems. On-board security and ocean-going navigation. The behavioural locks are solid and the parameters tight.' The Colonel's voice was dry, almost matter of fact. 'Believe me,' he said, 'I looked . . .'

'The lights,' Avatar said as firmly as his shaking teeth would allow.

'To cut those,' said Colonel Abad, 'I'd have to kill the ship's entire electrical system.'

'Then do it.'

'The entire system . . .'

'Sure,' Avatar nodded. 'I understand.'

The first thing Avatar saw was a tiny dance of light in the far distance, descending from the ceiling in a ragged two-step; slide and then stop, slide and then stop. A second firefly joined the first, followed by a third. Their dance taking them towards the deck.

Not fireflies, Avatar realized, his enemy, far off across the hangar, working their way down open steps in practised formation. The fireflies nothing but a faint splash of warmth between the bottom of a half-face night mask and the buttoned collar of a standard issue jumpsuit.

'How many in total?' he demanded.

All he got was silence.

'How many?' Avatar hissed.

Again silence, cold as the darkness. The Colonel was gone, along with the distant strip of lights. The cold pipes strung just above the deck no longer rattled. And the riveted plate below Avatar's feet was still, missing its heartbeat from the engine room beneath. Only the fireflies kept coming from far away across the deck.

Sliding himself through the open doorway, Avatar stepped rapidly sideways several times until he ended up behind a steel pillar. When he leant against it, the pillar felt no colder than his arm.

Cold was good if you got shot, according to the Colonel. It

reduced internal bleeding. Of course, it also slowed your concentration, which made it easier to get hit in the first place.

Three in here, how many more outside?

Avatar tried to call up the picture Colonel Abad had shown
him of that tiny helicopter just after it landed, doors popping
open and dark-suited toys spilling out onto the deck. Six
soldiers in all, maybe seven. Or was that eight . . . ?

Avatar shook his head, to free up his frozen thoughts, and
knew that if he didn't act soon the fireflies would be here and
there'd be no time left to unravel that one either.

Until he knew where the rest of the enemy were positioned,
silence was more or less the only real weapon he had. Silence
and surprise. Silence and desperation. Or how about silence
and being too cold to care?

No one was going to argue with that one.

Back hard to the pillar, Avatar flipped open the revolver
he'd stolen from the Khedive. Seven fat brass circles evenly
spaced in a ring, one of them already used. As he pushed the
cylinder back into place, Avatar realized this was it. Whatever
that actually meant.

The hammer pulled back with a muffled click, an internal
lever spinning the cylinder so that a fresh brass case presented
itself under the hammer's fall. Extending his shivering arm and
gripping his right wrist with his left hand, Avatar sighted along
the barrel at a firefly.

They were close now. Closer than he'd realized.

Time slowed and in the gap between the flash of the revolver's muzzle and its sharp bark, the vacuum of a passing slug
dragged a man's voice from his ruptured throat. The man Avatar
killed was at the back, the last of the three. It was luck, not skill.
He'd been trying for a body shot.

Instinct made the two remaining fireflies turn in horror to
stare behind them. By the time the first man glanced back,
Avatar was pulling his trigger again. This time Avatar's slug
took the man under his chin, deflected slightly on the inside
of his jaw and ripped apart his tongue, before liquidizing the
man's cerebellum. What was left of his occipital lobe splashed

against the back of his helmet. For all that, the soldier still landed on his knees, then crashed forward to headbutt the steel deck.

Shit mixed with the stink of cordite.

Roll, Avatar told himself, suddenly aware of the aftertaste of vomit in his mouth. That was what he should do. Avatar rolled, barely feeling the rivets that ripped into his shoulder. Then he rolled some more, stopping only when he clanged hard against a snaking pipe, the noise so loud it rang through the open area like a bell.

Instantly, a muzzle flared to his left, three quick flashes that sparked off the deck close to Avatar's leg, way too close. Rolling up and over the pipe, Avatar scrambled along its edge until he had thirty seconds of blind panic between himself and where the bullets had landed.

Adrenaline was flooding his body and for the first time in hours Avatar felt properly awake. Maybe that was what it took, what he should have done from the start; get someone to shoot at him . . . Now if he could just get them to give him their combat rations as well.

The gun the other man carried was squat, with a long magazine that curved away from him. Its barrel was the length of Avatar's thumb. Colonel Abad would have known the make, rate of fire and market price. Avatar just knew it looked dangerous.

Three shots, then another three. Each blip of the rifle's trigger registered in three fire fountains as the soldier swung his gun at random and bullets ricocheted in tight triplets from the floor. The man's big problem was that, despite the bug eyes of his official-issue combat mask, he fired blind. Avatar was just too bloody cold to show up on screen.

'So maybe I should be grateful,' thought Avatar sourly. Then decided not to waste the energy and rolled back over the pipe. All he had to do was keep going towards the stairs. Twenty paces later, Avatar stopped to looked back and again changed his mind. The soldier was still there, facing away from Avatar and staring intently at nothing much.

Avatar's options were keep crawling or else do the deed. Only he couldn't do that when the man's back was to him, though it was hard to know why turning round to die might be an improvement.

'Hey . . . behind you.'

Bursts popping through the darkness above Avatar's head. Different fireflies. When the man's clip finally hit empty, Avatar clambered to his knees and took a shot of his own.

Chapter Fifty-two

28th October

'I'm finishing a story . . .' Hani looked up, her head balanced on one hand and her elbow resting on her knee. 'But I can always end it now . . . ?'

She had her back to a wall and was sitting in late afternoon sunlight, on a small balcony recessed into the sloped glass roof of the *bibliotheka*.

'No need.' The chief librarian looked momentarily flustered, as if having caught herself being unforgivably rude. Which wasn't something that usually worried Madame Syria. 'I just didn't see you come in.'

'Are you sure you don't need the machine?' insisted Hani, holding up her borrowed laptop, its solar panels still outfolded.

'Mmmm?'

Madame Syria had been going to check the status of the library's electronic texts, when she noticed the balcony door was open. Obviously she had plenty of better things to do than this. And even if the core was dead and every e-book missing, as she rather suspected, she was still responsible for 1,250,000 real books, the kind people opened and held in their hands.

And anyway cultural vandalism was nothing new. Seven hundred years after the original *bibliotheka* began, Christian fanatics had destroyed all 500,000 of its manuscripts, including original works by Sophocles and Aristotle.

Even before that, the razing of the annexe on the orders of Theodosius had lost forever the *Alexandrian Geographica* and condemned Europe to a thousand years of the belief that Jerusalem was the centre of the world and that the world was flat.

'Madame Syria?'

The woman blinked to find Hani still patiently holding out the machine.

'No,' the woman said hastily. 'That's quite all right. I need to do something downstairs anyway.'

It was easy to forget a small girl, what with the chaos in the city as well as in the library, particularly when the child was so quiet and beautifully behaved. And Madame Syria didn't really begrudge the girl use of the computer. There were two non-web machines working downstairs, both outdated leather-bound models. Quite why only the three laptops out of seventy-five varied machines still worked was anyone's guess, though Madame Syria put it down to the fact that they'd been redundant models, stacked in a box in the lower basement, awaiting disposal. Originally there'd been five, but one had died almost immediately and one early yesterday. Fatal errors of memory, apparently, but then everyone had a few of those.

'I'm going to get a coffee,' said Hani. 'Would you like one?'

The chief librarian nodded without thinking and then frowned. 'I don't think your voice is programmed into the coffee machine,' she said apologetically, remembering too late that this was an irrelevance, the Zanussi was dead.

'There's a stall,' Hani looked round, as if about to impart a heavy secret. 'At the top of Rue Zaghloul. It's much better than the coffee here. When there *is* coffee here,' she added to clarify the matter.

'And His Excellency allows you to cross the road by yourself?' The librarian glanced over the edge of the balcony to the avenue below and suddenly realized just how stupid a question that was. Apart from an elderly man in a souf sat on a bench, the road outside was completely empty of traffic. Though a makeshift donkey cart sporting wheels borrowed from a motorbike was approaching from one direction, followed by a horse-drawn calèche, its leather roof raised against the possibility of rain.

She thought it was further proof of the child's good manners that Hani didn't point out that traffic problems were unlikely. Instead, the girl just nodded.

'Oh yes,' said Hani, 'I'm allowed to cross roads. In fact the bey allows me to do what I like.'

Madame Syria smiled and decided to go with the bey's niece to buy coffee. It was true that she really needed to use the child's machine but that could wait until Lady Hani finished her story.

Chapter Fifty-three

28th October

The glass girl was up ahead. Avatar saw her backlit through a halo of smoke that was his own cold breath. Her blue eyes watched him stagger up out of the gloom and, as he stumbled, she tossed her head, so that long blonde strands of her hair flicked through the air.

Avatar nodded his reply, the hard band of pain across his forehead tightening its grip, still held in place by invisible screws. His fingers were so numb he couldn't tell where the dead man's rifle began and his own flesh ended. Both of his weapons seemed a part of him, or he them; it didn't matter which way round, the result was the same.

He left the girl without saying goodbye, turning his back on the stained-glass memorial to a future not on offer to those like him, whatever his half-sister thought. In the Delta and along the river, the *felaheen* still used hoes rather than tractors. The only blonde girls he'd seen were rich tourists, out of their skulls on clubnite and still stuck at home in everything but actual place.

Avatar shot the next soldier without even noticing he'd seen the man. A single bullet shredding a larynx in a reflex action that saw Avatar's arm extended and the trigger pulled before Avatar's guts had time to knot with fear at what he was about to do; take his total up to four.

Another two soldiers swam into vision, radiating anxiety. They stood in the aquarium dark, arms stiff and bodies tensed. Wired into a command network as they all undoubtedly were, they'd have heard the others die.

Try mixing that . . . Avatar didn't doubt that he would, should he ever get back to his decks alive.

Stepping out from behind a pillar, Avatar raised his rifle and aimed at the nearest man. All the soldier had to rely on was equipment. Avatar had emptiness.

He pulled the trigger and felt his rifle buck. A second blip and the man behind tried to step forward on a shattered knee, only to stumble, pitching sideways as the remaining leg slid out from under him.

No prisoners.

Avatar walked forward and sighted along the barrel of his Taurus. The fallen figure shrinking into the deck, shoulders hunching as instinct kicked in and the man's body curled up to protect its vital organs from attack. Instinct based on millennia of experience. Instinct that hadn't yet adapted to guns.

Revolver in hand, Avatar crouched down and saw the figure flinch. The buckle at the side of the man's mask was a simple ceramic affair, tinted black as not to catch the light, the helmet's strap a fat strip of neoprene stitched to the lining. There were electrodes attached directly to the scalp of the person wearing the mask, though their purpose was uncertain.

Not that Avatar gave them much thought. He was much too busy staring into the pale blue eyes of a girl little older than him. Her broad face was set into something Avatar recognized instantly as acceptance. She still thought he meant to kill her.

As if he'd first bother to remove her mask. Except Avatar wasn't sure why he'd done that; unless, because it was the kind of thing Raf might have done? Certainly not because Avatar expected to find some blonde Soviet corn-daughter hidden underneath.

And she was Soviet. No other Army in Europe used women in front-line combat. A Soviet *Spetsnaz* ranger on an ex-Soviet liner come face to face with some Delta street bastard.

'Not even full Delta,' muttered Avatar to himself. Maybe half-Abyssinian or Danakil. It was hard to know. If a mug shot did exist of his mother, it was probably in the files of the UN or the Red Cross, along with blood type and a tissue sample.

'*What a fucking mess.*'

Some flicker of recognition in the blue eyes watching him

told Avatar that the wounded girl had logged the meaning, half recognizing his tone in what passed for consciousness amid all that endocrine stink of hope and fear.

And all the while, unanswered questions, mute but frantic, hissed from within the empty mask Avatar now held in his hand. They spilled out in a language he didn't understand, from a world he understood even less.

'Give me your rifle . . .' Avatar kept his own words simple. And though she didn't understand them, she followed his gaze until she saw what he saw and knew what he meant. But her hands remained white at the knuckle where they held her weapon tight to her body, one finger curled around the trigger and less than a shudder away from smashing her other knee, because that's where the muzzle pointed.

'Come on.'

A bullet to her head would have been Colonel Abad's solution, Avatar realized that, as he waited impatiently for the girl to process his demand and reach her decision. And in combat terms the Colonel was probably right. Of course, if she did something stupid then that would be Avatar's solution too . . . But all the girl did was uncurl slightly and push her gun away from her, leaving it to Avatar to kick the rifle away across the metal floor. Then he smiled apologetically and stamped on her good ankle, to cripple her other leg as well.

Once, just once, Avatar thought he might have seen his mother. Stood at the gates of St Luke's and staring intently through the ancient wrought iron bars at neatly-uniformed children who kicked a plastic football across melting tarmac or tried to dunk basketballs through a single hoop screwed to a classroom wall.

She looked old to him, but was probably not. A thin face peering from the folds of her heavy *hijab*. Her eyes had scanned the playground's movement seeking a point of silence. And the gaze she met was his. He was the one she watched, with a hunger so open it sent one of the sisters across the playground to find out who she was and what she wanted . . .

Avatar put a bullet through the head of a soldier standing guard outside the old bank vault. A single shot fired through the slightly open door. The *Spetsnaz* should have re-locked the safe after sending the others through. Except he couldn't, obviously enough, not with all the ship's systems down.

In reply, Avatar took a slug through his left arm which ripped up muscle and exited at the back. Only Avatar was so cold he hardly felt the blow and was too busy killing the first guard's partner to notice the blood which stained the canvas of his makeshift jacket.

Two left, maybe one. Up on deck where Avatar needed to be.

His mother was gone by the time Avatar brought his thoughts back to the long-forgotten and dusty playground. Gone from his memory and from the tall gates before Sister Carlotta even made it across the sticky tarmac.

Up ahead were more stairs and sunlight.

Flicking out the cylinder of his Taurus, Avatar discarded the dead brass and speed-loaded another seven rounds. His borrowed rifle already had a full clip.

Chapter Fifty-four

29th October

'It's paradise . . .' Hani's excitement filled the upper tier of the library, echoing off the inside of the giant pyramid to get lost among the books that lined row after row of shelves.

'*Hani!*'

'It is,' she insisted. 'Paradise. Jannah . . .'

Madame Syria stared up, towards the highest of the mezzanine floors where a small girl who shouldn't have been in the library in the first place, leant dangerously over a rail, while simultaneously pointing behind herself towards a dark shape on the horizon.

The *SS Jannah* had the classic profile for a great liner, a stepped ziggurat of cabins and suites rising high above the main deck along both sides, with the captain's bridge jutting from the ziggurat's front, like steel and glass flukes on a hammer-head shark. At the rear, a glass casino was suspended pod-like between tall towers. Everything aboard the ship was white, apart from the main deck, which was planted with a long promenade of palm trees and manicured lawn.

That the huge hull had originally belonged to a Soviet factory ship was a fact remembered only by nautical fanatics, shipping enthusiasts, Koenig Pasha and Hani.

'*Look!*' The girl practically screamed the word.

'*Hani!*' Madame Syria was torn between outrage and undisguised fear that the governor's niece might tumble over the edge to the marble floor far below.

'Look,' insisted Hani.

The chief librarian did what she was told, impressed despite herself. She'd only seen the *SS Jannah* once before, as a girl,

328

when the trimaran from Iskandryia to Syracuse had throttled back to let its passengers watch as the great liner cruised by.

'We've got to tell Uncle Ashraf,' Hani shouted, already halfway down the first flight of stairs. 'Really, we must . . .'

'Uncle . . .' No matter how often Madame Syria heard the child refer to the new governor of El Iskandryia by that name, it still seemed disrespectful. But then the child *was* his niece and a *mesdame* so . . .

Lady Hana bint-Abdullah al-Mansur, better known as Hani, hit the bottom of the stairs and grabbed the middle-aged woman by the hand, practically dragging her across the pink marble floor towards the exit.

'Paradise,' yelled Hani. 'It's almost here.' She'd shouted her message so often from the back of a calèche that her voice was now raw.

'What?'

'Paradise. The *SS Jannah*,' said Hani, her face split in a grin. 'It's true. Go on, tell her,' Hani insisted, turning to Madame Syria. The middle-aged librarian stared at Zara and then glanced over Zara's shoulder to a study door opening beyond.

'Excellency,' she said hastily.

Ashraf Bey scowled. In the study behind him were St Cloud, the Graf and Senator Liz, representing Paris, Berlin and Washington. All three had an opinion on the final sentencing of Effendi, all firmly held, all different. None of them wanted to give way on a single point. Everything, it seemed, but absolutely everything was a matter of principle.

Execution would play badly to the world's press. So they wanted Raf to agree to life imprisonment at Ras el-Tin. And this was before a man had even been found guilty . . .

Hani slipped her hand from Madame Syria's grasp, stepped politely but firmly around Zara who was blocking her from Raf's sight and stopped directly in front of her uncle.

'Solved it,' she told him, her voice little more than an intense whisper.

'Solved what?' Raf demanded.

'The riddle, obviously!' Hani's face exploded into a grin and then that was gone, leaving Raf looking at a quiet, satisfied smile. This too vanished as Hani noticed something on the study table behind Raf.

'Baklava!' said Hani in a tone something between outrage and admiration. 'You've got fresh baklava!' Without waiting to be invited, actually without appearing to notice Raf's other guests at all, she slipped through the door and into his seat.

'Hani.'

Politeness said not to answer with her mouth full, so Hani waited.

'My niece,' Raf explained and watched three faces shift their attention from him to the small girl and then back again.

'There's a ship coming into harbour,' said Hani when her mouth was empty, which took a while because Hani ostentatiously chewed the mouthful thirty-two times, as her late Aunt Nafisa had instructed. 'It's the *SS Jannah*.'

Tewfik Pasha had decided in advance what he intended to say and had prepared himself to overrule any objections. The talking box that Zara's brother found in the bilges had proved invaluable on both counts. An atelier on board the *SS Jannah* had spent the previous twelve hours hand-stitching a second jacket to specifications so strict that the Khedive had rejected the first attempt as inadequate.

The coat was modelled on a jacket his father had worn when he married the Khedive's mother, as seen on endless reruns of *Lives of the Rich and Infamous*. Cut from black silk and featuring minimal embellishment, the jacket's only decoration had been a thin piping of gold around its high collar. Unfortunately, the current Khedive's replica was both narrower across the shoulders and less tailored at the hips, although the atelier had worked hard to hide that fact.

At the suggestion of Colonel Abad, the Khedive had shaved away most of his beard, removing everything except the ghost of a goatee and the faintest trace of moustache. And, helped only by Avatar, he'd showered, dried himself and climbed into the immaculately-sewn costume; because that's what his new clothes were, a costume, the accretion of society's ideas on how a Khedive should look.

On Tewfik Pasha's head was a tarboosh. Over his heart was pinned a simple enamel and gold star. The order of the Imperial Crescent, first class. Even his choice of decoration carried a message. It was there to remind the waiting cameras that his ultimate allegiance (such as it was) went to Stambul.

And there would be cameras, dozens of them. That much was obvious from the myriad feeds he'd scanned as the *SS Jannah* steamed east towards El Iskandryia. A major city without electricity, without working computers, land lines, even cookers and cars. Its very nakedness drew the media like wasps to a honey trap. As the Khedive suspected his new governor intended it to . . .

Standing on deck with the injured Avatar slightly behind him, as protocol demanded, Mohammed Tewfik Pasha watched men the size of ants grab a stern rope and carry its giant loop to a waiting bollard. It took eight men to lift one rope and still they staggered under its weight.

When the rope was in place, a winch on the stern tightened, pulling the liner forward as a rope at the bow was loosened, removed from its bollard by another group of ants and carried forward, to be fixed around a bollard waiting up ahead. At which point the forward winch began to tighten. It was a laborious way to coax a liner along the edge of the Silsileh and perhaps there were easier ways to dock on Iskandryia's great sea wall, but this was the *SS Jannah*.

Stars, starlets and actual icons, whole galaxies of famous names were aboard. At least they were according to the *Hello International*. A *panoply* was the term they used. The reality was rather different. Late October/early November was definitely out of season and the constellation was confined to three minor genome-proteone heiresses, the elderly founder of LearningCurve GmB, two balding Bollywood lotharios, the Van der Bilt girl and him . . .

Ruler of a stricken city besieged on all sides by more-powerful nations who claimed to have only Isk's best interests at heart. Nations who, according to all the newsfeeds, still demanded that he give up Iskandryia's leading industrialist. And for what? To prove Isk was fit to join their nest of vipers.

Colonel Abad was right. It was an imposition too far.

Tewfik Pasha was scowling ferociously as he let an automated gangplank carry him down to the waiting dock, a fact that registered with everyone but him. He was too busy staring out over his silent city, looking beyond the crowded Corniche and the odd-angled pyramid of the *bibliotheka* to the green of Shallalat Gardens and a distant baroque palace that had, a century back, been the winning entry to the competition to design Iskandryia's railway terminus.

His scowl had everything to do with coming home and the state of his city. Nothing at all to do with the sight of Zara bint-Hamzah stood near the bottom of the gangplank or the fact she gripped the hand of Ashraf Bey as if her life depended on it.

Or was that her father's life?

'Your Highness,' she said, dropping Raf's hand.

Tewfik Pasha nodded to the girl and let go his scowl. But even as he fumbled for something appropriate to say, Zara's attention shifted away from him to her half-brother and something passed between the two as silent as thought and swift as electricity. Only then did she notice Avatar's injuries.

'I have a statement to make,' announced the Khedive loudly.

Camera crews surged. At least that was the appearance. What really happened was that the police cordon relaxed enough to let journalists flow though strategic gaps. They were getting good at that.

Cameras whirred, flashguns fired and questions were shouted.

And all the while the Khedive just stood there, counting down in his head from ten, elegant but slight in a simple black uniform. His face utterly impassive as the chaos broke around him. This was his version of courage. A refusal to engage immediately, to do from instinct what would please everyone else.

'You,' he said finally, reaching zero.

'Your Highness . . .' Having been chosen, the English woman with the lacquered blonde hair appeared uncertain which question to ask first. Too many needed answering, half of them involving the huge vessel moored behind him.

'How did you . . . ?'

'I own the SS Jannah.'

She looked at him, the rest of her question already dead on her lips.

'It belonged to my father,' the Khedive said with a shrug. 'Utopia Lines merely lease the vessel.' He could tell them how absurd he found this idea, that such an object should be owned by one person, but now didn't seem to be the time. If possessing a ship was absurd, then how much more so to possess a city, even a broken one . . .

The journalist looked from the Khedive to the liner, then back again. A tiny camera hummed in the air a few feet above her head; one lens focused on her face, the other fixed on whatever she had in her sights. 'Electricity,' she said as understanding suddenly lifted the frown from her face.

'You're going to use the ship to power El Iskandryia.' Enough capacity to power a small city, she was pretty sure that was in the liner's specifications somewhere.

'Power the city?'

It was a good idea, the Khedive was happy to admit that. But that wasn't why the liner had made her first land fall in forty years.

'No,' he said. 'Nothing so altruistic. After yesterday's unprovoked attack on the liner, SS Jannah needs a refit.'

Instant anarchy. Just add runout . . .

Ignoring the explosion of questions, Tewfik Pasha examined the crowd, his eyes skipping bland and blind over Zara and Raf, until they finally fixed on the man for whom he'd been searching. The Soviet ambassador, Commissar Zukarov.

'The attack was yesterday, at noon,' said the Khedive. 'Eight men in a Mi-24x Hind gunship . . . A Soviet-made attack helicopter,' he added. Though for most of those gathered on the Silsileh, including Commissar Zukarov, no clarification was necessary.

The Commissar was an elderly diplomat, waiting out his last years in a relatively unimportant post. And the Khedive had few illusions about the fact that Iskandryia was Zukarov's reward for a lifetime of doing exactly what he was told. In the man's face, the Khedive could see panic and fear, but no guilt. Which was what the Khedive had expected.

'It's possible the helicopter was stolen,' Tewfik Pasha admitted. But then pretty much anything was possible.

'They were terrorists?' The voice came from his right, a Frenchman.

'No,' said the Khedive, 'They were jewel thieves . . .' He paused to let the crowd of journalists assimilate that fact. 'At least, I assume that's what they were. They certainly broke into the safe.'

'I thought the vault aboard *SS Jannah* was unbreakable?' The English woman with the lacquered hair had re-found her voice. And the hunger in her blue eyes told the Khedive exactly how this story was going to play.

'Nothing is unbreakable,' he said carefully.

'Particularly not to a safe cracker with a thermal lance.' Avatar grinned, his voice street smart enough to suggest he knew all about things like that.

Flashguns fired.

No thermic lance had existed, but she wasn't to know that and nor was anybody else. The helicopter had been kept. The bodies Tewfik Pasha had ordered tipped over the side. As far as the Khedive was concerned, the press could report that as burial at sea.

'Was there a battle?'

The Khedive thought about that one.

'There was a short skirmish,' he said finally, with an apologetic glance towards Avatar and his bandaged shoulder. 'As you'd expect, security aboard the *SS Jannah* is excellent.' The

Khedive's lips twisted into a sour smile. Now he was beginning to sound like an advertisement for Utopia Lines.

'So the thieves were arrested?'

'No,' the Khedive said. 'They came armed and they were killed.' His gaze took in the Commissar, von Bismarck, the American Senator and that old man from Paris whose title kept changing. 'Except for two of them,' he added as an afterthought.

On cue, two burly crew members dragged the crippled Soviet girl down the walkway. Behind her staggered a small man, a revolver held to his cropped skull by a third crew member. Cameras fired, as the Khedive meant them too.

'Ashraf Bey.'

Raf stopped his whispered conversation with Zara and stepped forward. The bow he gave was slight, little more than a nod.

The Khedive raised his eyebrows. 'I'm putting these two in your charge.'

'Highness,' said Raf, and raised a finger. One of his uniforms instantly broke away from holding back the crowd. 'I'm transferring the prisoners to you,' Raf said. 'Take them both to the Imperial Free . . . And you,' Raf looked round for Hakim. 'Make sure they get full protection. And a doctor,' he added as an afterthought.

Protection from what Raf didn't say.

'Excellency . . .'

Raf turned back to the excited huddle of journalists.

'What is going to happen with Monday's trial?'

'In what way?'

'Will you continue as *magister* . . . Now His Highness has returned?'

'No, he will not.' The Khedive's answer was clear enough to reach the back of the waiting group. And even if it hadn't been, there were enough floating cameras and mics aimed in his direction to carry his reply to the waiting world.

'From now on,' said the Khedive, 'Ashraf Bey will be acting as city prosecutor . . .'

The gaze Raf met was unbending. A decision had been made publicly and was not to be broken. 'After all,' Tewfik Pasha continued, 'combating crime is a major part of any governor's remit.'

'In that case, will you still be allowing Miss Quitrimala to represent her father?'

'What case?'

The English journalist didn't seem able to answer.

The Khedive stroked his small beard, looking for the briefest moment exactly like his grandfather as a young man. 'As *magister* I will accept anyone the defendant chooses to appoint,' he said carefully. Although, in the circumstances, I would strongly recommend a trained lawyer.'

'But Quitrimala refuses to appoint his own defence . . . What's more,' the English woman's voice was taut with the human drama of it all, 'he categorically refuses to accept anyone appointed by the court.'

'Well,' said the Khedive, 'that is his right.' For the first time since Tewfik Pasha appeared on the jetty, he looked straight at Zara.

Hani sighed.

Chapter Fifty-five

30th October

The corridor was painted a drab institutional beige. Along its edges the dirty plastic floor tiles curled up to allow the floor to be sluiced clean. A relic from the bad old days when this wing had housed the insane, the incontinent and the politically inconvenient.

Three states that often went together.

At least they did under the Khedive's grandfather, after military doctors had finished their various forms of rehabilitation.

Raf moved quietly along its length, doing his best not to blink at the brightness bleeding in through windows opaque with grime. He wore no dark glasses and even five years' worth of dust and spiders web was not enough to soften the light.

Hakim and Ahmed he'd left hanging in the Athinos café oppose the hospital's front steps. Not very willingly Raf had to admit, but he'd overruled them with alarming casualness before making his way unannounced into the ugly concrete building. Along with the two guards, he'd left Eduardo, who was still in shock at discovering that 'the man', as he insisted on calling Raf, was governor of Iskandryia.

The façade of the Imperial Free had a preservation order on it, as did all the buildings that fronted the Western Harbour. The view from the sea was so famous that, years back, Koenig Pasha had decreed the skyline could not be changed.

When Raf had first arrived, the security guard inside the main door was watching Ferdie Abdullah, his eyes glued to a public screen, like somebody recently denied one of life's basic necessities. If he noticed the scowling young man with the flowers and Dynamo cap he thought no more about it.

Raf had returned the nod of a passing porter who was vaguely aware of having seen the visitor somewhere before, probably the last time the Dynamo fan came to see whoever he came to see. His fiancée from the size of that bouquet. No sane man would waste so much money on his wife.

Reaching the lifts, Raf had punched a button at random. He got out at obstetrics and took a different lift down two floors, got out again and used the emergency stairs to climb back past obstetrics to the deserted wards above. From there he walked the length of a corridor, until it ended at a large window.

Defenestration.

An ornate word for an ugly threat; but there were less messy ways to achieve what Raf wanted . . . Pulling a tiny voice recorder out of his pocket, he checked it was fully charged and working, then slipped it back into the leather jacket he'd borrowed from Eduardo, the battered one Eduardo had been wearing that night they went to the brothel.

Raf didn't really need to check the machine, since the Braun was brand-new and came from a boutique on the *SS Jannah*. He was just putting off what came next. And he already had the key code for the door in front of him. He'd got that from Hakim, who'd been guarding the impromptu prison cell when he got Raf's order to meet him in the loading bay behind Athinos.

And since the consultant had already made his rounds for the day and, other than Professor Mahrouf, only Ahmed and Hakim had authority to enter the cell, it was Hakim or Ahmed that the Soviet girl expected.

'Hi,' said Raf.

Her cell was small. The walls padded with cotton waste under hard canvas. There was one slit window, high up and barred. At its edges the floor had those sluice-friendly tiles which curved up under the padding on the wall. It was, in every way, as bleak as Raf had expected.

'I said *Hi* . . .'

She made no reply, just sat there in the orthopaedic chair, her legs wrapped in lightweight casts, her right wrist handcuffed to the chair's frame. An empty bedpan rested on the floor just out of reach and Raf caught the glance which said she wanted to ask him to hand it to her and then leave.

She didn't ask. Which was just as well. She'd been left like that for an hour because that was how Raf had told Hakim to play it.

'Just checking,' said Raf. He took a chart from the end of her bed and switched it on. Silk scaffolds shielded her broken, load-bearing bones. They were seeded with cells designed to deposit calcium and produce messenger RNA for pro/C, a precursor of the collagen found in bones. Also sourced from the *SS Jannah*, undoubtedly.

'Nothing but the best,' Raf said. 'But even with all that scaffolding, it won't be hard for me to smash them again, if that's what it takes.' He sat himself down on a bed next to the girl's chair, waiting for fear to happen.

It said a lot for her training that no panic reached her pale blue eyes. Instead her broad face fell into a mask of resignation, as if she'd expected no less – and she hadn't. All Soviet *Spetsnaz* rangers were instilled with a belief so absolute that the only thing awaiting them after capture was torture and death that it was practically hardwired.

'I've been told you speak English and Arabic,' Raf said as he took a notebook from the inside of Eduardo's scuffed jacket. He'd been told nothing of the sort. A full-face search of Iskandryia's intelligence database came up with as little as his, somewhat illegal, DNA trawl through the records of the Red Cross. The girl in front of him had never before been captured, or treated on a field of battle come to that.

What interested Raf was that Commissar Zukarov expressed so little interest in the prisoners. And the Khedive had given Zukarov a chance to comment, both on and off the record. All Zukarov said was, 'Not ours.'

Raf still needed to work out if that translated as '*Never ours*,' or '*Not ours now you've got them . . .*'

All the same, the girl understood some English. Enough for her brain to ignite verbal recognition patterns during a CAT scan. The two orderlies who'd chatted indiscreetly were plain-clothes. The white-coated radiologist was actually a police doctor. That, of course, had happened late last night and in a different ward.

'We could always do this the simple way,' suggested Raf.

The blonde girl just scowled, anger creating mental defences as she prepared herself to sever her mind from the pain awaiting her body. The separation never lasted, but everyone knew that occasionally people got lucky and died before their wandering mind got dragged back to hell.

'Maybe not.' Raf pulled out a snub-nosed Colt, also borrowed from Eduardo, and extracted an extra pair of old-fashioned metal cuffs from his coat pocket, flipping free one end. The Colt he put to the girl's head and the cuffs Raf flicked round the girl's free wrist, the left one, with a satisfyingly smooth flip. As manoeuvres went it was extremely professional, which was lucky. She was meant to think he did this all the time.

Snapping the cuff's other end to the bed's frame, Raf unlocked her right wrist, stood the girl up and walked her round to the mattress, his gun still at her head.

'On you go.'

With her left hand newly secured, the only way she could do that was lie face down. Securing her right wrist to the right side of the bed, Raf stood back. Then he yanked her ankles into position and fixed these with plastic strip cuffs.

Somehow, she still looked too comfortable.

So he took the pillows and when that didn't seem enough, pulled the sheet from under her, stripping the bed down to its striped mattress. After that, taking her hospital gown seemed obvious, so he ripped it in two from the bottom up and left himself with remnants still attached to her arms.

It was only when Raf pulled a gravity special and let drop the blade that he saw the girl tense. She was, he realized, watching him in a mirror across the room. Pretending not to notice, Raf slashed away the arms of her gown, leaving her naked except for two lightweight leg casts which looked disconcertingly like ankle warmers.

'Want to do this the easy way?'

Not a flicker of response.

With a sigh, Raf dipped into his pocket and pulled out a metal bar the size of a small torch. It was slightly pointed at one end, while at the other, a sheath of slightly-sticky clear plastic formed an easy-to-grip handle.

'You know what this is?'

She did. Every combat troop in the so-called civilized world could recognize a shock baton. They were the negotiators of choice for police forces across the world, not to mention for criminal elements from Seattle to Tokyo, combining all the advantages of maximum pain with minimal tissue damage. Batons didn't leave the kind of scarring that ended up on Amnesty posters, which was one undoubted reason for their popularity.

'I'm sorry,' said Raf, folding his fingers into a half fist, 'but there's something I need you to tell me And I need you to tell me it now.' His rabbit punch caught her in the kidney and urine darkened the bare mattress as her bladder emptied. 'It's kind of urgent.'

Walking to the head of the bed, Raf crouched down until he could see her face. Furious eyes challenged him and then he was wiping spittle from his cheek.

'Fuck it.' Raf stood up and wiped his face.

Instead of using the baton, Raf took his gravity knife and scratched a cross potent into her naked back, slicing just deep enough to draw blood. Then he stuffed a tissue into her mouth, gagged her with the cord from her gown and put the small recorder down on the windowsill. The time had come for Raf to go next door.

'Gregori,' said Raf.

Now, the small man stripped naked in the corner *had* been treated on a field of battle. At Fort Archambanlt to be precise, fifteen years before, on the Shari river in the southern wastelands of Tripoli. The name he'd given was Captain Gregori the Profligate, and a footnote still solemnly recorded a triage nurse's expert opinion that this was false.

What was much more interesting for Raf was that Gregori's DNA showed significant points of similarity to the blonde girl. Not enough points for him to be her father, but quite enough for him to be an uncle or cousin. Which fitted neatly with the Soviet habit of conscripting whole families, then keeping them together because the bonds that tied them were already imprinted.

The other interesting fact was that Gregori had surrendered voluntarily, not because he'd been wounded and unable to continue or brought to a halt by lack of ammunition. He'd taken one look at Avatar and put down his own gun seconds ahead of putting up both hands. Since *Spetsnaz* rangers didn't surrender, there was a meaning here that Raf wanted unravelled.

'You,' said Raf, 'on your feet.'

The naked man did what Raf expected him to do, which was stay slumped where he was.

'Up,' Raf insisted, producing Eduardo's gun. When Gregori still didn't move, Raf grabbed a handful of hair and yanked the man to his feet. A hood was needed and Raf had forgotten to bring one, so he stripped the case from a hospital pillow and used that instead, knotting its bottom tight round the man's throat.

Outside in the corridor, Raf spun Gregori in a circle, bounced him off a peeling wall and then spun him in the opposite direction. The man was still staggering when Raf pushed him through the door of the blonde girl's cell and untied the hood.

His partner lay naked and gagged on the bed, face down on a urine-blackened mattress, with blood running from a cross potent cut into her back. On the floor lay a discarded shock baton. If Raf had been Gregori, he'd have tried to attack Raf too.

A kick to the knee took Gregori to the floor, his fall unbroken because his arms were cuffed. Raf kicked him again for good measure, but Raf's snarl was not matched by the severity of the kick. He wanted Gregori scared, not injured.

'Who paid you?'

The man didn't even turn his head. Just lay on the floor,

curled into a tight ball, not the action of a *Spetsnaz* officer with Gregori's experience.

'Look,' said Raf, kicking him slightly. 'We already know you weren't acting on orders. So what we need is information on who instigated this attack.' He bent down and dragged the man to his knees. 'And it's information we intend to get.'

Raf walked over to the discarded baton and picked it up, Gregori's anxiety only really kicking in when Raf kept going towards the bed.

'Who,' said Raf, 'was behind the attack?'

He switched on the baton.

Gregori said nothing so Raf turned to the girl and put the live baton to her spine. The gag blocked her scream, but she still bucked in agony as muscles in her back locked solid. In the quivering aftershock, she pissed herself again. The baton had touched her spine for less than a second.

Raf breathed out, opened his eyes and turned back to the man.

'That's just a taste,' he told Gregori. 'Now we bring in the expert.' Toggling his watch to visual, Raf put a call through to Eduardo. 'Dr Lee? We're ready for you . . .'

The white coat came from a medical supply shop, as did the stethoscope Raf had given him earlier. And Eduardo only extracted the coat from its carrier bag and hung the stethoscope round his neck when he'd reached the corridor and was certain no one else could see him. He'd been assured by Raf that all CCTV cameras were still faulty, courtesy of Hakim's earlier word with the Imperial Free's security manager. Eduardo just hoped this was true. In case it wasn't, and because it looked cool, he was wearing shades. Copies of the pair usually worn by Raf.

'Excell . . .' He saw the frown on Raf's face and swallowed the rest of his word. 'I'm here,' he added, redundantly.

'Everything she knows,' said Raf. 'I want the lot.' He made to pass the shock baton to Eduardo, who shook his head.

'I always use my own.' Eduardo pulled a battered rod from his pocket, wrapped around with duct tape. 'It gives greater control.' Both Raf and Eduardo's batons came out of stores at Champollion Precinct and Raf had made Eduardo practise this little exchange until he was word perfect, but Eduardo was still pleased with himself. Raf had explained twice that getting it right was very important.

What they had to do was trick the man.

'It won't take long,' said Eduardo, pulling a tube of lubricant from his coat pocket.

Dragging Gregori to his feet, Raf reached for his makeshift hood and began to pull it over the man's head. The last thing Gregori saw before a pillowcase closed off his world was Eduardo leant over the face-down girl, rubbing KY between her buttocks.

The screams began before Raf even had time to spin Gregori round or bounce him off a wall. He did the spinning anyway.

Raf kicked Gregori's door shut with one heel, half closing off an animal howl that began low and ran the whole register before ending in juddering sobs. Even through the tightness of a gag, it was possible to hear the utter anguish of the person being tortured.

'You can stop this,' said Raf, pulling off Gregori's hood, 'any time you want to . . .

'Okay, your choice.'

Raf muttered into his watch and the next scream was longer, shuddering to a close in a muffled plea, spoken in no language understood by either of them, in all probability, no language that was human.

'She won't die,' said Raf, 'just wish she could.'

He pulled a sheet of paper from his borrowed jacket and skimmed it. At the top, a blue and yellow globe nestled within two curving sheaves of corn. Between the tips of the corn hung a red star. And beneath the globe rose a yellow sun, rising from the base of the two sheaves, which was bound round with red ribbon.

'Commissar Zukarov states categorically that you were *not*

involved in work for the Soviet Union, but you knew that didn't you . . .' Raf shrugged and skimmed the sheet. 'The Soviet Union disowns your actions.'

Gregori looked at him.

'You want to talk to me about that?'

The man didn't.

With a sigh, Raf muttered more words and the howls began again, animal-like and anguished, each one running into another until the very magnitude of the pain became unimaginable.

'Your choice,' Raf repeated. 'Your choice . . .'

Gregori held out for another ten minutes, during which he chewed the edge of his lip to ribbons. And then he caved, eyes blind with tears as he pushed himself to his feet and lurched towards where Raf sat on a dusty wooden chair.

'Whatever you need,' Gregori said desperately. 'Just stop your doctor.'

'Enough,' said Raf into his watch. The screams stopped dead. 'You want to go see her?'

Gregori shook his head. 'Later,' he said. 'When the shock goes. She won't be able to talk properly until then.' He looked, at that moment, as if he spoke from experience. 'What do you want to know?'

'Everything,' said Raf, except that he already did. The man and girl were there to confirm something. All the same, Raf let Gregori describe how *Spetsnaz* were hired out to the highest bidder for any currency harder than roubles. There were rules to guarantee no military action was counter-revolutionary but, in practice, any job could be made to fit.

Gregori's bitterness was unmistakable.

'You recognize her?' Raf pulled a photograph from his jacket. It showed the suit he'd left on the floor of the deserted house in Moharrem Bey. The technicians had done a good job with lighting, make-up and post-production. The woman looked only slightly dead.

'Yes . . . She died.'

'I know,' Raf said, 'I killed her . . . *Thiergarten*, right?'

Gregori nodded.

'Who both hired you and had tourists butchered to order . . . No,' Raf held up his hand when Gregori opened his mouth, 'that wasn't a question.'

The Soviet shrugged.

'So,' said Raf, 'who involved the *Thiergarten*? That *was* a question,' he added.

'I don't know.'

Raf had already figured this out for himself.

'What happens now?' the *Spetsnaz* asked. 'To me and Nadia.'

'Your cousin?'

'My niece. My brother's child.'

'Sanctuary,' said Raf. 'Asylum. New identities if that's what it takes. Help us and we will help her.'

Gregori smiled grimly. 'It takes time to recover from something like that.' He jerked his head towards the silent wall. 'And sometimes people never do, but you already know this, don't you?'

'Maybe,' said Raf, 'it will take much less time than you think. Now . . .' He pulled a final photograph from his jacket. 'Tell me if you've ever seen this man.'

Eduardo looked at Raf's outstretched hand, clicked the relevant bit of his brain into gear and shook it. And kept shaking until Raf patiently prised free his own fingers.

'Excellency.' Eduardo's smile was shaky. His eyes still tearful. All he'd had to do was click on a voice recorder when Raf said turn it on and click it off when Raf said do that; but the ancient recording of a Moslem girl being tortured kept repeating in his head.

'One of the best,' Raf said to Hakim, as Eduardo turned away. 'One of the best.'

Hakim looked doubtful.

'I mean it,' said Raf, and watched Eduardo shuffle away from Café Athinos, dodging traffic until he finally reached his ancient Vespa which was parked up next to the Corniche wall. It took Eduardo five goes to kick-start the machine.

The man cost Champollion less than the precinct paid out each week for fresh coffee and still counted himself lucky.

'Guard the hospital,' said Raf to the two men remaining, well aware that Hakim and Ahmed were really meant to guard him. By giving them other duties he freed himself up; they both knew that and were powerless to do anything about it. And besides, governors of Iskandryia were supposed to be impossible to work for, it went with the job description. 'Find the prisoners proper clothes,' he added as an afterthought, 'and get a doctor in to see to the girl's back.'

Raf caught the look in Hakim's eye. No matter what had really happened, an enhanced version would be round the precinct within minutes. His officers could be relied on to guarantee that his reputation lived up to its reputation.

'She'll live,' said Raf as he slipped on his shades and collected his own jacket from the back of Ahmed's café chair.

There were at least fifteen other cars on the road, now that the curfew had been lifted. They were old, battered and driven by grinning men who waved to friends and sometimes complete strangers. It was an irony of the EMF blasts that those whose vehicles were oldest were those least affected.

Garages were still shut but the electricity was back in a third of the city and stand-pipes were already being removed from at least one *arrondissement* which now had water. Shops were reopening. All of the newsfeeds had miraculously been restored. Foreign reporters were busy doing talking heads about how El Iskandryia was slowly getting back on its feet.

On his way out of the city, Raf halted the Bentley beside an over-flowing irrigation ditch and tossed in the tiny recorder. The woman on it had died long before he was born; and although the recording, smuggled at great risk from a cellar in Kosovo, had not been allowed as evidence at a later trial, a copy of the recording had found its way to Amnesty. Their 'democracy in action' radio advertisement was judged political and banned in twenty-four of the twenty-six countries in which it was due to run.

*   *   *

'What now?'

'His Excellency Ashraf al-Mansur . . .' St Cloud's major-domo was careful not to look at his master. Not seeing things he shouldn't see formed a substantial part of his duties. 'He *demands* admittance.' The small Scot spoke the word with such relish that the Marquis looked up and almost blew his carefully constructed, syncopated rhythm.

Luckily the object of his interest kept moving, eyes fixed into the far distance. Drugs, familiarity or fear had emptied the adolescent's smooth face of anything except boredom and an instinct for absolute obedience.

'Show him in.'

'Sir?'

'Show in al-Mansur.'

The major-domo bowed and withdrew, walking backwards from the chamber. When he'd trained at his own expense in Kensington, this hadn't been how he'd expected to spend his life.

'The Marquis will see you now.' He gestured politely towards a large door and the unacceptability of what lay beyond. 'You may find him . . .' The major-domo hesitated. 'A little distracted.'

Raf entered without knocking. Unlike the tiled, fountained and pillared Moorish fantasy that was Dar St Cloud, the Marquis' villa overlooking Cap Bon in Tunisia, the drawing room of his house at Aboukir could have been transported wholesale from Paris.

Gérard's *Cupid and Psyche* hung in pride of place on the far wall. An adolescent Cupid chastely kissing the brow of a blonde girl who stared wide-eyed straight at the door where Raf stood, her hands folded neatly below naked breasts. A *Vulcan Surprising Venus and Mars* hung beside it, a huge canvas edged in heavy gilt, with the frame so massive that it almost touched both ceiling and floor. And on other walls, endless young nymphs gazed innocent-eyed at lean shepherd boys, oblivious to their own semi-nakedness.

A Napoleon III sideboard was positioned directly beneath the Gérard, its top a single slab of horsehair marble cut from a quarry outside Milan. Along the top were ranged naked glass figures, mostly Lalique, and two decanters.

'Pour yourself a small drink.' The Marquis spoke without looking up or releasing the figure still sat on his lap (what with the shaved skull and baggy shirt, it was impossible to tell if St Cloud's companion was male or female). 'This won't take long.'

'It might,' said Raf, 'if we're going to cover who had Kamil Quitrimala kidnapped, why three tourists were butchered to order, a casino burnt and the pipe line to a refinery cut. And that's before we . . .'

'*Out*,' said St Cloud crossly. And the adolescent to whom he spoke disappeared in a flurry of colt-like legs and a flash of thin buttocks. The over-sized shirt was St Cloud's own, Raf realized; its use a badge of ownership or fondness received, perhaps both.

'Gang warfare for the casino and kidnapping . . . Psychopaths for the murders, variously dead, I believe. And I assume the Sword of God was behind the refinery, just as it was behind those outrageous EMF bombs.' The Marquis gave a smile.

'You assume wrong.'

St Cloud looked at him.

'What,' said Raf, 'do you know about the Osmanli Accord?'

'Less than nothing,' St Cloud's voice was firm. 'I never bother myself with politics.'

'So it would shock you to discover that, behind the scenes, Berlin needs French agreement to retain its spheres of influence . . . As does Moscow?'

The Marquis snorted. 'The idea that Berlin would ask anything of Paris is as unbelievable as . . .'

'The idea that someone French might demand a price of Berlin,' Raf said smoothly. 'Well, while you're at it, imagine that breaking Hamzah was the only result to matter in our little local crisis.'

'Hamzah Effendi?' St Cloud shook his head. 'Surely not . . .'

Raf nodded. 'Imagine everything else was just so much means to an end. So the question I have to ask is, Who would want to damage Hamzah?'

'Who indeed . . .' said St Cloud. 'I suspect we'll never know. Always assuming there was somebody.' He stood up from his elegant Louis XVIII chair, casually slipped himself back inside his trousers and made for the sideboard.

'Are you sure . . . ?' His hand hovered above a brandy balloon.

'Absolutely,' said Raf. 'Beyond doubt.'

'Your choice . . .'

St Cloud poured himself a generous measure of Courvoisier and swilled it round the balloon, bending close to inhale the heavy fumes. 'Of course,' he added as an apparent afterthought, 'even if this were all true . . . It doesn't change the fact that Hamzah is guilty as hell. And there's always the future ownership of that refinery to consider . . .'

'Plus the Midas oil fields in central Sudan and certain Mediterranean off-shore sites.'

'Quite,' said St Cloud. 'Now, should a senior official find himself in a position to facilitate the transfer of Hamzah's part of those holdings . . . After they've been legally forfeited by Hamzah, obviously. Then any country intent on consolidating its interests would undoubtedly be very generous.'

'Generous?'

'A commission is usual in these cases.'

'Five per cent?'

St Cloud looked shocked. 'One or two. Three at the absolute maximum.'

'And what would three per cent come to?'

The Marquis told him.

Raf decided to take that drink after all.

Chapter Fifty-six

1st November

The trial proper began two days after Raf's visit to the house at Aboukir. On the morning of 5th Safar 1472, a day that Raf thought of as Monday 1st November . . .

Within the first hour, Zara reached the inescapable conclusion that the man whose bed she'd twice shared was about to destroy her father. So now she sat at a long desk at the front of the temporary court and shuffled papers, while atrocity after atrocity unravelled itself on screen.

Atrocity was the word Raf used to describe what the judges were seeing. It wasn't a term to which Zara felt she could object.

Hani, however, sat at the back. And although the steady swing of her legs, which earlier had been flicking backwards and forwards to scuff the floor had stopped completely, she resolutely watched one of the screens. Her dark eyes darting from horror to horror; though whether to see more or allow herself to take in less was hard to tell.

She shouldn't have been on board the *SS Jannah* anyway, which the Khedive had declared Iskandryian soil for the duration of Hamzah's trial. But Khartoum had been strangely willing to be persuaded that he should accompany her, and the soldiers at the door had done nothing but stare at the cat on her shoulder. As a result, she now sat beside the skeletal Sufi in a makeshift public gallery, watching things she was pretty sure she didn't want to see.

The picture quality was terrible, the contrast too sharp, and the camera juddered with the reporter's every step, none of which really mattered. It was what the camera showed that counted. Oh, and spinning numbers near the bottom that gave time, date and an accurate GPS reading.

The ownership of the battleground itself was moot. So the location was translated underneath as 'North Eastern Sudan/Southern Egypt (disputed) . . .'

At first, as Raf gestured at the early images, inviting the judges, press and public to watch the evidence being presented, he'd thought the juddering was down to gyroscope malfunction in the original hand-held camera, but as the lens panned across another dead boy, fist stuffed into his mouth to prevent himself from crying out, he realized the gyroscope just hadn't been able to compensate for the photographer's shock.

Raf pushed a button on his control and the picture froze.

The assignment had both made and destroyed Jean René; turning the man into a living saint and consigning him to forty years of knowing his single most significant work was already behind him.

Raf stepped back to give the judges clear sight of the elderly, shock-haired Parisian, who stood in a witness box built overnight by carpenters at the Khedive's order.

'Who took these photographs?'

The elderly man stared down his hawk-like nose. 'You know who took those,' he said crossly. 'Why else would I be here . . . ?'

Raf smiled sympathetically. Nodding to show he understood the tumble of emotions through which the man must be going. 'Who took these photographs?' Raf repeated, his voice loud enough to carry to the public gallery.

'I did,' said Jean René.

'You did?' Flipping open a leather notebook, Raf pretended to check its screen. Working hardware, decent lighting and reliable power had ceased to be a problem the moment Tewfik Pasha relocated the court to the ballroom of the *SS Jannah*.

'You are a war reporter?'

'I was,' said the man bitterly.

'And you gave up when?'

The man's leonine mane of white hair rippled as he nodded towards the frozen screen, where the dead boy still lay with one fist in his open mouth. 'I gave up after that,' he said. 'How could I not?'

'And you became what?' Raf asked, glancing again at his notebook.

'I founded Sanctuary,' said Jean René, staring at the judges. His gaze bathed St Cloud, the Graf and Senator Liz in ill-hidden contempt. 'So long as countries like yours fight their wars by proxy there will always be work for people like me.'

Senator Liz opened her mouth but shut it again at a glance from St Cloud. Instead the three judges ignored the comment from a man famous for not pulling his punches when it came to apportioning blame.

'Excellency . . .' St Cloud's tone made it clear Raf could continue.

Only Raf was thinking, of nothing.

Less than nothing.

'Excellency . . .'

Raf came awake with a start, glanced at the judges and realized it was still his witness, but he had no questions for Jean René. Not real ones. Hamzah had been there, DNA matching marked him out as the soldier found on the battlefield by the Red Cross. His fingerprints, taken by a teenage Jewish nurse who hoped to reunite the boy with his parents, had identified Hamzah as the person who loaded and fired the HK21e machine-gun.

If that wasn't enough, the boy's inky thumbprint validated a typed confession found locked in a Chubb in Koenig Pasha's study; typed, it seemed, on an old Remington Imperial, to ensure no trace was left on any datacore. The confession had been witnessed by a certain Major Koenig Bey. A copy of this rested among the documents piling up in front of the three judges.

As for the defendant himself, guilt oozed from Hamzah's skin like sweat. Expensive and over-tailored though his clothes might be, they still hung from his diminished body like a beggar's rags. Everything about the man conceded defeat.

There was very little chance that Raf could blow this case. And inside his own head, Raf was already writing his closing speech, the winning address he'd make once all the evidence, both direct and circumstantial, had been heard. Once the transcripts, old newsfeeds and actual weapons had been examined.

The press were already his, Raf could tell that just from watching them. The public gallery were glued to every unfolding moment. It was undeniably time to wind up his examination of this witness and let Zara take the floor.

Flicking his eyes from the photograph on screen, back to where Jean René stood in the makeshift witness box, Raf opened his mouth to thank the man and did what he'd been avoiding doing all morning, somehow allowed his gaze to shift past René to where Zara sat.

Pain.

Absolute loneliness.

Enough of both to rock the courtroom around Raf.

If ever he'd needed the fox it was now. The fox would have known what to do because the fox always knew what to do. That was why it existed. To take from Raf the need to make those kind of decisions.

Ashraf al-Mansur, sometime ZeeZee, shuddered at this sudden understanding. Or else the courtroom shuddered. Whatever, something did as his eyes adjusted. And the rococo magnificence of the ballroom, with its borrowed ceiling, faux marble and fat gilded cherubs faded to a pixillated blur.

'Safety off,' said a gun.

Raf blinked at the half-memory and felt the cherubs reappear. Nothing had changed except for him and that change was so small, he wasn't even sure it was real. But then, he'd never been too sure about anything. Mostly he just accepted things. Accepted and then assimilated the accepting. Whatever he needed to become he became . . .

Some people regarded that as a psychologically adaptive advantage. Others knew it as negative capability. A few said, without quite realizing what they said, 'There but for the grace of . . .'

Standing beside Ka, Zac said nothing. He'd talked little enough when he was alive and now he was dead he spoke even less . . .

Ka thought that strange.

'Distance?'

'Half a klick and closing . . .'

It was an incredibly stupid weapon and the kid with the amulets didn't know why the manufacturer had bothered. But then the kid was just that, a kid. Someone too young to make the link between action and . . .

Everything that Raf had ever read about The Hague Convention suddenly ran like water through the parched soil of his mind.

'Did you actually photograph this man?' Raf turned to point at Hamzah who, for the first time since the trial had begun, lifted his head and looked around the well of the court. Maybe it was something in Raf's voice or else he too could hear clouds growling low like thunder.

Justice. That was what a court was supposed to provide. And he was Ashraf al-Mansur, Ottoman bey and supposedly governor of El Iskandryia, for the next few hours at least. Raf looked at Zara and then inside himself.

The living saint looked puzzled.

'It's a simple enough question,' Raf insisted. 'Did you photograph Hamzah Quitrimala?'

'Back then?'

'Yes,' said Raf heavily, 'back then . . .'

Jean René nodded.

'You photographed Hamzah Effendi as a child?' Raf said slowly, as if trying to get something straight in his head.

'I did. Yes.'

'Describe him.'

Puzzled, the elderly man glanced from Raf to the row of judges who sat watching from their raised bench. Above and behind them, alone at a higher bench sat the Khedive.

'Hamzah's over there,' said Raf. 'Not on the judicial benches. That is, if you need to take another look.'

Jean René hesitated.

'Tell us,' demanded Raf, 'how did he look?'

They stared at each other across the well of the court. And somewhere at the back of the bey's mind, thoughts continued to resonate until their growl manifested as a shiver which ran the length of his spine.

'Nothing unusual,' Jean René said finally. 'Scruffy. Wearing a man's shirt, trousers held up by a broken belt.'

'Broken?'

'The buckle was missing. The belt was tied round his waist. He had bare feet but then they all did. After a while, hot sand and gravel baked their feet to leather . . .'

'You've looked at this photograph recently?'

Raf paused, seeing Jean René look uncertain. 'It's a simple enough question,' he said. 'Did you dig out your photograph of this murderer?'

'Objection . . .' Zara was on her feet.

The Khedive shook his head. 'Objection overruled.' He turned to Raf, eyes hard. 'Presumably you have sound reasons for this line of questioning . . . ?'

Raf nodded. He had reasons all right. Half a dozen within his own head. Plus another, still stood, glaring at him. Although his main reason sat at the back of the court beside Khartoum, her eyes spilling over with tears as they flicked between him and Zara.

What was justice anyway?

Nothing most people would recognize. Nothing Hani had ever been given.

'Find the photograph,' Raf demanded. 'I want the court to take a good look at this killer.'

Finding the shot took a minute or two of skipping forwards and backwards, looking for the right image. And all the while, screens flickered with figures that came and went as Jean René trawled angrily through his notebook's data sphere.

A girl half buried in a sand dune.

Camels starved to a sack of fur and protruding bone.

A burned-out Seraphim driven by something reduced by flame to the texture of bitumen. Teeth grinning from a lipless mouth.

Images enough to make the ballroom fall silent and its gilded elegance suddenly appear frivolous and out of place. And finally, when it seemed not even the judges could stand another close-up of a dead child, Jean René found the picture for which he'd been looking.

A boy shading his face against the sun as he stared into a hungry lens. The shirt he wore lacked buttons and the trousers had been hacked short in the leg. At his feet rested an open water bottle and a radio.

Half a dozen amulets hung around his neck. Most were beaten silver or brass, with one no more than a bundle of hawk feathers tied tight with a leaf. But the last one, the one that mattered because it led aid workers to get wrong which side he was on, was a small cross carved from bone. The boy's eyes were hidden by thick dark glasses and a cigarette hung from his bottom lip, tendrils of smoke vanishing into the hot afternoon air.

Not that much older than Hani really.

'How old would you say this child was?'

'Irrelevant question.' Senator Liz Elsing was out of her chair.

'Overruled,' said the Khedive. 'The prosecutor still has the floor, as is his right . . .' Tewfik Pasha's smile was thin. 'Mind you,' he said, 'if this is the prosecution, I can't wait for the defence.'

'How old?' Raf repeated.

Jean René thought about it, looked at the screen and then back at Hamzah, an element of certainty leaving his face. Finally the man shrugged. 'I don't know,' he said. 'It's hard to tell.'

'Then perhaps we should find somebody who can tell us . . .' Raf stared at the public benches and a dozen cameras clicked. 'Presumably the *SS Jannah* has a doctor . . . ?'

There was silence while the judges tried to work out which of them Raf was asking. Finally they realized he was talking to the Khedive.

Tewfik Pasha nodded, reluctantly.

'And may I borrow your medical officer as an expert witness?'

The boy scowled, skin darkening under immaculately applied make-up. 'Of course,' he said. 'Provided the captain also agrees.'

The court recessed while the ship's medical officer was summoned. And then everyone waited again while a tall German woman introduced herself to the court and was sworn in.

'You are Lena Schultz?'

'I am.'

'And you trained where?'

'Heidelberg . . .'

Raf couldn't resist glancing at von Bismarck. The young Graf now leant forward and Raf knew he, at least, would regard her every word as absolute.

'You are the surgeon for the *SS Jannah*?'

She shook her head and dark hair flicked across to touch her cheeks. 'I am not a surgeon,' said Dr Schultz. 'I am a general practitioner.'

'I see,' said Raf, sounding as if he didn't. 'Can you tell me why Utopia Lines employ a general practitioner?'

She looked at him.

'Instead of medical software.' Raf paused, wondering how best to qualify his question. 'I thought that statistically . . .'

'Some people,' she said heavily, 'actually prefer the human touch.' *Some people* being rich. At least that was the inference.

'Really?' Raf shrugged. 'In that case, don't such people bring their own?'

'It happens, sometimes.' Her tone made it quite clear she didn't like that question or him. 'Now,' she said. 'You need me to present an opinion on a medical matter?'

'Sort of . . .' Raf pointed to where the boy still shielded his eyes from a sun that caught on the edge of his open shirt and cast its shadow across his bare chest and stomach.

'How old is that boy?'

The woman barely glanced at the image. 'Impossible to say,' she said firmly.

'Is he twenty?'

'Obviously not.'

'Six?'

She shook her head crossly.

'So you can say,' Raf told her. 'That at the very least he's older than six and younger than twenty . . .'

Sometime between my burning down a school and the killing of Micky O'Brian.

'You didn't say you wanted a rough estimate . . .'

'We can get specific later,' said Raf. 'At the moment, any kind of estimate would be good.'

One minute turned into two and still she gazed intently at the screen . . . Longer than was necessary, but Raf didn't hurry her. The cameras were hard at work catching every furrow of her brow, every tiny twitch that pulled at her mouth as she lost herself in thought.

'Was this boy well fed?'

From his place in the dock Hamzah shook his head, the movement entirely unconscious. And up on the bench St Cloud cleared a sour smile from his face so fast only Raf saw it come and go. There were other smiles, fleeting and bitter, from ordinary people on the public benches. Mostly from those, like Khartoum, who were old enough to have the memories.

Into Raf's head came thoughts of drought-twisted olive groves, crumbling irrigation channels, bushes on which apricots wizened before they were even ripe enough to be picked. Poisoned oasis and fields of millet being turned to straw by a sun that hung high overhead.

'Enough,' Raf insisted to himself and the images vanished.

'Well fed . . . ?' He shook his head. 'I think that unlikely.'

'In that case . . .' The woman hesitated. 'If the child was properly nourished then I'd put his age at nine, with a sixty per cent certainty. You have to look at the wrists,' she added, as if that explained everything. 'Chest too, to check development of the rib cage . . . Badly nourished, maybe ten, even eleven. My professional opinion is that the child is unlikely to be much older.'

'Court records say thirteen,' insisted Raf, and he made a point of double-checking the UN report in his hand

'Thirteen . . . ? Very unlikely.' Dr Schultz's stare was a challenge. 'Twelve if you must, assuming he'd been starved from birth. Except, of course,' she shrugged, 'if he'd been starved from birth, then disease would have killed him before this.'

'So definitely not thirteen?'

'*Ashraf Bey*'.

Raf turned round to find the Khedive watching him.

'Can you tell me where this is headed?' Tewfik Pasha's question was abrupt, but there was something unsettled in his eyes. As if the youth had only just become aware that he sat exposed in front of the world's press, acting as *magister* while the richest man in North Africa was tried for mass murder.

And there was one truth from which the Khedive could find no escape. It was widely known that Zara had taken al-Mansur as her lover. And for all that the bey wasn't a true believer, he still had *baraka*. A difficult quality to pin down, although luck, wisdom and blessing were in there somewhere. All those and an aura of strength which the poor believed clung like attar of roses to anyone who chose the stony path.

'Where is this headed?' asked Raf. 'Towards a conclusion, I hope.'

'It matters how old Hamzah was?'

Raf nodded.

'And to whom does it matter?'

To me, Raf almost said but he kept silent on that point. 'To the city,' he said instead. 'And also to you, as the city's *magister*, I presume . . .'

'Yes,' said the Khedive, 'you do.'

Raf looked puzzled.

'You presume,' Tewfik Pasha said with a tight smile. 'But then, perhaps somebody has to . . . Tell us why it matters.'

Raf picked up his notebook, tapped an icon for The Hague Convention and flicked to the relevant subsection. Ready to read . . .

'If a combatant is twelve or under at the time of a battle, s/he shall be exempt from direct responsibility and such responsibility lies with whoever issued the command . . .'

For a moment Raf thought the words were his, happening only in his head. Then he saw the fear on the face of Hamzah Effendi and realized the industrialist had also heard the gruff voice. As had Senator Liz, the young German Graf and a shocked-looking St Cloud.

Over on her bench, Zara began crying. Only Avatar looked at ease.

Chapter Fifty-seven

1st November

There'd been tears too from Hamzah when he finally realized who was speaking. Instinctively, the thick-set industrialist had straightened up, standing taller in the dock.

'*Ya Colonel*,' he said, sounding amazed.

'Lieutenant Ka.'

And then everyone in the court watched as Hamzah craned his head, looking round for his old commander. Only there was no Colonel Abad. Just a cracked radio held by Iskandryia's favourite DJ and a familiar voice that echoed from a wall speaker.

'You never did get to the source of the Nile,' said the Colonel.

Hamzah shook his head.

'But you still got me to safety. . .' The voice sounded content. 'Well, you got me to Koenig Pasha, which was almost as good. PaxForce wanted to kill me you know . . .'

'You're a radio?'

Colonel Abad chuckled. 'You might put it like that. Langley built me for counter-insurgency use in Colombia, then the Soviets patched in some ideology and relocated me to the Sudan. The CIA got me back eventually, ripped out the politics and offered me the Children of God.'

'But I was Islamic Fist, first battalion, company A.'

'No/yes . . . Well, some of the time,' conceded the Colonel. 'It wasn't always so simple . . .'

'You,' said Senator Liz to Avatar, 'bring that machine here.' Her New Jersey accent sliced through what threatened to become a conversation between old comrades.

Avatar did as he was told, placing the clockwork radio

carefully on the judicial bench in front of the American woman. The radio was small, battered and scratched along the bottom. Its shattered handle suggested someone had once kicked the thing.

'You can hear me?'

'Of course I can hear you . . . Senator Elizabeth Lee Elsing.'

'And you know me how . . . ?'

'Your face matches all points on a security photograph taken when Elizabeth Lee Elsing came aboard. Your voice profile fits exactly a phrase Elizabeth Lee Elsing recorded to control the strong box in her suite.'

'This thing is an appliance,' said von Bismarck. The expression on his face mixed revulsion with shock.

'An American appliance,' confirmed the box. 'Upgraded by Moscow and offered exile by Koenig Pasha, with the express consent of your own superiors in Berlin. A machine linked to software designed to win wars fought by children . . . Although, of course, their age was just an unexpected cost bonus. And *you* have this man on trial . . .'

'Are you saying you should be the one on trial?' St Cloud asked silkily.

'Obviously not,' said the box, 'I was thinking more that it should be all of you.'

'I suggest,' said the Khedive, when calls had been made, legal advice taken and the case reconvened later that afternoon. 'I suggest that we concentrate on one trial at a time.' He turned to Senator Liz. 'Do your friends in the CIA want to reclaim this box?'

She looked at the young Khedive as if he'd suddenly spat on her. 'Reclaim it?' the Senator said furiously. 'We don't even accept that we made it. The Soviets maybe. Although I wouldn't put it past Berlin . . .' She scowled bitterly at the young Graf, who sat carefully examining his nails.

Tewfik Pasha sighed. 'Your witness,' he said to Raf.

A hundred tiny pin-head lenses were set into the walls of the ballroom, Raf realized that well enough, but he turned to a wall-mounted CCTV camera to let the judges know he spoke direct to Colonel Abad.

'You recognize this man?' Raf asked, jerking his head towards Hamzah.

'I recognize his voice,' said the box, 'once suitable allowances have been made for vocal developments. And it doesn't matter if I say I recognize him or not. Protein pattern matching has already confirmed his identity.'

'Did he ever tell you his age?'

Colonel Abad stayed silent.

'You don't know how old he was at the time of the massacre?'

'*Massacre . . .*' The word was said thoughtfully, though whether that was because Abad was thinking or because elegant programming had anchored emotions to set logic sequences was impossible to tell.

'One hundred and fifty-three people died that afternoon,' said the Colonel. 'Two weeks before, according to UN reports, 1,002 refugees were reclassified as collateral damage when a poorly-targeted skySucker destroyed the oxygen over their camp. Seven days after, 503 died outside Wadi Halfa in a firefight between the Ragged Army and the Children of God. I note that neither of these incidents is down on record as a massacre . . .

'So your logic suggests,' continued the machine, 'that when 503 children kill each other it's not a massacre, but when one child kills 153, then it is. Have I got that right?'

'Answer the original question,' said Raf. 'Did he ever tell you his age?'

'Very few of them knew their age,' Abad said mildly. 'And it's unlikely that Ka was any different. But you could always try working it out. For example, your reports say Ka told the Red Cross he came from Azarat and his mother died when he was a baby . . .'

Raf waited.

'Didn't it occur to ask him from what?'

Glancing at Hamzah, Raf raised his eyebrows.

'Plague,' Hamzah said. 'That's all I was told. After the wells dried up and the crops died, she and my uncle walked north to Suakin and joined a caravan to El Makrif to get away from war.' Hamzah shrugged. 'So did everybody else.'

'Drought,' said Abad, 'War, plague and a migration of refugees . . . There were droughts in 89, 91, and 01. Beni–Amir conflicts from 87–91 and 98–03. Ebola in 91, 93 and 99–02.' The Colonel reeled off the figures, as if talking to itself. 'Migrations from 87–92, after which the UN closed the routes to stop refugees creating new vectors for the plague.'

'Which means,' Raf and Senator Liz said together, 'he was born in 91.' They'd been following the figures in their heads. The Graf was still busy writing out his sums longhand and St Cloud was doodling.

'Assume he was born in the spring,' said Raf. 'How old was he?'

'Nine on joining and eleven at the time of the *massacre*.'

Raf turned to where the *SS Jannah*'s medical officer sat near the front. 'Would you agree with that assessment?'

'It is perfectly possible,' Dr Schultz said slowly.

'Thank you,' Raf nodded to the bench. 'That finishes the case for the prosecution.' He glanced over at Zara. 'I imagine Miss Zara is impatient to make the case for the defence.'

St Cloud snorted.

'With the *magister*'s permission, this court will recess for ten minutes,' he announced, banging his gavel on its wooden pad . . .

After that, the rest was a formality. The judges decided two to one that there was no case to answer, with the dissenting vote being Senator Liz. Ernst von Bismarck went out of his way to stress that Hamzah was completely exonerated. Just to make doubly sure, he explained, to the amusement of the more up-scale newsfeeds, that this didn't mean Hamzah had been found not guilty. For the simple reason that Hamzah didn't need to be found not guilty. There was no case to answer.

In the seventy-five seconds it took Claire duBois' talking head to hit Television5, Hamzah mutated from a heavily-armed teen psychopath to traumatized drought-victim, stranded alone in the desert, trying desperately to carry out conflicting orders.

Chapter Fifty-eight

6th November

'If you don't move,' said the fox, *'you'll be late for Hamzah's party.'*

'Yep,' agreed Raf and reached for his cappuccino.

The power was back on at Le Trianon and the first thing the kitchens had done was whip up a fresh batch of ice cream for Hani, the kind made with vanilla pods. A glass flute of the stuff now sat, almost untouched, in front of her.

'Not hungry?'

Hani shrugged. A minute or so later, while Raf pretended not to watch, she stirred the ice cream to a pulp with her long silver spoon.

'You going to let her get away with that?' asked the voice.

'Probably.'

'You're talking to the fox,' said Hani.

Raf nodded.

'The one hidden in your head?'

He nodded again.

'Okay.' The small girl put down her spoon, then picked it up again. Le Trianon was absolutely her favourite café and vanilla supposedly her favourite flavour, but Hani obviously wasn't enjoying herself.

'Colonel Abad mended your fox?'

They'd been over this a dozen times. Raf couldn't bring himself to believe this was the real problem, but it was the point to which she kept coming back.

'That's right,' he said.

'How?'

'He took a look inside my head, then fixed a software glitch

365

that stopped the fox from being able to feed.'

'Did it hurt?'

'Too fast,' said Raf. 'I didn't even know it had happened.'

'And Colonel Abad doesn't really exist?'

'He's as real as the fox.'

Hani looked doubtful. 'How real is that?'

As questions went, this one was more difficult to answer. Actually, as questions went, that one was next to impossible . . . A software program designed to mimic the cunning and charisma of a long-dead revolutionary undoubtedly existed. It had led the Ragged Army, changed sides and then changed back again. Several times, from what it said.

The view of the *Washington Post* was that it was equal in intelligence to any human and therefore as dangerous. *Le Matin* disagreed, describing it as a military chess computer, a view also held by *Pravda*.

'I think it exists,' Raf said carefully.

'But you think the fox exists,' said Hani, brushing crossly at her fringe.

They were sat at a pavement table, even though the weather was cold and the first Saturday in November had brought fewer people than normal out onto the streets. And she'd brought him there because he knew she liked it, if that made sense.

'Zara's mother says that you're insane.' Hani's voice was matter of fact, although Raf caught the sideways glance that checked he wasn't angry. Only he was angry and had been since the trial was aborted five days before.

And in a way he was jealous. Raf sat back in his chair and closed his eyes. He was jealous of Avatar, for retrieving the Colonel. And furious with Zara, who'd known at least some of what Hani was doing.

'Uncle Raf . . .'

Raf opened his eyes.

'I'm sorry. All right . . .' Hani picked up her spoon and ate a mouthful of runny vanilla, as if that might make a difference. 'I should have told you.'

'Yeah, you really . . .' Raf swallowed the rest of his words.

'Forget it,' he said, turning to more important matters. 'You don't like vanilla ice cream anymore, do you?'

'It's okay.' Hani shrugged.

'What happened?'

The nine-year-old thought for a second. 'I grew out of it,' she said. 'It happens.'

A butler met them at the steps. He wasn't anyone Raf had seen before. And if he seemed surprised to see a blond young man in dark glasses and drop-pearl earring holding the hand of a small black-haired child he didn't let it show. At least not that much.

'Ashraf al-Mansur,' said Raf.

'We're here for the party,' added Hani.

'Can I ask if His Excellency is expecting you?

His Excellency? Raf smiled. That was a new one.

'This is the Governor of El Iskandryia,' Hani said crossly. 'He doesn't need an invitation.' She squeezed Raf's hand, as if she thought the butler's question might have upset him.

'Hamzah is expecting me . . . Expecting us,' Raf corrected himself.

'Very good.' The man turned, obviously intending to leave them on the doorstep until Hani pushed her way in with a sigh.

'English,' Hani said loudly, as the butler stalked away down the corridor, back stiff with disapproval. 'Madame Rahina's price,' she added more softly.

'For what?'

'For not throwing a complete tantrum about you and about Avatar.' Hani sounded like a middle-aged woman discussing a small child, rather than the other way round.

'Come on . . .' She set off towards the drawing room, without waiting for the butler to return. And Raf let himself be tugged towards a babble of voices filtering through an ornately-carved door.

The Long Drawing Room at the Villa Hamzah, so called to distinguish it from the Square Drawing Room on the floor above, was decorated to Madame Rahina's taste. Which mostly involved European wallpaper in green and silver stripes, gold velvet sofas and faux Persian carpets from a place called Axminster. At least that was where they came from according to the fox, who layered little bubble facts over every object until Raf ordered it to stop.

'Ashraf . . .'

Hamzah Effendi stepped forward, hand outstretched and grabbed Raf's own, wringing it hard. 'You found us then . . . ?' The barrel-chested man stopped and grinned at his own stupidity. 'Of course you found it. You've been here . . .'

'Several times,' Raf agreed.

'But not as often as me,' said Hani smugly and let go his hand to scoot away across the carpet to where Zara sat, with a cup of Earl Grey, talking stiltedly to the Khedive.

'I remember when she was never going to set foot in this house again,' said Raf. He spoke without really thinking. As the fox kept reminding him, he did a lot of that.

'She told you?'

Raf nodded. 'Months ago. After the beating. When I was patching her up.'

'I didn't know it had happened until later,' Hamzah Effendi said flatly.

'You had other things on your mind.'

The industrialist glanced at Raf, then realized the comment was no criticism. 'Yes,' he said, 'I did. And I have you to thank for . . .'

Raf stepped back and held up both hands. 'I was there to *prosecute* you,' he reminded Hamzah.

'Ah,' said St Cloud as he materialized beside them both. 'So that's what you were doing. We did wonder.' He flashed Raf a smile and, when it wasn't returned, the Marquis just shrugged and lifted a champagne flute from a passing tray.

And as the young waiter stopped dead, embarrassed not to have realized that St Cloud needed a drink, the elderly Frenchman finished his first glass, put it back and took another.

'Most kind, dear boy,' he said lightly . . .

'Don't you think,' St Cloud said to Raf, 'that our host should rescue his daughter from having to talk to that little idiot?' He jerked his head towards the sofa where Tewfik Pasha still sat with Zara, while Hani squatted impatiently on the arm.

'Maybe she likes talking to him,' said Raf.

The industrialist raised his eyebrows and went to do as St Cloud suggested.

'What percentage?' Raf demanded, the moment Hamzah was gone.

St Cloud looked him.

'What percentage of the Midas refinery do you currently own?' Raf didn't bother to keep the anger out of his voice.

'Seven per cent, maybe eight . . . Enough to make Hamzah respectable, not enough to make a difference. It's in all the records.'

'And you wanted more?'

'More?' St Cloud spread his hands and smiled mockingly, although Raf found it impossible to tell if he was the person being mocked or if the man was mocking himself. *'Moi?'*

'Does Hamzah know it was you?'

'Me what . . . ? Even if that were true,' said St Cloud, taking a glass from Raf's hand and finishing it, 'which I obviously deny, he can't touch me any more than you can. My advice is take his cash and leave it at that.'

'Discussing money?' said Ernst von Bismarck as he joined their small group. The German ambassador didn't know whether to looked shocked or intrigued.

'Ashraf Bey's just reward,' St Cloud said smoothly. 'It's bound to be vast. Which I gather is just as well . . .'

'These Arabs.' The Graf's voice was serious. 'Debts matter to them. You must let him give you something. I'm told you didn't when you saved Miss Zara from that mad assassin . . .'

St Cloud laughed. 'Which mad assassin would that be?' he asked. 'The mad *Thiergarten* one?'

The Graf paid no attention. 'People tell me Hamzah Effendi was very hurt . . .'

'Give me something?'

Ernst von Bismarck looked surprised. 'What do you think

this is about?' His gaze took in Zara, Hamzah and the Khedive, Senator Liz, Captain Bruford from the *SS Jannah* and General Koenig Pasha . . .

'Such a miraculous recovery,' said the Marquis. 'For which we must all be heartily grateful, no doubt.'

'And then there are those two journalists,' added von Bismarck. He ran together their names and stations, as if they were part of the same thing. 'Both of whom are desperate to interview you . . .'

'About the city's miraculous recovery, no doubt.' St Cloud shrugged. 'It's amazing how fast Iskandryia managed to get back on its feet. One's almost tempted to suggest things were not quite as bad as the world believed.'

He raised his eyebrows.

'Believe me,' said Raf. 'Those EMF bombs inflicted enormous damage.'

'Oh I'm sure that's true. I can even believe that all the cars and trams were affected and all the phone lines. But just imagine, every single electricity substation, every gas processing plant, the entire IOL network and all of the power supplies to all of the local newsfeeds, even the pumps to the mains water supply . . . Everything, suddenly dead, as if someone somewhere threw a big switch.'

'*He knows,*' said the fox.

'The e-bombs were real,' Raf reiterated.

'And as I've already said,' repeated St Cloud, 'I don't doubt that for a minute.' He twirled his empty champagne flute until it hung upside down. At which point a waiter hastily appeared, bearing a silver tray full of freshly-filled glasses.

'You do realize, don't you?' said von Bismarck. 'That the reappearance of Abad leaves us with a major problem . . .'

'I rather imagined,' Raf said, 'that you'd all fight over ownership while pretending to be friends . . .' Reaching for a passing glass of champagne, he casually killed it and took another. 'Isn't that what diplomacy is about?'

'So young,' said St Cloud, 'and yet so cynical.'

The Marquis turned his attention to the German ambassador.

'And where Abad is concerned there is no *us*. Paris wasn't part of making the hideous thing, or subverting it come to that.'

'Soon,' said Raf, 'you'll be telling me you didn't know Abad still existed . . . Or where he was hidden.'

'We didn't.' St Cloud shrugged. 'At least not officially, and that's what counts. Mind you,' he added, 'we certainly intend to be part of trying the monster.'

'*Assuming it can be tried*,' said a voice. But the fox's comment was lost, because somewhere across the other side of the Long Drawing Room Hamzah nodded to Avatar, who hammered a whisky glass down on a wooden overmantel.

'Your Highness, gentlemen, ladies . . .' Hamzah should have got an *Excellencies* in there after *Highness*, but having had a speech carefully prepared by Olga he'd decided at the last minute to do without notes.

He knew exactly what he wanted to say.

This was payback time, in its way. He had a room full of notables, most of whom didn't want to be there but knew better than to refuse. 27.3 per cent of the Midas Refinery belonged to him, which was why St Cloud, its urbane public face, joked uneasily at the edge of a group that included Ashraf Bey and that young German.

St Mark's relied on Hamzah's generosity for its recent scholarships. He could see the headmaster across the room, a drab Christian Brother wrapped in dirt-coloured tweeds. The city's famous library still needed new glass, somewhat urgently after the recent bouts of rain. Madame Syria was smiling fondly at Hani, but she'd been less happy earlier, when she'd been talking to Zara about the library's need to find finance for repairs.

The two thick-set men in suits, stood over by the door, they headed up the Kharmous and El Anfushi crime families and were both doing their uncertain best to look happy at finding themselves in the same room as Mushin Bey, Minister for Police.

'Your Highness, Excellencies, ladies and gentlemen . . .' Hamzah draped one arm heavily around Avatar's narrow shoulders. 'I don't think any of you have been formally introduced to my son Kamil.'

'Avatar,' insisted Avatar, but his heart wasn't really in it.

On the other side of the boy stood Madame Rahina, her face dark as thunder, her arms heavy with new and unwanted gold bracelets. And it was obvious that Hamzah was as oblivious to his wife's smouldering anger as he was to the tears running down his own broad cheeks.

'Very clever.' Senator Liz handed Raf a fresh glass of champagne and instantly a waiter materialized to spirit away his dirty glass, depositing it on a passing silver salver. Both waiter and salver-carrier were models of professionalism, right down to the shoulder-holstered guns under their left arms. Hamzah might be everyone's favourite son but he was still taking no chances.

'What was clever?' Raf asked.

'Taking the Colonel into protective custody.' The Senator's smile was tight. 'Can a synthetic intelligence be tried for crimes against humanity?' She shrugged. 'Thanks to you, I think we're probably about to find out.'

'Only if it's first possible for software to be extradited . . .' Raf said lightly.

The woman opened her mouth and forgot to close it.

'And that's always assuming the Khedive accepts the extradition papers. Which he probably won't.'

'What?'

'Colonel Abad has asked for political asylum.'

'On what grounds?'

'That it won't get a fair trial elsewhere.'

'Then try the thing in El Iskandryia,' said the Senator. 'I don't see that being a problem. If you can stand having the reptiles crawl all over you again.' She glanced at C3N's Nick Richardson, accidentally caught his eye and immediately smiled.

'I hear you're going to put Colonel Abad on trial,' St Cloud said, about five minutes later, when he tracked Raf down to a window seat overlooking the grey waters of the Mediterranean. 'If Paris can be of any help . . .'

Raf shook his head. 'It's not going to happen.'

'Are you sure?'

'Oh yes,' said Raf, taking another sip from one glass too many. 'As sure as anything.'

'Such certainty in one so youthful.' The Marquis shrugged. 'The sign of true breeding. And yet, a German recently suggested to me that you were a fake and that, for undisclosed reasons, Koenig Pasha has been colluding in this pretence.'

'Really?' said Raf. 'I'd love to meet this person.

'That might be difficult. She died in the basement of a derelict house. After someone took out her throat.'

'*Which is what happens,*' said the fox, '*if you build your city on top of a graveyard. The dead forget to stay dead.*'

Raf raised his glass to his lips and wondered why St Cloud was looking at him, then realized the glass was empty, again.

People nearby looked surprised when the fox made Raf click his fingers but the fox was too tired to care. It needed more champagne and then some sleep. A long dark sleep with no dreams. But most of all it wanted this party to end before Hamzah got round to making more speeches.

It just knew Raf was going to offend the man.

'She was right,' Raf told the Marquis, once both their drinks were refreshed and a nervous young waiter had vanished. 'Your woman got it right. I'm not a bey. I don't belong in El Iskandryia. My name isn't Ashraf al-Mansur . . .'

He watched the man walk away.

'I doubt I'm even Berber,' Raf added quietly, to no one in particular. 'Hani probably isn't my niece.' He glanced across to where the small girl stood next to Zara, half listening to someone, half staring at Raf. 'Maybe I'm just someone who got lucky . . .'

'*Uncle Ashraf.*'

Everyone in the room was looking in his direction, Raf realized. Hamzah, in particular, was waiting expectantly for something.

'He wasn't listening,' said Hani. She sounded obscurely proud of this fact. 'He was probably talking to his fox.'

'His what . . . ?' Zara sounded puzzled.

'It's a long story,' Hani told her. 'Weird too.'

'Well,' said Zara. 'Are you going to take Dad's money this time?'

'Your reward.' Hamzah's grin had become slightly anxious.

'No,' said Raf. 'I really don't think . . .'

What stopped him finishing his sentence was the anguish that flooded Zara's face, when she realized he was about to hurt her father's feelings again.

'The thing is . . .' Raf paused.

'*Oh really!*' said the fox. '*The thing is what?*'

'The thing is,' said Raf carefully, 'my niece needs a dowry. And since she can't hold property for herself . . .' He didn't make Iskandryia's laws and pretty soon he was going to stop trying to uphold them. 'I thought perhaps His Highness and Hamzah Effendi . . . As trustees?'

Tewfik Pasha looked shocked and then resigned, Hamzah looked delighted.

'You want all the reward to go to Hani?' It was Zara who spoke.

Raf nodded and saw St Cloud shake his head in disbelief.

'It's a large sum.' Koenig Pasha sounded doubtful.

'Good,' said Raf, 'maybe it'll be enough to keep her out of trouble.'

Hani stuck out her tongue.

Later, when everyone had gone back to talking to each other, mostly about Hani's fabulous new-found wealth, St Cloud reappeared at Raf's side. 'Well,' he said, 'you won't take my bribe and you won't take Hamzah's . . . That either makes you unbelievably stupid or even more dangerous than I imagined.'

'I'll settle for a drink,' offered Raf.

'And I'd get you one,' St Cloud said, 'but your pretty little girlfriend thinks you've had enough.'

'*She's right,*' a familiar voice said in his head, but Raf shushed the fox into silence. There was something about St Cloud that required absolute concentration.

'$50,000,000 . . . That's a lot to turn down.'

Behind his dark glasses, Raf blinked. 'Money,' he said flatly, 'isn't everything.'

Or was that life?

'Maybe not,' said St Cloud. 'But if ever I need to buy you, I can see it'll have to be with something other than cash.'

'I'm not for sale.'

'Everyone is for . . .' The Marquis looked at Raf and then shrugged in disgust. 'People like you,' he said, 'fuck up the bell curve.'

'I'm impressed.'

'I'm not.' Raf looked round the discreetly-lit drawing room. The elegant invitations with their gilt edges, china clay surface and hand embossing had given the party's duration as 2.30–6.30 p.m. and it was now just after 10.30 p.m. Raf had sobered up somewhat, mostly with the aid of proprietary alcohol inhibitors and, as yet, no one showed much sign of leaving.

'They don't dare go,' Zara said.

Raf didn't ask how she knew what he was thinking, just accepted it as something he'd have to get used to. Like the smell of her skin or the fact she looked better in old trousers and a silk cheongsam than any other woman in the room looked in that season's Dior. And there was a surfeit of that season's Dior.

There was one other thing about her. At no time had she tried to shoo Hani away, even though Hani had glued herself to Zara's side from the moment she arrived to the point she dropped in her tracks, dead to the world. And it was Zara's Chinese silk jacket that now made do as a blanket, covering the small girl who lay curled up on a sofa.

'Marry me,' said Raf.

It was Zara's turn to blink.

'You want to get married because I gave Hani my coat?' Zara smiled. 'I saw you check to see the kid was okay,' she added, by way of explanation. 'Then I saw you notice the goose bumps on my arms. You're not the only one who can play detective.'

'That's finished,' said Raf. 'I resigned ten minutes ago as Chief of Detectives. Ibrahim Osman gets the job. The Khedive will be appointing a new governor in the morning . . .'

'Koenig Pasha?'

'The Khedive seems keen to take the job himself,' said Raf. 'Apparently there's nothing in law that says the city needs a governor.'

'There's nothing to say it needs a Khedive . . .' Zara's voice was louder than it should be. With a rawness that he'd missed earlier.

Raf looked at her. 'He proposed, didn't he?' said Raf, suddenly understanding what had been right in front of his face.

'Oh yes,' Zara's voice was bitter. 'Despite the fact I'm apparently your lover. It seems he simply couldn't help himself . . . One way and another, it's been quite a night for proposals.'

'Then I take mine back,' Raf said hurriedly.

'No,' said Zara. 'Don't . . . If you do that I won't have the satisfaction of turning you down as well.'

'That's your answer?'

She was about to nod when Hamzah and Madame Rahina jostled their way out of the crowd. Zara's mother had changed her outfit, but still wore head to toe Dior and smelled of some number Chanel that was impossibly difficult to find. She also sported a scowl and an air of barely-restrained fury at the way her husband had hooked his arm through her own.

'So what are you two up to?' Hamzah asked brightly.

'Oh,' Raf glanced at Zara. 'I was just asking her to marry me.'

Hamzah's grin died as his wife yanked herself free. Unfortunately, even on tiptoe, she remained too short to spot the Khedive over the heads of her other guests.

'By the window,' said Zara, 'sulking.'

'So,' Hamzah asked, 'it's agreed? You're going to marry Raf . . .'

Zara shook her head. 'Not a chance. But Hani's busy trying to persuade me to move into the al-Mansur madersa.'

Which was the first Raf had heard of it.